THE INFECTION
By Craig DiLouie
©2011, 2021 Craig DiLouie. All rights reserved.

This is a work of fiction. All characters, events, things, and places portrayed in this novel are either fictitious or used fictitiously.

Scripture quotations are taken from the Holy Bible, New Living Translation, ©1996, 2004, 2007. Used by permission of Tyndale House Publishers, Inc., Wheaton, Illinois 60189. All rights reserved.

Cover by Jacqueline Druga. Layout by Brent Nichols.

Published by ZING Communications, Inc.

www.CraigDiLouie.com

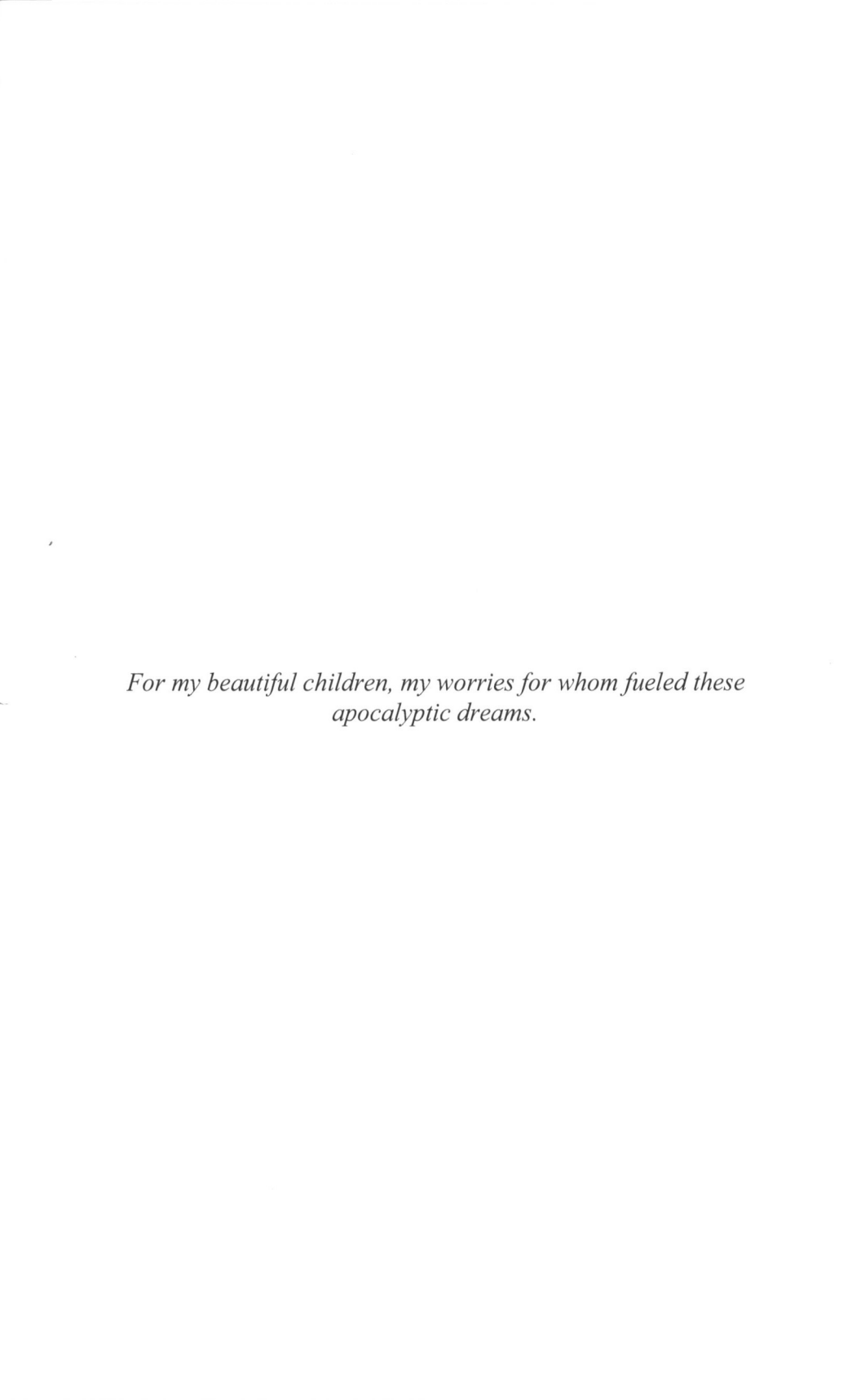

For my beautiful children, my worries for whom fueled these apocalyptic dreams.

PRAISE FOR THE INFECTION

"Gripping...DiLouie carefully recreates our society and our military...then proceeds to bring the horror, devastation, and heroes we require."
—*Fangoria*

"Not just another zombie story...a disturbing, nightmarish read."
—David Moody, author of *Hater*

"An absolute joy to read...If you want a book that will disturb you and give you the creeps, check this one out."
—Peter Clines, author of *Ex-Heroes*

"Brilliant and terrifying!"
—Jonathan Maberry, author of *Patient Zero*

"*28 Days Later* meets *The Mist*...a definite page-turner right from the get-go all the way to the insanely intense final scene."
—TheGOREScore.com

"A page-turner of the highest order...one of the most emotional, unsettling and satisfying takes on the zompocalyse yet to see print."
—Necroscope

"*The Infection*...is that rare novel...that 'happens to you.' You are not merely a reader but a victim of the hell it portrays."
—HorrorReview.com

"One of the best zombie books I've read."
—*The Fringe*

"A progressive nightmare that ends with the reader standing alongside humanity at the gates of hell."
—*Hearse-Say*

"Inventive and fresh, offering an insider's perspective on pain and terror."
—*Shock Totem*

"DiLouie's writing has a gripping authority that makes the reader not so much suspend disbelief as throw it away to join the wild and frightening ride."
—*Alberta Views*

"While *The Infection* is incredibly strong in its action sequences and far above average character development, the best part of the book is the strikingly original horrors in this new world."
—AllThingsHorrorOnline.net

"Captivating...I could not wait to start reading again every time I had to put it down."
—TwistedCentral.com

"A road trip through hell."
—Zombies & Toys

"DiLouie has created a vivid world of mayhem and destruction."
—Doubleshot Reviews

"An entirely new way to look at the apocalypse."
—ZombieSlam.com

"Goes from moments of stillness and calm to breakneck madness at the drop of a hat."
—RevolutionSF.com

"Beyond the regular apocalyptic novel."
—LivingDeadMedia.com

"A unique brand of zombie/post-apocalyptic horror that genre readers should not miss."
—Strange Amusements

"A frighteningly nightmarish twisting of the zombie formula."
—AwilltoAct.com

"Rises well above other books in the zombie genre."
—Xomba.com

FOREWORD

A quick survey of apocalyptic fiction, and especially of those works that concern themselves with some version of the zombie, shows that a lot of these writers are getting their toys from the same toy box. If you've read more than a handful of zombie books, you know what I mean. You see, time and again, the steely eyed, but emotionally damaged, hero. The badass heroine who somehow pulls herself together to save the day. The hapless and recently bitten survivor, who somehow proves to be immune from the virus. The protracted death scene of a beloved friend. The retreating military in shambles. You've seen all this before, right?

Of course you have. They've become beloved mainstays of the zombie genre.

They are, for lack of a better word, archetypes.

Not that there's anything wrong with archetypes, mind you. Archetypes are archetypes for a reason. They're the proven tools of all storytellers. They're emotionally satisfying. They're a familiar connection in an environment meant to be otherwise shocking and dissonant. You'll even find a few of those archetypes in the pair of books you currently hold in your hands.

The important thing about archetypes, though, is not their recurring use, but what the storyteller does with them. Good storytelling is not a mere chemistry experiment, after all. One doesn't simply throw the ingredients together, like in the classic hydrogen peroxide and potassium iodide marshmallow experiment, and crank out a story bubbling over with excitement. To give readers what they love, while the all the while giving them something completely unique, a writer needs to understand subtlety. He or she needs to know when to go for the headshot, and when to linger on the heartache. When to shout, and when to laugh. When to love, and when to go numb. There's no formula for that, either.

The best writers slog their way toward that understanding, and in the process, develop real empathy for their characters, for they have shared the struggle together. That takes more than blind luck and raw talent. It even takes more than a good editor. It takes guts. And if anyone is brave enough to make that journey through the dark, it is Craig DiLouie.

Sitting on the corner of my desk as I write this are the original paperback editions of *The Infection* and *The Killing Floor*. Their spines are cracked; their covers tattered. Inside, nearly every page has something written on it, notes to myself about how DiLouie managed to pull off the magic that he did.

You see, I write in books. I'm one of those people.

And I make no apologies for it, either. I think of books, first and foremost, as the food upon which my imagination feeds. When I look at my sagging, groaning bookshelf, I see an extravagant buffet. One can never have too many books. The good ones are precious. The great ones are sacred.

But I'm a writer too, and because of that, I also think of books as tools to help me become a better writer. That's why I write in them. It's my way of engaging the text in the most immediate, and intimate, way possible. It's an act of devotion made easier now that I do most of my reading on my Kindle, but when I first encountered the pair of books you now hold, I had yet to give in to the convenience of eBooks. Hence the chicken scratch scrawled onto nearly every margin of these two books.

I read through my marginalia before sitting down to write this appreciation of Craig's achievement, and one theme kept coming up page after page.

Real, honest to God emotion.

These books are a zombie lover's dream…or, maybe, nightmare? I can't be sure. But I do know that they contain proof that Craig DiLouie is one of a small group of genre authors who not only have the knack for good storytelling, and for a wild effulgence of the weird, but also for genuine sentiment.

So much of modern horror lives in the gutter. Horror, as a general rule, and as a genre, has embraced everything from torture porn to parody to surrealism to tramp-stamp wearing bad-assery. If Horror were a girl at your school, she'd be the one all the guys ask out on dates but never bring home to meet mother.

You see where I'm going with this, right?

Horror has earned a bit of a bad rap because it is so very welcoming to all comers. Whatever you're into, Horror has a sub-genre for you. From the apocalypse to xenophobia, we've got you covered. We've even got tentacle porn, for those of you who like your Lovecraft wearing fifty shades of gray. That openness has led to some truly exceptional fiction, but it has also led to a lot of really, really bad stuff. In truth, the bad, volume-wise, far outweighs the good.

Which brings us back to authors and their toys.

Far too many writers working today are content, I think, to give us mere violence as a stand-in for genuine storytelling. They use the archetypes of the genre like pieces on a game board, and give them all the emotional inflection of a grocery list. We've all heard that the reason zombie stories resonate with us is because we are fascinated with the survivors. We want to be those survivors. At least a little. We want to live in their world. For a short time, anyway. Ultimately, we want to come back to the safety of our workaday lives, but it is fun to dream. Few authors, though, have the emotional intensity necessary to make those dreams seem real.

Craig DiLouie, I'm happy to say, is one of those few.

His *Infection* series is a testament to that. These books are gloriously weird, terrifying, and, at their core, painstaking explorations of the reasons we want to go on fighting for life.

I don't want to spoil the journey that lies ahead of you by saying too much about plot.

That would be unfair to you.

But I will say this pair of volumes holds a place of honor in my library. They are heavy with marginalia for a reason.

Because they matter to me.

I'm hoping they will mean as much to you.

Joe McKinney
Helotes, Texas
September 4, 2014

THE INFECTION

FALLING DOWN

Ethan reached the end of his patience trying to explain how to solve factoring equations when everybody started falling down.

Hacking at the blackboard with a piece of chalk to guide his teenage students through a third example, he heard the first distant scream. The chalk broke in his hand, and he accidentally scratched the board with his fingernails. A shiver of revulsion coursed through his body.

He peered at his algebra class over the rims of his glasses. "Let's try that again."

Engaged by his personal tone, some of the kids smiled back. The rest slouched at their desks and stared out the window at the green lawn washed in spring sunshine.

Finishing the example, he slapped chalk dust from his hands and said, "Okay, who wants to take a crack at this one? Where would you begin to solve for *x*?"

"Wow," several of the students shouted at once. Two of the boys stood to look out the window.

Ethan frowned. "Come on, guys. Butts in seats. We've only got fifteen minutes left."

"There was an accident," Trevor Jackson said. His eyes gleamed with excitement. "A bunch of people are lying on the ground out there. It's crazy."

Another scream in the distance. Ethan took a few steps toward the window. The kids stood to get a better look outside.

Footsteps pounded the hallway outside. Ethan turned just in time to see two teachers jog by his classroom. A door slammed.

He took several steps toward the hallway now, wondering if there was some type of emergency, if he should be doing something special to protect his kids.

"What's that sound, Mr. Bell?"

"I don't know," Ethan murmured.

He knew. Why deny it? It was screaming. Screaming that wouldn't stop. Screaming that went on and on and on. Whoever was screaming was in extreme, unending pain—strong enough to make them howl at the top of their lungs for minutes. And there seemed to be a lot of people doing it—some outside and some inside the school, in the classrooms down the hall.

He now wondered if he should be here at all. His wife was at work. Their toddler, Mary, at day care. He took another step toward the door. Would he get fired if he left?

Trevor's face contorted. Then he fell screaming.

Blood spurted as he cracked his nose on the floor. The other kids shrank back with surprised yelps. Trevor lay on his side with his back arched, arms outstretched, hands splayed into claws.

His eyes bulged. His mouth screamed at a volume Ethan hadn't believed possible.

Ethan felt the urge to run.

"Do something!" Lucy Gall shouted at him.

He glared back at her with wide, watery eyes. "Yes, I'm going to call 911—"

Lucy fell. Her body jerked in little spasms on the floor. The crotch of her jeans flooded with a dark stain. Then she screamed loud and shrill enough to damage eardrums.

The students shouted at each other to do something. One of the boys got down on his knees and shook her.

His eyes rolled back into his skull, and he fell over.

It's in the ventilation system, Ethan thought. *Something's in the air all around us.*

Five more kids fell within seconds of each other, spilling desks and scattering notebooks.

They screamed.

Moments later, Ethan was outside his body, watching himself run with the remaining students in a blind stampede to exit the school. In the hallway, they raced over the trembling, screaming bodies of teachers and students, as if they were parts of an intricate obstacle course. They bolted out the school's steel doors and into sunshine and relative quiet.

He froze in his tracks. The street beyond the lawn was a tangled mess of crashed vehicles. Plumes of smoke rose above the city in the distance. Now new waves of sound assaulted his ears: car alarms, horns, sirens and, rising up above it all, the distant sound of thousands upon thousands of mouths screaming in unison like an auditory glimpse of hell.

This is everywhere.

He kept running. Students toppled around him as if cut down by an invisible scythe. The screaming filled him with blind panic now, an irrational fear of the supernatural, as if actual demons were at his heels. A motorcycle roared by, its spilled rider cartwheeling through the air. In the distance, a plane fell from the sky. These things barely registered in his consciousness. All he could think about was Mary's safety. He had to get to her.

Please God, spare her. Take these kids. Take Carol. Take me. If anything happens to my little girl, the world will end.

He got into his car and started the engine. The radio sobbed hysterically at him. He turned it off, and that was when he noticed the screaming had stopped. Twitching bodies carpeted the lawn. Those who escaped the attack walked among them trembling and hugging their ribs in shock.

So rapid was the transmission of the mysterious virus that swept the world over a period of just forty-eight hours, so sudden the onset of disease, that scientists would later claim that it must somehow be linked to human-engineered nanotechnology. Some kind of weapon that escaped the lab. The government traced the origin of the pandemic to a village near secret facilities in China, but they'd never find out the truth. And Ethan would never teach again.

After three days, the screamers woke up.

TWELVE DAYS LATER

THE SURVIVORS

They are refugees forced from everything they consider home, searching for a safe place. They have become nomads, living on whatever they can find. But mostly, they're survivors. They're good at surviving because they're on the road and they're still alive. They have done the things one had to do to survive. They have all killed, or they wouldn't be here.

They haven't lost anybody since Wednesday, when they buried Philip in Wilkinsburg. There are five of them now. They sit ramrod straight in the hot dim passenger compartment of the armored personnel carrier. Rifles between their knees, they pass around a bottle of water. They sit in a tense silence, mouths slack, sweating in air that is twenty degrees hotter than the unseasonably warm May weather outside. The air stinks of sweat and grime and diesel combustion. Between the engine, the squeal of the treads, and a steady drumming sound, they have to shout to make themselves heard, and nobody has the energy to do that. Punctuated by sharp metallic taps, the drumming grows louder until it drowns out the Bradley's six hundred horsepower engine. The survivors are perpetually a second away from screaming.

The drumming is from hands. The tapping sound is from jewelry. Bracelets and watches and wedding rings.

The people outside know they're in here, and they want in.

The survivors wonder if they've killed everything for which they want to live. Wonder if it might grow back again, given enough time, if only they can find sanctuary.

The survivors are adaptive. People who will do whatever it takes to survive naturally don't trust others. But to travel the road, one must be in a gang, and to survive the experience day after day, as they have, that gang must function as a single protective organism. Each has been tested by violence, and if they failed, they all would have died. They know this. At this point, after what they've seen and done, this sense of responsibility to each other is what keeps them from collapsing into hysteria or catatonia. Fear, sorrow, guilt, rage: these and other emotions are just as dangerous as the infected outside and must likewise be killed.

They're bound for the Children's Hospital based on a theory. They have the Bradley, weapons, and the illusion of safety as long as the rig's engine keeps humming and its treads keep moving. They need supplies, though, especially water and diesel. They need to find a place unspoiled by Infection, where they can rest. The simple fact is they can't keep fighting like this. You can only win so many fights before it feels like you're losing.

They sense a subtle shift in the atmosphere, a sudden drop in temperature. Outside, it begins to rain. The drumming fades as the infected lose interest in the vehicle. The damned fill the air with plaintive cries as they melt away into the rain.

Anne alone does not appear to be stripped to a single bare electric wire. She sits in the back near the exit ramp, across from the cop, a place of respect among the survivors as whoever sits there is the first to leave the vehicle and the last to reenter. The others admire and try to imitate her cool. Sarge may be the commander of the Bradley, but they consider Anne their leader because without her example and unfaltering aim with the scoped rifle, they'd all be dead. They know she'll do whatever it takes.

She has two long scars on her left cheek and a short one on her right. The survivors assume she's ex-military and imagine she has a romantic and violent past. Anne doesn't tell them she has an overwhelming feeling that once they finally stop moving and find a place of rest where they can be truly safe, she's going to burst inside out with a scream of guilt, terror, and anguish.

Hours earlier, they'd found Sarge's infantry squad in the parking lot of a Walmart. The soldiers lay mangled like road kill around a strange device. Piles of dead infected, tangled in a line of concertina wire, surrounded them. The dead stared wide-eyed into oblivion. Many of the bodies were badly burned and emitted a sickening, sweet barbecue stench. Bits of charred clothing fluttered in the light breeze. A few infected stumbled blindly among the remains, gnawing on human meat from a dismembered arm or leg. Crows shrieked in protest as the Bradley approached at forty miles an hour. Then an enormous flock of the birds exploded into the air, dribbling morsels of flesh from bloody beaks as they filled the sky.

Sarge cut down the few infected in the area with several bursts from the Bradley's machine gun. Outside, he warned the survivors not to step on any of the bodies.

Of course we won't, they told him. *We'll respect your dead.*

"It's not a matter of respect," he said. "These people are rotting. Gases are building up inside their bodies. See how bloated they are? They can burst and spray fluids. You could catch the bug."

Six days ago, the Bradley had dropped off the squad of six soldiers—who were supposed to operate on their own in the field for three hours—and then withdrew for the badly needed repair of the vehicle's steering. The soldiers had tested a non-lethal weapon against the infected that used active denial technology. They deployed a line of concertina wire, set up their device, and blasted a klaxon to attract any infected within hearing range.

The device, shaped like a large hoe attached to the face of a basketball backboard, is a transmitter that beams energy waves that penetrate the skin and produce an intense burning sensation. The idea is that whoever is subjected to this reflexively tries to avoid the beam and submits. It didn't work on the infected. They only became enraged and attacked until their flesh sizzled, and even then they still attacked until they fell down.

Another Bradley had been tasked to pick up the soldiers, but it never came because by the time it left on its mission to recover the squad, the soldiers were already dead. Sarge knew this but had to see for himself that it was true. These dead boys were his people. They'd served together in Afghanistan. He placed his hand over his heart, a gesture of respect he picked up from the Afghans, and collected their dog tags.

"The device is supposed to be angled to trigger a burning feeling from the neck down," he told the others. "See how it's angled up? That's not an accident. They were desperate. In the end, they tried to burn out the eyes of the infected. They tried to blind them."

Is it okay to take these guns? they asked him. *They're better than ours. Will you teach us how to shoot them?*

"I heard about another test of long-range acoustic weapons, over in Philadelphia, that also failed," Sarge went on. "The device was supposed to cause intense pain in the ear using a certain frequency of sound, but it actually attracted the infected. They came in hundreds and killed the unit that deployed it. Pointless."

A pack of dogs yelped in the distance. Somebody, far away, fired an automatic weapon, which set off a brief crisp flurry of gunfire that sounded like the pop of firecrackers.

"None of the non-lethals worked," Sarge said. "The only thing that can stop these motherfuckers is a rifle and the will to use it."

The armored personnel carrier smashes into the abandoned traffic jam on squealing treads. Its twenty-five tons shoulder aside a minivan and crush the front of a sports car into metal pancake. The words BOOM STICK are neatly stenciled in white paint on the side of the turret, near the gun barrel. The rig plows into a pair of infected and flings them down the street in a fine red mist. The Bradley emerges from the intersection and grinds to a halt, its engine idling. The vehicle fills the street, flanked by stores topped by low-rise apartments. Using the vehicle's periscopes, its three-man crew scans the bleak, shattered landscape visible through a smoky haze. The rain has stopped. The sun is shining again.

In the back, the survivors cringe. Stopping is bad. They finger their weapons as Sarge wedges his way into the back and squats, sweating in his camouflage uniform and helmet. The commander is a large Black man, and his size makes the cramped passenger compartment appear even smaller. As always, he looks at Anne when he wants the civilians to do something. They appear to have some sort of unspoken agreement about the sharing of authority.

"Drugstore," he says. "Once you're out, it's on the left."

"Locked up?" says Anne.

"Not that we could see."

"Any signs of forced entry?"

"The door looks fine and the windows are all intact."

"No damage, then?"

"I saw no vandalism, no fire or water damage."

"Cleaned out already?"

"No, that's the thing. From what I could tell, there's still stuff on the shelves, and plenty of it."

The survivors allow themselves a brief smile. The store hasn't been looted or damaged. They'll be able to get supplies. Not everything they need, but something. Every useful item they can find is a piece that must be fitted into the puzzle of survival.

"How many infected on the street?"

"None living."

"It's worth the risk," Anne says, and Sarge nods.

"Show time," he says.

Ethan takes a deep breath to steel his nerves. He fidgets with his M4 carbine and tries to remember what Sarge told him to do if the weapon jams: slap the magazine and pull the bolt back. Observe the firing chamber and release the bolt. Then tap it and squeeze off the next round. If a double-feed, detach the mag and drop the rounds. Assuming he has time and presence of mind to do all this while a swarm of infected race hell for leather at him while shrieking their inhuman cries of recognition and rage.

He is certain that he's living on borrowed time and that one day he will be killed or infected. He was a math teacher; he understands probabilities. Every day, just to live, he has to give it everything he has. If just once he's a little slow, or takes a wrong turn, or is in the wrong place at the wrong time, they'll catch him.

How many days can a man go on like that? Never be a little slow, never take a wrong turn, never be in the wrong place at the wrong time?

It's true his body and mind have risen to the challenge. But while his body is fast dropping fat and becoming more toned, he often feels stabbing pains in his back and neck, especially after sitting in the Bradley for hours. The truth is he's a middle-aged man and not in top shape. His mind similarly has sharpened, ever vigilant for threats, purged of the pop culture nonsense and petty worries that plagued the middle class before Infection. But the stress is slowly damaging his mind and steadily shaving time off his lifespan. Ethan is rising to the challenge, but he doesn't know how long he can keep this up before he'll finally break down.

In the end, he knows the odds are stacked against survival. The infected spread disease through violence. Possessed by their aggressive pathogen, they're meat puppets, totally expendable and intent only on finding new hosts. They drink from gutters and toilets. If they get hungry, they eat the dead. They have nothing to lose. They run through fire and bullets to reach their prey. If you're standing, they punch you. If you're down, they stomp you. When you stop fighting back, they bite and infect you. The pathogen penetrates the blood through saliva in the bite and enters the central nervous system. From there, it mainlines into the brain, where it proliferates in the limbic system and produces rage. The pathogen is so strong, so virulent, it paralyzes you in seconds and takes total control in minutes.

And then you become one of them.

In the beginning, there weren't as many of them. Ethan never imagined how terrifying another human being could be in a world where all people had become predators or prey. Now the predators appear to outnumber the prey, as least in downtown Pittsburgh. Either that or, just as likely, the prey is hiding. The power has been out for days, and it's hard to imagine how people are living behind their locked doors and drawn shades without food or plumbing. In just a few more days, this city will be unlivable.

It's horrible to think that his students are out there somewhere, hunting him.

"I'll drop the ramp, and then we'll move the rig about twenty meters down the street and park it in the first alley on the right," Sarge tells them. "You'll have to put your own eyes on the street. There are a lot of buildings, a lot of windows."

The survivors not only have to watch out for the infected, but for other survivors living in the neighborhood, who might fight to protect the store.

Gnawing a wad of gum, the cop says, "Sarge, we didn't get a chance to tell you. We're all sorry. You know, about what happened to your guys back there."

The survivors nod in sympathy, but they're uncomfortable. They're sorry they didn't find the soldiers alive, partly because it would have been a relief to turn over responsibility for their safety to somebody more qualified. On the other hand, if they'd found the soldiers alive, Sarge might have left them stranded and gone off with his infantry to fight.

The soldier gives the cop a sharp glance. She blushes and adds, "If you need a friend, you can talk to me. That's all."

"I have no friends," Sarge says. "All my friends are dead."

The ramp eases to the ground on whining hydraulics, flooding the compartment with smoggy sunshine and the acrid stench of burning chemicals.

The survivors exit the Bradley and fan out to establish three-sixty-degree security as Sarge taught them to do. Anne says she'll clear the store of infected before the group enters. Wendy, the cop, says she'll provide backup. Then the Kid insists on coming, but Anne tells him to stay and watch the street.

They disappear into the store guns first.

The Kid grins, dressed up like something from a reality show about teenage bounty hunters with his black T-shirt, urban BDU pants, bulletproof vest, and SWAT cap. He chews on a toothpick as he scans the street through the close combat optic of his M4.

"Is the end of the world not killing you fast enough, Reverend?" he says.

Paul pauses while lighting a cigarette then finishes and takes a drag. He exhales a long stream of smoke and picks up his shotgun. "This makes the apocalypse just a little rosier for me."

"Isn't that God's job?"

A shadow flickers across the black reverend's face, but he says airily, "God sent us you, my boy."

The Kid stops grinning. He's not sure, but he believes the old man just zinged him. He's easily zinged. Even the slightest remark makes him anxious, confused, and angry. Oblivious, Paul takes another drag and coughs into his fist. He has already forgotten the exchange. The Kid envies that kind of cool that comes with age. For the Kid, every interaction has enormous stakes.

"I hope it rains again, a really big rain that washes all this shit away," Paul says.

The Kid admires the thought. "Me too, Rev."

Wendy appears at the door and gives the all-clear. The survivors enter the store as the Bradley pulls away in a burst of exhaust. The big rig crumples another car like tin foil before staging an abrupt turn into a nearby alley.

Inside, Paul marches to the nearest secluded corner, drops his pants, and craps loudly into a five-gallon bucket covered with a toilet seat. He finishes his cigarette while clutching a roll of toilet paper. Next to him sits a bag of lime, which he'll dump into the bucket to cover up the smell. The Kid envies the way the others can eliminate their waste so casually. He needs privacy to be able to go, but privacy isn't a preferred survival trait these days. Privacy means clearing a room that might be occupied by the infected, a move the others consider an unnecessary risk. It means being vulnerable. And it involves the risk of being left behind if the group is forced to bug out.

Anne touches the Kid's shoulder and tilts her head toward the door. She has chosen him to stand guard and be their lookout. He whines briefly but does what he's told. He asks her to find him some batteries and candy. Oh, and a new toothbrush.

The survivors picked up the Kid three days ago. Cut off from the Bradley by a large swarm, they were saved by the ring of an old metal windup alarm clock on the next block, which distracted the infected long enough for them to escape. When they returned to the Bradley, they found the Kid grinning like the proverbial cat.

He refused to give his real name, Todd Paulsen, because Todd Paulsen was a loser in high school suffering a grinding avalanche of petty humiliations. Todd Paulsen is dead; the Kid killed that loser himself, and long live the Kid. The apocalypse, for some, is turning out to be filled with second chances.

The survivors were grateful and admired his ability to innovate. They invited him along and he accepted. Everybody else he knew was dead or infected. He felt safe alone and had done very well for himself, but it wasn't fun if nobody saw him doing it.

Growing up outside cliques, the Kid wondered what it'd be like to be one of *us* instead of *them*. Even among this tight-knit tribe of survivors, he was the newcomer, and he thought he'd have to suffer some type of hazing. But nobody cared, too occupied by their own survival. Then a magic thing happened. Two days ago, driving in the Bradley, Anne cleaned his glasses for him, a touching maternal gesture that made him feel like a full citizen of this group.

Last year, John Wheeler, a giant senior, picked him up in the cafeteria during study hall and dangled him over a garbage can in front of forty other students who watched with a mixture of tension, *schadenfreude*, and blunt relief that Wheeler wasn't doing it to them. The trick was always to stay in the middle of the herd. The trick was never to stand out. They were good at that. But with his good grades and clumsy adolescent skinniness, Todd Paulsen stood out. The teachers called him smart, and some of the other kids hated him for it. Then other kids hated him too, without knowing why, just to be safe.

John Wheeler fell down during the Screaming, and that means he's one of the infected. Many kids who were in study hall that day, the ones who cheered and the ones who did nothing out of fear, are either dead or controlled by the pathogen. For all the Kid knows, he's the sole surviving witness of what happened to Todd Paulsen during those terrible five minutes. Yet he can't stop reliving it, just as he can't stop reliving all his other minor humiliations. It's easier to shed your name than your baggage.

He wishes they were all alive just so they could see him now: the Kid, driving with a group of adults armed to the teeth, fighting through an apocalyptic wasteland. They'd absolve him of his humiliations with their admiration and respect.

They'd know that they'd never be able to fuck with him again because this time, he has a gun.

Wendy finds some plastic bags at the cashier and hands them to the others. Panic buying cleared most of the shelves before Infection put an end to consumerism, but there are still useful things here. She discovers a squashed plastic container filled with packages of beef jerky behind the open register, a great find. Some idiot rifled the register for its cash but left food on the floor. It goes into her bag. She finds a full pack of matches, a large bag of salt, children's vitamins, mosquito repellent, condoms, a bottle of sunscreen. It all goes into the bag. She finds a bottle opener, which she puts in her pocket.

Next, a pack of Bazooka gum, a valuable find. She spits out the old wad of gum from her aching jaws and pops in a fresh piece. She finds a box of tampons and displays it like a trophy to Anne, who merely nods as she scoops cans off the floor.

Ethan pauses in one aisle and picks up a three-subject spiral-bound notebook. He turns the blank pages as if skimming an old love letter. He brings the book to his face and breathes deep. When he lowers it, Wendy sees tears welling in his eyes.

"You okay, Ethan?"

"No," he says. "I mean, yes."

She reaches to pat his shoulder but cancels the gesture. Leaders in a crisis are not tender. Leaders in a crisis are strong. She has to be strong.

He adds, "Where would you begin to solve for x? I remember now where we left off."

"You sure you're okay?"

"Yes. Sometimes I forget where I am. Or rather when. I'm fine now."

"Why don't you go see if you can find something worth taking in the pharmacy?" she says. "Especially tranquilizers and sleeping pills. Prazosin for the bad dreams. Look for vitamins, gauze, antibiotics, Ibuprofen—hell, anything we can use."

"All right."

Wendy still considers herself a cop, which is why she still wears her uniform and badge. To her, symbols matter, especially in a time of crisis. The other survivors agreed at first, looking to her as an authority figure, but not anymore. To them, she's a valuable member of the team but otherwise just another refugee, no different than them. She can't understand why they put so much trust in Anne when she fights even harder and takes even bigger risks for the group. Wendy just wants to help. To serve and protect. The fact is, a lot of cops died back at the station so she could go on doing her job. She owes a debt to the dead.

They have witnessed the end of the world one horrible scene at a time, each as potent as the last. Pillars of smoke rising from burning communities. The sprawling wreckage of a crashed Boeing 727 scattered for miles along the highway among blackened, half-melted cars driven by charred skeletons. The infected feeding on the dead. Screaming on the radio instead of music and commercials.

For Wendy, the most crushing thing she's seen is all of the abandoned police cars once manned by people sworn to protect life and property but now swept away in the violence. The breaking of the Thin Blue Line signaled the collapse of law and order. It meant every man for himself. The infected took only minutes to wipe out half her precinct. The other cops saved her life, salvation she must continue to earn.

Strangely, the uniform probably extended her lifespan. The survivors all wear dark colors, various shades of black, tan, and gray. Paul, for example, is still wearing his black clerical suit with its white collar. They're sharp, they're the best of what's left, but they're largely here by accident. In the early days of Infection, they'd spill from the Bradley, and the infected would rush straight at anybody wearing bright colors. Red excited them most. And everybody who wore red died or became infected. Those wearing orange and yellow were next. It was Philip who figured that out. The financial analyst, dressed in a grimy black suit and gray tie, said they were all alive because they picked the right clothes the morning the slaughter began.

"Something's coming," the Kid cries from the door.

They hear a low rumble. They feel it as a subtle vibration in their feet. The survivors gather around the Kid. Anne increases the magnification on her scope and aims her rifle down the street. The sense of vibration migrates up to their knees.

She lowers the rifle. "It's a tank," she says in wonder. "A really big tank. Coming fast."

The tank smashes through an abandoned police barricade, scattering trash and rats. It's close enough for the survivors to take in the scratched and gore-splattered composite armor and massive barrel of the tank gun. They feel the roar of the engine deep in their chests. The treads shriek like a massive bird of prey.

"Um," Ethan says with a frown.

"That's an M1 Abrams," the Kid says.

"Does this mean the government is still functioning?" Paul asks.

Wendy grins. "I think we might be saved, folks."

"Get down," Ethan says.

The cop waves her arms. "Hey. We're in here!"

Their teeth vibrate. Bottles of household cleaner topple from the shelves. The windowpanes rattle in their frames. The dust dances on the asphalt.

The tank's turret swivels and aims its massive gun directly at the store.

"GET DOWN!"

The tank's machine gun fires in short staccato bursts. The survivors throw themselves to the floor as bullets crash through the windows and clatter against the walls.

"Stop it!" Ethan screams.

Wendy buries her face in her arms. Above her, the bullets rip through the air and destroy everything in their path. It sounds like somebody rattling screws and pieces of glass in a metal can next to her ear. Pieces of plastic and cardboard rain on her like confetti.

Then the firing stops.

"Is everybody all right?" she calls.

The tank turns roars past the store on steel-clad treads. The ground shakes. Shards of glass from the broken windows tinkle to the floor. The air flows thick with glittering dust and particles.

"Everybody, stay down," she says.

Wendy stands and goes to the door. She peers out at the rear of the tank, now already two blocks away, just in time to see small arms fire open up on it from apartment buildings on both sides of the street. A Molotov cocktail streams down from a third floor window and bursts against the rear of the tank, briefly setting it ablaze. She flinches. Why are those people shooting at the tank?

The Abrams grinds to a halt in a cloud of dust and returns fire with its machine guns while its turret swivels and raises the main gun to aim at one of the apartment windows.

The tip of the 105mm barrel erupts in a blinding flash. Wendy gasps and jerks her head away as the heat and light strike her with an almost physical force. The apartment building sneezes its contents onto the street in a massive explosion of dust and swirling debris. Wendy glimpses flying people and furniture in the avalanche. The massive cloud of smoke ripples and seethes down the street, plunging the survivors into virtual darkness.

"What the hell is going on?" the Kid shouts from the floor.

"I don't know," Wendy answers.

"Change of plans, I think," says Anne.

"Why is that?"

Anne replies, "That tank is going in the same direction we are."

The atmosphere is still filled with soot and ash from fires burning in the city, making the sunset spectacular with lurid alien colors. The survivors camp for the night in a service garage at a car dealership. After clearing the building, they black out the windows with paint and make sure all the doors and windows are locked up good and tight. Every nook and cranny of the Bradley's interior is filled with the tools of survival, which they carefully unload to establish their camp: flashlights and batteries, Coleman stove and propane tanks, waterproof matches, utensils, bedrolls, and gallon jugs of water. They set out a chemical fire extinguisher and a battery-operated carbon monoxide detector.

Cockroaches scuttle from the light into dark spaces. Empty cans, wrappers, and rotting food litter the floor. Others have used the garage as a refuge before them, fellow nomads who left graffiti messages and original and copied photos of loved ones on the walls. Paul and the Kid explore them with their flashlights. The light beams play across the images of people smiling in happier times before Infection, now dead or missing.

IF YOU SEE THIS MAN DALE, TELL HIM JESSIE IS STILL ALIVE AND HEADING NORTH TO THE LAKE. THE INFECTED ARE NOT PEOPLE ANYMORE: KILL THEM OR BECOME THEM! IF YOU ACT LIKE YOU ARE INFECTED THEY WILL NOT ATTACK YOU. ←THIS IS A LIE!!! IF YOU SEE THIS BOY, PLEASE TAKE CARE OF HIM AND TELL HIM HIS MOMMY LOVES HIM WITH ALL HER HEART. INFECTION TAKES LESS THAN THREE MINUTES. THE ARMY IS SHOOTING ANYTHING THAT MOVES SO KEEP YOUR HEAD DOWN. KILL THEM ALL!!! YOUNGSTOWN IS FREE OF INFECTION. ←LIE!!

REPENT, FOLKS, THE END IS ~~NEAR~~ HERE!!!!!

The survivors often have access to information such as these messages, which others have scrawled on this wall in fear and boredom and need. As usual, almost none of it is useful.

"Do you think it's true, Reverend?" the Kid says. "Are the infected not people anymore?"

"I don't know."

"Do they even have souls? Or have they already crossed over?"

"I don't know that either, Kid."

"What are they, though? Are they still men? Or animals? Machines?"

This time, Paul doesn't answer. His flashlight illuminates the faces on the wall, some of whom are dead, others infected.

It's hard to say what they are, he thinks. *Whatever they are, they're not human, but they're still our loved ones. We still love them, perhaps even more than before Infection. When somebody is gone, it's easy to remember only the good things about them. No wonder so many people can't pull the trigger and accept death or infection themselves.*

When Sara came at me, I couldn't do it either.

"Is killing them murder, Reverend? Is it a sin?"

"No," Paul says.

Ethan takes out his dead cell phone and stares at it. It doesn't ring. He returns it to his pocket. He thinks of Philip sitting in the back of the Bradley with his tie neatly knotted at his throat and his briefcase open on his lap. As the disaster unfolded, the businessman tried for days to call his broker to buy stock in home security and healthcare companies. He drooled over the killing he'd make shorting the airlines. He saw home-based power generation as the next big thing. He speculated about pharmaceuticals and trucking and water and agribusiness. The other survivors listened with polite disbelief.

Philip's broker in New York didn't answer the phone, making the man steadily more anxious. Philip said economics was simply the study of who got the pie. Infection, like the Screaming, was just another economic shock creating winners and losers, and those who could shift their investments from the losers to the winners fast would earn the biggest return. But that required a broker who answered his goddamn phone. It seemed particularly important to him that he convince Anne of his theories, but Anne would listen wearing the expression one usually brings out when rubbernecking a crash, and say nothing.

Philip started shouting into the dial tone, demanding share prices in Remington and Glock and Brinks. Then the grid failed, and he lost his signal. He was cut off now and became quiet and morose. In Wilkinsburg, while picking through the ruins of a convenience store, he saw a copy of *The Wall Street Journal* with the wrong date, sat in the ashes, and let the infected take him.

They find the dead man in a dark corner, his feet sticking out from under a tarp. They pull the tarp back to reveal the desiccated corpse sitting with its legs spread and the top half of its head exploded up the walls behind it. The corpse wears a brown uniform. This man was an employee of the Allegheny County sheriff's office. His gun is missing. Somebody has taken his shoes.

Killed, or killed himself.

Wendy kneels next to the corpse and unpins the man's star-shaped badge.

"What are you doing?" Sarge asks.

"Collecting a dog tag," she says tersely.

The soldier nods.

Anne approaches, rifle slung over her shoulder, and tells them dinner will be ready in a few minutes.

Sarge watches her closely. "Does this place remind you of anywhere in particular?"

Anne looks around at the garage as if seeing it for the first time.

"I think I was born in a place like this," she says.

Sarge nods.

She adds, "We need to talk about that tank."

"We should have followed it," Wendy says.

"The tank was going to the Children's Hospital," Sarge tells them. "Just like us."

"An isolated unit then," Anne says. "Just trying to stay alive."

"That tank was the first evidence of a functioning government we've seen in days," Wendy cuts in. "It was a patrol. We could try to find the base where it came from."

"No," Sarge says. "The tank has no base. It's going to the hospital to shell it. That tank is going to rain fire on it with every bomb and bullet it's got."

"That can't be true." Anne is at a loss for words, it's so absurd. "Why?"

"Containment. They were ordered to do it. You have to admire the dedication even while you laugh at the stupidity. The hospital was overrun nine days ago, and Infection has already spread far and wide. But just a few days ago, the military shifted from containment using non-lethals to deadly force, so they ordered the hospitals, the source of Infection, to be attacked. The tank commander is only carrying out his orders, even if they came a week too late. Its infantry escort is gone now, its base has probably moved, and every resentful shitbird in the city is apparently trying to kill it, but that tank is going to complete its mission."

"How sure are you about this?" asks Anne.

Sarge shrugs. "I know how the military has been responding. It fits."

"So what do we do?" Wendy says.

"We find another hospital. Preferably one that isn't being bombed."

"There's Holy Cross, across the river," Anne offers.

"Which river?"

"The Monongahela. In the south."

They already decided that a hospital is the ideal place to settle for several reasons. First, few people would even think to enter one. They're taboo places. Charnel houses. Unclean. After the Screaming, the infected were picked up from the ground one by one and brought to hospitals, but there wasn't enough room, so the government requisitioned schools, hotel ballrooms, indoor arenas, and similar spaces to accommodate the millions who'd fallen.

The hospitals filled to overflowing. They stacked the screamers like cordwood in the corridors. So many people required care that medical students were handed licenses, and retired healthcare workers got drafted. When the infected woke up three days later, they slaughtered and infected these people, making the hospitals epicenters for death and disease.

The hospitals are rich in resources, however, and they're defendable. Specifically, they have medical supplies, food and water, lots of space, and emergency power. And most if not all the infected are long gone, compelled to search for fresh hosts for the bug.

Anne adds, "It's worth the risk."

The three nod. The group's next move has been decided.

Wendy touches Anne's elbow and motions her aside. The two women walk through the service garage. Everywhere, they see evidence of work abandoned suddenly by the resident mechanics.

"What branch did you serve in?" Wendy says.

Anne shakes her head almost imperceptibly.

"I appreciate your service," Wendy continues. "But I'm the highest civil authority here. It would help if you acknowledged me as such in front of the others."

Anne regards the cop in the gloomy half-light emitted by the camp's LED lanterns.

Wendy clears her throat and adds, "We have to function as a team."

"You know, I didn't believe in evolution before," Anne says. She inspects a car muffler lying on the floor like the bone of a giant animal. "Now I do. We're natural selection in action. So many other people died because they wanted to die. They fought tooth and nail to survive, but they didn't want to live while everybody they knew and loved died or became infected."

"You're talking about survivor's guilt."

"Yes. We all have it. The question is whether you're going to let it kill you."

Ethan calls out to them. Supper is ready.

Anne adds, "You go on taking crazy risks like you have to prove your leadership, and you will let it kill you."

Wendy stares at the woman for a moment, unable to speak.

"I'm just doing my job," she says finally. "I'm responsible for these people."

"That's fine with me. I don't care who's in charge. I'm just trying to find refuge and help the group find it too."

"So you'll acknowledge me then," the cop presses.

"No," Anne says.

Before the world ended, the cop woke up alone at five each morning in her small apartment in Penn Hills. She showered, ironed her uniform, and wolfed down an energy bar. She put on her crisp short-sleeve black shirt over a clean white T-shirt and stepped into her black pants. She attached her badge and pins before pulling on her bulletproof vest and Batman belt.

She reported to work at six in the morning carrying a tall cup of coffee. After roll call, she started her patrol car, told the dispatcher she was in service, and drove to her zone. Most of the time, the dispatcher called about dogs barking, suspicious characters walking through backyards or hanging around playgrounds, loud music, and domestic violence. She pulled over speeders and drunks, wrote up accidents and graffiti, gave people lifts to the nearest service station when their cars broke down. She isolated crime scenes and canvassed homes for witnesses to murders. Some days, she got so bored she could barely stay awake. Other days, so busy she ate nothing but donuts and Slim Jims.

She watched other cops act aggressively to control every encounter and tried to imitate that impersonal, in-your-face attitude. After several months on the job, she began to view most people as idiots who needed to be saved from themselves. She wrote tickets, threatened wife beaters, ate dinner in her car, waited for the next call on her radio. After a twelve-hour shift, if she didn't have to work late, she went home.

Though a large part of her job involved either cleaning up or eating other people's shit, she was proud of being a police officer and loved her job. Then the world ended, and she never felt so important or needed. A part of her rejoiced in being a cop in a lawless world. In the land of the blind, the one-eyed man is king.

The survivors share corned beef cooked on the Coleman stove with stewed tomatoes and served on paper plates on a hot bed of cooked brown rice, with canned pears for dessert. As much as they're sick of eating food from cans, they wolf down their meal. The Kid feels a piercing stab of regret as he realizes he'll probably never eat Buffalo wings again. It's odd to focus on such a trivial thing when faced with so much loss, but he realizes he's going to have to mourn the lost world one little bit at a time.

After dinner, Paul lights a cigarette and smokes in silence while the others take turns having sponge baths behind a nearby car. Wendy, breathing angrily through her nose and holding back tears, gets the solar crank radio working.

"—not a test," the familiar electronic voice says. "This is the emergency broadcast network. This is not a test. Today's Homeland Security threat level is red for severe risk. Remain indoors. Obey local authorities. Avoid individuals displaying suspicious or aggressive behavior."

One by one, the survivors chime in with the announcer and chant, "When encountering military units or law enforcement officials, place your hands on your head and approach them slowly and calmly. Do not take the law into your own hands. Respect life and private property—"

Sarge turns off the radio. "I think we can all agree that today was as bad as yesterday."

They nod glumly.

"On the other hand, Sergeant," Paul says, "we're all still here. I would consider that one for the win column."

"Amen, Rev," the Kid says.

Anne returns from her sponge bath and nudges the Kid's shoulder.

"Here's your new toothbrush."

Outside, they hear the howls of the infected and the tramp of hundreds of feet. Distant gunshots and shouts. Then it's so quiet they can hear the blood rushing through their veins.

In the dim light of the lantern, Ethan accepts a sleeping pill from Wendy and dry swallows it. He lies on his bedroll in T-shirt and shorts and relives his last conversation with his wife and child until he becomes groggy. His final coherent thought before falling into a deep sleep is a vague recollection of a Greek myth in which sleep and death are brothers.

His nightmares are exhausting trials of lurid colors and feelings, extremes of good and evil, symbols of guilt. He finally dreams of a warm evening at home, his wife pink and happy in a cherry bathrobe, holding their daughter on her lap in a rocking chair next to the toddler bed. The familiar ritual of getting ready for sleep. But the walls turn dark and sooty with ash and cluttered with graffiti tags and photos of missing children. A bullet hole appears in the window behind his wife's head. She's still smiling as she smells her daughter's hair, but her face has turned gray, her mouth and chin stained black. His little girl isn't moving. He doesn't know if she's breathing.

His wife licks the back of her head as if grooming her. As if tasting her.

FLASHBACKS: ETHAN BELL

Nine days ago, Ethan woke up in an empty bed with his heart pounding against his ribs. He found his wife in the bathroom, putting on mascara in front of the mirror with her mouth open. Mary sat on the floor, imitating her. Ever since the Screaming three days earlier, he panicked when he didn't know where his family was. He suffered nightmares in which they fell screaming. He tried not to think of his students who actually did.

"I need coffee," he said. "Where are you going, hon?" He added a quick wave and grin at his daughter. "Hi, Mary!"

"Work," said Carol. "I have to work today."

"Hi, Daddy," Mary said.

"But you weren't going to go to work until Thursday."

"Uh, today is Thursday, Ethan."

"No," he said, then smiled broadly for Mary, who'd fixed him with a keen stare, worried he was upset. "You should stay home again today. A lot of people are doing that."

"Ethan, we talked about this," his wife said, her own smile genuine. "We're all still freaked out, but the country has to get moving again. Too many things are up in the air. And we need money coming in. We have to eat."

Mary said, "No talking."

"The schools are still closed," he pointed out.

"They need room for the screamers."

"Don't call them that."

Carol snorted. "You actually want me to call them SEELS?"

"We should show a little respect, that's all," he grumbled.

Sudden Encephalitic Epileptic Lethargica Syndrome, or SEELS, was the formal term adopted by scientists to describe the mystery disease. Aside from naming it, scientists knew very little about it. Some said it reminded them of Minor's Disease, with its sudden onset of pain and paralysis caused by bleeding into the spinal cord. Some wanted to explore exploding head syndrome, frontal lobe epilepsy, maladies related to the functioning of the inner ear. A group of scientists wrote a letter to the President demanding widespread sampling of air, soil, water, and people for novel nanotechnology agents. They warned the worst may be yet to come.

Equally puzzling were the ongoing exotic symptoms exhibited by some of the victims of the new disease. Echolalia, for example, the automatic repetition of somebody else's sounds. Echopraxia, the repetition of others' movements. And, in some cases, "waxy flexibility," the victim's limbs staying in whatever position they were last left, as if made of wax.

Nobody could explain why some people had these symptoms and others didn't, just as they couldn't explain how the disease chose its victims or how it appeared almost spontaneously around the world. There were very few real facts, only hundreds of theories that tried to force these facts into a narrative that made sense.

"Look, Ethan. They'll reopen the schools soon. In the meantime, why not go to the school and see if you can volunteer at the clinic? A lot of people need care around the clock."

"Maybe," he said.

"It might do you some good," she said tartly, cutting him down with a single glance at his tangled red hair and stubble. "Get out in the sunshine a bit. It's time, Ethan."

"All right, I probably will," he lied. He had no intention of leaving the house. "Leave Mary here, then. Last night, when I was up late watching some TV, there was some kind of rioting going on all over the West Coast. I'd like to keep her close to home."

"We live in Pennsylvania. And Mary misses her friends at day care. They're holding a special candlelight vigil today for the SEELS."

"No talking!" said Mary. She was upset her parents were talking to each other and not to her. "My talking!"

Carol got down on one knee to work things out with their two-year-old, asserting their adult right to have a conversation, but the fact was the conversation was over.

Ethan made a cup of coffee, kissed them goodbye, and went back to bed. He'd been up all night again watching the news.

He woke with an uneasy feeling to the sound of sirens in the distance. Sitting up, he yawned and pulled on a T-shirt and a pair of sweatpants. Sunlight shined into the second floor bedroom picture window, which offered a spectacular view of downtown that had cost them an extra twenty thousand dollars on the house list price. Ethan and Carol had moved to the city from Philadelphia during the previous summer, and she'd insisted on having a view. It was early afternoon. He needed another cup of coffee. Then he glanced out the window and saw plumes of smoke rising up from downtown, over which helicopters swarmed. The sirens wailed.

"God," he said. He'd just known something bad was happening. He found the remote and clicked the television on.

The news reported riots throughout the country, across the world in fact, focused on the hospitals and the clinics, following the same path as the Screaming epidemic. Panicked mobs were firebombing the clinics. Families of victims armed themselves and had taken up positions outside the clinics. And the screamers, who'd lain in a catatonic state for three days, were waking up and committing acts of violence.

"Holy crap," Ethan said. His heart raced in his chest.

He dialed his wife, but all circuits were busy. Should he drive to the day care and get Mary? Then drive to the bank and get Carol? What if she were already driving here? What if she were trying to call him right now? He hung up the phone and paced, racked by indecision. Surely, if there was a crisis this big, Carol was already on the move. If he left the house, he'd never find her.

He felt paralyzed. He needed some time to think. He needed more information. He went downstairs and turned on the TV in the living room. A newsman sobbed through evacuation instructions.

"Nobody knows anything!" he shouted at his empty house.

He hit redial on his phone repeatedly but kept getting an all-circuits-busy signal. Then the news cut to video recorded by a helicopter accompanied by the breathless monologue of a reporter describing the scene.

A group of people surrounded a family of four in a tightening circle in the middle of a busy downtown intersection. The man stepped in front of his wife and kids. The other people rushed in. The man punched one, and then they beat him and his family to the ground and kicked them for a while and tore the children limb from limb. The screamers ate their remains while the man and his wife lay on the ground twitching.

"Jesus Christ," Ethan said at the edge of tears.

The reporter was screaming, "The SEELS are changing. Oh God, oh God, they're attacking people, they're attacking everybody they see, they're eating the children!"

Ethan turned the TV off and went back upstairs to watch history unfold from his picture window. Towers of smoke dominated the downtown skyline. It was chaos down there. Across the street, he saw his neighbors' houses standing in a neat row.

One stood dark and silent, the living room window painted with streaks of dark fluid.

What is that? Could they be here already?

Pale faces looked back at him from an upstairs window of the house directly across from his. The three Tillman kids. Their father, Roger, paced downstairs in the living room with one of his big hunting rifles.

Roger had the right idea: bunker down. Ethan stared at their house for a long time and tried to think about what came next: collect his family. Then food, water, defense. But everything was fuzzy. He couldn't focus on these things beyond abstractions.

A hole appeared in the window with a sound like a wine glass breaking in the sink. Roger Tillman lowered his rifle and squinted up at him through a puff of gun smoke from his porch. Ethan backed away from the window in a dry-mouthed stupor.

Why did Roger do that? Jesus, he could have killed me!

He retreated to the bathroom, locked the door, and sat on the toilet. Long minutes passed, and nothing happened. He sat there until he started to feel safe again.

The gunshot made him realize how serious the situation was. *What am I still doing here? I have to find my family. I have to find them now and get them to a safe place.*

Ethan ran to his car and drove to the bank and then the day care but both were closed, locked and empty, just as he'd feared. He saw many terrible things, but later, he'd remember the entire drive only as a blur. As darkness fell, he returned home and paced his house, alternating between rage at Carol for not coming home and blind panic that what happened to that family on TV might have happened to his wife and precious little girl. He howled in torment until he realized he was starving and needed food. He drank more coffee instead and watched the news in the dark and hit redial on his phone until he fell asleep.

For the next few days, he sortied out in the car anywhere he thought Carol and Mary might be but couldn't find them. The trips became increasingly dangerous. Each morning, he woke up hopeful and each night, he passed out from exhaustion in a state of near suicidal despair. The days began to blur together until the power failed. There were no more sirens downtown, only sporadic gunfire. He realized he had plenty of meat in the freezer that he should cook before it spoiled, but the gas stove didn't work either. He ate as much as he could from the refrigerator and washed it down with the cold dregs left in the coffee pot and then went back to staring at his cell phone, willing it to ring and feeling sick. He tried to pour himself a glass of water but the plumbing didn't work. He hadn't filled the tub or any gallon jugs. For some reason, he'd thought the plumbing didn't need electricity to work. He stared at the faucet, feeling helpless rage at his own impotence.

He tried to call his wife again, but his cell phone couldn't get a signal. The collapse of the power grid had cut off phones, cellular communication, and the Internet. Ethan was completely isolated from his family now. From everything. He knew all about the mathematics of probability. Finding them at this point would be like finding a needle in a haystack—a haystack soaked in gasoline and blazing.

That night, he lay curled in a fetal ball on the bed and cried into his wife's pillow, unable to even look inside his daughter's room out of fear of losing what was left of his mind. A machine roared to life outside, and he rose in utter darkness, grateful for the distraction. Across the street, Roger Tillman had a generator going, and the house blazed with light under a beautiful night sky filled with stars. Ethan ran his hand over his scraggly new beard and questioned his very manhood. That Roger really knew what he was doing. He had a gun, generator, food, water, and his family under wraps. He'd prepared for the apocalypse. He'd thought of everything, while Ethan had whined and paced.

Black shapes and shadows flickered around the Tillman house. A man ran from the darkness into the pool of illumination created by the bright porch light. He bolted straight into the front door and bounced off with a startling crash, howling in pain and rage. Then ran back again, and again. A woman appeared at the edge of the light on wobbly legs, dressed in a torn tracksuit and holding onto a purse slung over one shoulder. Her head jerked in little spasms like a bird as she walked to the living room window and peered in as if looking for somebody to ask directions. She punched the window until she put her fist through it. Her arm sprayed blood as she fell to the ground twitching. Another woman took her place.

Within minutes, the house was surrounded. Some crawled into the broken window. Roger banged away at them with his rifle, but now dozens of people, drawn to the light and noise, poured in through every window and door. Jane Tillman howled like an animal, *Don't you touch them you motherfuckers, I'll kill you, I'll fucking cut you.* Roger roared, *Get back, get back, there's too* many. Shadows flickered inside the Tillmans' living room. A table lamp spilled, its bulb popping in a flash of light before the room plunged into darkness. The rifle banged several more times. The muzzle flashes lit up the dark. Then the shrieks for mercy began.

Moments later, the house stood quiet except for the buzz of the generator and the screamers stumbling around the illuminated porch, drawn like moths to the light and sound.

Ethan returned to his bed and fell into a deep dreamless sleep until a crash jarred him awake.

Footsteps clomped downstairs.

Somebody is in the house.

He almost called out but didn't. He knew it wasn't Carol. He realized then that he'd lost hope that she'd bring Mary home, and that it was time to get out of this house if he wanted to survive the week. The threat of death was once miles away, but now it was crashing through his front door.

There are people in my house who can't be spoken to or reasoned with. Things of nightmares that are now wild animals and hunting me even though they are not yet aware of my existence. Creatures that will claw and bite me until I'm dead or become one of them. Some of them wear faces that I know, but they're not human anymore.

The first step was to get out of here.

The sun burned over a smoking America, and its first rays filled the bedroom with dim red light. Ethan stuffed a backpack with clothes, photos and trinkets, and a hairbrush from his wife's drawers. He found a tiny yellow rubber airplane on the floor, a toy left there by Mary days ago, and pocketed it. He wanted to take as much of them with him as possible. The floorboards creaked downstairs. He picked up his baseball bat and felt its reassuring weight in his hands. Here we go, then.

Footsteps in the den, the room he and Carol used as a home office. Moaning in a female voice. Whatever it was sounded more like a woman in mourning than a monster. As he descended the stairs, however, he could feel the air thicken. The woman sensed his presence and growled deep in her throat. His heart pounded against his ribs. Books and papers crashed to the floor in the den. The woman yelped and paced. She shouldered the walls as she moved. He forced himself to breathe in and out, in and out, as his bowels liquefied. Feeling the weapon in his hands, he wanted to rush in there and bash her brains out, but the moment passed and left him feeling drained and even more terrified.

Ethan slipped out the front door and ran to his car parked in the driveway. He saw a neighbor and waved, glad to see a familiar face, but the man howled and raced toward him with murder in his eyes. Something snarled and thrashed in the rosebushes behind him. Ethan jumped in his car, started the engine, and stomped the gas pedal as his neighbor threw himself against the door with a heart-stopping bang. The car roared as it built speed.

"Get out of the way!" he cried and jerked the wheel.

People raced from driveways and lawns. A woman bolted into the passenger side window, cobwebbing the glass and leaving a red smear clotted with tufts of hair. A man surged into the back door, bounced off, and then ran alongside, pounding on the glass with bloody fists until he lost his balance and fell hard against the blacktop. Ethan swerved to avoid hitting an overturned truck and other people running at him like human missiles.

He leaned on the horn, but the sound only attracted more. The shapes impacted and bounced off the car with loud bangs, leaving blood and dents and cobweb fractures. Sobbing, Ethan drove past a burning house with a burning tree in its front yard. The car plowed into a snarling woman in a red dress and sent her flying over the roof. Another blurred against the door, cracking her nose against the window and leaving a long squirt of blood.

"Stop it!" he howled. "Fucking stop it!"

The neighborhood began to turn from residential to commercial. He glanced at his rear-view mirror and saw a horde shrieking twenty yards from his bumper. He became aware that an old Beatles song played on the car's speakers. His pursuers began to lag behind. They gave up the chase and watched him go.

It's over. He made a ragged sound that was part chuckle, part sob. *Thank God.*

By the time he glanced back at the road, it was too late to avoid the mob running at him. The car plowed into their bodies and flung them over the car like ragdolls. One became stuck like a nightmarish hood ornament, flailing with its one good arm. The crumpled hood sprayed scalding water onto the body and windshield. Ethan, half blinded, gunned the engine. The man detached with a howl and got caught in the right wheel hub, which broke the body with an awful cracking sound. The car jerked to the right. Everything went black.

Ethan awoke on the sidewalk, stumbling away from his car that rested half-smashed against the wall of a department store. He tried to run but instead fell to his knees vomiting. He was holding his backpack.

Behind him, shrieking. The tramp of feet.

One of the department store's display windows was broken. He climbed in and limped through the store past selections of men's ties and belts and leather shoes. Several men clawed their way inside and gave chase at a loping gait, hunting him as a pack through the cosmetics department.

They yelped as they gained on him. Ethan dropped his pack and ran blindly, gasping for breath. One of the men appeared at his side with a snarl. A second later, he lunged and tackled a mannequin Ethan had just passed and began beating and biting it. Another pushed over a second mannequin and stomped its face. The rest snapped at Ethan's heels. Inspired, he saw a mannequin at the end of the aisle and ran straight for it.

The mannequin's fists belched flame and smoke. Ethan threw himself to the ground as his pursuers toppled around him.

Ethan lay on his back dripping sweat and gasping. He looked up at his savior, a petite brunette dressed in a black T-shirt and jeans. Her hair was cropped short. She had a hard look about her, as if she'd been born to kill people and had been doing it for years. Her face was disfigured by fresh scars. Her eyes looked old.

She helped him to his feet and handed him one of the pistols. She pointed at the wounded men who writhed and keened on the floor in widening pools of blood.

"Finish them, and you can join us," she said.

That was how Ethan met Anne.

THE HOSPITAL

The Bradley mounts the steel cantilever Liberty Bridge and crosses its five hundred-foot main span over the Monongahela River at a careful pace. There are a few abandoned cars cluttering the four-lane bridge, but "Sarge"—the nickname he gives civilians so they feel comfortable around him—isn't taking any chances. He knows a National Guard artillery unit destroyed several bridges in the area in a misguided effort to contain the spread of infection. The last thing they need is to drive through a big hole and plummet more than forty feet into the muddy waters below.

The density of vehicles thickens as the Bradley approaches the other side of the river. Several lanes are blocked by lines of cars stacked in front of abandoned makeshift barricades. Piles of corpses draw flies in front of a machine gun mounted on a heap of sandbags. The Bradley speeds up and passes the scene, popping skulls under its treads.

The armored fighting vehicle rolls into the South Hills neighborhoods. Sarge opens the hatch for a look around in the open air and sees more barricades and piles of corpses. Some of the barricades apparently held; some were overrun. Either way, it didn't matter. Even if they held, Infection was everywhere, eventually making barricades meaningless. Plastic bags and bits of garbage dance in the wind. A shredded T-shirt hangs on the branches of a tree, waving bye-bye at him, while another tree burns energetically like a giant torch, scattering heat and sparks and ashes. A pair of military jets fly high overhead, a reminder the government is still alive, still fighting its own people.

The houses here are covered in graffiti. After the Screaming left more than a billion catatonics twitching on the ground all over the world, volunteers in these communities worked with local authorities to search each house for victims and get them to a place where they could receive care. Orange posters, still taped to streetlight poles, encourage citizens to call tip lines to report SEELS for pickup. Black Xs are still sprayed on many doors marking houses that have been searched and cleared of victims of the disease. The tragedy is that by helping the screamers avoid starvation and dehydration, a lot of good people selflessly planted the seed of their own destruction.

Some houses have other graffiti on them; as people fled their homes, they sprayed messages, and other refugees added their own, using the houses for communication. Names and dates. Missing persons. Directions and wayfinding. *Going south. Avoid the police station. Don't trust Earl Felt, coward ditched us. Bill, I'm going to get grandma.* Other messages warn travelers of infestations, give opinions on everything from purifying water to effective killing methods, or offer trade. Some of the graffiti are simple tags. Newly formed militias claiming territory. Boasts of kills and time served. Totemic symbols scrawled by people in a hurry. Arrows. Biohazard signs. Skulls and crossbones.

The infected stumble and hold their heads, wailing in a constant state of real and metaphysical pain. They glower and bare their teeth at Sarge as he drives by in the armored vehicle.

☣

The survivors find the tall muscular man on his front porch wearing a bathrobe and boxer shorts. The man shouts and waves a pistol in his right hand and a battered folded-up umbrella in his left. All the neighboring houses have a large black X painted on their front doors; the Screaming apparently wiped out this community and left this man its sole survivor.

"This is my neighborhood!" He fires a round with his pistol and kills a running infected, who falls sprawling on the sidewalk. "You ain't welcome here!"

The Bradley's gunner sizes up the man through the periscope and says, "I think we found somebody who might be big enough to take you, Sergeant."

Sarge snorts and says, "I like his spunk. He's a fighter."

"Spunk as in crazy," the gunner says. He has the square jaw of an action movie hero and wears a Dora the Explorer Band-Aid on the left cheek of his stubbled face. "Crazy as in a threat to all of us."

"If crazy disqualified membership, there'd be no club in this rig. Ha."

"I thought the plan was we want survivors, not fighters. That's what you said."

"Fighters are useful too," Sarge says cryptically. "We can't do job interviews, Steve. We're a man short. Let's invite him on. If he blends, he blends."

"You're the boss, Sergeant," the gunner says with a shrug.

The man roars: "Kids used to play on this street!"

Crack. Another infected falls. *Crack.* Another.

Sarge says, "Something about him reminds me of Randy Devereaux. Remember Devereaux?"

"Not really, Sergeant. I hardly knew him."

"Right," Sarge says. "You're right. That's my bad." Steve and Ducky, the driver, are new to the Bradley, replacements for the previous crew, who were claimed by the Screaming nearly two weeks ago back in Afghanistan. Two weeks and an eternity. The replacements barely had any contact with the Bradley's infantry squad, the boys who survived the Taliban and the Screaming and then flew all the way home to die in a Walmart parking lot in Pittsburgh.

"This is a nice place to live!"

Sarge calls out to him, but the man ignores him. If he doesn't trust the military, maybe one of the civilians can coax him. Anne volunteers to get out and do the inviting. While the Bradley stands idling, she approaches with her hands up, palms out.

"What's your name?" she asks.

The man glares at her sideways then waves her off. "Aw, you don't live here neither."

"My name is Anne. There are five of us, plus the crew—"

The pistol cracks in the man's hand twice and drops two distant running figures.

"I am making my stand!" he announces to the sky.

"Come on, get in," Anne says. "You can come with us."

"I said step off, bitch!"

Sarge laughs, shaking his head, while the gunner grins.

"But we want you to come with us."

"Too dangerous out there," the man tells her. He waves his umbrella over his head. "It's raining zombies!"

Crack crack

He fires again several times at distant figures running down the street. At long range, barely looking, he doesn't miss. One of the kills, Sarge sees it clear, is a headshot. The infected's head snaps back, and he's dead in the blink of an eye.

Steve says, "Is he actually hitting anything with that peashooter?"

"Yeah, he is. In fact, every shot hit a separate moving target and brought it down at between twenty-five and thirty meters."

"You're kidding."

"I'm not a kidder, Steve."

"With a handgun, though? Wow, this guy is amazing."

"No, you're right," Sarge says. "He's crazy. Radioactive."

He calls out to Anne, who jogs back to the vehicle.

"This is my home! My land!"

Crack crack crack

Sarge lowers the telescopic seat and closes the single-piece hatch.

"How long do you give him, Sergeant?"

"I don't know, Steve. Longer than most. Not long enough."

They reach the hospital. The survivors fan out.

The reverend runs his hand over his salt-and-pepper stubble and takes in the massive hospital looming against the graying sky. The air is cooling, and he can feel the tickle of tiny raindrops on his face. Dull thunder grinds in the distant ether, like God moving his furniture across Heaven's floor.

Now this is good weather for an apocalypse, Paul tells himself. A gray sky against which black birds swarm. He found the past two weeks of May sunshine jarringly discordant with the end of the world. The diseased walking blindly past flowers in bloom. *(Earth abides.)* The dead rotting away on lush green grass and in overgrown gardens, slowly eaten by bacteria and insects and birds and animals. By the very soil. *(Yea, the earth abides.)*

Paul wonders if God, who also abides, is as impervious as the weather to mankind's sufferings or if, like the grass and the animals and the insects, his creator is getting something out of it.

The drizzle turns into a spring shower. The survivors set out buckets to catch the water and decide to wait out the downpour inside the hospital instead of the Bradley. They navigate a cluster of abandoned ambulances and dead bodies and enter what is supposed to be the emergency room but instead looks like a burned-out slaughterhouse. Signs of extreme violence are everywhere in this place. Charred bodies litter the floor under a thick layer of ash and dust. The walls are painted with dried blood.

"When the first infected woke up and spread out into the city, the first responders brought the victims of the violence here, to the hospital," says Ethan. "Gift wrapped for the rest."

"It looks like some concerned citizens then showed up and firebombed the place," Wendy says. She kicks at the ash and raises a small cloud of black dust.

The place gives them the creeps. The hospital seems eerily deserted except for the charred dead. It's not hard to imagine doctors and nurses hurrying across this noisy room to greet hardworking first responders bringing in broken and dying people for lifesaving treatment. But this is where Infection started. After the Screaming, the people who fell down were brought here. Three days later, they awoke to slaughter and infect the people who'd worked around the clock to keep them alive. They killed families come to maintain their anxious vigil. Then they went out into the city in the early morning hours, driven by the pathogen's simple programming.

Attack, overpower, infect.

Now it's a killing floor. A dead place. Sarge regards a bloody wheelchair crumpled in a corner, the walls above it riddled with bullet holes. Wall-mounted electronic medical devices hang uselessly. Disturbed by movement, black ash swarms in drifts in the air, acrid and bitter.

Ethan searches the faces of the others for encouragement and finds none. They look as damaged as he feels. The place has an almost supernatural aura about it. As familiar as the hospital is in some ways, in many ways it feels like the unknown.

☣

Paul wishes the dead had come back to life to eat the living. That there was truly no room in hell anymore, and the end of days had come. Because then there'd be evidence of a supernatural cause instead of just a bug created in a lab by men to kill other men, or whatever it was that started all this. There'd be evidence of a hell and true evil and Satan. And if there is a Satan, there is a God, and if there is a God, then death isn't the end, but the beginning. Man's suffering over a lifetime is nothing compared to an eternity of bliss in God's direct presence. To see the dead rise is to see the end of days and with it, the end of faith—the beginning of certainty. With such certainty, Paul would willingly walk into the embrace of the dead and let them tear him apart and eat him. Didn't Christ suffer more on the cross? What use is this old fleshly cage when paradise awaits the spirit?

His wife always laughed at him when he watched films about Satan visiting the earth with a plan to end the world, only to be stopped by an action hero with a shotgun. He'd cheer for Satan to get on with it. He'd yell at the action hero: why are you fighting God's plan? Let Satan win already so we can all go to Heaven!

☣

"We can't stay in this room," Sarge says. He crosses his arms and nods to Anne. "What's our next move?"

Anne shakes her head. She looks back at him with raised eyebrows.

"We treat this like climbing a mountain," Wendy says. "It's too big. So we conquer it in stages. But first we need a base camp."

"Sarge has military experience," Anne says in a quiet voice. "I think we should ask him what he thinks we should do."

Sarge nods at the transfer of authority, which he expected. "There are some simple tactics for taking down a building. Wendy, that analogy of yours was actually very good."

"Go ahead, Sarge," the cop says. "It's your show."

"All right," he says. "Here's how I see it. There are three things we need to do. One: secure a piece of this building for ourselves. Two: strip it down of anything that we can use that will keep us alive. And three: avoid obvious signs that the building has new ownership. We all agreed on that?"

The survivors nod.

"The crew and I will get the rig under cover. Out of sight, but not too far. Anne and Paul, find a janitor's closet and get as much bleach as you can. Mops and rags. Then find a broom."

"You want us to clean this room?" Paul says, incredulous.

"No. Later on, we're going to make it exactly as it was before we showed up. We'll need to get rid of our footprints, and we'll need the broom for that. Okay?"

They nod.

"And while you're doing it, take a look and see what kind of supplies might be around we can come back for later," Sarge adds.

"Got it," Anne says.

"Wendy, Ethan, and the Kid will go up to the third floor, seal themselves in, and then start clearing it of anything living." Sarge grins. "Then we do the cleaning. We'll need to scrub that level from top to bottom with bleach and air it out before we can move in. But only the rooms on the side of the hall away from the windows. Don't clean the rooms with the windows, since again we don't want to advertise to anybody that the building has new ownership. Just seal those rooms and leave them. Okay? Once we get all that done, we can do some exploring."

The survivors agree. It's a good plan.

When Paul's wife fell down during the Screaming, he arranged for her care in their home. The next day, he visited the hospital, where exhausted first responders and volunteers still delivered scores of twitching bodies, and tried to provide counseling and strength to the families of the victims.

He expected the Spirit to tell him what to say, but nothing came. Feeling hollow, he rolled up his sleeves and helped empty bedpans for hours. That night, he held a special service. The church was filled to standing room only. Many held candles as a symbol of their vigil, their hope for the fallen to wake up. This wasn't going to be a typical service. Paul simply wanted to speak for a few minutes and offer comfort to his flock through the power of prayer. He had no sermon planned. The Spirit would move him, would speak through him at last.

Looking at all the anguished and weeping faces on the benches, he began by asking rhetorically why this happened.

For long, agonizing minutes, the Spirit said nothing. He was on his own.

He cleared his throat and said, "John, chapter thirteen, verse seven: 'Jesus replied, "You don't understand now what I am doing, but someday you will."'"

Several in the congregation nodded. They waited for him to continue, but he fell silent. It wasn't enough for him to say the Lord works in mysterious ways. Not nearly enough.

Why would God allow this to happen? He couldn't fathom it. The standard arguments raced through his mind justifying God's existence in a world in which God allows evil to happen to good people. *God's creation has free will, and that includes the free will to do evil.* But what evil did his Sara do? *God allows evil to thrive in a world corrupted by original sin.* But weren't the sins of Adam and Eve and everybody since, including Sara, washed away by the blood given by the sacrifice of Jesus Christ? *Evil is complementary to good.* But how could Paul see anything good in a world without his beloved wife?

God is testing us. God is trying to teach us something.

No, he decided. *God isn't teaching.*

God was punishing.

Paul told the congregation, "The good book also says: 'And if you fail to learn the lesson and continue your hostility toward me, then I myself will be hostile toward you. I will personally strike you with calamity seven times over for your sins. I will send armies against you to carry out the curse of the covenant you have broken. When you run to your towns for safety, I will send a plague to destroy you there, and you will be handed over to your enemies.' Leviticus. I intend to learn why these verses were written. I intend to learn the lesson God is trying to teach us through such harsh discipline."

His congregation didn't like his message. They didn't want to be forsaken. They wanted answers. They wanted comfort and mercy. They stared back at him with terror.

The Old Testament God of justice was back, and Paul, who'd worshipped and studied and preached the good news of the New Testament God of mercy and love all his life, didn't know what God wanted from him. For two days, he prayed. Sometimes, he prayed for understanding. Mostly, he prayed God would show mercy and bring his Sara back to him.

Two nights later, his prayers were answered. His wife rose in her nightgown, her eyes black and cold as a serpent's, and lunged shrieking for his throat.

☣

The survivors climb the stairs to the third floor. Wendy and the Kid volunteer to clear it while Ethan guards the stairs so nobody can get in or out. They leave him huddled in a corner, terrified at being alone.

The Kid walks ahead of Wendy, scoped carbine shouldered and ready to fire. He jerks the barrel back and forth as he scans for targets, though he's not paying much attention to what he's doing but instead imagining what he looks like to the beautiful, blond cop. He wonders if Wendy is impressed with his warrior skills. He loves his new M4. He wishes it had a laser sight. That would be so cool. She walks behind him and to his right, holding her Glock in her right hand and a flashlight in her left. Their footsteps disturb the dust that carpets the floor.

The Kid bends over with an explosive sneeze, followed by another.

"Shit," he says, his face burning. "Sorry about that. That wasn't very ninja."

The cop offers a grim smile. "We're not trying to be ninja. We're here to clean up, not sneak around."

"Oh, right."

"You know, I'm never going to get used to calling you Kid."

His mind reels at this. "You don't like it?"

"I'd rather call you by your real name."

"It's Todd," he says. "But don't tell anybody else."

"I promise," she says. "It's our secret."

He says nothing, flustered and afraid he might blurt out something stupid and irrecoverable.

Wendy motions for him to stop. "You ready to shoot that gun, Todd?"

He nods.

"Then let's clear this hallway." The cop calls out, "Hey! Hello? Anybody home?"

A woman bursts from one of the recovery rooms. Dressed in hospital scrubs stained with dried blood down the front, she jogs toward them with a bark. The survivors tense. The ammonia smell of piss assaults their nostrils and makes their eyes water.

"Who?" says the Kid.

"You," says the cop.

The Kid wishes he could set his carbine to full auto and let it rip like in the movies, but Sarge said not to do that. Sarge said you don't need *suppression*. You just need to stop somebody, running right at you, with as few rounds and as little energy as possible.

The Kid doesn't aim at the woman's head, which offers only a small lurching target. Instead, he aims at her center torso and squeezes the trigger. The M4 fires a burst of three bullets.

The center of the woman's chest explodes. She stumbles, wincing and smoking, against a wall and topples to the floor.

The man turns the corner and lunges at them from behind. Wendy wheels and fires her Glock. The bullet enters his left eye socket, scrambles his brain and shoots the mess out the back of his head. He collapses without a sound, dead before he hits the floor.

"Nicely done," the Kid says, feeling drained already.

"I swallowed my gum," Wendy says.

The corridor echoes with howls and the tramp of sneakers, dress shoes, high heels, bare feet. Wendy and the Kid freeze. They stand back to back with guns ready.

They thought the hospital would be largely emptied, but they were wrong.

☣

Sunlight can't reach this part of the building where it's now perpetual night. The corridor connects the emergency room with the guts of the hospital. Paul and Anne search for supplies along its length. Their breathing and footsteps sound far too loud in their ears. Paul lights the way with a highway flare that reveals bloody handprints on the wall. Bodies lie on the floor. The air reeks of bleach and rot. Water drips somewhere close. A door slams far away. Paul's shoes crunch on the scattered remains of a smashed jar of tongue depressors. Rats scamper along the walls before disappearing into the dark.

"I made a mistake, Reverend," Anne says, shattering the silence.

"What kind of mistake?"

"The kind you regret."

Paul grunts. He doesn't know what to say. This is survival. He doesn't think it's possible to be alive today without having regrets. He's trying hard to keep his moral compass aimed in the right direction, but the harsh truth is morality is a luxury at a time like this. There's plenty of guilt to go around. He wishes there was just a little forgiveness. But even guilt is a luxury reserved for those still alive and feeling safe enough to experience it.

He pauses in front of a door and holds up his flare.

"Custodial," Paul reads. "I think this is it. It's unlocked."

Too late, he understands Anne wasn't talking to him as a fellow survivor. She was speaking to him as a man of the cloth. *Sorry, lady,* he wants to say, *that well has run dry at the moment.* He realizes he knows so little about the people on whom his life depends on a daily basis. He glances at this petite woman holding her powerful scoped rifle and the satchel filled with ammo and thinks, *Take the gun away, and she could be a housewife. A dentist. An actress doing local theater. President of the PTA.* The only part of her he has really cared about, however, is her natural talent with the rifle. Her talent at killing that has kept him alive for so long while other men, better men, have died.

"Reverend, did you have to kill somebody you love?"

Paul remembers Sara getting older, and how, on some level, he saw her as a mirror reminding him that he was getting older. He didn't like it. *Dying? Beats getting old*, Sara used to say. She had a great attitude about it. He often wondered about the strength of his faith if he was afraid of getting old and dying. But even then, his mortality was still just a frightening abstraction. Not like the past nine days, during which he has been continually and painfully aware of the thin layer of ice separating life and death. You walk along, and you fall through, and then either there's a Heaven or there's only oblivion. Sara used to joke, *If you want to be remembered for a really long time after you're gone, die young.*

He remembers lighting a cigarette in the alley behind his house several nights after the Screaming. So late at night, it was practically morning. He'd tossed and turned and barely slept. The neighborhood twenty-four hour convenience store was open, and he bought a pack of cigarettes to satisfy an incredible sustained craving he felt upon waking. Now here he was, smoking for the first time in years. Beating an addiction takes belief in a higher power, and while his faith in God helped, the strength of his marriage got him to finally kick the habit. Now Sara lay on a bed inside his house, connected to an intravenous bag, and here he was, standing in the alley lighting up and blinking at the head rush. He coughed, but by the third drag, he was hooked again. Like riding a bike. He enjoyed the quiet. A dog barked and stopped. For the first time in the past few raw days, he felt something like an inner peace. At least one itch had finally been scratched.

A figure appeared under the streetlight at the end of the alley, a small silhouette. Paul squinted at it for a few moments, unsure it was even a person until he realized it was growing larger. Moving toward him. It passed a light fixture mounted on a neighbor's garage, and Paul caught a glimpse of its terrible face. It was breathing hard and running at Paul as fast as the average human being can run. It was doing the hundred-yard dash, and Paul was the finish line. For several critical moments, Paul was outside his body, watching himself do nothing. He wasn't sure he could move; his legs had turned to water.

He started to feebly ask, *Can I help you?* He barely finished the sentence before turning and sprinting back into his backyard. He locked the gate behind him while his heart hammered. Hissing like an animal, the man paced outside the gate. Paul walked carefully back to his house on wobbly legs, still filled with dread.

Inside, Sara sat on the edge of her bed. Waiting for him.

"No," Paul says. "I haven't killed somebody I love. Have you?"

"Yes," Anne says.

☣

The doors at the end of the corridor open. A snarling man races from the gloom. The Kid fires a burst that obliterates his face. The man is followed by a swarm of infected that pours into the corridor and fills it with their horrible sour stench. Todd falls back, firing and dropping bodies.

Wendy keeps pace at his side, covering him with her pistol. The beam of her flashlight glitters across red eyes. The Kid's gun jams, and he stares at his weapon in numb surprise. The cop empties the Glock into the snarling faces, drops the mag, loads another. The Kid wrestles with the bolt until a howling woman lunges at him with hands splayed into claws. Holding the carbine sideways in front of his body for protection, he slams it into her gray face and breaks her nose. She falls back shrieking, and a giant of a man in a paper hospital gown stomps toward him with clenched fists like sledgehammers. The top of his head erupts in a geyser of blood, and he disappears. Wendy is still shooting.

Jaws chomping in a blind rage, the first woman comes back at the Kid. Wendy stops firing. He hears a scuffle and the crack of her police baton striking bone. The Kid shoves the infected woman against the wall and smashes the carbine into her face repeatedly until she slides down the wall leaving a smear of blood. Panting, he turns and sees Wendy fighting two men twice her size and kicking the shit out of both of them. He clears the jam in his carbine and signals to her, murder in his eyes. She backs away just in time for him to gun them down with two bursts fired from the hip.

They stand quietly for several moments, unable to speak or move, utterly drained. Just breathing. A pall of gun smoke hangs in the air.

"You kick ass," he says finally.

"It's the training."

"That was way too close."

"We're okay."

"You'll have to teach me your judo skills sometime."

"Wait," the cop says. "Do you hear that?"

The Kid shakes his head. His ears are ringing too loud. "I can hardly hear *you*."

Ethan, Anne, and Paul rush into the corridor.

Anne says, "We heard the shooting and came as fast as we could."

"Sounded like a war up here," Paul says. "You okay, boy?"

"We're okay," the Kid tells him.

"Quiet," the cop says. "Something is coming."

The survivors train their light and weapons on the doors at the far end of the corridor. A strange sound comes to them that slowly reveals itself as something familiar. Chewing. The sound of an animal chewing a piece of meat, oddly loud in their ears.

"What the hell is that?" the Kid says. He winces as a fresh wave of sour milk stench assaults his nostrils with an almost physical force.

"Wait," Anne says. "Quiet."

A baby is crying.

Ethan takes two steps forward before Anne grips his arm.

"It's a baby," he says, his eyes wild. "A little baby. Oh, God."

Paul grunts in surprise. He holds his dying flare high, hoping to see better. A baby in the hospital, alone in the dark. A miracle baby. How did it survive? What has it been eating? Is it infected?

"That's not a child," Anne says.

The creature pushes the doors open and slithers through. The survivors flinch and take a step back with exclamations of horror and revulsion. It's a giant worm, half as thick as a car and twice as long, with an enormous blank face made up of wrinkled folds of skin. The creature appears to be blind. It propels itself toward them using tiny appendages, something like a cross between giant warts and tentacles, that cover its body. It looks sick, its body pale and covered in purple bruises, trembling as it slithers, starving.

Ethan sobs in horror, unable to comprehend the existence of such a repulsive thing. His concept of reality is disintegrating. It's as if the map of the world were now blemished with big blank spaces marked with the thickly scrawled warning: HERE BE MONSTERS.

The worm plows into the dead and pushes their bodies against the sides of the corridor.

"Can it see us?" Wendy whispers.

The monster pauses in front of one of the bodies and nuzzles its hair. The massive blank face cracks open, revealing a gaping black maw ringed with shark-like teeth. It begins to absorb the corpse headfirst with a slurping sound.

"Oh, God!"

The creature shudders and resumes its feast, cracking bones. Chewing.

"We need to get out of here now," Ethan says. He can't stop shaking.

"What do we do?" says the Kid. "Anne?"

The creature mews like a baby wanting milk.

Anne shoulders her rifle and says, "Kill this abomination."

☣

Gunfire fills the corridor as the survivors vent their fear and revulsion, draining their magazines into the thing. The bullets sink into the mottled gray flesh of its face with no apparent effect.

The worm abandons its grisly meal and lurches forward, its movements jerky in the strobing light of the muzzle flashes.

Ethan lowers his smoking carbine. How can it be killed? Does it even have a heart or a brain? Even if it were just a giant worm without a brain or heart, the amount of ordinance they're throwing at it should be tearing it to shreds. Yet here it comes. The creature appears to have some type of bony plate on its face that is thick enough to absorb their firepower. He sees it differently now, not as an aberration but as a form of life perfectly designed for tunnels. That would mean it's vulnerable on its sides but not its front.

What about its other end?

Something whirs in his brain and clicks.

He roars at the other survivors, "*GET BACK!*"

THE INFECTION ♦ 49

The creature's rear end leaps into the air, revealing itself as a second head with another hissing mouth ringed by giant sharp teeth. It lunges with surprising speed and force, leapfrogging its front and landing among the howling survivors.

They run. Wendy pauses at the top of the stairs and squeezes off a few more shots with her Glock before following the other survivors down.

"It's right behind me," she cries. "Keep going!"

They exit the stairs and enter the emergency room. Anne points to the Bradley parked outside in front of the floor-to-ceiling windows, the barrel of its 25mm automatic turret-mounted gun aimed directly at them. Slanted rain pelts the armor. Sarge sits in the open hatch and waves at them with both arms.

"Get down!" Anne screams.

The cannon fires. The windows burst, and the inside of the emergency room dissolves in a series of flashing explosions and enormous clouds of smoke and dust. The survivors eat ash on the ground, faces buried in their arms.

The vehicle trembles as the gun fires again: *BUMP BUMP BUMP BUMP BUMP BUMP,* vomiting empty shell casings down its metal chest.

The firing finally stops. The dust and ash swirl in black clouds.

The survivors are screaming.

☣

Gripping his AK47 rifle, Sarge climbs out of the Bradley and leaps down onto the ground. He shouts their names as he races into the hospital. The impossible creature he saw is now a quivering, smoking ruin smeared across the floor. He hopes he hasn't killed the other survivors in the bargain. The Bradley's cannon is a sledgehammer, not a scalpel, and it's best to be nowhere near where its rounds are falling and exploding if you want to live. He had no choice; he heard all the shooting upstairs and brought the Bradley back in case they needed to make a quick exit. He calls the others' names again and is relieved to hear voices shouting behind the reception desk. He finds them covered in black ash and ringed around the Kid, who kneels holding a bleeding wound on his arm. The cop screams and pushes the barrel of her Glock against his head while he pleads for his life and the others shout at her and each other.

"It's dead," Sarge says. He wipes rain from his face. "The thing is dead."

"We've got a bigger problem right now, Sarge," Anne says.

"My point is we're okay now. So let's just be cool and put these guns down."

"He got cut by the thing's teeth," Anne says. "Wendy is right. He could turn."

"I'm not doing anything unless that happens," the cop says.

"How long is incubation?"

"Somebody his age and size? Three minutes, tops."

"Who has a watch?"

Ethan spits on the face of his watch and rubs it with his thumb.

"Counting down," he says.

"I'm just trying to protect us!" Wendy says, panicking.

"You're doing the right thing," Anne tells her. "You're doing fine, Wendy."

Tears stream down her face. "I don't want to do this."

"We know. The Kid knows it too."

Anne takes a step back and raises her rifle. She's got the boy's head zeroed. If Wendy doesn't shoot, she will.

And they wait. Ethan marks the time aloud. The survivors hold their breath while the Kid listens to his life ending in ten-second increments. He once pictured a heroic end for himself, but this is getting put down, covered in filth, like an animal.

After everything he's been through, he will die from a friend's bullet. He wants to remember something important, hold onto a beautiful memory or thought he can take to the other side with him, but his mind is a raw blank. He wants to pray, but all he can remember is the one he used to recite each night as a child.

"Now I lay me down to sleep," he rasps. "I give thee Lord my soul to keep."

The survivors back away in a widening circle.

"And if I die before I wake, I pray thee Lord my soul to take."

He clenches his eyes as Ethan counts down the final ten seconds of his short life.

"Zero," Ethan says.

"But I'm still me," the Kid says.

He laughs until it turns into hysterical crying. Wendy drops to her knees and hugs him. Sarge jogs back to the Bradley to get the med kit.

The cop's tears join his. "I'm so sorry," she tells him. "I'm so, so sorry."

"I want my mom," he says.

☣

Todd Paulsen sits on the floor in one of the recovery rooms. Anne unscrews the cap on a plastic gallon jug and pours water into a bucket. Todd wearily pulls off his ruined bulletproof vest, ripped and slashed by the thing's teeth. He is skinny and normally doesn't like taking his shirt off in front of other people, but right now he doesn't care. He peels off his T-shirt and reaches to scratch a spot between his bony shoulders. He feels hollow, numb. Completely drained. If he weren't so scared of never waking up, he'd be asleep already. He didn't know death was so terrifying. It was always an abstraction to him, sometimes even a romantic one. He could afford such foolishness before today because before today, he was immortal. Now death is in his hair and skin. It lurks in the empty moments between the beats of his heart. Non-existence. Nothingness. And all the world with its beauty and horrors will go on without him as if he never existed.

What was it the preacher was always saying? The earth abides. The earth, in other words, doesn't give a shit.

Todd takes the sponge from Anne and goes through the motions of washing himself by the light of an LED lantern. His arms are filthy with ash. The black dust contrasts with his pale torso, which gleams white like a dead fish. He's ashamed of his body and his weakness. He cried in front of them. The adults. He faced death, and he cried. He couldn't think of even one beautiful memory. And worst of all, at the moment he thought he was about to die, he couldn't remember his mother's face.

"Would you rather be alone?" Anne asks him.

Todd shakes his head. He's already alone.

Anne says, "Here, let me help you."

She takes the sponge, wrings it out and wipes down his face and neck. She does it expertly, like a mother would.

Somebody knocks at the door. Sarge enters carrying his helmet.

"We need to talk, Anne."

Anne glances at Todd and responds with a slight shake of her head.

Sarge nods. He squats in front of the boy, who cringes, his expression vacant.

"How's the arm?" he says. He points at the bandage covering Todd's wound, which the Bradley's driver had carefully cleaned and stitched up with needle and thread.

It hurts like hell, but Todd doesn't answer.

"Keep it clean, soldier," Sarge adds. "The bug going around ain't the only infection we got to worry about."

"I'll take care of him," Anne says. "You might want to check on Wendy."

Sarge appraises Todd with a hard stare and a tight smile. "I just wanted to say you did real good today, Kid. You're a tough little sumbitch, you know that?"

After he leaves, Anne nudges the boy and whistles.

Todd smiles.

Wendy sits on a sheet of plastic on the edge of the bed in another recovery room. Her hands won't stop shaking. Slowly, she removes her Batman belt—heavy with handcuffs, gun, Taser, baton, extra magazines and pepper spray—and sets it carefully on the plastic beside her. She takes off her badge and pins, and places them next to the belt. She unbuttons her uniform shirt, balls it up and puts in a plastic bag. She unhooks her bra, grimy and soaked through with sweat, and hangs it to dry out. After a quick but thorough wash, she examines herself in the mirror while brushing her wet, tangled hair. She recognizes the face and body, but her eyes look like somebody else's. Her face and perky chest once earned her a lot of attention. Wendy knows she's physically beautiful; she's heard it said enough times to be sure. She knows it made some men want her. She knows it made them angry. Then it saved her life when the man who'd hurt her most got her out when the infected came howling through the door.

She raises her left arm and inspects a thin red line across her ribs. The creature's razor-sharp teeth grazed her flesh. *Son of a bitch.* Not deep enough for stitches, but enough to draw blood. Enough to plant virus and infection.

Christ, she was about to shoot Todd in the head, and she was at infection's door herself.

Would she have done it?

If she had to do it, then yes, she would have. Murder one, or help murder all.

Would she have then shot herself if she felt herself turning?

The answer is yes. More readily than shooting one of the others, in fact. The realization surprises her. Some of the cops at the station never accepted her, yet she was still a cop. Many cops had an us-against-them mentality about the communities they policed. Wendy was trained in that culture and adopted it as her own. She was still one of *us*. Nobody had as much authority as her when she patrolled the neighborhoods in her square. Up until she held her gun against that teenage boy's head, she saw the other survivors as civilians, people who weren't her equals but instead ungrateful charges. She no longer feels that divide. She thinks: *We are fast becoming a tribe.*

Somebody knocks, and she tells them to wait while she pulls on a black T-shirt.

Sarge enters the room. He glances up and down, an appreciative nod. It's so subtle, he doesn't realize he's doing it, but Wendy can read the language of attraction without trying. She pointedly looks away and pins her badge to her belt. The soldier clears his throat and gets down to business.

"I brought you some more water, so you can wash your hair if you want," he says.

"Just did it. See?"

"Roger that. Well, take it anyway, for later. It's rainwater."

"Does the building have any water in its tank?"

"It does. A lot, in fact, but we're saving it for drinking and cooking. Tonight, we're washing with good old rain."

"Well, thank you," she tells him. "What's our situation?"

"Steve and Ducky swept the rest of the floor. It's clear. No infected, and no giant slugs with teeth either. I think we're secure. Now we're clearing out the bodies and cleaning up the place."

"You need a hand?"

"No, no. This is just a social call. You rest. You've been through hell."

The cop sits on the bed with a sigh. "All right."

"Hey, uh, Wendy..."

"Yes?"

The soldier takes a deep breath and says, "I wanted to say thanks."

"For what?"

"For what you said about my boys yesterday. I appreciate what you said. So, thanks."

☣

Ethan, Paul, and the Bradley's crew drag the bodies downstairs on plastic sheets. Change spills from the corpses' pockets. This work done, they mop the floor with a strong bleach solution. The gunner and the driver retreat to one of the recovery rooms to set up the Coleman and try to get supper going. The idea of food makes Ethan want to vomit. The bleach makes his eyes sting. He and Paul decide to try the roof. The hospital has turned out to be a chamber of horrors, and they're craving some fresh air and a little time and space to wrap their heads around it all.

He now regrets that decision. The stairwell is pitch black. The air is stale and musty. He can't remember how high the floors of the hospital go. He doesn't know what fresh terrors await him up there in the dark. His clumsy footfalls sound like thunder in the stillness. After three flights, he's out of breath.

He can't stop thinking about the wormlike creature that attacked them. That these things are another of the horrible children of Infection is obvious. But are they a mutation, a freak? Or an entirely new life form? Were they once men? Or did the bug jump species? He has a terrible feeling that the emergence of this creation may signal a fundamental shift in the ecology of the planet. The infected violently spread disease and cannibalize the dead. They're a plague and an enemy that has humanity on the run, and that's bad enough. But this is new.

The balance of nature is changing. A new world is coming in which humans may no longer be at the top of the food chain. The thing appeared to be a bottom feeder, another eater of the dead. There's plenty of that kind of food to sustain a large population of these monsters, depending on how much they need to eat. What'll happen when they can no longer feed on the dead?

It took a 25mm cannon to kill it.

They reach the top of the stairs and find the door unlocked. Some of the hospital staff must have fled onto the roof to get away from the Infected rising from their beds. But the roof is bare of the living or the dead. Ethan walks with care, feeling exposed under the massive twilight sky.

The rain has mostly stopped, but the ground is still wet, and the air feels heavy and humid. They walk to the parapet. Over the roofs of the houses and low-rise buildings, they see downtown Pittsburgh in the distance, across the river. The tall buildings stand dark and derelict. The Grant Building is on fire and veiled in smoke, an incredible sight. Pillars of smoke rise from a dozen smaller fires scattered across the city. They hear the distant crackle of gunfire at the Allegheny County Jail to the east.

"Reverend, why did those people leave their photos in that garage?"

"I don't understand you."

"The parking garage where we stayed last night. People passing through there before us left photos of their families and friends on the wall. Some were Xeroxed posters, but others were actual photos. Why did they do that?"

"Just saying goodbye, I guess."

"I don't think I want to say goodbye."

Paul shakes his head and says, "I don't even know how."

Bonded by their grief, the men watch the sun go down and the Grant Building burn in the twilight. Even after everything they've gone through, it's still sometimes hard to believe what has happened to the world they once lived in. People and buildings and phone calls and TV shows and grocery shopping and the normal pace of life, all gone now, maybe forever. An entire world and its history to mourn. The gray sky occasionally spits. The warm drizzle washes away the ash and the filth from their faces. They stand there without speaking for over an hour while Paul chain-smokes.

This high up, the apocalypse seems almost peaceful.

"The end of the world doesn't happen overnight," Paul murmurs. "It takes its sweet time."

The sky turns dark. They decide to head back. Ethan notices that somebody sprayed the words HELP US in bright orange paint across the hospital roof.

He says, "It may never end."

FLASHBACKS: WENDY SASLOVE

The Screaming changed everything. Millions of people lay helpless and twitching on the ground. Thousands died in accidents. Fires burned out of control. Entire towns suffered without electricity or running water. The survivors walked dazed through the streets. Distribution of everything from food distribution to internet access to mailing Social Security checks was completely disrupted. Entire industries such as insurance folded overnight. Governments and businesses struggled to continue operating as one out of five people simply fell down, broke everything in the process, and took all their knowledge with them in a massive brain drain. The country reeled from the shock.

Seventy thousand people fell in Pittsburgh alone. The police department was devastated. Some three hundred out of nearly nine hundred police officers had either fallen down or simply taken their guns home, locked their doors, and refused to return to duty. Burglaries soared as people broke into homes abandoned by the fallen. Arson was rampant as communities, terrified of another outbreak, burned homes with the screamers still inside. Frightened people took their guns to the local grocery store, which became scenes of panic buying and looting.

The cops remaining on the job dug in, marked their territory, and held it with force. They cracked skulls and exchanged gunfire with street gangs and vigilantes. They cleared the streets and protected firefighters and helped to recover the fallen. The police stations became forts in hostile territory. They were used to dealing with murderers and drug dealers and other criminals. Now everybody was the enemy.

The cops worked around the clock. In just three days, they already made a difference. The power was on, food was delivered to stores, and the fires were under control. For now, that was enough. They geared up for another big push to recover the fallen. Humans can live up to nine weeks or longer without food but can't go more than a few days without water. Thousands were still missing and had to be found and transported to one of the new emergency clinics as quickly as possible.

Meanwhile, people continued to gather at the hospitals each day. Most were pilgrims searching for missing loved ones. It was common to find screamers without any identification on them, as their wallets had been stolen. Sometimes, screamers were found without any clothing at all, as they'd been raped while lying helpless on the ground. The pilgrims arrived filled with hope, clutching photos of friends and family. They stood in line all day awaiting their turn to go inside, sit in front of a computer, and try to track down their loved ones in the SEELS database. As a counterpoint, several hundred people also came shouting and carrying angry signs and concealed weapons. Terrified of another outbreak, they demanded stronger isolation measures for the fallen, calling for their removal to quarantine camps outside the city.

These two groups of people naturally hated each other and were kept separated by police mounted on horses. A line of riot police guarded the front of the hospital, intimidating in their black body armor, helmets with clear plastic visors, yard-long hardwood batons, and tactical riot shields. Three-man arrest teams formed a second line.

Wendy was in one of these teams. In the old days, the cops used to form a line, charge, and bash skulls until the street emptied. The tactics changed over the years. Now snatch teams were sent into the crowd to strategically arrest troublemakers and remove them from the scene. The idea was to prevent a protest from turning into a riot that could rage out of control. They barely had the resources to counter protests. A large-scale riot might spread and become the end of law and order in Pittsburgh.

Word passed down the line that the new mayor had enough of the protests and was cutting off all public access to the hospital at four o'clock.

The cop on Wendy's left, Joe Wylie, shook his head and spit.

"Bullshit," he said. "This ain't a Nazi state. Shit, I lost people in the Screaming too. These people have a right to find their family."

"We don't have the manpower," Archie Ward said. "Or, in Barbie's case here, girl power."

Wendy said nothing, staring forward wearing an expression of sullen professionalism. She knew better than to take the bait. She chewed her gum.

Archie added, "The mayor's right. These people here tie up how many cops every day? We don't have enough people. We're running on empty, Joe."

"I don't mind the overtime. And right is right."

The sergeant shouted into his megaphone. He told the crowds to disperse.

They screamed back, *No!*

Another sergeant, the overweight old cop they called John-John, sang out in a comical World Wrestling Federation voice, "Get ready to *rumble!*"

"What do you think, Barbie?" Joe said.

"Doesn't matter what I think," Wendy said. "We got our orders."

"Shut the fuck up," Joe said.

"Jesus Christ, rookie," Archie said. "You're either the dumbest broad or the best politician I ever met. Either way, you'll go far at the Pittsburgh PD."

The words hurt her, as usual, but she'd never give them the satisfaction of knowing just how much they did. Her expression never changed, just as her opinions were always neutral and noncommittal. All she showed them was her game face.

The line of mounted police cantered off the street. The phalanx of cops in front of the hospital pulled on their gas masks. Some clashed their batons against their shields in a warlike rhythm, and the rest joined in. Wendy knew these men. Despite their sympathies for one or even both factions, they were hoping the crowd would refuse to disperse, and they could let off some steam stomping ass. Joe and Archie grinned at the prospect.

The cops fired tear gas grenades, which burst in brilliant white clouds. The crowds recoiled from the growing pockets of swirling gas. They cried and coughed as the gas attacked the mucous membranes in their eyes, nose, mouth, and lungs. The cops lowered their visors and crouched, tense, waiting for the signal.

Wendy felt a strong hand grab her ass and squeeze.

"Too bad you're not a screamer, Barbie," Joe Wylie said, his voice muffled by his gas mask. "I'd keep you in the spare bedroom."

Even now, even after the Screaming, even after the thousands of smaller but equally horrible tragedies that followed, some of these men were still trying to break her. She wasn't broken yet.

"If you ever touch me again, I swear, I'll take you out," she told him.

Joe grinned. "So there is somebody in there behind the mask. Nice to meet you, finally."

Wendy attended the Training Academy two years ago with forty other cadets. All cadets experienced some type of degrading hazing treatment, and with three of four police officers being men, they were hard on women—especially a beautiful young woman like her. They made her scrub toilets and clean laundry and fetch coffee. She'd taken it all in stride. Meanwhile, she excelled in firearms training, Taser certification, CPR and first aid, high-risk traffic stop training, and the rest—all of it. The other cadets hit on her, but she'd had neither the time nor interest in taking romantic risks with men. But then she met Dave Carver.

Dave was different. He was a detective—older, experienced, adversarial against the world. He smelled like her cop dad used to smell before he retired, like cigarettes and strong coffee. Dave was also different from the young men her own age in that he seemed so sure of himself. He could take or leave Wendy's looks while seeming to be engaged by her personality and energy. He told her stories about drug dealers and bureaucratic hassles and the time he used his gun during a liquor store robbery. It was only later that she learned he was married and she had a reputation.

Dave's friends were hard men, and they could be cruel. After graduation from the Academy, she got assigned to her zone and started doing real police work. But the hazing didn't stop. Instead, it spread, like infection, throughout Patrol, men and women alike. Through bad luck or somebody's malice, she'd been assigned to the same station as Dave Carver and his friends.

Wendy had worn a mask ever since.

The whistles blew. The line of cops surged and crashed into the crowd. The batons rose and fell, driving people back or beating them to the ground. The line quickly dissolved as everybody became lost in the expanding white clouds of gas.

Wendy slammed into a man with her shield and knocked him back. She raised her baton at a couple holding handkerchiefs over their faces to warn them off. People shouted at each other in the smoke. Wendy felt detached, as if moving through a surreal dream. The desperate faces flashed by, weeping and coughing and screaming. She swung her baton at a man, who stumbled away, blood pouring into his eyes from a jagged tear in his scalp. He didn't seem to be critically injured, so she pressed on.

As far as some of her brethren were concerned, she was at the bottom of the pecking order. But she was still better than these fleeing people. In the larger pecking order of society, they were all lower than her. She was cop. They were civilians.

She flinched at the roar of gunfire. Moments later, Joe Wylie staggered out of the clouds, his plastic body shield riddled with blackened holes, and crumpled to the ground in a heap.

Wendy pulled him out of the chaos until other cops hoisted him onto a stretcher and rushed him into the hospital. By the time the gas cleared, they found two other critically wounded cops lying on the ground among moaning protesters. The cops had identified four shooters; they were dragging one they'd caught behind the hospital for swift justice.

These were not ordinary times.

The sergeant caught her watching them. He gripped her arm with a hand like iron and pulled her roughly away toward the police station, which was four blocks east of the hospital.

"I'm assigning you to recovery operations until the end of your shift, Saslove," he barked. "Check dispatch to find out where the teams are going tonight. Move your ass."

Wendy walked to the police station, dumped her riot gear, and caught an hour's sleep under a desk. For the next twelve hours, she looked for screamers. Her search team found sixteen, half as many as the night before and one-fifth as many as the night before that. At six in the morning, exhausted but buzzing with coffee and the dregs of adrenaline, she returned to the police station and entered Patrol. Some of the cops gathered around a TV set. They shook their heads at the news. Riots in the western states. A wave of violence spreading inland from the coast.

Most of the military was still deployed overseas and in disarray from the Screaming, with only some units having flown back to the homeland. The police was the main line of defense, and in city after city, that line was breaking.

Not here, the officers swore. They were tired and angry, but they were holding their ground, and they weren't going anywhere unless it was on a stretcher.

"Turn that shit off," somebody yelled, and they did. The windows were open and a cool breeze wafted through the big squad room. Somebody produced a bottle of scotch and shared splashes in Styrofoam cups. "Get ready," he said. "They need you out there. Get ready." Wendy was bone tired and covered in bruises. Her jaw and skull still ached from earlier in the night, when somebody clocked her while her team intervened to prevent the looting of the Whole Foods store.

John-John handed her a cup. "You done good, rook," he said. He winked and punched her lightly on the shoulder. "Keep it up."

You done good, rook.

She smiled, her jaw aching.

"Throw in a blowjob and he'll make you Officer of the Month," one of the patrolmen said with a sneer. He flinched as another cop jabbed him in the ribs with his elbow. "What?"

"Lay off," the other cop said. "She's one of us."

John-John raised his cup and declared in a loud voice, "Sometimes, it seems the only time a cop is called a hero is when he takes a bullet. Well, today, we got three heroes. That's right. But I say you're all heroes, every day, and especially right now, in the middle of this goddamn apocalypse. So here's to our guys still in critical condition at Mercy Hospital, and here's to all you ugly dicks who won't give up. You guys are my heroes. Here's to you, Pittsburgh's finest."

She's one of us.

The cops emptied their cups and held them up for refills. Somebody turned a radio on and tried to make it a party. Everybody stood around awkwardly in their uniforms and Batman belts, holding their drinks. The alcohol burned Wendy's throat and made her feel alert and loose at the same time. Bracing.

A dispatcher entered the room and blustered, "I need somebody to take a domestic disturbance, and everybody's committed. We're getting flooded with calls."

"Give it to the commander," one of the cops called out, and everybody laughed.

The dispatcher rifled through his slips. "Sound of breaking glass on the street," he read. "Man heard screaming in alley."

The officers chanted, *Tell it to the commander!* until the man left red-faced and roaring. The cops cheered. They were dead tired. They needed a break. Wendy had completed six twelve-hour shifts virtually back to back. In just a few hours, she and the other police officers in the room would have to pull another shift.

Until then, they were officially off duty.

The radio played an old song that reminded her of summers as a child. A very old song recorded before she was born. Some of the younger cops moved to the music. They nodded and shifted from one foot to the next, trying to unwind. Wendy couldn't remember the band, but the song took her back to one particular summer when she was ten years old, maybe eleven. She remembered riding a bike down the driveway past her dad, who stood hunched over the open hood of his big police cruiser, working on the engine. Her bike's handlebars had multicolor tassels that streamed in the wind. She remembered the sound of lawn mowers and the smell of fresh-cut grass. A boy kissed her that summer. His name was Dale. There was a tire swing hanging by a thick rope from an old oak tree in his backyard, and he kissed her there. The memory gave her butterflies. For a few seconds, she fell asleep on her feet.

She opened her eyes. Men shouted in the foyer. The officers looked at each other, some frowning, others laughing. A scream pierced the air. Everybody froze and glared at the doors. More screaming. Stomping feet. The cops bristled.

The Raspberries, Wendy thought. That was the band.

The doors burst open. People ran into Patrol and grabbed at the nearest officers, who shoved them back with shouted obscenities. The cops nearest Wendy dropped their drinks and reached for their batons. Wendy did the same. The cops flailed with their batons while others tried to cuff the assailants. More rushed in howling, dressed in paper gowns and hospital scrubs.

"Son of a bitch bit me!"

Cops fell. Wendy saw a man bite down on a cop's arm and shake his head like a dog, ripping flesh. She struck the man with her baton and knocked him down. The cop sank to his knees, shaking, his eyes glazed, and toppled onto the floor. Everywhere, it was hand to hand fighting. The batons rose and fell, but for every attacker clubbed to the ground, more took his place.

John-John gripped her arm.

"Go tell the lieutenant we're under attack," he roared. "Go, rook, go!"

She bolted down the hall and entered the Detectives section. A man grabbed her in a headlock. She struggled, but other hands held her. She heard guns crashing back in Patrol.

"Stop fighting, Wendy," she heard a familiar voice.

She opened her eyes and saw Dave Carver surrounded by a group of burly detectives in cheap suits and bad ties, glaring and flushed and breathing heavily. They reeked of stale coffee.

"Let go of me," she cried. "I have to see the lieutenant."

"He's busy," one of the detectives sneered. "What's going on in Patrol, rookie?"

"They're killing them. I'm serious—they're killing them!"

"What are you talking about?"

"She's drunk. Smell it on her breath."

"Who the hell is shooting in the station, rookie?"

"Just let her talk!"

The detectives released her. Wendy caught her breath and said, "We're under attack. Civilians dressed in hospital clothes. They had no weapons." The truth hit her. "They're screamers. Probably from Mercy. They've woken up, and they're crazy."

Dave said: "How many?"

"Forty. Fifty. Maybe a hundred. I don't know. Maybe more. It's wall to wall in there. Every patrol officer was committed." The screaming and gunshots in Patrol had been replaced by growling in a hundred throats. A fist banged on the door. Then another. They shrank back.

"This is bullshit," a detective said.

The others glared at the door.

Dave said, "Is everybody armed?"

Multiple fists pounded now.

"Where's Patrol?" a detective cried. "Where the fuck is Patrol?"

Dave touched her shoulder and said, "Get behind me, Wendy."

The door shook on its hinges. Splinters flew.

The detectives took out their guns and aimed them at the door.

"Let's go, let's go, let's get this over with," somebody said.

The door exploded inward, and people ran screaming into the room. For a critical moment, nobody did anything; their attackers were just regular people—unarmed, sick people. Some of the detectives yelled, *Stop, or we will shoot*. A moment later, somebody fired his gun, and they all started shooting, roaring like madmen, one running forward and emptying his shotgun at point blank range into the gray faces. But the screamers were already in the room, and the fighting quickly turned hand to hand.

Wendy stared, horrified, unable to move. Some of their attackers were police officers. She saw John-John tackle one of the detectives, scattering files and a computer from one of the desks. She aimed her Glock.

Dave grabbed her arm. "Get out of here! We're not going to make it!"

She shrugged him off. "Fuck you, Dave."

"Wendy, get out now!"

"They need my help!"

"We're done!"

She fought him, but he was stronger than her. He dragged her to the window and shoved her onto the fire escape.

"Survive," he said.

"Come with me then," she pleaded.

"All right, babe. I'll be right behind you. I promise."

He turned away before she could respond, blazing away with his hand cannon. She climbed down the fire escape and waited in the vehicle yard. The guard booth stood empty. From here, the sounds of gunfire ground together in a constant roar. The muzzle flashes lit up the windows like lightning. Dave didn't appear at the fire escape. The detectives were backed against the wall and giving it everything they had.

Wendy stood helpless, her fist clenched around her Glock, her eyes flooded with tears.

The shooting sputtered out. The windows filled with dark shapes stumbling aimlessly, silhouetted by the glare of the station's institutional fluorescent lighting.

The entire station was wiped out in minutes, and she hadn't fired a single shot. Her ears rang, and the loss of sleep over the past few days hit her hard.

Lay off her. She's one of us.

She raised her pistol with both hands and aimed it at the windows above her.

"Help me! Please help me!"

A woman ran down the alley in a nightgown, waving her arms.

"Stay right there," Wendy said raggedly. Her training kicked in. "What's the problem?"

"My husband is hurt," the woman said, her eyes wild. "He's bleeding."

"Okay, did you call 911?"

"The lines are all busy."

"Where do you live, Ma'am?"

"Just over there."

You can't do this. You need to report what you saw.

Another voice in her head countered: *What you saw couldn't have happened.*

"Let's go," she said.

They entered the house. Wendy felt dizzy. Details in the scene jumped out at her: a pale man dressed in pajamas lying on the floor, bleeding from the head. A table lamp, still on, sitting on its side on the carpet and casting long shadows. Family photos on the wall. A TV with the sound off, showing a worried news anchorwoman. A broken pot and the dirt and scattered remains of a plant. A baseball bat freckled with blood drops.

"Officer, are you okay?"

Every time she closed her eyes, she saw the mob run screaming into Patrol.

"Tell me what happened here, Ma'am," she said mechanically.

"I hit him on the head. You can arrest me, if you want. But take care of him first. Please!"

Wendy inspected the wound.

"What's your name?"

"Lisa."

"Okay, Lisa, come over here. He's got a scalp wound. That type of wound bleeds a lot. I'm going to elevate his head a little so that it's above the heart. There. He needs to get to a hospital, but he's going to be okay. In the meantime, I want you to sit here and put pressure on it."

Wendy stood, fighting tears, and tried to call 911. The circuits were jammed. She saw the couch and wanted to lie down on it for just a minute. Maybe five minutes. Just a little while—

"I had to do it," Lisa was saying.

"Uh huh," Wendy said in a daze. She glanced at the TV. The anchorwoman was crying, mascara running down her cheeks in black lines.

"He was threatening our boy—"

"This man—?"

"My husband."

"You say your husband attacked your son?"

"Then I stopped him. I heard him wake up and went to find him. When I saw him holding Benjamin down and biting him, I grabbed the bat and hit him on the head. I had to do it."

"Was he one of the people who fell down? One of the screamers?"

"When he woke up, he must have been confused, because he'd never hit Benjamin. He loves that boy more than himself."

Wendy took a step back. Her hand flickered around the handcuffs on her belt. She drew her Glock. She frowned. She was finding it impossible to think straight.

"You can remove your hands now, Lisa. I want you to back away from him. Now."

Lay off her—

"Okay," Lisa said. "But he's still bleeding—"

She's one of us—

The cop raised her gun and fired. The sound of the discharge filled the house. The man's head exploded and splashed up the wall.

The woman wailed like an animal caught in a steel trap. She fell to her knees and hugged the man's broken face against her chest.

"You killed Roy!"

Upstairs, a teenage boy snarled and slammed his fists against a bedroom door.

Wendy holstered her gun and walked out the door into the night.

"Why did you do that? Why? Why?"

The woman's screaming followed her down the street until it became just one of many voices rising up from the city like a demonic choir.

MEMORIES

Todd wakes up in a bed in a warm and windowless hospital room after a long dreamless sleep. He's exhausted even as his body tells him he overslept. *You're still here, Todd old man. Still truckin'.* Wrapping his blanket around his bare shoulders, he shuffles blearily to a bucket in the corner and empties his bladder. His stomach growls. Outside, he finds Paul in the hallway, whistling as he mops the floor with a strong bleach solution. Todd finds the sight reassuring. He's not used to being alone.

"Hey, Rev," he says.

"Morning, Kid."

"Wow, we just got here, and they got you mopping floors already. Too bad there isn't more need for preachers in the post-apocalyptic world."

Paul pauses in his work with a smile. "On the contrary, son, a true minister is no stranger to working with his hands. It's a form of prayer. Good for the soul. You ought to try it sometime."

"Are you trying to turn me into an atheist?"

"Ha," Paul says.

"Anyhow, my soul needs some coffee, or it's not doing anything today."

"Go around the corner and look for the lounge. We've got it set up as a common room. I'm sure Anne saved you something."

Todd sets off, his blanket forming a train on the floor behind him. "Thanks."

"Good to have you back, Kid."

Todd grins. "The Kid abides, Rev. The Kid abides."

☣

Ethan wanders through the pathology department and marvels at the expensive equipment now gathering dust in the gloomy light of his lantern. Everywhere they go, he sees signs of a world that has fallen down. He's searching for useful things but hasn't found anything. A large centrifuge sits on a laboratory table. People were working here when the infected got out of their beds, and they left in a hurry. Ethan sees an overturned chair with a crisp white lab coat still clinging to the back. A crushed test tube on the floor.

He pauses in front of a cabinet filled with delicate glassware, test tubes, and beakers. They're clean, but he avoids touching them. Germs are the greatest threat to his survival right now, and his instincts aren't very discriminating. In the corner, an emergency liquid nitrogen tank catches his eye. He stares at it for a long time. The nitrogen is stored under pressure, so they might be able to siphon some off into a container to make a crude bomb. If they don't blow their own hands off first. They might dump it on the infected and flash freeze them. As long as they don't freeze their own arms solid in the bargain.

Liquid nitrogen is a dangerous laboratory material. Probably best to leave it alone. He considered it worth thinking about, however. In this world, everything must be evaluated as a potential weapon. Of the five basic survival needs, security now ranks first.

Ethan fiddles with a fluorescence microscope, but it sits dark, inert, lifeless without electricity. The room is filled with hundreds of thousands of dollars' worth of dusty lab equipment. He recognizes an incubator, decides not to open it. It strikes him again that scientists studied disease here. Not scary diseases like AIDS and Ebola, no, not in a lab like this, but dangerous nonetheless: cancer, diabetes, emphysema, bone disorders. The pathologists examined tissues and blood and urine to figure out what was wrong with people. Doctors used these tests to treat people with all sorts of disorders and extend their lifespan. Researchers looked at the smallest living particles in the human body and tried to understand what hurt them and how they adapted to being hurt—knowledge that could be used to diagnose some diseases more easily, treat others and even cure.

Now the healers have all gone, possibly never to return.

Ethan wonders what great and noble things they might have accomplished.

☣

He once thought he understood what severe stress was like. He and Carol both worked hard at their jobs. They juggled dinner and day care and doing the dishes. They survived the dramas of raising a little girl who was deep in her terrible twos. Life was full of responsibilities, bills, errands, miscommunication, and petty conflict. It was hard, but he'd consider that sort of stress a breath of fresh air after what he's been through these past ten days, with the Sword of Damocles poised over his head and hanging by a thread. The human body wasn't meant to experience this level of fear for this long. Getting this close to death for too long can turn your hair white and break your mind.

He and Carol coped as best they could, but every so often, they bickered. They bickered as they prepared dinner and as they ate it and as they cleaned up and put Mary to bed. They each knew how far they could go, and no further, to needle the other person without getting a major reaction that would upset their toddler. Every once in a while, somebody would go too far, and there'd be hurt feelings. When this happened, the bickering escalated, and either Ethan or Carol would storm away from the table out of fear of shouting in front of Mary.

One night, nobody walked away, and, witlhout really understanding what he was doing, Ethan shouted, "Carol, stop it, stop it, just stop it!"

Carol sat back, stunned, while Mary, busily pouring her cup of water into her mashed potatoes, stared at him with eyes like saucers, her mouth hanging open.

Ethan smiled at his daughter to reassure her everything was okay.

"How dare you shout at me in front of her," Carol hissed.

"I said I don't want to argue. So stop it."

"I'm not the one shouting."

"STOP IT."

"Why don't you shut up?"

They shouted over each other for the next minute until he couldn't take it anymore and stormed out of the house seeing red. He walked for an hour, his mind boiling as he played the argument over and over in his mind and hating all of it. As his anger dissipated, he felt the first wave of panic over what they'd done to Mary. He needed to talk to Carol. He hurried home.

Ethan found his wife and daughter upstairs on the rocking chair in Mary's room. Carol was reading her a story from a hardcover compendium of *Curious George* stories.

"Are you happy, Daddy?" Mary said.

"I'm very happy," Ethan said.

They gave her a glass of water and tucked her in with her dollies. Then they turned out the light and left her to sleep.

Carol went downstairs for coffee, and Ethan trudged after her.

"I'm sorry I yelled," he said.

"I'm sorry too."

The next thing he knew, he was bawling with his head bowed and his shoulders shaking, and Carol held him, telling him everything was okay.

"I didn't like the look on Mary's face," he said.

That heartbreaking look of confusion, fear, guilt that her parents were fighting.

He surprised himself by crying. He hadn't cried in at least ten years, when his mother died. But that look haunted him. That look of broken trust and loss.

"Kids blame themselves for everything," he added. "I don't want to fight in front of her. I don't want to ever fight in front of her again. We're supposed to be protecting her."

Carol understood. They each promised it wouldn't happen again. They made up and went to bed feeling better about their marriage. As Ethan lay in the dark that night, trying to sleep, he vowed to preserve Mary's pure innocence and joy as long as he could. She would slowly learn over time that the world was a hard and terrible place. But he'd fight that world as long and as hard as he could to protect his little girl from its dark truths.

☣

In the third-floor lounge, the survivors sit around a small table and share a breakfast of peanut butter on crackers. They wash it down with instant coffee sweetened with honey and lightened with powdered milk. An espresso machine gathers dust in the corner next to a small refrigerator nobody is interested in opening. Corporate art decorates the walls. The stale air smells like dust. The LED lantern casts long shadows behind a fake potted plant.

"I think we can all agree we need to continue searching the building," Anne says. "I'd like to lead a team to look for supplies. Food, water, drugs, and anything else we can use."

"If it's all right with you, I need to sit that one out," Sarge says.

"Got to work on the Brad?"

"No, I'd like to take my boys and find the emergency generator. We might get some lights going again. Charge our electronics. Maybe even get some news of the outside world."

"Wow," Wendy says with a smile. "That'd be nice."

"Hooah," says Sarge.

"Don't tell me you have to go into the basement," Anne says.

Sarge shakes his head. "No generator in the basement. If a water main broke or there was some type of disaster where fire hoses or sprinklers would have to be used, it could get flooded out too easy. Hurricane Katrina taught everybody that. No, this hospital has a mechanical penthouse. High and dry on the top floor. That's where it'll be. Me and the boys will take care of it."

The survivors eat in silence. Sarge pours himself more coffee, smiles, and adds, "Don't you worry about me. The only people going into the darkest, most dangerous parts of the hospital today will be you."

"Don't leave without me," Todd says as he shuffles into the room. "But first, give me some of that coffee and my pants back."

"How's the arm?" Wendy says.

"Sore as hell, but I'll live."

Anne pats the empty chair between her and Wendy. "Have a seat, Kid."

Todd grins in his blanket and glasses and battered SWAT cap. He sits and extends his hand to Anne for a shake. "Todd Paulsen. Nice to meet you."

Paul aims his shotgun into the darkness. A flashlight, wrapped around the barrel with electrical tape, illuminates the area with its sharp beam. The Remington 870 tactical pump shotgun features a short pistol-grip stock and recoil pad. It packs seven twelve-gauge rounds. He likes the gun because it's dependable, and it'll stop anything smaller than an elephant.

They pass the radiology department. Down the corridor, on the right, they find the chapel. Paul looks at it in surprise. He'd forgotten the hospital would have a chapel. The survivors look at him, questioning, and he nods, yes, he'd like to see it.

The small room looks like a miniature church, complete with red carpeting, dark wood pews and a stained glass wall that was probably backlit when the power worked. Hymn books are scattered on the floor. Dead flowers crumble in their vases, and most of the candles have melted.

Ethan takes the candles that are still usable and puts them in his bag. The others stand by the doorway, watching Paul, who picks up the hymn books and stacks them on the lectern with care.

He looks at the arched ceiling overhead, closes his eyes, and remembers the last time he spoke as a clergyman. After the infected rose, he kept Sara tied to a bed for three days. He fed her, bathed her, changed her bedpan while the world ended outside. He even tried an exorcism, commanding demons to abandon her body while she shrieked and strained at her bonds.

Time blurred until he realized people were probably flocking to his church for comfort, and there was nobody there to give it. He had a responsibility to his congregation that was just as great. Exhausted from lack of sleep, he put on his clerical uniform and staggered out into the night. People sobbed and screamed in distant houses as he walked to the church in a daze. The infected ran howling down streets and alleys, breaking into homes and attacking their occupants. Paul arrived at his church to find it had been attacked. The dead lay in heaps surrounded by clouds of flies. The streetlights shined through the stained glass windows in a ghostly shimmer. The carpet squished wetly under his feet. The infected had eaten the children on the altar. And he thought, *Isn't this what you wanted, Paul? The End of Days?*

The signs of violence were everywhere in this place. There were as many infected lying on the ground as those who weren't. His congregation had put up a fight—for their children and their sanctuary. The massive wood cross mounted behind the altar, the symbol of his faith in a divine sacrifice that made life everlasting possible, loomed impotent over the carnage. Rage boiled up inside him. Infection had invaded and defiled this holy place. Infection had raped his wife's blood. And he, personally, had not been touched.

Dawn brought the singing mob marching down the street out of a haze of smoke, sweeping him along. Middle-class suburbanites carrying shotguns and baseball bats and crowbars and kitchen knives and garden tools. They shouted and sang and waved banners proclaiming: DEFEND OUR HOMES and WE SHALL NOT BE MOVED. One carried a Bible and a large wooden cross. There were hundreds of them. The vanguard roared and dragged along eight infected, who struggled against handcuffs and ropes tied around their necks. The men stopped in the middle of an intersection, threw the ropes over the traffic signal, and hauled the infected kicking and gasping in the air. Paul pushed through the clapping mob for a better look until he was satisfied Sara wasn't one of the victims. The air smelled like smoke. The infected hung by their necks and jerked and twitched until they died. The mob cheered. They shot the corpses with their guns and sang "The Star Spangled Banner" until everybody joined in, tears running down their cheeks.

Paul found it hard to breathe. People noticed his clerical collar, shook his hand, and shoved him to the head of the column, chanting, "Bless us! Bless us!" A man with a mullet and a hunting bow standing on the hood of a car pulled him up and clapped him on the back. Paul looked down upon the cheering crowd in anger and didn't trust the Spirit. What could he say that they wanted to hear? Should he tell them God was on their side and approved of them murdering their brothers and sisters in broad daylight? Should he rouse them to torture and murder more of them with a hymn, maybe "Onward, Christian Soldiers"? Then he realized how scared they all were. The faces looked up at him with raw hunger; if ever they needed the strength and hope of Christ's love, it was now. They were quiet except for the cries of their babies. A pair of military jets roared overhead in the gray, smoky sky, followed by the boom of distant explosions.

His heart opened. He raised his hands and blessed the mob.

"Your war is just," he told them.

For a war to be truly just, its soldiers must kill with love, not hate, he thought. This was perhaps the first war in history where the combatants killed those they loved most.

People at the edge of the crowd screamed. Drawn by the noise, infected rushed from nearby lawns and gardens into their midst, punching and biting. Shotguns and handguns roared in a motley cluster of shots, followed by triumphant shouts. Men traded punches over a bitten and newly infected teenage girl lying twitching on the ground.

"Brothers and sisters," Paul sang to them. "The Lord is with you. Do not be afraid."

More infected ran into the crowd, which sent tremors of panic rippling through it. Some people ran away, while others huddled closer together for protection. They stumbled over the newly infected who lay twitching under their feet. A swarm arrived howling, and the mob began to break and tear with screams and gunshots and running feet. The fighting went on and on, the mob slowly dissolving like a wounded whale surrounded by sharks, flailing and dying one bite at a time. Paul soon found himself alone. He watched the last clumps of people throw away their banners and flee, leaving dozens of bodies on the ground. A small knot of fighters made a stand in a smoky haze, shouting at each other and firing their shotguns, until the infected overran them.

Paul opens his eyes and is back in the hospital chapel, his face upturned toward the ceiling.

He offers a silent prayer for the dead and then sings aloud in a rich baritone voice, "Amen, amen, ah-ah-men."

The other survivors stare at him wearing stricken expressions. Wendy wipes her eyes with the palm of her hand. Paul wonders if he said something while reliving that horrible day so vividly. He realizes his own face is wet and that he's crying.

He realizes he wasn't singing at all. He was moaning. He didn't remember what happened so much as relived it.

But he can't remember what happened afterward. The fighters made their stand, and they died in the smoke. Then nothing more.

☣

They all know about flashbacks. The experiences are so real, so visceral, they can swear they've discovered a legitimate form of time travel. But unlike the type of time travel one might find in, say, the movies, with this type of time travel, they can't change the outcome. They're doomed to relive the past without being able to change it. And no matter how many times they visit the past, they will never truly comprehend it.

☣

The survivors enter the gift shop guns first and clear it the way Sarge taught them. They break into teams, fan out along the walls, and circle back to the door.

"Clear," they sound off. Then they start looting.

Ethan is again struck by the sensation that the world has become a giant museum dedicated to the day the world ended. The magazines and newspapers sitting in their racks still trumpet dramatic headlines about the Screaming. He runs his fingers over the greeting cards, pauses in front of a selection of stuffed animals and shiny balloons that proclaim IT'S A BOY! and FEEL BETTER SOON! and HAPPY MOTHER'S DAY!

Behind him, Wendy opens a dead refrigerator and empties its bottled water and juices into cloth shopping bags packed onto wheelchairs, which they're using as carts. Paul lights a cigarette with a tired sigh and sits on a stack of magazines. Todd scoops candy and gum and shoves it into a bag slung over his shoulder. Anne prowls the other shelves with her flashlight, snatching up aspirin, nail clippers, deodorant.

Todd holds up his bag of candy, shakes it and says, "Trick or treat."

Ethan says, "Do you think they remember who they are?"

"You mean the infected?" Todd says.

"Do you think their consciousness has been replaced, or that they're still trapped inside their bodies, forced to do things they don't want to do by the disease?"

"I'd hate to think they're still in there, watching themselves attack people and being helpless to stop it," Wendy says. "Either way, killing them is mercy."

"Maybe when the infected dream, they remember who they are," Todd says. "It would be nice to think that." He frowns. "Or completely horrible."

Ethan picks up a stuffed animal, squeezes it, and drops it to the floor. "I'm wondering if they still love us. If they recognize us and love us while they attack us, even as we recognize them and love them while we kill them."

Paul's head jerks up. He stares at Ethan.

Anne says, "Nobody likes these questions."

Paul says, "They're the only questions worth asking."

☣

The door to the mechanical penthouse is locked. Sarge and the crew go out to the Bradley to recover the demolition kit, which contains a few blocks of C4 plastic explosive and detonators.

They're going to cut and mold a wad of C4 onto the doorknob. Stick a detonator into it. Let the wires run out until they get to a safe place. Then trigger the detonator, and BOOM. The soldiers have a casual but deep appreciation for the stuff. You can throw it and kick it, and it won't blow up on you. Light it on fire, and it burns nice and slow, and you can heat an MRE on it if the area is properly ventilated, as Sarge did many times back in Afghanistan.

Mold it wherever you want it to go in whatever shape you want it, pop in the detonators, and you can take down buildings.

They move fast, rifles shouldered and aimed, communicating with hand signals. Papers and loose trash flutter across the parking lot. The parking garage where they hid the rig under a tarp doesn't appear to be occupied, but swarms have a way of appearing as sudden as a flash flood. They're used to playing it safe. Caution is now second nature to them.

Once they're back in the hospital, the soldiers relax a little.

"Are we safe here, Sergeant?" Ducky says. "In this building?"

"Safe enough at this moment." This is Sarge's stock answer to that question. He credits staying alive and sane this long with taking this hellish journey one day at a time. One moment at a time. Speculating about what he doesn't know is a waste of energy he needs to stay alive.

"I mean, are we going to stay a while?"

They climb the stairs. Sarge shrugs and says, "I think we should. It's a good place."

"I thought the idea was we'd train a civilian combat team and use them as security until we found some friendlies."

"That's still the plan, Ducky."

"The civs seems to think we're going to live here."

"Yes, we're still trying to find the Army," Sarge tells him. "No, we don't need to advertise this fact to the civilians. Do you even know where the nearest friendlies are? Because I sure as hell do not. Our battalion technically doesn't exist anymore. We've heard nothing on the net in days."

The soldiers reach the top floor and pause to catch their breath. The gunner drops to one knee and plants the C4 charge.

"There's always the camps," Steve says as he works. "The FEMA camps. The closest one is in Ohio, right?"

"Which we don't even know still exist, Steve. If they ever did. We've heard of lots of refugee camps and Army elements that either moved by the time we showed up, or were never there in the first place. I'm not interested in risking our safety for rumors, especially if it means driving all over Ohio on a quarter tank."

"Hey, I'm with you. I'd like to stay. I wouldn't mind if we bunkered down here until the whole thing blew over. Let the gung-ho mo-fos take care of it."

"I don't want to stay here forever. The Army is out there still fighting somewhere, and we've got to find them and help. But these people need a rest. We need a rest."

"Roger that," Steve says.

"I look at it this way," Ducky says as they retreat down the stairwell. "Every hour we sit here, more people die that we could be helping. So how long are we staying if we are staying?"

"At least a few days," Sarge says. "A lot can change in a few days. We're still taking this one day at a time."

He remembers what the Boy Scouts taught him about having the right frame of mind for survival: STOP, short for stop, think, observe, and plan.

"What if we decide to move on, but the civs want to stay?"

"I don't know, Ducky. I honestly don't. I don't own them. They're not in the Army."

"Fire in the hole!" Steve calls out. The soldiers crouch and plug their ears.

The C4 explodes with a clap of metallic thunder that rolls down the stairwell, followed by a wave of smoke and a strong chemical smell. The warped metal door hangs on one of its hinges then snaps off and flops to the side.

The soldiers stand and dust themselves off.

"The truth is we really need them," Sarge says. "They've gotten good." He offers his crew a grim smile. "In fact, I'd hate to piss them off."

☣

God is good, and death is evil, so why does God allow people to die? That was a question Paul was never been able to answer during his ministry. When he was ten years old, a plane crashed and scattered burning metal and body parts across miles of scorched and bruised earth. More than two hundred people died, including his mother. He experienced the full gamut of grief, from denial to anger to bargaining to guilt.

The guilt was the worst. He'd been asleep when she left for the trip, and it haunted him that she could be taken away so suddenly, without even a final goodbye. By the time he reached the acceptance phase, he'd aged beyond his years. He'd aged because he'd become aware of death and the fragility of life.

A minister came to the house frequently in the weeks following the crash to offer consolation to Paul and his father.

"If God loved my mom, why did he let her die?" Paul asked him.

"I don't know," the minister said. "What I do know is it was her time to cross over."

"To Heaven?"

"To be with God, who made her. Your mother didn't die. She underwent a transition. It's painful that you'll have to wait to see her again. But you will see her again."

Paul wrestled with his next question, feeling insecure about asking it.

Finally, he said, "Is God going to make me die, too?"

The minister smiled. "We all die, Paul," he answered. "But you won't die for a long, long time. The world is a hard place. But it's also wonderful. You've got a lot of things to do here."

Paul spent the next few days thinking about what Reverend Brown said. Over the years, he not only began to accept the loss of his mother, he decided to become a minister. He loved superheroes, couldn't get enough of them on TV and in comic books. Here was a real superhero, somebody who fought the evil of death every day and helped other people conquer their fear of it.

He turned out to be good at it. He spent hundreds of hours in grief counseling with dying people and their families. He offered whatever comfort he could. When they had nobody else, he even helped with chores and bills. He felt he made a real difference in people's lives. He helped the dying accept what was happening to them, and to Paul, there was simply no greater gift than some degree of confidence that they weren't dying, but crossing over. Crossing over not into oblivion, but to a better place to wait for loved ones they'd left behind. Yet a part of him always felt like a sham because he, himself, remained terrified of dying.

Rita Greene wasn't a regular churchgoer, but when she was diagnosed with bone cancer and rushed into a painful treatment regime including chemotherapy and surgery removing part of her pelvis, her family asked if Paul would visit with her. He agreed.

He came to her home and sat by her bed while she shook with a fever that wasn't a fever but instead a side effect of her treatment. The drugs she took killed growing cells in her body, both the fast-growing cancer cells and the normal, healthy cells in her mouth, stomach, intestines, hair follicles. Some days, he was told, she felt so well, she'd go out to her garden and work on her daffodils. Today was a bad day. The fact was, she was declining fast.

They exchanged small talk while he tried to put her at ease. He gave her a compilation CD of jazz, which her son said she liked to listen to while tending her flowers. He explained why he'd come and that she should consider him another form of support.

Rita said the hardest part for her was the weight loss, her hair falling out, the general sickliness. She hated looking in the mirror and seeing what the cancer and its treatment had done to her. Plus she was a woman who liked to get up and do things. She hated being inside, trapped in bed.

He asked, "Are you afraid of what comes next for all of us?"

"We all got to go sometime. It's my time, is all."

"How are you feeling about leaving Jim behind?"

"He's a good boy. He'll find his way."

"You're a very strong person," Paul said.

Rita coughed. "I got no choice about it."

"And do you feel you're right with Jesus?"

"I don't believe in Jesus, Reverend," said Rita.

Paul stared at her. "But of course you do."

"No, I don't."

"You've been coming to worship at my church for years."

"That's right. Our church is a lovely community, Reverend. But I never really believed any of it."

"Oh," he said.

"No offense, Reverend."

"You don't believe you're going anywhere special, yet you're not afraid?"

"Why should I be? Like I said, I got no choice."

Paul stared at her, unsure what to say. Based on his experience ministering to the dying as well as the living, he'd always agreed with the sentiment there are no atheists in foxholes. Rita Greene proved the exception to the rule.

"Reverend," she said. "Read me that passage from Ecclesiastes. The one about the seasons."

"Uh," Paul said. "Of course." He cleared his throat and recited from memory, "'For everything there is a season, a time for every activity under heaven.'"

"Mmmm," Rita said. She smiled and closed her eyes.

"'A time to be born and a time to die. A time to plant and a time to harvest. A time to kill and a time to heal. A time to tear down and a time to build up. A time to grieve and a time to dance...'"

He stopped. Rita had fallen asleep.

Her son Jim met him in the kitchen. He was a large man who worked in construction. He told Paul that he was taking it hard. They sat at the kitchen table to talk.

"Chondrosarcoma," Jim said with revulsion. "I never heard that word before a week ago. And here it comes, the thing that's going to kill my mom. Goddamn cancer."

Paul nodded.

"Hey, Reverend," Jim added, "what do you say to people when you do grief counseling? What technique works the best?"

"Well, the hardest part is giving our loved ones permission to die," Paul told him. "Some people go on trying to interact with them even after they're gone. They'll go on talking to them because they don't know how to move on."

"So what do you say to these people to help them?"

Paul took out a pen, pulled a napkin from a neat stack on the table, and drew a thick black line on it.

"It's a line," Jim said.

"I tell people their past is on one side of the line, and their future is on the other," Paul explained. "I tell them they have to acknowledge they're crossing this line, and things have changed. They've got to let go and accept the change so they can move into the future."

Jim grunted as he let the visual sink in.

Paul looked at the line and imagined it didn't separate the past from the future, but life from death. On the left, a tiny life of joy, hardship, searching, and wandering. On the right, either eternal joy in union with the Creator, or eternal oblivion—an endless, mindless, terrifying darkness—each of us alone, each of us forgotten, each of us nothing.

☣

The hospital appears to grow larger and more complex as the survivors explore its depths. They mark their progress with a can of fluorescent paint. All the phones are off the hook. Ethan picks one up and places it against his ear just to rediscover the old, familiar act. He dials his home number and listens. The phone doesn't ring. Nobody answers. He places the phone carefully back on the receiver. Then he hurries to catch up with the other survivors, who have stopped in front of a door.

The sour, rancid smell of the dead is strong here. Ethan places a rag soaked in cologne over his mouth and nose and fights the urge to gag.

"We have to check every room," Anne says.

The others nod, reluctantly, and step inside.

Ethan explores the walls with his flashlight. They're covered with crayon drawings on construction paper, crude depictions of homes and mommies and daddies and family pets and suns with big yellow rays coming out of them. Sprayed with dried blood.

"Oh, Jesus," he says. "Oh, Jesus."

"This was the day care," Wendy whispers.

Like a trapeze artist afraid of vertigo and falling a long way, Ethan tells himself not to look down. For some reason, the infected don't want prepubescent children. They don't try to infect them. It may be the pathogen doesn't see them as viable hosts. Or perhaps it places a higher value on them as nutrition, as the infected murder children and feed on their remains.

He knows the floor is littered with rotting meat and bones. Little skulls.

Ethan can't breathe.

Anne shines her flashlight in his face. "Ethan?"

He moans and swats at the light.

"He's losing it. Get him out of here."

As the survivors retreat from the day care, Wendy steps on something soft, which pops with an organic squeak.

She aims her flashlight down and illuminates the floor.

"Anne," she says, her voice thin. "Oh God, Anne, come quick."

The floor is littered with translucent, fleshy sacs filled with a mucus-colored slime. As the beam of light from Wendy's flashlight crosses the sacs, pale worms inside the fluid become agitated and thrash, making the sacs wobble and stretch.

The sacs are eggs. The room is infested with eggs.

Anne appears at her side and looks down. She says nothing.

"What do we do?" Wendy asks her. "You know what they are. If they hatch, we're dead."

For a single long minute, Anne doesn't answer. She holds a bandana against her face, her eyes wide and watery.

"We burn them," she says finally.

The soldiers sweep the gray concrete walls with light as they look for signage that will orient them to the layout of the hospital's mechanical equipment floor. The rooms are filled with boilers, pumps, piping, and makeup air units used to provide heating and cooling to the building, all of it sitting dormant under an exposed ceiling coated with fireproof foam.

Sarge doesn't doubt the hospital has emergency backup power. All hospitals have it because outages can happen unexpectedly, causing monitors, oxygen pumps, and other lifesaving equipment to fail. What he doesn't know is whether the generator burns natural gas or diesel.

If gas, it might have a backup propane tank that would be useful for heating water and cooking. But if it's diesel, they can refuel the Bradley as well as produce electricity.

Sarge stops in front of two bright yellow, twenty-ton machines that look like a cross between a tractor and a train locomotive. The hospital has two generators wired in parallel, each rated at two thousand kilowatts, and what appears to be a big backup fuel tank.

"Hallelujah, boys," he says with a grin. "It's diesel. Check the tanks. We could be mobile."

The soldiers laugh and whoop. They hang their lanterns and get to work inspecting the generators. They're natural grease monkeys and know their way around internal combustion engines. They check the oil and batteries and measure how much diesel is in the tanks. Each generator can hold up to a hundred fifty gallons, while the Bradley holds one-seventy-five. And that doesn't count what's in the backup tank. It's been ten days since the infected put this hospital out of business, so the fuel may have deteriorated a little, but it should be all right.

"Good news and bad news, Sergeant," Steve says.

Ducky says, "The bad news is the generator tanks are empty. The emergency systems automatically turned on when the power failed and drained them. The *good* news is the backup tank is full."

"Hot dog," Sarge says.

"Yeah, it's about time luck got on our side."

Once they get it working, the generator will burn its fuel to generate force that turns a crankshaft. The crank will turn a rotor inside a stator, which will create a steady magnetic field. As the rotor passes through the field, electrical current will be generated in wires that it houses. The current will flow to whatever circuits they assign for loading.

If it works, they'll have light, refrigeration, cooking, air conditioning, heat, and power for electronics. Plus enough to top up the Bradley's fuel tank.

"All right, let's find the breaker panel and set up our loads," Sarge adds. "Then we can take this baby for a spin."

☣

Wendy peels off her grimy clothes, dumps them in a bucket and tosses in some washing liquid she found next to a pile of bloody laundry. Anne also strips down and steps under one of the shower heads.

"Wow, it feels good to be out of those clothes," Wendy says. "It also feels scary. I'm not sure I like it."

Anne points to the inflamed cut along her ribs. "Where did you get that?"

"Worm teeth," Wendy says. "I didn't know I had it until after. I don't think the worms are infectious. Either that, or Todd and I are very lucky."

"Well, that cut looks infected with something. You got a fever?"

"Honestly, I've felt feverish ever since the Screaming. Almost two weeks ago."

"Make sure you take care of it. Your immune system is weak from stress and lack of sleep. If your temperature goes up, take some aspirin and antibiotics."

"I'll take care of it, I promise."

"You do that, Wendy. We need you."

Wendy smiles at that and for the first time becomes aware of Anne's nudity. The end of the world and its forced survival diet burned off any excess fat and left sinewy muscle on the woman's petite frame. Anne has the body of a gymnast.

"You're beautiful," Wendy says.

Anne stares at her in surprise. A smile crosses her face, but her hand flickers at the scars on her face, and the moment passes.

"I might have been once," she answers.

"Come on, ladies, let's go," Todd calls from the locker room. "I haven't had a shower in two weeks!"

"Don't let him peek, Reverend," Wendy says. "We're counting on you to protect our honor."

"Your honor is safe for exactly three minutes plus drying time," Paul calls back. "Let me know when you're ready, so I can start counting down."

Wendy and Anne turn on the faucets, which groan for several moments before spraying a steady stream of cold water.

"Start it now!"

Wendy steps under the shower head. The water's sensual, cold bite electrifies her body. Closing her eyes, she finds it easy to imagine being under a waterfall. The building's water was designated for drinking and cooking only, but Sarge said quick showers would be a great way to celebrate their taking the hospital back from Infection and reminding them what they're surviving for; the others eagerly agreed to the luxury.

Wendy closes her eyes and feels the water drum against her head and shoulders. Lathering up her hands with a bar of soap, she laughs as she washes herself.

"Two minutes!"

Wendy pours a handful of shampoo into her palm and massages her scalp. Soapy brackish water swirls down the drain between her feet. She marvels at how precious water is now. Standing under the downpour, she feels rich with its wealth. Drunk on the luxury of being able to wash herself like this.

"One minute!"

"Shit," she says. She frantically washes her dirty clothes before Paul calls time. They turn the faucets off.

"Now can I peek?" Todd says.

"No!" Wendy answers. She adds to Anne, "We're going to have to find that kid a girl soon."

The women towel down, put on hospital scrubs and slippers, and hang their clothes to dry. Then she grins.

"You know, for a few moments there, I actually forgot all about it," Wendy says.

Anne says, "I don't want to forget."

☣

Eleven months after entering the Academy, Wendy was sworn in and told to report to Zone One. The Northside neighborhoods would be her territory for the foreseeable future. Her first day finally arrived. She woke up after only a few hours of sleep filled with energy and too nervous to eat anything. She downed a cup of coffee and took a hot shower. She tied her hair back into a bun and considered getting it cut short. She carefully laid out and then put on, piece by piece, over black bra and panties, her crisply ironed uniform and pins and badge and Batman belt, conscious of a mundane cop ritual that was still novel to her. She fussed over getting rid of every speck of lint. Then she stood in front of the mirror and worked on her game face.

At the station, after orientation, she was told she'd be partnered with a senior officer named Kendrick, a grizzled, overweight cop with a permanent scowl. She held out her hand to shake, and he gave her a long incredulous once-over, which concluded with him shaking his head.

"I hope fucking Dave Carver isn't the only thing you're good at," he said.

Wendy put on her game face and said, "I'm not fucking Dave Carver."

"If you say so, rook."

"But you're right, I was good at it."

Kendrick snorted with laughter.

"All right, Cleopatra. Let's get going. One more thing, before we go out today. We're going to be in some rough neighborhoods, but remember there are a lot of good people who call those neighborhoods home, so show some fucking respect out there."

Wendy appreciated the perspective. She nodded. They reported to the dispatcher and entered the garage, where they found their cruiser.

"I'll drive, rook," he growled. "You don't do anything unless I say so—*what?*"

"I said, 'Okay, Officer Kendrick.'"

"If you think I'm being hard on you because you're a woman, fuck you."

The squad car left the garage. They drove around their territory for a while and stopped at a Dunkin' Donuts for breakfast. Wendy went in and returned to the car with a box of donuts and two tall cups full of coffee. Kendrick wolfed down the donuts and drank his coffee then settled into his seat with a contented sigh. He watched the street with the dull gaze of a basilisk. Wendy guiltily prayed that something terrible would happen, and she'd do some real police work on her first day. She pictured the dispatcher calling out, *Car crash with injuries*, or, *Robbery in progress* and, *Shots fired*. Maybe she and Kendrick would catch a drug deal in progress. Maybe there'd be a man on one of the city's many bridges, threatening to jump, and she'd have to talk him down. She fidgeted in her seat.

"This is the job, rook." He slurped his coffee. "You hurry up and wait. And wait."

The radio blared, "CD to all units."

There'd been a break-in and stabbing. The dispatcher gave the location and advised the suspect was still in the house. He'd broken in through a window, punched the occupant to the floor, robbed her and cut her up. By the time the dispatcher finished, Kendrick had started the car, turned on the lights and siren, and replied that they were en route.

The car lurched into traffic and roared toward the scene on squealing tires.

"Hold on to your ass," Kendrick said.

"Every unit in the zone must be on its way," Wendy shouted over the siren.

"We'll get there first. Excited, cherry?"

Wendy tried not to smile through her game face.

He whistled. "First day on the job, and you might get a collar. Lucky kid."

The dispatcher was firing updates over the radio when Kendrick yanked the steering wheel and brought the squad car to a screeching halt in front of the house.

They got out of the car. Kendrick pulled out his shotgun. Wendy drew her Glock and ran to the house at a crouch.

They pounded on the door and took a step back.

"Police!"

The door opened and an old woman waved them in.

"He's gone," she said. "He left when he heard you coming."

"Where'd he go?" Wendy demanded.

"Up there," the woman answered vaguely.

"Hold it a second, rook," Kendrick said tersely. "Ma'am, are you hurt? Did he cut you?"

The woman touched her face and frowned. She appeared confused. "I don't remember. He might have."

Kendrick's face turned purple.

"In any case, I'm okay now."

"Which way did he go, Ma'am?" Wendy said.

"I already told you. He's up there. On the roof."

Behind them, other cars rocketed to a halt in front of the house, spilling cops.

"What a waste of time," Kendrick muttered.

"Can I get you a glass of milk, officer?"

Sergeant McElroy showed up, talked to the woman for few minutes with clenched fists, and called the dispatcher to report the call as unfounded.

He jabbed Wendy in the chest with his finger. "Congratulations, Sherlock. You caught your first big case."

She spent the end of her first shift filling out the incident report.

☣

Clean and pink and dressed in plain green hospital scrubs, the survivors wolf down heated cans of ravioli in the lounge. They eat their meal with bottles of red wine that before the world ended would have been considered expensive. The showers cleansed them of the days' old stink of fear. They're starting to feel human again.

As the time approaches six o'clock, they chant a countdown. When they get to zero, nothing happens. The survivors stare at the ceiling, their hopeful expressions wilting in disappointment.

"Bummer," Todd says.

The fluorescent lights blink to life.

The survivors gasp in amazement. Then they cheer.

"Ladies and gentlemen, I give you civilization," Sarge says.

"Fantastic," Ethan says. "It almost feels normal."

"How much of the building is powered?" Anne asks.

"We isolated the power to a section on this floor that includes this lounge plus the pathology department, brain clinic, OBGYN, nursing administration, and all our rooms."

"How long will we have it?"

"The generator runs on diesel like the Bradley. After topping up the rig, we've got enough fuel to have power for forty days if we use it an hour a day."

"I need to charge my cell phone," Ethan says.

"There's probably still no service, though," Paul says.

Ethan shrugs with a sad smile.

"Sorry," Paul adds. "That was a stupid thing to say. Anything is possible."

"It's all right. I want to have the phone ready. Just in case. I have to be ready."

"I hear you."

Todd says, "I'm going to juice up my phone too. I can't wait to hear music again."

"Are there any windows we need to black out?" Anne asks Sarge.

"I think we're good," Sarge tells her. "We turned off the lights in all the rooms with windows."

"Somebody should go out and check to make sure no light is leaking out of the building."

Sarge frowns at the risk. "If you think that's wise."

"If somebody sees the light, we're not safe."

"True," he admits.

"We're acting like we're safe here, but we're not. We've only explored a small part of the building. Yesterday, we found a bonafide monster and killed it. Today, we found a room infested with its eggs. There could be more of those things, not to mention more infected, right under our feet on the second floor. Right over our heads on the floors above. We can't worry about both them and other people coming in from the outside wanting to take what's ours."

"All right, Anne," Sarge says. He feels sour now, as if a fine party has been spoiled. "Who do you want to go out and check? The power will only be on for an hour, and it's starting to get dark. Whoever's going had better get moving."

"I'll do it."

"Not alone. If nobody else wants to go with you, I will."

"Thanks, but I'd rather go alone," she says. "I'll be fine."

"I'm not at all sure that you are," Sarge says.

"So it's decided."

Anne cleans her hands on her pants and walks out the door. The survivors stare at the empty doorway in a stunned silence.

"Are you really going to let her leave like that by herself?" Wendy asks Sarge.

The big soldier shrugs. "She don't belong to me."

"She wanted to go," Paul says. He shakes his head. "She practically ran out of here."

"I'm not going anywhere," Ethan says and pours himself another tall cup of wine.

☣

The soldiers wheel in a television on a cart and plug it into one of the power outlets. The screen fills with snow as it flickers to life. Sarge fiddles with the antenna until a coherent image resolves: a military officer standing in front of a blue curtain and giant map of the United States mounted on an easel board. The image lurches for a moment, stretching like a fun house mirror, and then snaps back.

"Whoa," Todd says as he eats a chocolate bar. "This isn't the usual emergency broadcast crap."

The speakers roar white noise, under which they can hear the officer murmuring like a ghost behind the walls. Sarge fiddles with it a while. Then he gives up and turns the sound off.

"Who is that guy?" Wendy asks. "Do you know him, Sarge?"

Steve snorts. "He's the chairman of the joint chiefs."

"The who?"

Sarge explains, "The highest ranking military official in the country, besides the President. That's General Donald McGregor. Ran the show for a few years in Afghanistan. He's a tough sumbitch."

"Any idea what he's saying?"

"It looks to me like he's giving some type of press conference."

The survivors stare at the unstable image raptly, their brains tickled by the sensation of watching television again. Drunk on the feeling they're no longer alone.

Ethan points at the map. "It's shaded. Like a weather map. See? Pretty much all of Pennsylvania is red."

"I guess we're in for some hot weather."

"That's not a good color," Ethan agrees. He squints at the grainy image. "Philly and New York are shaded a really dark red. That can't be good either. But eastern Ohio, outside the major cities, is yellow. Yellow's better than red, right?"

The survivors shrug, but nobody objects either.

He adds, "If the chairman would move his ass out of the way, we could see what's going on out west."

"The chairman looks profoundly unhappy about the current state of affairs," Todd says, his mouth full of candy.

"Washington, DC is shaded dark red," Wendy says. "I wonder where the President is."

"At Mount Weather in Virginia, most likely," Sarge guesses. "The emergency bunker. Anybody in government who made it out of Washington when the screamers woke up, that's where they'll be now."

"At least there's still a government," she tells him. "We're still resisting. That's something."

Sarge nods. "Yeah, that's something. We're still in the game. I hope we're winning it."

The survivors pour fresh drinks, lean back on the couches, and watch until they grow bored.

"Is there anything else to watch?"

"When does *Game of Thrones* come on?"

They laugh.

"Thank you for coming to my important press conference," Todd says in a nasal voice, watching the general talking on the TV screen and imagining aloud what the man is saying. "My strategic assessment is we're all fucked. Any questions?"

☣

Before the end of the world, Todd wouldn't be caught dead watching television, which he considered an opiate for the masses and a big waste of time besides. He grew up on the internet. He'd spend hours staring at his PC, flitting from one site to the next. One of his favorite things to do was engage total strangers in obnoxious debates about weapons, tactics, and rules in *World of Warcraft* and *Warhammer 40,000*, his favorite games. He called this nightly ritual "doing the time warp." He'd sit at his computer after dinner and, after several hours that flew by as if only a few minutes, his mother would nag him to go to bed.

One night, seven months earlier, as he sat hunched over his keyboard dying to piss, she'd yelled his name from downstairs, which he dutifully ignored. It was his policy to never answer his parents' first call, only the second.

Less than a minute later, she yelled again.

"WHAT?" he roared in a blind rage.

"Come down!"

"I'll *never* finish this post," Todd complained with a dramatic sigh.

He froze at the bottom of the stairs. Sitting on his living room couch was April Preston, wearing jeans and a sweater and glasses.

April was a senior. April was popular. April was beautiful, even with her glasses on.

"Hey," he said, recovering.

"Hi," she said with an awkward smile.

"I thought you might want to say hello," Todd's mom said. "You go to the same school."

"Different grades," Todd said.

"Right," April said.

"April's car broke down," his dad said. "We just called AAA."

Todd nodded. "Excellent."

"Do you want a Pepsi or something, April? Something to eat?"

"I'm all right. Thanks, Mrs. Paulsen."

"Do you need to call your parents?"

"I already did, thanks. My dad's coming to get me."

Todd studied April while they talked. Her presence here made him nervous. She never did any harm to him personally, but he considered her an enabler to those who did. She dated them. Apparently, she found total jerks irresistibly attractive. *You're abusive to people who are younger and weaker than you AND you play football? Wow, you're so hot!*

Now she was in his house. Even his home was violable, apparently. They could just walk right in. He pictured her telling everybody at school what a dorky house he had, what dorky parents. She would imitate them: *I just called AAA. Want a Pepsi?*

She didn't look particularly threatening, however. In fact, she looked as nervous as he felt. He felt an impulse to do something chivalrous. Maybe he could impress her, and she'd tell everybody at school how cool he actually was.

His parents left the room. April stared at her hands resting on her lap.

"Must be great to be a senior," he said.

She smiled again and nodded.

"Um. Are you going to college?"

"I'd like to go to college," April said. "I'll probably end up at Penn State. You?"

Todd started. "Me? I'm not sure yet. I mean, I'd like to go, I definitely will go, but I haven't chosen a school yet. Graduation seems like an eternity to me."

"Well, you're smart. You'll probably get your pick of schools."

Todd didn't know what to say. April had violated the first law of the jungle, which is to never praise above average intelligence. You could be a great athlete, a great musician, a great consumer of twelve-ounce beers, but never a great student. He began to see her as outside the game, operating by different rules. In her last year of high school, she already seemed like an adult. His ears rang, and his entire being felt warm and flushed at the compliment. He was used to being complimented, but only by authority figures—his parents and teachers, mostly—never by other students. Never by his peers.

He began to see himself as outside the game as well, entering a world where a reputation for smarts would be an asset instead of a source of embarrassment and fear. For the first time in a long time, Todd felt hopeful.

Another impulse: he wanted to talk to her all night. Then his dad returned to tell April that her father was outside, waiting for her.

Todd looked at her with hope, but the spell was already broken. Tomorrow, they'd return to the same building that defined their lives, and they'd have no relationship. He felt like he'd been given an unexpected gift, while at the same time cheated.

"Well, I'll see you around, I guess," April said.

"Good talking to you," Todd told her with formal gravity, meaning every word.

Months later, the great game of high school ended with the Screaming. April was one of the majority that didn't fall down. Todd still wondered sometimes what happened to her. He hoped she made out okay. She was one of the good ones.

☣

The survivors drift away one by one. Wendy goes back to her room to clean her Glock and refill her magazines with bullets. Sarge wants to work up a sweat with some exercise. Ethan, drunk and slurring his words, scoops two unopened bottles of wine and announces that he's going to his room to recharge his cell phone.

Todd shows Steve and Ducky his crudely stitched forearm and asks them if they ever heard the story of how he got wounded. He asks them if they had to choose between a pistol with thirty rounds and a *katana*, which would they want to fight a zombie horde with?

The crew shake their heads in irritation and excuse themselves to check on the emergency generator.

After they leave, Todd grows even more bored. He lists aloud all of the things he misses the most. A big, fat, juicy steak, for starters. French fries. Buffalo wings. Anything cold to drink. His PC and his X-box game console. Friday nights at the hobby store. *World of Warcraft. Warhammer 40,000.*

"I wonder how much time we spend each day doing things and not actually knowing we're alive," Paul contemplates. He drains the last of his wine and stares at the bottom of his cup.

"So what do you miss the most, Reverend?"

Paul grimaces, shaking his head, and leaves Todd to watch the crumbling image of the tired general by himself.

☣

Sarge mentally counts his pushups—*twenty-one, twenty-two*—his shirt off and his thickly muscled torso slick with sweat. A medallion engraved with the image of Saint George, the patron saint of soldiers and Boy Scouts—and the victims of plague—dangles from his neck. He has been sitting reclined in the Bradley for over a week—which is like being forced to sit on a tiny couch playing a violent video game, one in which people actually die—for ten days straight. His brain is exhausted while his body has been going soft. Exercise will reboot both. Rest means refit.

His mind wanders to mountains looming over a sprawling base built of sandbag bunkers and huts and tents surrounded by timber walls and concertina wire.

Chinook helicopters pound over the valley with their Apache escort. A patrol toils across a distant hill. Soldiers laugh and clean their gear and piss into PVC tubes stuck in the ground. This is Afghanistan.

"Forget it," he thinks aloud. "Just forget it."

The first Chinook falls out of the sky and crashes into the mountain. It breaks into pieces, spilling bodies as it rolls into the valley.

He quickens the pace of his pushups. His heart races.

A knock at the door.

The soldiers at the base crumple onto the dirt.

"Not yet," he says, *thirty-seven, thirty-eight, thirty-nine—*

The bodies start to scream.

The person knocks again.

He stops, panting. So close. He came so close to forgetting.

"Come in," he says.

The door opens, and Wendy enters. She watches him wipe the sweat from his body with a towel. She stares at the bear paw print tattoo on the left side of his chest. He looks away, feeling naked.

"Has Anne come back?" he says.

Wendy smiles and nods.

"Good," he says.

She reaches into her mouth and extracts a chewed ball of Bazooka gum. She sticks it to the doorframe.

"Good," she says.

"So," he adds.

"So," she says.

The cop takes a step toward him, holds his face in her hands, and kisses him gently on the mouth.

He forgets everything.

Ethan sits on his bed in the bright fluorescent light. He stares at his phone, lying inert on the floor, while drinking red wine out of a Dixie cup. The phone is connected to a power outlet. The power from the emergency generator will shut off in fifteen minutes, and he wants to make sure his phone is charged.

It's starting to hit him that they're safe and might live here a while. Ever since he fled his home with nothing but a backpack, his every waking thought focused on staying away from the infected when he could and killing them when he couldn't. After that: water, food, shelter.

Now that all his basic needs are satisfied, his mind already is looking to other needs. New clothes and toiletries. Some DVDs to kill the time. Exercise equipment. Some art on the walls. And, perhaps most important, a project that will give him a sense of purpose, that will allow him to start living again instead of simply surviving. Rescuing other survivors, maybe. Starting a greenhouse.

Anything to keep out the other emotions that continually threaten to invade his mind. For ten days, he has felt fear, panic, and little else. Now guilt, depression, and boredom. A crushing sense of isolation and homesickness.

He misses his wife. He misses his little girl. He misses his old life.

We were lucky, Carol. We were stupid.

He takes another long sip of wine. It's a ridiculously expensive vintage, but he's put down so much already, his taste buds right now couldn't tell the difference between a fine Bordeaux and Mad Dog.

Ethan takes out his backpack and places a series of artifacts on the bed. A hairbrush with his wife's hair still tangled in it. A yellow rubber airplane, a promotion from an airline during a family vacation to Florida. Plastic piggy; Mary picked it up while playing in a park and wouldn't part with it. A grimy little teddy bear that squeaks when squeezed; Mary used to make it talk back to her in a falsetto voice during pretend conversations. A hair clip. A card his wife gave him to express how glad she was that he hadn't been taken from her by the Screaming. Ethan knows the words, written in her fine handwriting, by heart. A wood spirit carving, the face of a bearded old man. A little blue Buddha on a keychain; Carol frequently toured spirituality but couldn't commit to religion. A photo of her from before Mary was born. Another of them smiling at their wedding, hastily ripped out of its frame before he fled the house. Several wallet photos of Mary when she turned one. The edges are worn from constant handling.

He has dozens of other photos, but they're all on his computer at his house. He wants to think that he can go back there one day and get them. That someday the infected are all going to drop dead or some scientist will invent a cure, and he can go home.

Sarge returns to consciousness with an intense sensation of butterflies in his heart. The beautiful cop pulls away. He gazes after her sadly, wondering if he did something wrong.

But she says, "Will you hold me?"

"Yes," he says, surprised at how relieved he feels that she's not leaving.

"Just hold me for a minute?"

"I'd like that."

Wendy guides him gently to the bed and pushes him down. She curls up next to him. They lie together on their sides, spooning, his large arm wrapped protectively around her stomach.

"This is nice," she purrs. "Jesus, I feel really safe right here. Oh, fuck, yes."

Sarge feels the warmth of her body against his. He smells her hair. The sensations are intoxicating; he hasn't been with a woman since before his deployment to Afghanistan. A long time. He wonders if he can touch her in other places but doesn't make a move. He's afraid of spoiling the moment.

"Do you mind if I sleep here tonight?"

"You can sleep here," he tells her.

"Sarge?"

He frowns at her tone. The moment was spoiled after all. A part of him expected this all along. She's going to ask him why he prefers Anne as leader. He doesn't want to have to explain the deal he made.

Instead, she says, "Do you think we have a responsibility to other people anymore?"

"What do you mean?"

"You're a soldier. I'm a cop. We swore an oath. We have our duty."

Sarge thinks of Ducky, willing to risk everything to find friendly forces and get back in the war.

"We do," he agrees.

"What if this really is a safe place? Are we allowed to stay here and try to be happy? Or are we obligated to find others like us and see what we can do to help?"

"I don't know, Wendy," he says. "I honestly do not know."

He wants to kiss her again, but she has fallen asleep in his arms. She's a different person in sleep, so beautiful and innocent it makes his heart ache. His arm is sore from the weight of her body, but he doesn't care.

She moans briefly. She winces at some inner pain. Her cheeks are wet with tears.

"I'll protect you," he whispers.

Paul stands in the dark on the roof facing north, gazing into more darkness. The fluorescent lighting made him feel nervous and exposed. It, or the wine over which he silently mouthed the Sacrament almost without thinking, gave him a royal headache. He believes he understands why Anne left. He felt a similar yearning to go out into the night. The dark can be a safe place. In the dark, nobody can see you. *Sanctuary is what we all wanted, and now we fear it. We fear its illusion of safety and choice, its utter fragility.*

He lights another cigarette, careful to conceal the flame of his lighter. He coughs on a cloud of smoke. His throat feels scratchy and raw. He's already planning his next cigarette. He has fresh packs making a comfortable bulge in the pocket of his jacket. He finds renewing his old habit good for the nerves. A habit is reliable. Right now, lung cancer is the least of his worries.

He thinks about the first man he killed. A woman, actually, in the beverage aisle of Trader Joe's market. The woman came running, and the shotgun, held in his shaking hands, seemed to weigh a hundred pounds. He barely remembers firing it—by that point, his heart rate skyrocketed and his vision had shrunk down to the size of a small circle. He couldn't control his hands. The roar of the gun startled him, and he flew back against the empty shelving; then he ran screaming for help.

When he returned with the other survivors, he found the woman lying on the ground, her head splashed down the aisle, stone dead. His legs gave out, and he cried. Over time, he has gotten better at killing, but he still regrets every one.

The only man he actually wishes he ever killed was that first infected who came running at him out of the darkness in the alley behind his house. When he tries to sleep at night, that hateful face lunges out of the dark, flooding his system with adrenaline. He has killed a dozen infected, wounded perhaps twice that, but that one man still terrifies him. That one man has become more than a memory; he's a symbol of Infection and the hate and fear it has imposed on his life. If Paul could only go back in time, he would fight and kill the man with his bare hands.

He sighs and wonders what Sara would think about the new Paul if she were still alive. He takes comfort in the understanding she loved him and would want him to survive no matter what the cost. She'd tell him to kill the thing in the alley. She'd say: *You are my man, and I love you more than myself.* She'd say: *Survive, baby.* She'd say: *Kill them all.*

He can't remember what happened to her. He remembers the grisly slaughter at the church, the mob, the battle with the infected. The next thing he knew, he was huddled in a corner in a temporary shelter set up by the government. He can't remember anything else but wants to know what happened. Sara was claimed by Infection. Knowing will not affect that outcome. But he'd like to know. Or rather, he'd like to remember.

The sky is covered with flying clouds that hide the moon. For a few minutes, it's so dark, it's easy to imagine he's in a spaceship hurtling lost through the void. Slowly, his vision adjusts, and he can make out details in the urban nightscape. He sees the headlights of a small convoy of vehicles driving far to the west. The warm glow of a campfire in the corner office of a high-rise office building. A bright red line emerges from the darkness in the northeast, like a glowing cut.

He watches the line grow larger, curving, a glowing red scimitar. Fire. A big fire on the south side of the river. He can already smell the smoke. Hear gunshots and screams. People and infected alike are in flight.

Paul shudders. If the fire goes on spreading, there will be a bloodbath tonight as thousands are flushed out of hiding onto streets filled with infected. Many will come this way. There are few other directions they can go.

Already, down at the edge of the parking lot behind the hospital, he can see gray shapes moving in the dark, writhing and pushing against each other like maggots.

☣

Ethan's head reels from the wine, and he can't think straight. He picks up the cell phone, his heart pounding loudly in his ears, and turns it on. The image tells him there's no service available in his calling area, another reminder the entire power grid is down. Cellular networks use radio base stations. These systems in turn use power, and there's no power because the people who run the power plants, provide fuel to the power plants, and maintain the power distribution system are all dead or infected or hiding. He feels a crushing headache coming on.

During his family's last vacation together, they joined a group helping baby turtles make it to the sea. The female turtles leave the sea to dig a hole, lay up to two hundred eggs in it, and refill it with sand, the same as they've done for millions of years. After the turtles hatch, instinct draws them to the sea. As they emerge from the sand, predators, lying in wait, devour them. Most die; few survive. Only one in a thousand survive the journey. It's a heart-wrenching thing to watch, but there's no morality here, no overarching narrative, no guarantee even one would make it. There's only life and death and survival of the fittest. This is nature. As Paul would say, the earth abides. The earth is blind to suffering and justice and happy endings.

A part of him believes his family is alive. He pictures Mary hiding alone in a closet, scared and crying for her mommy and daddy; the image rips the heart out of his chest. If she's alive, she's a needle in a burning stack of needles. He wouldn't know where to look, and he knows he wouldn't survive five minutes on the streets without the protection of the other survivors and their big fighting machine. One in a thousand survive: they're innocent, but so few make it, and the rest are culled, and there's no reason for any of it. He can't believe his family is dead, though the rational part of his mind knows this must be true. Ethan understands he will spend the rest of his life being broken, stuck in the past, unable to say goodbye.

The lights cut out; the soldiers have turned off the power for the night. He paces and drinks straight from the bottle in long, painful gulps. His vision blurs with tears. His organs feel like they're in free fall. Ethan coughs on a mouthful of wine, vaguely aware that his right hand is bleeding and alarmingly swollen and throbbing with pain. *My family is dead.* It feels good to scream. *What did my little girl think when the infected beat her to death?* He becomes aware of other people in the room. An LED lantern being turned on. He throws the bottle.

Did she feel any pain?

Voices cursing.

Did she wonder where her daddy was?

Hands on him, pushing him down.

Was she still alive when they started EATING HER, while I did NOTHING?

Voices pleading.

WHY, WHY, WHY—?

Ethan lies on the bed screaming, his eyes wide, arching his back against the hands that hold him down. His consciousness swims through a haze of guilt and rage, briefly focusing on Anne's face, hovering overhead, just before he feels the jab of a needle in his arm, and his vision fades to black.

FLASHBACKS: TODD PAULSEN

The government closed the schools after the Screaming. For Todd Paulsen, this meant the possibility of early summer vacation.

Four whole months of freedom. No more furtive darting through the crowds in the hallways between classes. No ritual humiliations during gym class. No awkward moments trying to secure a seat on the school bus. No fantasizing about walking into the school with a machine gun and hunting down every jock asshole who ever hurt him. He prayed the school system would stay screwed up until the end of the summer. The Screaming had culled the assholes; graduation would claim most of the rest. Then next year, he'd be a senior at last.

The only thing that kept him sane since entering high school was the Lycans, the war-gaming club down at Lycan Hobbies. Most of them were guys attending the local college. He counted them as his best friends. He pretty much worshipped them. They were basically geeks like him, but they were much more self-assured and worldly. In fact, to them, *geek* wasn't an insult, something to be ashamed of, but instead a simple, apt, and mildly amusing descriptor. They even dated girls and discussed their dating casually, without fanfare. They assured him that high school could feel like prison, but college would be better, so be patient. This tantalizing thought had kept him sane all year.

That and Sheena X, the high school chick who worked the register at the store and usually sat with her feet up on the counter, chewing gum and reading comic books. Sometimes, she even participated in the gaming on Friday nights. She would typically show up wearing red skinny jeans, Converse All Stars, and a black T-shirt with SCREAMO or some band name scrawled on it. Often, she wore a matching studded belt and wristband. On colder days, she wore a tight sweater vest. Her hair, dyed black, fell over one eye. She'd show up at the store with new obsessions. One week, it was getting suicide scars tattooed on her wrists. Another, making a movie based on the songs of Island Def Jam and Joy Division and Garbage. For the next three weeks: Johnny Depp, Johnny Depp, Johnny Depp. Todd usually communicated with her in an overexcited, virtually shouted stream of consciousness, but instead of rolling her eyes at him and mouthing, *Freak*, Sheena X simply stared and nodded sagely.

They accepted him, more or less, as he was. They were his port in the unending storm that was his adolescence.

The club played several tabletop miniature war games but usually *Warhammer 40,000*, set in a space fantasy universe where the Imperium of Man, far flung across the Milky Way galaxy, was in constant conflict with powerful alien species. For many teenagers, music and fashion offered outlets. For Todd, it was gaming. He'd painstakingly collected and painted a company of a hundred Space Marines, war machines, and bosses, allowing him to participate in smaller games as well as big games, three thousand points and up, that played out over days.

The Lycans had just gotten a new codex for urban warfare and had been trying it out in a contest between Space Marines and massive swarms of Tyranids. The table presented the ruins of an ancient alien city. The Space Marines' mission was to secure the city within several turns and set up a defense in time for a massive Tyranid counterattack. Todd and Alan had just taken the city before the Screaming, and now that school was canceled, he was itching to get back to the game. Alan had fallen down, but his opponents were okay, so the game could continue.

Lycan Hobbies, however, remained closed three days after the Screaming. Todd called Sheena X at home. She explained to him that the owner's wife had fallen down and that he was out of his mind trying to find his brother, who was missing.

"Wow," said Todd. "So do you know when he's going to open the store again?"

"I don't know, dude. What are you doing up this early? You're *never* up this early."

"Sirens woke me up. It's like non-stop sirens out there. Some kind of fire or something."

"I can hear them here, too."

Fires were a common occurrence since the Screaming. A lot of heating devices—ovens, irons and so on—were left on when the Screamers fell down. Natural gas systems weren't being properly maintained. Power lines were still falling.

"So anyway, do you think he would just let us in so we could finish up our game?"

"*Todd*, what the fuck?"

He launched into a recap of the first night's gaming. She hadn't been there that night. Surely, if she knew how great it was, she'd understand his impatience at continuing the contest. He'd had a simple strategy, he said. He and Alan had sent armor—two Venerable Dreadnoughts with plasma and auto cannons, flanked by Land Speeders armed with missile launchers and heavy bolters—pushing hard through the city to secure it. When the infantry caught up, he sent half to mop up the remaining resistance and the rest to establish a defensive perimeter in a horseshoe shape. Then the Tyranid counterattack suddenly appeared, a real party made up of Tyrannofex, Termagants, Tervigons, and Hive Guard led by a Swarmlord with three Tyrant Guard—

"*Enough*, Todd," Sheena said.

He felt his stomach fall into his feet. "I'm sorry," he said tentatively. His mind raced to figure out what he'd done wrong.

"I don't give a shit about *Warhammer* right now. My dad *fell down*, Todd."

"Now he won't bug you anymore," he offered.

"I know I don't like my dad very much," Sheena X said in a strained voice. "I know he can be a real asshole when he wants to be. But I didn't want *this* to happen to him. I didn't want him to go into a fucking *coma*. I didn't want half his foot to get chopped off by the fucking *lawnmower* he was pushing when he fell down." Her voice became shrill. "*Okay?*"

"Okay, Sheena," he said, feeling chastened and more than a little shocked by her language. "I get it. You know, my mom fell down, too."

"I *know*, Todd. Maybe you should be thinking about her instead of that stupid game."

Anger flared in his chest. She'd made him feel childish for enjoying *Warhammer 40,000* when he'd always understood it was a game adults played too. It wasn't stupid. And his mom was fine. Dad put her in a special facility where she was getting around-the-clock care. He also tried to get Todd to see a therapist, but luckily they were all booked up with new patients after the Screaming—indefinitely, it seemed.

Why would he need a therapist, anyhow? He was at home sick, lying on the living room couch when the Screaming happened, fast asleep; he'd missed the entire thing and had to see it on TV later. Half the school's bullies were in a catatonic state, and the school itself had closed. His mom was sick like the other Screamers, but he knew she'd be okay. They'd all be okay. He had tremendous faith in the government's ability to solve problems like this. A cure was coming.

Todd racked his brain for something to say, maybe something funny that would ease the tension.

She sighed. "I've got to go, Todd. My *mom* is yelling for me."

"All right."

"Oh my *God*," Sheena X shrieked. "I can't believe it!"

"What? What is it?"

"Mom says Dad is waking up!"

Todd laughed. "That's great!"

"I have to go. Bye, Todd!"

Todd hung up with a grin. If Sheena X's dad was waking up, so was his mom.

His grin evaporated. *And so are all the others.* Like John Wheeler.

And they'll reopen the school. Maybe even keep school going past the end of June to make up for the lost time. Todd felt deflated at the thought. God had a crappy sense of humor.

The phone rang. That would be his dad bearing good news. He picked up the receiver.

"Todd, listen—"

Can't they all just stay asleep one more month?

"Hey, Dad. Are you calling about Mom?"

"Listen to me. I don't have much time. That barricade isn't going to hold. We have nothing to fight them with—"

"Aren't you at work?" His dad worked in an office as an executive. In one of those big cubicle farms like you see in *Dilbert*. He was a big man at work, with a lot of people reporting to him.

"You need to get my gun. It's in a shoebox on the top shelf of my closet. Make sure you get the bullets too. Don't leave the house. Shoot anybody who breaks in. Shoot to kill."

Todd laughed. "Dad?"

"They're coming in. DON'T RUN! STAY TOGETHER! FIGHT! Todd, I don't know. I *don't know*. We're fucked. I love you, kid. I do. Yeah. I guess that's it. Take care of yourself."

A flurry of shouts at the other end of the phone.

"Dad?" Todd said into the dial tone.

He smelled smoke through the open window. Sirens wailed from all parts of the city. Other sounds ripped the air: screams. And splashes of gunfire, startlingly loud. Something big was happening. Todd looked out the window but saw nothing out of the ordinary. Just his boring little typical suburban street washed in bright May sunshine. Every lawn perfectly manicured; even the front yards of the homes abandoned by the screamers had been well tended by charitable neighbors. Looking at this gentle scene, it was hard to believe that even the Screaming had happened.

He called his dad back several times but kept getting voicemail. He checked the major news sites and read headlines about widespread rioting along the West Coast. Then Todd called his dad again. He left a message, trying to figure out what to do next to keep his growing sense of panic at bay a little longer.

He looked down at the street again and saw a big cop in a motorcycle helmet marching down the sidewalk.

"Hey, officer!" he called. "Do you know what's going on?"

The policeman looked up at the window, showing his gray face and wet, blackened chin.

"Are you okay?" Todd said.

The man ran up the front walk of his house and disappeared from view.

"What the hell is he doing?" Todd mumbled to himself, both alarmed and amused.

He heard the front door crash open. The motorcycle cop came banging up the stairs.

"Oh, crap," he said.

Stomping in the hall. Todd threw himself onto the floor and crawled under the bed as his door flew open, knocking half the Space Marines off his dresser to sprinkle the floor.

The cop paced around the room, sniffing the air. Flooded with panic and fear, Todd lay under the bed and tried not to breathe. The emotions reminded him of school, the strange feeling that everybody hated him. He watched the cop's boots track blood across his carpet. The minutes ticked by. The cop continued to pace and knock things over. The room was filled with a rancid sour milk stench. Todd breathed through his mouth.

After an hour, the cop left. Todd heard him enter the bathroom and splash in the toilet. Then the man came back, coughing wetly, and resumed his march around the room.

After a few hours of this, Todd eventually fell asleep.

He woke dry mouthed and sweaty with a massive urge to piss. He almost cried out in confusion but remembered the danger he was in. He had no idea what time it was; the sun had gone down, and he could barely see his hand in front of his face. The maniac cop was no longer pacing but was still in the room. Todd could smell his sour stink and hear him breathing in quick shallow gasps.

He wondered if the man was sleeping. Should he risk moving? The thought of leaving the security of his hiding place paralyzed him with fear. He didn't know exactly what the cop would do to him if he caught him, but just the idea of being dominated physically by a stronger man electrified him with revulsion. He stalled by fantasizing about his dad coming home and warning him just in time that the cop was there, saving his life. Then he fantasized about Sheena X coming over to check on him and saving her life, which gave him a painful erection. An hour went by like this while the night breezes delivered the sounds of screams, squealing tires, and gunfire through his window.

He had to do something soon, or he might be trapped under this bed for another full day. He crept toward the edge of the bed. The policeman panted like a dog. He wondered what to do next. A part of him wanted to stand up and make a run for it on pure adrenaline, but this notion was quickly overruled by his tiny but growing voice of common sense. *Do nothing and you're going to die, old man. So do something.* The bedroom door was open and the cop was somewhere to his left. If the man was facing the door, he'd see Todd. If not, then Todd might have a chance.

He slithered like a snake and paused to peer at the dark form swaying on its feet in the darkness. The cop faced the corner. The white motorcycle helmet bobbed as the man breathed in his little shallow gasps, his shoulders shrugging in rhythm.

This is really freaking ninja.

Todd slipped out of the room and gently closed the door behind him. He tiptoed to his parents' bedroom and emptied his bladder into the sink in the en suite bathroom. Then he pulled boxes down from the top shelf of his parents' closet until he found a heavy blue shoebox. Inside were nestled a small handgun, box of bullets, and sheet of paper. He took the sheet to the window and squinted at it under the light of nearby streetlights. It was a note from his dad to him saying the gun was loaded and had no safety, so don't even think about touching it if he ever found it.

Awesome. He picked it up.

The gun roared in his hand and punched two smoking holes through the wall. He blinked in the afterglow of the flash, his ears ringing and his nose burning from the gun smoke.

"Holy crap," he said. His voice sounded muffled in his ears. "Aw, jeez. I barely touched it."

Dad's gonna murder me for that.

The cop roared and banged on his bedroom door. Todd ran to the hall, braced his legs, and aimed the pistol with both hands. His hands started shaking. The door shivered and splintered under the blows. He took a deep breath and tried to calm down. *Picture the outcome*, he thought.

He envisioned the cop bursting through the door. He imagined squeezing the trigger and putting two in the man's chest and one between the eyes. He pictured the crazy cop dying before he hit the floor.

"Screw that," he said and lowered the pistol.

He ran down the stairs, stepped into his shoes at the front entry, and bolted from the house. He collided with a snarling woman coming up the driveway. The gun went off in his hands again. The woman fell.

"Crap, sorry," he said and kept running into the night.

He became winded after a few blocks and slowed down, cradling the gun carefully against his chest. He heard the tramp of feet and hid as a pack of growling people ran past. People screamed everywhere. On the next block, a house burned without a single fireman on the scene; he could feel the heat on his face. Changing direction to avoid the fire, he approached a group of people huddled on the ground near the wreckage of a horrible car crash in the middle of an intersection. He wanted to ask if they were all right, but the tiny voice of common sense warned him to stick to the shadows. One of the cars was on fire. The flames glittered on the broken glass that carpeted the ground.

He got a closer look at them as he passed. They hunched over a body, pulling out organs and chewing noisily. The light crawled across their gray bloody faces. He fought the urge to retch.

Picture them eating something nice. Fried chicken. They're eating a bucket of fried chicken. Crispy fried chicken with a side of fries. That's all. No big deal.

Bad idea. The contents of his stomach leaped into his throat, and he vomited noisily against a brick wall, helpless, his eyes filled with water. When he turned back, one of the eaters looked right at him. He knew they were different—crazy, demonic, even—but they couldn't see in the dark, could they? He clung to the wall, trying not to move, yet shaking uncontrollably. The woman was topless, her chest wet and darkly stained. The firelight gleamed in her black eyes. Todd stared wide-eyed at her bare, full breasts. She lowered her head to resume her grisly meal.

People are turning into cannibals. Some kind of zombie. What the hell is going on? Where am I supposed to go?

He wanted to find a computer or TV so he could see what was happening. A phone so he could call his dad again. Maybe his dad was dead. He tried not to think about it.

Sheena X. He decided to go to her house, help her barricade the place, and wait out this zombie apocalypse together. He was rolling a fantasy of them sharing the pain of their parents being dead—followed by the realization they were in love, and a huge make out scene—when the infected ran howling out of the dark.

Todd bolted in a blind panic. *Jesus God. These people want to kill me.* The very idea sapped the energy from his legs. Made him want to sleep. His mind swam in panic. *If only*, he thought. *It's not fair*, he thought. *The gun*, he thought. He remembered the pistol in his hand.

He turned as the first infected bore down on him, a big man wearing a T-shirt soaked through with blood and sweat. Todd squeezed the trigger on reflex without aiming. The bullet entered the side of the man's head just above the ear and turned half his skull into a spray of blood and skull fragments. The man staggered and wagged his head as if sneezing, shaking free pieces of brain, and then collapsed. The death of this monster struck Todd as nothing short of a miracle.

"Yeah!" he cried.

More came howling out of the darkness. He had to wait until they got close so he could be sure he'd hit them. But if they got too close, he'd panic and run, and then they'd get him. Todd blanked out his mind and breathed through his nose. He pictured the scene as an online first person shooter game and let his hand-eye reflexes take over. He shifted his aim and fired as the infected approached, hoping he had enough bullets.

"I am invincible," he sang off key, wishing for a soundtrack, then stopped, unable to remember the rest of the words to the song. The fight was over in seconds. He surveyed the bodies of five infected lying on the ground moaning and thrashing.

He approached the twitching bodies carefully, watching for any who might make a last-second movie lunge and deliver a mortal wound that would be just payment for letting his guard down. One was a police officer. Todd was curious about him because he shot the man three times, but the cop kept getting up and coming at him until the last bullet destroyed the right side of his head. The mystery was solved easily; the man wore a bulletproof vest.

Todd pulled the vest off and put it on himself. It was a little big, and it was heavier than he'd thought it'd be, but he loved it. He'd seen them on TV, of course, and had always wanted one. He thought it made him look bigger, bulkier, tougher than what he usually saw in the mirror.

He sensed that he could be good at this—surviving in a post-apocalyptic world.

Looks like school is out forever. The thought almost made him happy.

He reloaded the gun and continued his march. After a while, the sky lightened; dawn was coming. He had to get off the street soon. His heart pounded as he approached Sheena X's house.

Just wait until she gets a load of me in this gear. She'll be all over me.

The porch light was on, as if she were expecting him. Lights blazed in the house. The door was ajar. He rang the doorbell and waited.

Todd backed away.

"Aw, Sheena..."

The screen door banged open. Sheena X stumbled out of the house, twitching and gray-faced, the front of her T-shirt soaked with blood, her hair still combed over one eye.

"No," he said. "Oh, no."

"*Rah, ruh,*" she snarled.

"I'm sorry, Sheena."

Todd raised the gun and fired. The bullet punctured her skull and splashed her brains onto the screen door. She collapsed, leaving a puff of smoke and bloody mist hanging in the air.

The crash of the gunshot echoed down the street and mingled with millions of similar sounds all over the city, rising up to the sky as a single chaotic roar.

Todd sat on the ground in a daze. He wasn't sure what he felt. Then it hit him. Shaking uncontrollably, he hugged his knees and bawled.

THE FIRE

The survivors stand on the hospital roof and watch the growing fire consume western Pittsburgh. The sky glows red as buildings continue to burn downtown, soar up into the sky on powerful convection currents, and rain back down as particulates. The air grows thick with heat and smoke and falling ash. The night is alive with gunfire and screams.

"Paul was right," Anne says. "It's huge. And it's moving."

"Gone," Wendy says. Her voice cracks. "It's all gone."

Sarge says, "We've got to get out of here. Tonight."

☣

The survivors race in and out of their rooms in the glow of LED lanterns, throwing bags and supplies into the corridor. Their shadows flicker across the walls. Shouts echo in the gloom. A box rips open and spills cans across the floor. A handful of bullets clatter and roll like marbles. The survivors don't want to leave. They don't want to go outside at all. But they have no choice. If they stay here, they'll die.

The spreading fire produced a massive migration. Pittsburgh is on the move. The fire flushed thousands of people out of their hiding places and into the streets to mingle with the fleeing infected. The number of infected is growing by the minute, and they're all headed this way.

"What about Ethan?" Todd says.

Sarge glances at Anne, who shakes her head.

"He's coming with us," the commander says.

"Damn right he's coming," Paul says.

"I got him."

The soldier grabs the front of Ethan's shirt and pulls him to his feet. He curses as the man spews half-digested ravioli and red wine onto the floor. Then he heaves Ethan up and over one shoulder.

The survivors hustle down the stairs in a train and dump their supplies at the entrance of the hospital. Sarge drops Ethan in a heap in the vestibule and turns to scan the outside parking lot using his rifle's night vision close combat optic. The optic amplifies ambient light thousands of times and creates a grainy image rendered in green. He can make out figures shambling through the parking lot.

"Where's our ride?" Todd says, his voice edged with panic. He realizes that Steve and Duck went to retrieve the Bradley, and if they don't come back, the survivors will be stranded.

"It's coming," Sarge growls. "I'll cover forward. The rest of you, go get the rest of our shit."

Anne touches his shoulder, asking the unspoken question, *Do you need me for anything?*

"Light," he says.

They have flashlights, but turning one on right now would be like ringing a dinner bell. Instead, he needs fire—flares, Molotovs. He doesn't have to explain this. Anne knows what to do.

He thinks about Wendy. It was always nothing to take care of himself, but now he's worried about her too. It's hard to aim a rifle when your heart is pounding. He pushes his worries away and breathes slowly and steadily until he regains complete control of his nerves.

Crowds of infected flow through the cars in the parking lot. A pack breaks off with strident cries and pound toward the hospital. Their eyes gleam bright green in Sarge's optic.

They never stop searching for us. Sarge pulls the trigger and cuts them down with several bursts.

☣

Steve and Ducky scurry between the rows of abandoned cars in the parking garage, guided by their night vision goggles, rifles held in the aiming position.

The sounds of distant fire and chaos fills the air like white noise. The characteristic *ping* of the sergeant's AK47 cuts through the din. The man is blazing away down at the front of the hospital. Steve takes a moment to look out from the second floor of the parking garage. He sees the muzzle flashes.

"Let's go," Ducky hisses from somewhere ahead.

Steve nods. He wants to help the sergeant, but the best way he can do that is to get the Bradley down there as fast as possible.

He trained to fight to protect his country, but he never trained for this. Of course, he's scared. They're all scared, all of the time, even in their dreams. But more than that, he hates, with every atom and every fiber, killing other Americans. The first time he did that, he stopped being a soldier. He trusts Sarge and will follow his orders as long as it helps keep them all alive, but Steve isn't in Sarge's Army anymore.

A noise like a foghorn stops them in their tracks. Next comes a deep, rumbling, phlegmy cough. Steve and Ducky crouch behind the hood of a car and scan the area. Something big moves through the far end of the garage. Big enough to push vehicles out of its way.

"What the fuck is that?" Ducky says. "One of those worms?"

"No. Yes. I don't know."

Steve turns on the SureFire flashlight mounted on his rifle and aims it at the thing moving through the gloom. The flashlight has a red lens that makes the beam barely visible to anybody not wearing night vision goggles. On the NVGs, the light appears a brilliant green. The beam plays along the smooth, hairless flank of something massive striding through the garage.

"Some kind of elephant or something," Ducky says.

"Or something. At least it's moving away from us."

The thing shoulders aside an SUV and sets off a car alarm.

Ducky pats Steve's arm and says, "We'd better get moving."

They find the Bradley where they left it in the corner. Steve pulls at the black plastic tarp, exposing a yellow happy face stenciled on the vehicle's side.

Another sound distracts them. Something making a wet clicking sound deep in its throat.

The soldiers stop, look, listen. They aim their carbines into the darkness.

"We don't have time for this," Steve says.

"Leave the tarp," Ducky tells him. "Just get in the rig."

Steve stares at the source of the noise, a squat stumbling shadow. At first, he believes it's a child on a tricycle, the noise a squeaky wheel. Then the shape reveals itself.

"Jesus Christ," Ducky says.

The creature looks like a little sickly albino baboon wobbling on grotesque legs articulated like a grasshopper's. Its little barrel chest heaves as it takes rapid wheezing breaths. Despite its shocking appearance, it appears almost harmless, a bizarre mutation thrust into a hostile world, barely equipped to survive, a pale and hungry thing.

"Kill it," Steve says, his skin crawling with revulsion.

At the sound of his voice, the baboon thing stops, fixes its gleaming eyes on Ducky, and roars, showing rows of teeth. A moment later, its nose wrinkles and the elongated face shakes with a massive sneeze, spraying a cloud of mucus.

Ducky raises his carbine and fires, but the thing is already flying through the air. It lands with a thump on the soldier's chest and chomps down on his body armor.

Steve aims his weapon but hesitates. He doesn't have a shot. Ducky reels and screams for help.

Steve pulls out his knife and closes in. He slashes. The thing shrieks in pain, and a jet of scalding oily liquid shoots up his arm.

And then it's gone, vaulting into the air and landing ten feet away, where it briefly whines and hisses before disappearing into the dark with a series of flying leaps.

Steve races to collect his rifle until stopped cold by Ducky gasping, "I'm hit."

Sarge drops an empty magazine, pops in a fresh thirty-round mag, and chambers the first round in a single rapid, fluid motion. He fires a burst and cuts down an infected racing at him. Sarge got the rifle from a dead Taliban fighter, who probably got it off a dead soldier long ago during the Soviet occupation. He treasures the rifle for the simple fact it almost never jams. It's rugged and reliable, if a bit inaccurate. Between the close combat optic he retrofitted onto it and the close range of less than a hundred meters, however, he drops bodies at a steady pace.

He misses his first shot and curses. He's tiring, getting sloppy. He fires again, and the snarling man goes down wearing a surprised look on his face.

Sarge knows he can't keep this up much longer. Anne must show up with the flares and Molotovs, or the Bradley has to come and get them all out of Dodge. If neither happens soon, the infected will take him, and that will be that.

His eyes sweep the parking lot and evaluate every detail as a threat, an asset, or nothing. The robot has taken over; he's in complete survival mode now, every part of him focused on fight and the option of flight. Being under fire in Afghanistan gave him the ability to look at the world as a palette of survival. He finds it bizarrely unsettling to be in combat, firing his rifle steadily at close targets standing out in the open, without worrying about the snap of bullets flying past his ear. When he blinks, sometimes he sees insurgents running at him at a crouch instead of infected. Time is compressing. He doesn't know if he's been out here minutes or hours.

No matter how many of them he kills, they never quite feel like the enemy. Even after all of the atrocities he's seen, he can't bring himself to hate them.

The worst is when they come at him wearing military uniforms.

Flares arc through the night and land among the derelict cars. Their fierce orange glow reveals scores of moving figures.

Anne taps his shoulder then raises her rifle, peers into the scope, and takes down a running woman with a colossal bang and flash of light.

"It's about time," he grunts and resumes firing.

Anne is a different sort than him. Anne has enough hate for both of them.

The asphalt vibrates with stomping feet.

"Swarm!" Wendy cries. She stands nearby with her Glock held ready in case any infected get close.

Todd lights a Molotov. "I'm on it!"

The infected bob among the cars, blending into a howling mob racing through the night toward the six survivors.

"Molotov out!" Todd calls out.

The flaming bottle soars through the air and hits one of the infected in the chest, bursting into a wide sheet of fire that turns it and five others into screeching human torches.

"Good throw, boy," Paul says and yells, "Molotov!"

The flaming bottle arcs over the infecteds' heads and bursts on the roof of a station wagon. Maniacs race through the fire, the clothing on their arms and legs igniting with flaming gasoline, and continue running at the survivors until Wendy cuts them down with her handgun. The fire flares briefly before fizzling out.

"It's starting to get dicey out here, Sarge," Todd says.

"Shut up, Kid," Sarge says. "This ain't nothing."

Actually, the kid's right, they're in deep shit. The enemy is relentless and inexhaustible. His own tiny force is tired, scared, and fighting with a limited supply of ammunition. In the long run, the infected will either overrun them or force them back into the hospital, where they'll be killed by the expanding fire or stuck barricaded behind some door for who knows how long.

Unless the Bradley gets here first.

He sizes up his next target. The red dot in the close combat optic hovers on the man's chest. He squeezes the trigger. The view shakes violently, and the man drops. Then another. And another. Bankers and housewives and bakers and students and firemen. All infected, all dying.

Behind him, Wendy and Paul open fire. The infected press in on the flanks. Somebody throws a Molotov and Sarge hears the bottle shatter dangerously close; he can feel its heat.

A loud metallic shriek fills the air.

"What's that sound?" Paul says. He sweeps the parking lot with his shotgun. The gun fires with a deafening roar and cuts a howling woman almost in half.

Sarge grins. That sound is the cavalry arriving just in time.

The Bradley slams through a row of nearby cars on its screeching treads, its main gun flashing and thundering. Sarge sees the familiar BOOM STICK on the side of the turret. The red tracers stream toward the far end of the parking lot, where the cannon rounds rip apart infected and vehicles alike and fling them into the air in a series of mushrooming fireballs. The survivors watch this incredible violence until the Bradley grinds to a halt.

The tail lights wink. The ramp drops, promising safety in its dark interior.

☣

Ducky Jones sits in a semi-reclined position in the driver's station in the left front of the hull, hands on the steering yoke and foot working the pedals, eyes glued to the center periscope that offers night vision. He shifts into higher gear using the transmission's selector lever. As the rig builds speed, he scans the gauges arrayed across the dashboard with a single glance before returning his attention to the periscope. To his right, the five-hundred-horsepower Cummins engine hums loudly as it propels the heavy vehicle forward on its treads.

He works the accelerator and brake pedals with his left foot instead of his right. His right leg has gone numb below the knee. The bruise on his hip has grown to the size of a grapefruit and continues to throb steadily like a drum made out of pain. The agony is incredible. He wonders if this is what it's like to be shot. To donate bone marrow. He wipes sweat from his face and stifles a moan. Deep down, he knows he's growing weaker by the moment, that he is, in fact, dying a little at a time.

Ducky was a ten-year-old military history freak when the September 11th attacks shocked the country. He made a decision that day to become a soldier. Years later, he made good on that decision and enlisted. By that time, the ideals of fighting for freedom around the globe had deteriorated into the usual lies, betrayal, and corruption. It was a valuable lesson on a fact of life: that which is pure is precious but easily corrupted. He was still idealistic enough, however, to believe that something could be pure. He loved his country and wanted to serve. Maybe he could do something good. He still believed one man could make a difference. At least he would get to see history up close and maybe make some himself instead of just reading about it.

The Army became his life. He lived on the base and had Army friends and dated women his friends introduced him to. He complained about the Army constantly, but he loved it like a second mother and would deck anybody who dared criticize it. He thought about death philosophically and accepted the fact that one day he might die for his comrades in combat. As he saw war up close and personal in Afghanistan, his ideals faded even further; he watched the Army built a clinic in a village and then saw the Air Force accidentally bomb its school. But he still believed in one thing that was pure and could never be corrupted—the sacrifice of comrades for each other in combat. He believed that dying in combat, while fighting for the man next to him, was a truly honorable death, which it was.

Ducky never imagined he might die of a bizarre infection growing in his body, planted there by some sickly mutant horror, while driving out of the burning ruins of a major American city. There is no honor in this total war, this war of extermination, only futility and waste. There will be no medal for him. No historian to record his deeds. Possibly, there isn't even a country anymore for which to die. Instead, he'll die with people he barely knows in the ruins of a country he loves at the end of history.

Not what he imagined at all.

The simple fact is Ducky is still fighting the pain and driving the vehicle because he's living on borrowed time and is willing to give that time to help these people stay alive themselves a little longer. There must be some honor in that.

The Bradley plows into a downed telephone pole, smashes it to splinters, and drags a tangle of insulated cable and chunks of wood clattering after it. The gunner and commander sit at their stations in the cramped dark compartment and grip the handles used to maneuver the turret and fire the weapons. The gunner uses a periscope with night vision. The commander sees what the gunner sees using an optical relay.

Sarge squints at the display. "There's something wrong with the ISU."

The gunner shakes his head.

"I can't see shit, Steve," Sarge complains. "What the hell now?"

He taps the display, which accomplishes nothing. Under the familiar reticle, flickering green blobs glow bright, which he interprets as fires. Off to the left, he can see little bursts of pale green light which, he knows from experience, are muzzle flashes; there are people out there shooting. He can make out a road sign announcing ROUTE 22, 376, the Penn Lincoln Parkway. But the rest makes no sense. His visual is filled with bizarre shapes that seethe across the screen at different speeds in multiple shades of green, as if the relay were on a bad acid trip.

"I saw a sign," Sarge says. He activates the comm and says, "Take the next exit for Parkway West, Ducky."

"Wilco," Ducky says, his voice strained.

They're almost home free now. Once they reach the highway, they'll break west and escape the conflagration.

He adds to Steve, "Not that it matters. We could get on the eastbound highway and still go west. It ain't like somebody's going to write us a ticket for driving the wrong way, right?"

Except maybe Wendy. He suppresses a grin. It's an odd time to be thinking about her, but he can't help it. He wonders what she sees in him. Aside from the uniform and the values it represents, he doesn't consider himself anything special—a "big lug," the kind of guy that beautiful girls like her often consider a valuable friend, not a lover. Most girls like that fall for the gunner with his square jaw and surfer build.

Steve says nothing, glued to his periscope.

"You all right, Steve?"

"Not now, Sergeant," the gunner says, his voice tight.

"What do you see? What's going on out there?"

Steve turns away from the periscope with a wince. Sarge's heart skips a beat in alarm. The gunner's face is taut. Droplets of sweat glisten on his forehead. His eyes gleam like those of an animal caught in a steel trap.

"See for yourself."

"But..."

"There's nothing wrong with the equipment."

"This interference..."

"What you're seeing is *real*."

"Steve..."

"Look, Sergeant. Look again."

Sarge concentrates on the images on the commander's optical relay. He gasps as the tumbling, seemingly random shapes coalesce into monsters.

The Bradley hurtles down the road, punching cars out of the way or flattening them, surrounded by a ragged column of creatures joining the exodus out of the burning city. Little baboons hobbling on insect legs. Lumbering and tentacled behemoths. A leathery wall impossibly covered with screaming human faces. Giant balls of flesh, like ticks bloated with blood, strutting on spindly tripod legs. A thing with massive lobster claws where its hands should be. A half dozen other species. And of course, a refugee army of infected. Their chatter and wails compete with the constant roar of the rig's engine.

The fire appears to be flushing everything out of its hiding places tonight. The conflagration soars into the air behind them, flows into the sky, and comes back down in a constant rain of ash on this parade of monsters.

"What are these things?" Steve asks in a childlike voice. "What does this mean?"

☣

The survivors look at each other with gaping eyes in the dark hot interior of the Bradley, gasping for air and scarcely able to believe they're still alive when so many others were either claimed by the infected or burned alive in the fire. Every breath astounds them. Their bodies are slick with sweat, and their old street clothes, still damp from washing earlier in the day, cling to their flesh. It's so hot, it feels like they're being cooked in a microwave. They can barely move, half-buried in boxes and bulging plastic bags and gallon jugs. Cans and bottles roll around their feet and clatter as the Bradley takes a sharp turn.

Anne is content to be back on the road. There's familiar comfort in the drone of the engine and the smells of fear and body odor and burning diesel. They're safe here, for now, in the Bradley's dark and sweltering metal stomach. She opens a bottle of water, takes a long pull, and passes it on. She welcomes the road. This is where she's meant to be.

Sitting across from her, Wendy covers a private smile with her hand.

Anne stares at her and wonders what could possibly be worth smiling about right now.

Wendy catches her watching and says, "Did you ever do something on a crazy impulse, and it turned out to be the best idea you ever had?"

"No," Anne says. She struggles to remember a time when that might have been true.

The cop frowns and turns away. Anne didn't mean to offend her. Sometimes, she feels like she no longer knows how to be a real person and connect with other real people in a real way. Everything she thinks, feels or remembers ultimately winds up taking her to a dark place in her mind where people die over and over. She doesn't know how to tell Wendy that she lived most of her life obeying her impulses, and that they eventually got everybody she loved killed.

☣

"Ducky's hurt," Steve says. "He says he's okay, but I think he's hurt real bad."

Sarge says nothing. He waits for the gunner to continue.

"There were things in the garage, Sarge. *Monsters*. Dark shapes that flitted around the cars, always just out of sight. Then we saw one. A giant bloated thing covered in elephant trunks that boomed like foghorns. When it made that sound, the trunks stuck out straight and shook. Like something out of a nightmare. It pushed cars out of its way like they were nothing. Made you want to puke just to look at it. Then we saw a little white hairless monkey with thick insect legs, barely able to walk. It was sickly, diseased. It could barely see. It was in pain. It was like a newborn, Sarge. A freak of nature that somehow survived against all odds and was walking along making this weird clicking noise in its throat. Kind of sad, like a little kid looking for his family..."

"Steve. *Steve.* What happened after that?"

"The little bastard jumped on Ducky. The only way I could get it off was to cut it with my knife. Ducky went down, saying he was hit. The thing had sharp teeth and was biting around Ducky's throat, so I assumed that's where he was wounded, but I couldn't find even a scratch. His neck was wet, but there was no blood. So I asked him where he was hurt, and he said his hip. The little fucker used its teeth like it used its arms and legs, to hold on. It was...I don't want to say what it did to Ducky's hip, but it was unnatural. It...stabbed him with this big stinger between its legs, like a barbed scorpion's tail. The puncture left a massive bruised lump. He insisted on driving. I had to help him into the rig. He could barely walk."

Steve stops talking. Sarge takes a moment to rub his eyes. Outside, the horde of infected continue making noise like a house being slowly ransacked, barely audible over the loud pulsing hum of the Bradley's engine. He hears no more gunfire.

"Ducky," Sarge says into the microphone attached to his helmet, "do you copy?"

"I'm okay, Sergeant," the driver answers.

"How's that wound?"

"I said I'm okay."

"We'll pull over at the nearest safe point and get it looked at."

"By who? Who's going to look at it?"

Sarge doesn't know how to answer. The fact is they have little in the way of real medical supplies. Little medical knowledge, no medevac. They are completely on their own.

Ducky says, "I'm fit for duty. So let me do my job while I still can."

Sarge nods grudgingly. He doesn't know what to say. Perhaps he should just say thanks.

He grits his teeth. "You sit tight. We're going to find help for you."

"Sergeant, I just wanted to say—"

The air fills with an enormous roar of rage so pervasive, at first Sarge is convinced it originated inside his own head.

☣

The survivors flinch at the sound and stare at each other with big watery eyes. The roar stops as suddenly as it began. They hear massive pounding footsteps outside and a sudden *boom* that makes the rig tremble like a gong. The sound rattles through their bodies and hums in their brains, knocking out every thought as effectively as high voltage. They wince and cup their ringing ears in the aftermath. Then another *boom* jostles them, its aftermath vibrating deep in their chests.

The roar again, filling the air, followed by another *BOOM*. The rig speeds up, lurches, corrects itself. Wendy sees Paul huddled with his arms wrapped around his ribs, his eyes clenched shut and his mouth working silently. She never saw the reverend pray before. She finds it deeply disturbing, the idea that even the Bradley is unsafe.

The roar never seems to end. It cascades in waves of endless despair and rage that scrapes its talons over the chalkboard of her nerves. It fills the air so completely she struggles just to breathe through it. She still has enough sense to understand that whatever is out there, it's big and powerful and angry. She has a moment to wonder about the size of its lungs. Then her mind blanks out as the terrible sound of the attack builds and builds. The sound finally punches its way out of the paper bag of Wendy's mind, and she screams, the sound tinny and lost like a child shouting in a deafening wind. She reaches out, and Todd clasps her hand tight as another impact jostles them violently against the boxes and each other. Todd lashes out with his other hand and pushes at the boxes in blind panic. Across from her, Anne shouts something while Paul grimaces and cups his ears with his palms.

The siege lasts years; it lasts minutes. The thing outside loses interest and lags behind. The last tremor dissipates through the Bradley's armor and their bones. The final roar fades, leaving behind a powerful ring in their ears and a tingling vibration deep in their chests. The thing cries plaintively in the distance, as if sad to see the Bradley go and calling for its return. Wendy gasps for air, her heart clanging in her chest like a bell. She sees the terrified, pale faces crying in the dark and barely recognizes them. She touches her mouth, unsure if she has stopped screaming yet.

The Bradley crashes through an abandoned military checkpoint, and then the survivors are free of Pittsburgh at last. Behind them, the city burns like an early sunrise.

FLASHBACKS: SERGEANT TOBY WILSON

Combat Outpost Sawyer had all the beauty of a heavily fortified shantytown. But the mountains were breathtaking. This was the roof of the world.

Afghanistan, land of the Afghans.

As the Bradley topped the crest and drove along the escarpment, Sarge, sitting in his telescoped seat with the hatch open, got his first good look at the outpost that was just another island in a vast archipelago of little firebases scattered across the mountains.

The soldiers here called it Mortaritaville.

Sawyer lay perched on the valley's long slope, a sprawling little compound of sandbag bunkers and huts and tents around which sturdy timber walls and rows of C-wire had been erected. From here, along the ridge, it appeared tiny and weak. The series of ridges commanded the base. From these heights, Afghan fighters could drop mortar rounds right into the middle of the compound and then scoot behind the ridge and disappear from view. The nearest helicopter support was twenty-five minutes away. No wonder the boys here were reported to be so fatalistic, living in this remote place in almost total isolation, with an enemy that could strike from anywhere at any time and often did.

The Bradley caught up to a "jingle" truck, a high-axle vehicle painted in bold and bright colors and jingling with hundreds of shiny bangles. Luridly painted female eyes stared at him from the rear bumper, as enigmatic as a cat's. The truck was open in the back; several men sat inside, wearing the baggy trousers and loose tunics typical of Afghan men.

Smiling in the dust cloud raised in the wake of their truck, Sarge waved.

The men glanced at each other until one of them nodded, apparently giving permission to another man to wave back shyly.

There we go. We're making progress now. Salaam, bud.

Hares scattered from the road and took refuge among the rocks.

These men were elders and their retainers from one of the villages in the valley, on their way to attend a pow-wow at the base. For some years, the Pashtuns in this wild region of Nuristan Province, so close to the Pakistan border, welcomed the

Americans. The land here was heavily forested, mostly conifers; while a majority of Afghans scratched out a living in farming and herding, the people here had cut timber since the days of Genghis Khan. They sold it to Jalalabad, Mehtariam, and Pakistan. The jingle truck Sarge followed, in fact, was probably filled from top to bottom with firewood most days. The Taliban were oppressive and bad for business, so the locals celebrated when the Americans threw them out. Soon, however, Kabul enacted laws restricting trade with Pakistan. The locals grumbled but cut the Americans slack, as the Americans built roads and schools and regularly doled out gifts—school supplies, milk, prayer rugs.

The Taliban remained active in the area. The region was a corridor for insurgents crossing over to and from Pakistan. Inevitably, the locals got caught in the crossfire. The Air Force dropped a smart bomb on a village and missed the target, a mid-level Taliban commander, by ten minutes, instead killing thirteen civilians, including several children. As a result, the locals threw their support to the insurgents against a foreign military they now saw as infidel occupiers. Fighting raged across the valley for the six months, accounting for thirty percent of all combat in the brigade. The Afghan National Police station in the closest village to the east had been attacked so many times that the police were permanently demoralized. Without local support, the Americans controlled nothing outside their compound.

And so this meeting had been brokered in an attempt to stop the fighting.

Two Bradleys, loaded with heavily armed combat infantry, now drove to the base as a demonstration of strength. Sarge was glad to be in the point vehicle. For most of the trip, he enjoyed the beautiful scenery rolling by without eating the other vehicle's dust.

The truth was he loved Afghanistan and had even learned to love its people. The Afghans lived close to life and death. This was one of the places of the world where it was still common to see nomads living off the land. It was a very old place. Numerous armies had marched through it—Greek, Persian, Indian, Mongol, British, Soviet. The Afghans had beaten the British and the Soviets and had nothing to show for it; centuries of warfare had impoverished the country, and many people here lived as they had for thousands of years, in ignorance and poverty.

Sarge had grown up in Los Angeles searching for something he couldn't name. He found it briefly in the discipline and opportunities of the Boy Scouts, but after that ended, he saw little in his future. He spent his late teenage years gang banging on the city's hard streets as a corner dealer and later as muscle. He killed a boy three days before his twenty-first birthday, but they never caught him for that. A month later, his girl dumped him, and he smashed windshields in a drunken rage all the way up two blocks of Hillcrest until the cops finally showed up. He took a swing at one and they did a Rodney King on him. In court, he was given a choice of prison or the Army.

Five years later, he deployed to Afghanistan. Found himself sitting in a Bradley, watching M1 Abrams tanks drive across fields of poppies overlooked by the wild mountains of the Hindu Kush and endless blue sky.

And that thing he'd been searching for, he'd found it.

The column followed the jingly truck into the base in a blinding cloud of dust. The men piled out of the truck. One hoary specimen, his eyes white with cataracts and sporting a long white beard, scowled at everything. The colonel and his staff emerged from a large tent set up for the meeting, and they shook hands all around. The old man with the beard stood off to the side and refused to shake. Noticing Sarge, he spat and said something in Pashtun, ending with *Yabba dabba doo*!

Sarge knew the expression but had never heard it spoken. It was Afghan slang roughly translating as, "falling crates that knock down houses." During the invasion in 2001, the Americans dropped boxes of food to the villages. Some landed on huts and destroyed them, which struck Sarge as a perfect little parable of the trouble with good intentions.

One of the other Afghans, the man who'd waved to him from the back of the truck, laughed and said, "Do not take it personal. He thinks you are Russian. He thinks you are all Russians."

"He's got a long memory," Sarge said. "Maybe he thinks I'm British."

"Ha. Perhaps. English and Russians alike died here. I hope you will do better, my friend."

"*Inshallah*," Sarge said. If God wills it.

The Afghan laughed with feeling. "There is a path to the top of even the highest mountain," he exclaimed, quoting an Afghan proverb. Then it was Sarge's turn to laugh.

More jingle trucks pulled up to drop off more village representatives. The squad in Sarge's Bradley dismounted in full battle rattle. The place now swarmed with locals and heavily armed soldiers in a melee of salutations and small talk. The colonel ushered his guests into the big tent for tea, and then all was quiet again in the compound.

A dollar got you fifty afghanis, the local money. Sarge had seen a lot of Afghanistan and particularly enjoyed visiting the larger bases that had a market day where you could buy local food, crafts, anything. He loved the food, especially the rice *pilau*, and ate it the way the Afghans did, using *naan* flatbread as a utensil to scoop the food. But in these smaller bases, there was nothing to buy, and nothing to do except duck bullets.

Sarge talked to Devereaux about the base and its vulnerabilities for a few minutes and then decided to join a few of its grunts sitting and smoking on buckets and ammo crates in the protective shadow of a concrete bunker. This little nook of safety apparently passed for the base's lounge.

"Welcome to Mortaritaville," one of the soldiers said. "Got any cigarettes?"

Devereaux did, and they all got along fine trading jokes and war stories and ripping open MRE pouches looking for candy. Sarge found a comfortable spot on the ground with his back against a wood bin holding water bottles. The soldiers were already laughing at Devereaux. The boys in the squad called him "the Afghan" because he loved to tell big stories. The smallest firefight became an epic starring him and the Bradley. Sarge loved this part of Army life. Shooting the shit and busting balls.

"Black and White don't matter to me, Sergeant," Devereaux was saying. "I wouldn't mind being a Black dude like you if there weren't so many douchebags. I'd rather be White because there are more White douchebags than Black douchebags, and so the odds of somebody being a douchebag to me are less being White. Does that make any sense?"

"None whatsoever," Sarge replied with a smile.

"As long as I'm not an Afghan, I'm good," another soldier said. "Everybody's a douchebag to the jinglies. This place has been douchebagged since the dawn of fucking time."

The meeting dragged on all day until the Afghan leaders piled into their jingly trucks and started the long drive back to their villages. They smiled when they left, which the soldiers took as a good sign. Word went around the colonel made good progress in getting the locals back on their side. Sarge understood he and his boys would stay the night and rejoin their unit near Mehtariam tomorrow morning. The valley filled with a familiar mechanical sound, and he looked up to see a pair of Chinook helicopters pounding air, escorted by a single Apache attack helicopter.

One of the Chinooks wobbled and fell out of the sky. It crashed into the mountainside and broke into pieces that rolled into the trees in a massive cloud of dust.

"Whoa," Devereaux said. "Did all y'all see that?"

The soldier next to him shook his head in wonder. His nose wrinkled, and he said, "Man, that sure smells funny." Then his eyes rolled up into his head, and he collapsed.

"Medic!" Sarge roared. He knelt next to the man to check his vital signs. "We need some help over here!"

But soldiers were falling everywhere onto the crushed stones.

They began to scream.

The colonel ran out of the tent.

"Get to your posts! We're under attack!"

The Apache veered and collided with the other Chinook, bringing both down in a spectacular, hundred-yard-long eruption of dust, stones and metal.

"Holy shit," Sarge said. He ran for the Bradley.

He sat in the commander's station, heart pounding against his ribs. What happened to those men? Were they dead? If this were a biological or chemical attack, weren't they all exposed?

If the Taliban had done this, the gloves would come off. They were begging the world's best military for wholesale extermination, and they'd get it.

The rest of his crew didn't come. He shifted into the gunner's seat and worked the periscopes to scan the heights for possible enemy attack.

The screaming stopped. Sarge almost cried with relief. After several moments of pure silence, the compound filled with shouting voices. Sarge sat for three hours, talking occasionally to the commander of the other Bradley on the radio, trying to find out what he could. Martinez and Thompson, the driver and the gunner, still hadn't shown. He assumed the worst.

Somebody banged on the side of the Bradley.

"You in there, Sergeant?" It was Devereaux. "Answer me, goddamnit!"

Sarge popped the hatch and emerged blinking in the late afternoon air.

"I'm good," he said. "How about you? Your boys okay?"

His comrade nodded, his eyes glazed and his face pale.

"We're managing," Devereaux told him.

"Where's my crew?"

"They're down, Sergeant."

"*Goddamnit*," Sarge said fiercely.

Devereaux added, "They're putting the wounded in that big tent where they had the meeting. The base suffered twenty percent casualties from whatever the hell just happened."

One in five men was down. It was incredible.

"What's our alert status? Why is everybody walking around?"

"The colonel just dropped security to thirty percent," Devereaux said. "I heard somebody say they heard the RTO tell the colonel this is happening everywhere, and the colonel is figuring it's not an attack. Right now, he's arguing with the captain over whether to send a unit out to look for survivors at the place where those helicopters crashed. The captain is refusing orders. He doesn't want to go. Says we might still be attacked."

"What do you mean, 'everywhere?'" said Sarge. "You mean the whole country?"

"*INCOMING!*"

Soldiers ran everywhere, seeking cover. Devereaux dove into a mortar pit, leaving Sarge to look for the source of the fire. The mortar round fell short and exploded just outside the base's timber walls in a flash followed by a giant cloud of smoke and dust. A machine gun opened up from somewhere on the rocky heights, sending plunging fire into the compound. Small arms fire flashed across the distant hills. Sarge flinched as he heard the first hissing snap and twang of bullets as they flew past his ears.

He climbed back into the Bradley and maneuvered the turret to align the rig's cannon with the MG position at the top of the ridge.

It's the locals. They fell down screaming too, and they think it's us who did it to them. Christ, there are seventy thousand NATO troops in the Sandbox and nearly thirty million Afghans. Twenty percent casualties would be fourteen thousand NATO troops but SIX MILLION Afghans. If they think we did it, we're toast. They slaughtered the goddamn Red Army for a fraction of the offense.

He fired. The rig's big gun sent rounds arcing to crash into the heights. The MG fire stopped.

Big Dog 1, this is Big Dog 2, come in, he heard over the radio.

"I'm here, Big Dog 2," he said as he scanned the heights for his next target.

"The Mark 19 is down!" somebody yelled outside.

Mortar shells burst in the compound. A rocket propelled grenade hit the Bradley—an amazing shot—and glanced off before exploding in the air, raking its armor with shrapnel.

Big Dog 1, we've got reports of fire from the police station. Can you confirm?

"Identified," he said into the mike. "I'm spotting hostile fire from the ANP station, Big Dog 2. Insurgents have taken the building. That, or the ANP has gone hostile."

They're all yours, Big Dog 1. Happy hunting.

He dropped a score of rounds onto the building, which crumbled under the fire.

"Target," he said.

Oh my God, he now heard over the radio. *Oh my God.*

"Big Dog 2, this is Big Dog 1."

Then he saw. The Afghans were sending plunging fire down into the tent where the fallen soldiers had been placed. The radio filled with angry voices.

We need fire on that goddamn hill!

The human condition is to survive. When a man is just surviving, he has been carved down to the animal he once was. And animals largely think of their own survival. It's all about fight or flight, and a lot of times, the animal in you wants to run blindly to safety. What makes a soldier a good soldier, Sarge knew, is when he's properly trained to control these impulses. What makes a soldier brave, even noble, is when he's willing to sacrifice his own safety for his fellow soldiers.

Soldiers ran into the open to draw fire, trying to distract the insurgents away from shooting at the tent, and were getting cut down. Sarge counted two bodies writhing on the stones, bleeding, and a third lying completely still. Another soldier stood in the open on a carpet of spent brass and links, firing steadily into the hills. It was Devereaux.

"The Afghan" is going to have one hell of a story to tell if he survives this. He rained suppressing area fire onto the enemy positions along the ridge.

The radio steadily filled with traffic.

We've got hostiles identified in the open to the north and east. They're crossing the minefield.

The insurgents were launching a full-scale attack. They spent their first wave on the minefield. Two more waves followed closely on the heels of the first. Then it would be hand-to-hand fighting among the hooches. Hundreds of insurgents were in the assault.

Combat Outpost Sawyer was about to be overrun. Sarge could hear the distant voices shouting, *Yalla yalla!* One of them cried, *Allāhu akbar*, and the rest took up the shout. The volume of fire intensified. Hand grenades burst near the bunkers.

Jalabad says we're getting zero air support.

"Medic!" a man screamed.

Enemy in the wire, we've got enemy inside the wire.

A line of claymores exploded, sending geysers of dry earth and wood splinters soaring into the air. As the soldiers retreated, they blew up everything behind them.

Sarge couldn't move the Bradley, not while he was shooting. He wasn't a mobile cannon, but instead a pillbox, his own personal Alamo. He scanned his forward sectors, looking for targets, but the air had filled with smoke and dust. Small arms fire crackled around the bunkers. He saw a fire team abandon a burning building and fall back to the next defensive line.

Grenades burst around his rig. The Bradleys were now in front of the Americans' position, not behind. A Molotov cocktail streamed high into the air and landed on the rear of the turret, shattering and flaring to life.

The first insurgents came into view. They fired AK47 rifles and crouched low as they ran.

Sarge opened up with the Bradley's M240 machine gun at close range and cut them down. Small arms fire rattled off the vehicle's armor. He saw an RPG team set up near one of the hooches and point at the other Bradley. He switched back to the cannon and armed it.

"On the way," Sarge hissed. He punched the firing switch. The insurgents exploded in a series of fireballs.

As his visibility deteriorated, he kept it hot with the cannon, trying to stall the insurgents' advance.

We've got air support.

A single Apache helicopter flew through a hail of fire, dropping Hellfire missiles onto the insurgents running in the open toward the flaming base. The soldiers cheered. Its missiles spent, the helicopter set up its first strafing run with its machine guns. The guns buzzed, raining death from above.

Every man living in this valley must be here, trying to wipe us out over a horrible misunderstanding. And with the insurgents caught in the open between Bradleys in front and the Apache behind, we're going to wipe them out over that same misunderstanding.

The fighting raged past sunset. The soldiers shot flares and exchanged fire with the insurgents in streams of tracers. Sarge spent the night in the gunner's station. Outside, the wounded screamed and screamed. By the time dawn finally came, the surviving insurgents had melted away into the dark. More than a hundred bodies carpeted the rocks and were stacked around the scorched and broken bunkers.

The dazed survivors stumbled among the ruins of the base. Sarge found Devereaux and the other boys of the squad, all of them miraculously unscathed, and bear hugged them. Devereaux told him the colonel had received orders to shut down the base and bring everybody to Jalabad, where local American forces were consolidating. He found out his crew was still in the tent and that they remained catatonic but were otherwise unharmed in the fighting.

"This entire country must hate us right now," Devereaux said. "How do you come back from that?"

"Welcome to the Suck," Sarge told him, but the old Army complaint rang hollow. He walked toward the big tent, wondering what was going to happen next. The war had suddenly changed. Quite possibly, so had the world.

Twenty yards from the Bradley, an insurgent silently prayed and choked on his own blood where he lay. It was the laughing Afghan who'd waved to him from the back of the truck and translated the old man's curses.

Looking at him, Sarge raged at the waste of life.

"We didn't do this to you," he said. "Before you die, I want you to know that. We didn't do it. All this fighting was for nothing."

"God hates you," the man said. Then the lights in his eyes went out.

Several weeks later, as Pittsburgh burns behind him in a ruined America, Sarge will think about his comrades serving overseas. Only a fraction of the military deployed abroad was brought home after the Screaming. He will wonder how they are doing over there, the thousands left behind in the wild parts of the world. He'll wonder whether the boys in the Sandbox ever made it home. Whether they're now shooting at Americans instead of Afghans. If he ever sees them again, he'll say, "*Pa khair raghla.*"

Thank God you arrived safe and sound.

THE TRUCK STOP

Wendy staggers out of the Bradley's oven heat onto a wide open parking lot under a glaring, overcast sky. The scorched air dries the sweat on her face instantly, cooling her skin while giving her the strange sensation of being baked. She breathes deep but coughs on air heavy with a tangy burnt chemical smell.

A large building sprawls in front of her under a massive sign announcing GAS and ALL YOU CAN EAT BKFST and CAR WASH. Two canopied fuel islands flank the building, one promising gas for vehicles and the other diesel for big trucks. Without power, the building appears dark and desolate. The parking lots are all empty, dotted with random litter that flutters on sudden hot breezes. She imagines truckers filling up their rigs during their long hauls in and out of the Keystone State, heading into the greasy spoon for coffee and a piss. Then the moment passes. These days, she knows, people can see ghosts. They're all around, if you know how to look. All you have to do is remember the past. Conjure up some memory of the dead world.

She gasps on the smoky air. The very atmosphere has been burned. It smells like lung cancer. Impossibly, little gray snowflakes tumble gently across the barren landscape. It takes her exhausted brain several moments to understand that these flakes are hot ash. That they are, in fact, the cremated remains of Pittsburgh, drawn into the atmosphere on massive convection currents and scattered on the winds. One twirling piece of ash lands on her shoulder and she tries to brush it off, leaving a smudge of gray dust that might once have been something living.

Pittsburgh is still burning. Wendy turns and stares at the vast wall of smoke rising above the smoldering ruins of the city in the east, surrounded by heavy particulates.

"Everything I knew was in that town," she says hoarsely. Her throat feels raw and dry and scratchy from the heat and the screaming. "Everything and everybody I ever knew in the world."

The place where she was born, and the place where she was raised. The house where she smoked weed for the first time, and the house where she lost her virginity. The school where they educated her about the basics, and the school where they taught her to be a cop. The station house where she worked, and all the neighborhoods she patrolled in her square, and the mall where she shopped for clothes, and the supermarket where she picked up her groceries, and bars where she drank a few beers on the weekends. The theater near her house where she watched dozens of movies with friends and dates, the hospice where her parents died, the hospital where her niece was born, the restaurant where she fell in love with Dave Carver, the old Crown Victoria squad car that was like a second home to her.

These places, and all the people who filled them with their lives and played a part in hers, both large and small, all burned into ash. All lost in the fire. And all of her past lost with it. It's too much to comprehend, too horrifying to even imagine.

"I can't believe it's gone," she says.

She turns to see if anybody is listening to her, but nobody is there. The other survivors wander alone and dazed across the empty lot until stopping as if some invisible leash ties them to the vehicle. They've gone as far as they can from each other without being completely alone. She wants to go even further.

Patting the Glock on her hip to feel its reassuring weight, Wendy walks toward the highway.

☣

Ethan wakes up on warm asphalt with a splitting headache. He feels like a piece of chicken left in the oven too long. He opens one eye and clenches it shut as the glaring silver sky painfully blinds him. Blinking tears, he tries again. Slowly, his eyes adapt to the light, and he can make out figures on a wide parking area in front of a simple shoebox-shaped building. *Truck stop. We're at a truck stop.* Woods and hills beyond. They've not only left the hospital, they've abandoned Pittsburgh entirely. *Just what the hell happened last night?*

The last thing he remembers is the sharp prick of the needle sliding into his arm.

He tries to bring the dark figures into focus. His glasses are missing, and he has trouble seeing distances. The blurry figures coalesce into the other survivors standing scattered around the asphalt. Anne is ransacking the Bradley. The soldiers drag the struggling driver into the shelter of one of the fuel islands. Ethan wonders if they're infected. His immediate instinct is to play possum. He closes his eyes and tries to ignore his aching bladder.

"Where are we going to go?" somebody asks. "Is anywhere safe?"

Ethan knows the voice; it is Paul speaking. He suffers a sudden sense of *déjà vu*, a flashback to one of the endless nightmares he dreamed last night. He opens his eyes and tries to sit up. The air is hot and tinged with smoke. His shirt is covered with a dried red crust. Not blood; vomit. The acidic smell triggers the dry heaves. He groans on his hands and knees, his vision blurred with tears, and spits into the dust. He wipes his eyes and notices the other survivors watching him.

"Water," he croaks. His voice sounds alien to his ears. His tongue feels like a piece of leather.

Anne exits the Bradley and drops a box onto the ground, where it bursts open and spills cans across the asphalt. She draws one of her handguns and marches toward him. The other survivors drift closer.

"Can I have some water?" he says.

Anne kicks him in the ribs, hurling him back onto the warm hard ground.

"Motherfucker," she says.

The sudden stress makes his stomach lurch again. He writhes in the soot, struggling to breathe, retching.

Anne kneels next to him, grabs his curly hair in one fist and shoves the barrel of her pistol into the soft flesh under his chin. The sky darkens as the winds shift.

"We were attacked," she hisses close to his ear. "We were attacked and you weren't with us. We had to carry you out of there. We had to *carry* you. You let us down, Ethan."

"Don't you do it, Anne," Paul says.

Ethan glares up at her. "Yes, do it."

Anne recoils. "Are you trying to die? Is that it?"

"I don't care anymore."

"You want me to do it because you can't do it yourself. You're a coward. I could do worse. I could leave you here for *them*."

He hesitates. She's right. He has no hope of finding his family, and without his family, he has no hope at all. But he doesn't know how to die.

"I'm sorry I let you down," he says. "If you want to scapegoat me for something, that's fine too. It doesn't matter anymore. So do it, if that's what you want."

"He knows what he did, Anne," Paul says. "What's done is done."

"Who trusts him?" Anne says. She glares at the other survivors. "Who here trusts him now? This isn't about justice, Reverend. It is about survival."

"We all know what's at stake here. You think we don't know?"

"Leave him alone," Todd says shrilly, his voice cracking.

"It could have been any of us," Paul adds.

He stands over Ethan with his shotgun. Ethan realizes these people aren't his friends and that he doesn't really know them.

"Do you want to live or not, boy?" Paul asks him.

"I want to live," Ethan says through gritted teeth. "But I'm sick of surviving."

"That's not an answer," Paul tells him. "We've got to know we can count on you, or Anne's right, we've got to part ways right now. It's a simple question. Can we count on you?"

"Yes," Ethan says.

"Step aside," a commanding voice booms.

Sarge pushes into the ring of survivors. The soldier glares down at Ethan. "You're coming with me."

☣

Anne returns her large handgun to its leather shoulder holster and heads back to the Bradley. The supplies she left on the ground are already gray with a light coating of soot, a depressing sight. She feels an overwhelming urge to hit the road. Paul blocks her path and glares down at her from his large grizzled head. The gesture would be enough to intimidate anybody except her. She sidesteps and continues to the vehicle.

"We need to talk, Anne," he calls after her. "I have something I need to say to you."

She rummages through the boxes until she finds a battered camouflage cap, black paisley bandana, and bottle of water. After fitting the hat on her head, she unscrews the cap of the bottle and soaks the bandana before tying it over her face.

"We all look up to you," Paul says. "If things get really bad, we all look to you to tell us what to do. Even if we think you're wrong, we still do it. Because we believe."

Anne clasps her metal canteen onto her webbed gun belt.

Todd watches her closely. "Where are you going, Anne?"

Paul says, "But there are some things you don't get to decide. Like who stays and who goes. Who lives and who dies. You don't get to make those decisions. It's not up to you."

Todd adds, "Why can't we get out of this ash and make some plans? We need a plan."

Anne squints up at Paul's face and sizes him up.

"I'm going for a walk." She picks up her scoped rifle. "You're in charge."

She heads off toward the distant trees.

"I wouldn't do that by yourself," Paul says.

"You're not me."

"When are you coming back?" Todd asks nervously.

Anne ignores them, marching with a purposeful gait that takes her onto the highway. Tiny figures move in the distance along the road. The only vehicles are abandoned wrecks, their doors hanging open. Her ears still ring painfully from the screaming monster that attacked them.

She needs to be alone for a while. She relishes the sudden sense of space. She never asked to be a leader. And she certainly doesn't want anybody believing in her. Anne knows they're all going insane one day at a time, and each of them—at different times, depending on the individual—will crack under the stress. And if one of them cracks, that person could put them all at risk. Like Ethan. He suffered some sort of breakdown and endangered all of them. The man already has a bad habit of firing his weapon with his eyes closed. He's simply not as cool as the others in a fight. Anne was willing to overlook these things, as Ethan has good instincts about obtuse threats such as the tank firing on them and the worm monster having a second head. He also came up with the idea of the Molotov cocktails. He's a smart man, smarter than the rest. He makes a real contribution. But if he's cracking up, he's a liability. He'll take up space in the Bradley, consume scarce resources; worse, he won't cover their backs.

Then they'll have to make a tough choice as a group. Anne would rather not wait until people get killed before that decision is made. If it were up to her, the man would have been left behind at the hospital last night. Which would have been sad, but necessary. They simply can't take care of him and hope to survive. Everybody has to pull his weight, or they're all dead.

About a mile down the road, a burning vehicle pumps oily black smoke across the highway's westbound lanes. She peers into her scope and sees a pair of olive green vehicles, one a Humvee with its headlights on and behind it, a burning military flatbed truck. Anne squints, hoping to see more, but everything is blanketed in ash. Visibility is steadily diminishing. Across the landscape, tons of ash flutter to the earth in drifting clouds of black snowflakes.

Anne slings the rifle onto her shoulder and walks west.

Sarge and Paul and the other survivors are getting sentimental, she knows. They're getting to know each other. Becoming friends, even. They think they're a tribe now. They're forgetting that being sentimental is a luxury at a time like this. They're forgetting the only reason they have this luxury is because they've been tough as nails. Because they all pull their weight.

She senses the others are leaving her behind. But they aren't moving forward, they're regressing. They're hoping they can once again be who they were before the world ended.

Anne can't go back.

She shrugs the rifle into her hands and approaches the Humvee at a cautious pace.

She almost trips over the first body. Four dead soldiers sprawl on the ground amid broken weapons and scattered empty shell casings. Their heads are eerily missing. Something decapitated them and left the rest.

Inside the Humvee, a tangle of voices compete for expression across the ether. They resolve into a single urgent female voice, *Patriot 3-2, Patriot 3-2, this is Patriot, how copy?* The radio blasts white noise for ten seconds. Then the message repeats.

Something rustles in the trees and sighs.

☣

Wendy trudges through the ash along the road. She pauses to take in the hellish gray landscape warped by shimmering heat waves. The giant wall of smoke continues to rise over the smoldering ruins of Pittsburgh like a distant storm. Heavy particulates flow steadily into the sky, riding pulses of heat. The highway races east in a long straight line that dissolves in the haze. Figures toil in the distance—refugees of the inferno. Tiny headlights glimmer in the ash fall. She wonders what it would be like to lie down in the warm soot in the gulley below the guardrail and surrender herself to the earth. Philip did that, she remembers. He was tough as nails, but one day he saw a *Wall Street Journal* with the wrong date and sat in the ashes, and that was that. He became numb too. He couldn't handle seeing his world die. When you find yourself envying the dead, you're not long for it.

Stopping at the hospital was a mistake. They invested their hopes in its promises. They believed they'd found a place where they could at last feel safe. But that isn't the world they live in. All those hopes—of living instead of barely surviving, of having some sort of future after the end of Infection, of being able to dream again—were blindly and cruelly crushed. In this world, giant faceless things haunt abandoned buildings and duel with armored fighting vehicles in the dark. In this world, entire cities burn to the ground, and everything you ever knew and loved becomes converted into tons of ash floating in the upper atmosphere. In this world, the children are dead. It's best not to hope in this world. The safest bet is to keep moving and never stop.

The only thing giving her strength right now is that brief moment of contact she experienced with Sarge last night. The memory of it still burns in her chest. She went to his room on impulse, intent on dropping a hint, maybe flirt a little. *I see you*, she wanted to let him know. *You see me, and I see you too.* She kissed him and fell into blissful nothingness. She told herself the world was ending, and love was in very short supply, and so you had to grab it where and when you could find it.

Wendy and Sarge are made of the same stuff, she believes; that's what attracted her to him. He's a soldier without an army, a centurion still fighting though his legion is dead; she's a cop in a lawless land, the last enforcer of the old justice. Then she slept in his arms and never felt safer. It amazes her how just a simple man could make her feel that safe in a world this dangerous.

Wendy passes a motley group of refugees, some wrapped in blankets, others carrying backpacks and umbrellas, others decked out in goggles and respirators. All are armed with knives, crowbars, baseball bats, and even makeshift spears.

She decides to hail the next group she passes. "Hello. You all right?" They ignore her, walking by in a daze, their hair and shoulders covered in ash.

"You're going the wrong way," a man says, flashing gray teeth. A woman notices her badge and belt and asks if she's a cop.

"Where are we supposed to go?" the woman says.

Wendy pauses to spit out her gum, which has become gristly with dust. The woman watches it fall into the cinders with longing.

"My advice is keep going west," Wendy tells her. "Get as far away from Pittsburgh as you can."

"Is there a rescue station on this road?"

A man with a bleeding ear shouts, "ARE YOU FROM THE FEMA CAMP?"

"I don't know of any FEMA camp, sir."

"WHAT?"

A small crowd gathers. The refugees shiver in the heat and stare at her with a mixture of hope, resentment, and shock. The man who shouted stumbles, briefly disoriented, and then shouts again, "THERE'S NO HELP AHEAD? WE'RE ON OUR OWN?"

"I don't know of any rescue station or FEMA camp anywhere. I'm not here in any official capacity. I'm with another group of people leaving the city after the fire."

"We lost everything," the woman pleads. "We have no food. Some guys with guns back there on the road took the last drop of water I had. Where am I supposed to go?"

"Where were you cops when those monsters were ripping my family apart?" a woman says, her eyes glazed with fever. Most of her hair and eyebrows were burned off, and the right side of her face is covered by a filthy, bulky bandage. "I called 911 and nobody came. Nobody came, and now Edward is dead. Edward and Billy and Zoe and little Paul. Now you show up and try to tell us what to do? Where the hell were you, lady?"

The angry crowd presses in.

"I'm sorry," Wendy says. She wants to explain her situation—that her precinct was overrun, that she's on her own, that she can't help them—but they don't care. She's a symbol to them. They look at her with hungry, feral eyes gleaming from the folds of bundles of rags tied around their heads. They cough loud and hard into their fists, struggling for enough air to scream.

A woman reaches for Wendy's face and hisses, "Give me something."

Wendy takes a step back and places her hand over her pepper spray dispenser. She senses a dangerous line forming—knows it's there because it's about to be crossed. The crowd closes in.

A man wearing a cowboy hat and carrying a walking stick marches past and yells, "Hey, now! What are you bugging that pretty gal for? There ain't no rescue coming, and there ain't no police. She ain't no cop. Get over it."

The crowd turns and flinches at the echo of gunshots.

"There you go, officer," the man says, still walking. "There's some guys back there with a truck robbing people and shooting anybody who fights back. You want to be a cop? Do something about it."

☣

Ethan follows Sarge and pauses at the sight of the Bradley. The rig looks like it lost a brick fight. Dents and scratches pockmark the welded aluminum armor. Several plates on its side are missing.

Sarge turns and sees him lagging behind. "You okay?"

"I could use a drink of water."

"I'll get you water after we do this thing, all right?"

"Okay."

"Anne can be a little rough."

"It doesn't matter," Ethan says, meaning it. The truth is he feels completely numb. He doesn't feel pain. He doesn't feel anything. "What happened to your tank?"

"Those plates are explosive reactive armor. It protects the rig by exploding outward when something comes at it trying to explode inward, canceling it out."

What could have hit the vehicle with that much force?

"What happened last night?" Ethan says.

"There was a big fire," Sarge tells him. "See all the ash starting to rain down on us? That's what's left of Pittsburgh—west of the Monongahela and the Ohio, anyhow."

"What about the Bradley?"

"The gates of hell opened. If we hadn't dropped smoke, I don't think we'd have made it. That thing was kicking the shit out of my rig. Come on."

Ethan shakes his head in amazement. *That thing*, Sarge said. This was not the average infected and probably not a worm either. The commander obviously had no idea what he'd been fighting in the dark. As Ethan suspected, there are other children of Infection, possibly an entire family of monstrosities.

If there's something out there that can take on an American armored fighting vehicle, the human race might have to give up its claim on the planet.

He has often speculated about what could have caused the pandemic. As an educated man, he refuses to believe the cause is supernatural. Infection is spread by viruses, bacteria, and parasites, but none of these explain the bizarre mutations. In the days following the Screaming, scientists speculated about a nanotech weapon that escaped the lab. Could nanotechnology create such monsters?

Ethan once again finds himself entertaining an alien colonization theory. Consider an alien race in a distant world that wants to propagate itself across the galaxy. Instead of spaceships, it sends seedlings out across the cosmos, which eventually rain down on Earth to colonize the resident species' DNA, mutating the natives into adaptations of the alien species and its ecology. The creatures are sickly at first because they're still adapting to Earth's environment. They eat the dead but are starving because their alien digestive systems can't extract sufficient nutrition from it. While they turn the dominant species against itself through Infection, they burrow into the darkest spaces in abandoned buildings and adapt and multiply. Over time, they grow stronger until they eliminate the dominant species and complete the conquest of their adopted world. *It makes sense. Why else would they target our children for immediate extermination?*

Or perhaps the aliens are indeed coming in spaceships, but they're terraforming the planet before the ships arrive, eliminating the resident species in the process. Which means humanity is not fighting aliens, but the wildlife of the aliens' home world. These things are repulsive, but they're not evil in the sense that they want to hurt humans purely out of malice. They're hunting people for food. In one sense, they might as well be millions of hungry lions roaming the streets, hunting and eating people simply to survive.

The worst part is the human race will probably never truly understand what killed it.

His family needs him more than ever, and he'll keep looking for them. He wonders if this is why he feels so calm—because he's surrendered what's left of his sanity to the delusion they're alive.

I'll keep searching for you, Mary. I'll never stop.

He's tired of running away and hiding. He never should have done it to begin with. He should have stayed in his car and searched for his family until he found them or died. Terror stopped him then, but he's losing his capacity for fear.

They approach a figure sitting on the ground propped against a gas pump. The man is pale, underweight, his cheeks sunken, his eyes dark and bruised. His arms rest withered and useless at his sides. Ethan finally recognizes him as the driver—what's left of him, anyway. The gunner kneels and tries to give him water.

Sarge says, "You're smart, Ethan. I'm betting you can figure out a way to fix him."

Ducky Jones lost thirty pounds since Ethan saw him last night in the lounge. The man is almost visibly wilting in front of him, coughing feebly, his breath rapid and shallow. His dark, intelligent eyes flicker at Ethan with a mixture of fear and hope. There's still a man in there.

Ethan holds his gaze respectfully for several seconds. Then he looks down at the revolting thing that protrudes from his hip.

☣

Todd enters the truck stop cautiously, violating Anne's standing rule of never going anywhere alone. Anne's rules mean a whole lot less to him today, however. The monster changed the game last night. How can they hope to survive with horrors like that out there hunting them?

Like most victims of bullies, Todd is highly sensitive to what other people are feeling, and the best word he can think of to describe the mood right now in the group as a whole is *deranged*. Deranged and black, raw, angry. In other words, morale is shit. They're becoming people who don't care, people who are losing hope and otherwise have nothing left to lose. Damaged goods. They're close to giving up.

Inside the lobby, he has a choice of restaurant, convenience store, or public restrooms. As much as he'd like to take a private dump on a real toilet, there's no way he's going into a public restroom alone. The store looks interesting. The shelves have been rifled, but whoever did it left most of the stuff behind. He might find some good loot in here. He remembers Wendy wants a pair of toenail clippers.

His nerves crawl with the oppressive feeling the group is falling apart. Anne and Wendy wandered off to who knows where, Paul is emptying the Bradley's guts into the ash under the pretense of organizing their supplies, and the Bradley's driver is dying at the fuel island. Anne was ready to blow Ethan's head all over the pavement.

What about Todd? Nobody wants to listen to him. They obviously think of him as just a kid. But he won't abandon this group. He feels a very strong loyalty to it now. Groucho Marx once quipped that he'd never want to be a member of a club that would have him as a member. Todd wants to be a member of the club almost entirely because they offered him membership. America already feels like a distant dream. This tiny tribe is his nation now. These people are not mere tools used to help collect food and stand guard while he sleeps. They're much more than that. They're something like family to him.

It's true he doesn't know them well, even after days of fighting together against terrible odds. All anybody talks about is how they plan to survive the next ten minutes. It's not like people are going to open up during the apocalypse about their hobbies. Where they went for vacation last summer or their favorite flavor of ice cream. They have intense flashbacks but never talk about their separate pasts from the time before Infection. The past right now seems less real than the monster that attacked them last night. The past is also too painful to recall willingly, bringing to mind too many lost things. Todd likes the other survivors, but his interactions with them, while having life and death stakes, have been largely superficial. He feels his deepest connection with the group itself—feels safest, in fact, interacting with the others through the medium of the group.

But if there's no group anymore, what or who is there to be loyal to aside from me, myself, and I?

A bell tinkles as he enters the store, sending his heart galloping in his chest. The place smells musty. The air feels flat, dead. He foot nudges a two-liter bottle of Mountain Dew and sends it spinning across the floor. He flinches at the noise and raises his rifle to sweep the store for targets.

Maybe coming in here by myself wasn't such a good idea. Another scare like that, and I'll drop dead from a stroke.

Having a closer look at the dusty shelves brings further disappointment. Most of the merchandise is still sitting on the shelves or hanging on hooks, but there's no food, water, medicine. Instead, almost all the stuff are products specifically marketed to truckers who have to live on the road for as long as a month at a time. Movies and audio books, CB radio equipment, road atlases, electric frying pans, toasters, DC adapters, coffee makers, and TV/VCR systems.

Todd wonders what a trucker would do with a coffee maker and then realizes, looking at the packaging, that all these devices are DC powered. And the DC adapters allow AC devices to run off DC. An epiphany follows. Most appliances don't work anymore because they need AC power, and the only way he knows to make AC power when the grid is down is with an emergency generator that runs on diesel or propane or natural gas.

But DC comes from batteries.

They could run all this stuff off car batteries. Of which there are plenty lying around, courtesy of the fact that their drivers are either zombiefied or dead.

Looks like being a whiz at science has finally come in handy. He realizes that he has hit some sort of jackpot.

Wendy marches through the wasteland, her Glock held at her side. She's a police officer, still on duty, still protecting life and property. Perhaps the last cop left in Pittsburgh. Perhaps the last government employee still doing anything. Once she left, the crowd followed her for a while but eventually gave up and resumed their long walk west. Apparently, they didn't have much faith she'd be able to stop the bandits and recover their supplies. The truck stop is far behind her now, perhaps a mile, perhaps more. The chemical fog hems in on all sides, reducing visibility to less than fifty yards. Ahead, the headlights of a large vehicle shimmer in rising heat waves.

She hears gunshots and puts on her game face.

The absurdity of the situation nags at her, however. What is she supposed to do, arrest these people? And then what? There are no more courts, no more judges. No more jails or wardens either. The entire legal system is gone. There's only frontier justice now—the law of the gun, with justice dispensed one bullet at a time. *Is that it, then? Am I supposed to kill them?* Even sheriffs in the Wild, Wild West had judges and jails and a community they could count on.

She clears her scratchy throat and considers her next move.

Perhaps I should yell, "FREEZE, POLICE" before shooting them, she thinks with bitter humor. Read them their rights before opening fire and cutting them down in cold blood for doing something that used to be illegal when there were laws and a government.

She ain't no cop, the man said.

Wendy stops and returns her Glock to its holster on her belt. *Ain't no cop*, he said. And he was right.

The realization of this simple fact feels as pleasant as her heart being torn out of her chest.

I did my best, she thinks, trying to remember the fallen whom she once considered her tribe, but she can't recall their faces. Even Dave Carver is just a blur. She has a pounding headache and is starting to feel light headed.

Time to go back. To her new tribe.

Wendy removes her badge, runs her thumb over its edged details, and puts it in her pocket. This done, she turns and begins walking back toward the truck stop.

In the land of the blind, the one-eyed man is not king. He is not king because nobody recognizes him as king. The others don't even know he's there.

Wendy coughs long and hard on the smoke and soot, her lungs on fire. When it's over, a smile flickers across her face. If you're still alive after part of you dies, it's like being reborn. She will survive this.

The gunshots escalate back at the truck and the headlights shake and blink out. Screams echo across the asphalt. The darkness closes in around her.

Wendy breaks into a run. Her decision to stop being a cop probably saved her life.

☣

Anne steps cautiously among the trees, her body taut and her rifle shouldered and ready to fire. She blinks away the sweat that drips into her eyes from under her soaked cap. Her finger twitches near the trigger. Each step is planted carefully, one foot following the other, taking her deeper. She's a hunter now. She doesn't yet know what she's hunting. Her quarry is present but not known.

Sighing in the trees. She can hear them now, their guttural clicks. Communication that is like ancient speech but also as mindless as insect mating. The things scamper playfully through the bushes and leap into the trees, releasing clouds of soot that make the little bastards squeal and sneeze.

They're like children, she thinks, and then banishes that painful thought. Unlike the other survivors, Anne doesn't question why she's here. Doesn't constantly compare herself, the world around her, and what she's doing in it to the time before Infection. Anne has survived so far because she successfully locked away her past. She doesn't need to remember it to continue atoning for it. She has learned to truly live in the moment.

The ash blankets the treetops and drifts in the air, obscuring everything green and creating a virtual twilight. Eyes glimmer in the haze. Dozens of red eyes burn in the dark spaces of the forest. She takes another step forward.

Foliage thrashes as the creatures scamper across the treed ground. The air fills with guttural clicks and squeals. Even the squeals sound like language. They know she's here. She's no longer hunting but observing. There are too many to fight; it's not worth the risk.

Anne raises her rifle and peers into the scope. She conducts a slow sweep until stopping at a small group clustered at the foot of a massive oak. The crosshairs come to a rest on a blank little elfin monkey face, blandly chewing, its mouth stained. As if sensing it's being watched, the creature bares bloody teeth and glares with pure malice. She moves the rifle and watches the others shove handfuls of some furred animal into their mouths.

She cries out and falls to her knees, weeping with racking sobs, her shoulders shaking with each burst.

The forest comes alive with hoots and shrieks.

"It's just a dog," she says. "Just somebody's old dog."

Anne stifles the next sob and wipes her eyes. She hates them with every ounce of her being. She raises the rifle and aims it at a snarling face. She exhales and squeezes the trigger.

The rifle fires with a flash and bang that fills the forest with a rolling roar. The creatures bound shrieking through the undergrowth. The rifle lurches hard against her shoulder as she fires again. She sees a little skull explode before the view in the scope jumps.

"I'm going to kill you!" she screams at them, her voice ringing through the trees. "Do you hear that, you little freak bastards?"

Her dog had an almost supernatural talent for catching Frisbees.

Anne shoots another, and the rest leap into the trees. They appear to be baffled by the distance over which she is reducing their numbers one by one. The little things bare their teeth and throw handfuls of their shit in her direction. She fires again. And again. A group breaks from the woods and leap toward her on their insect legs. She cuts them down. She fires until her rifle clicks dry. They sense her hesitation. With a massive howl, the children of Infection rush at her all together. She drops the rifle.

"God damn you," she sobs. She tastes salt and soot in her mouth as they rapidly close the distance in great leaping bounds. "God damn you for what you've done."

Anne raises her handgun and rains death upon them.

☣

Paul pulls a large sack out of the Bradley and curses as it splits open in his hands and spills cans and bags of rice onto the gritty asphalt. He can feel the ash settling on his hair and shoulders. This project is converting him to paganism. Getting these supplies sorted is like something out of a Greek myth expressing the usual cruelty of the gods toward mortals who crossed them.

He reenters the hot and dim interior of the Bradley, his back aching at having to walk stooped, and rummages through the three neatly rolled MOPP suits that he found earlier. The soldiers at the government shelter wore suits like this, and they had respirator masks. He finds one with the filter already attached and pulls it over his head. The inside smells like rubber and ass, and it feels mildly suffocating, but it works. He no longer feels like he's inhaling sandpaper. He raises the mask until it rests on top of his head, sits and lights a cigarette.

Where are you, God?

Paul has not prayed in weeks, ever since Sara came at him with her hands stretched into claws. He always found conversing with God a path to inner peace and unlocking the solutions to problems.

Why have you forsaken us?

He wonders if this is some type of test for humanity and possibly for him personally. If it is, it's not a fair test. Imagine a school where the students have to guess what the question is on a test before they give their answer. And if you answer wrong, the teacher kills you.

Dear God, help me remain your servant. I only want to serve you and glorify you through good works and spreading the good news of your son's resurrection.

He thinks about that. What has he done to help, other than endless work with the shotgun? He wonders if he's still invited to Heaven. Jesus' teachings don't appear to apply to this holocaust. Those who followed to the letter God's prohibition against killing died fast.

He was so close to giving up entirely. He remembers standing near a wall in the government shelter as the other refugees evacuated. The people crowded against the doors while Paul pretended to pray over rows of body bags arranged against the wall. He intended to stay behind after the others left. He wanted to stay behind because he was going to zip himself up inside one of those bags and lie there, pretending to be dead, until God came for him.

Instead, Anne taught his hands to war.

God already ended one wicked age with water, a great heaping flood that covered the earth and drowned it. Then the waters gave and Noah, stepping down from his ark, saw the washed-away ruins of the great cities covered in rags of seaweed, the thousands and tens of thousands of bloated bodies half-buried in the mud.

Noah was tested. But God talked to Noah.

Speak to us, Lord. Tell us what you want.

He steps on his cigarette and thinks bitterly that perhaps there is a Noah out there, building his fortress for the righteous, and Paul simply isn't invited. That God has abandoned him.

He's no Noah. He knows that. He feels he has much in common with Job, however.

God asks Satan what he thinks of Job, a truly pious man. Satan answers that the only reason Job loves God is because God blessed him with riches, health, and family. God gives Satan permission to test Job. First, all his property is destroyed. Then a massive wind kills his children. Job continues to praise God, lamenting that as the Lord gives, so the Lord takes. Satan next afflicts him with boils. Sitting in cinders, Job laments but forgives God.

Finally, unable to endure, he curses the day he was born. He realizes his life has no meaning and believes there's nothing for him to do but die. He doesn't understand why God created man to suffer. It's a good story. Paul can relate to all of it.

God comes in a whirlwind and tells Job that it's not for him to question God, as God is king of the universe, not accountable to his creations for anything, including their approval.

Paul always saw this as a cop-out, that God gave Job an answer that basically boils down to: *I'm God and you're not, so don't ask me to justify myself.*

But at least it was an answer.

Talk to us, God. If you won't even talk to us in this time of darkness and sorrow, why should we give you any allegiance?

The Jews grappled with the Holocaust for decades. They tried to reconcile their belief in a just and merciful God with the millions worked to death and gassed and fed to the ovens in the death camps. Paul wonders what humanity will make of God when and if this plague ever ends. If God doesn't need mankind's approval, he may sacrifice it.

The Old Testament God rewarded such waywardness in his creation with pestilence and slaughter. But as Job basically said, what else can you do to me that hasn't been done?

Paul dons the respirator mask and steps out into the early twilight created by massive smoke clouds slowly writhing across the sky. He spends several minutes watching as the green landscape continues its slow dissolution into a powdery gray wasteland. He thinks of the other survivors wandering across this wilderness, alone and without hope. This is a place where people face themselves and learn what they really are.

In war and adversity, we learn our true nature as humans. On our deathbed, our curse as earthly beings. In a place like this, we gaze into a mirror at our image rendered naked in cruel honesty— at who we really are as people.

His knees popping, he stoops to brush soot off the supplies. He organizes them for repacking into the Bradley. Lanterns, Coleman stove, propane tanks, bedrolls, and all the rest, including his tattered copy of the Holy Bible.

Lord, would you have destroyed Sodom if I was there?

Abraham argues with God to spare Sodom and Gomorrah, saying he shouldn't destroy the innocent along with the wicked. He asks God if he'd destroy the city if fifty innocent people live there, and God says he wouldn't. He asks God if he'd destroy it if forty-five innocent people live there, and God says he wouldn't. And so he bargains with God, forty, thirty, twenty, finally settling on ten. Paul always wondered why Abraham didn't ask for mercy if even one innocent man or woman lived there.

Paul decides that he must make himself a righteous man to save the world from God's wrath, but he doesn't know how. This is a world where the righteous are easily culled.

He prays for guidance, but again, God doesn't answer.

"Oh Lord," Ethan says.

He remembers seeing stories on the news about poor kids from the developing world who were flown to hospitals in the United States to have giant benign tumors removed. The kids were grotesques, carrying twenty to thirty pounds of flesh on their faces. The tumors were large masses of tissue forming as a result of cancer cells reproducing at an abnormally accelerated rate.

Ducky has something similar growing out of his hip, but it's not a normal tumor. It's a monkeylike creature curled into a fetal ball, breathing with its own tiny lungs, apparently asleep. Ethan can see where the driver cut the pants of his uniform to release the growing creature. Now he understands why the soldiers were carrying the driver here, away from the other survivors. They didn't want the others to see Ducky like this.

Sarge asks the driver how he's feeling. Ducky's gaze shifts to Sarge, but otherwise his expression doesn't change.

The gunner shakes his head. "He barely has enough energy to breathe right now."

Sarge looks at Ethan. "So. You're the smart one. What do you think?"

Ethan examines the thing growing out of Ducky's hip, careful not to touch it. It's like cancer, but more than that: a true parasite. He can't believe his eyes; the man's entire body has been completely rewired to give everything it has to the growing creature. The thing apparently reorganized Ducky's organs and is pressing on his bladder, making him piss himself nearly continuously with a foul-smelling pink fluid.

Fascinating, almost miraculous, from a scientific view. Horrific and revolting from a human standpoint.

"We don't have much time," the gunner says.

"Time's up, Doc. Can you fix him?"

"I don't understand what it is exactly you expect me to do here."

Sarge extends his service knife to Ethan. "Can you fix him?"

Ethan almost laughs but stops himself. Sarge isn't the kind of guy you laugh in front of when one of his people is dying.

Sarge adds, "I sterilized it. It's clean. And we've got plenty of alcohol and gauze."

"He can't survive an amputation."

"Ducky's a tough sumbitch." He smiles weakly at the driver. "We'll booze you up good, Ducky. You won't feel a thing."

"Sarge, I'm sorry about your man," Ethan says carefully. "But there's nothing anybody can do."

"Did I make a mistake hauling your ass out of that hospital?"

"Sarge, you're not really thinking straight. A procedure like this would take a team of real doctors most of a whole day in a real hospital. I'm a *high school math teacher*. I'm just smart enough to know that anything I do will kill this man. Look at this small wound here that's still weeping; he must have tried to cut it off himself in the Bradley, and the pain stopped him. At some point, I assume the parasite will detach, as you can see legs forming here, but right now there's an entire system of veins supplying blood to it. I cut into this mass, and even if Ducky's heart didn't fail from the shock, the loss of blood would surely—"

"Holy shit," Steve hisses. He pushes himself away from the driver and falls sprawling on his ass.

The parasite's eye is open. It studies them each in turn. The head, fused to the rest of the body-shaped mass of tissue by a thin film of clear mucus, begins to stir. The men gasp with revulsion. Ducky looks down at it, his eyes wide with helpless terror.

The creature is becoming aware. It's literally being born right in front of their eyes.

"It ain't nothing, Ducky," Sarge says, his voice fragile. "Don't even look at it."

Ethan points to the thing's face and says, "See how it's able to move, but Ducky isn't. The parasite is now stronger than its host and is—"

He leaps to his feet and bolts across the asphalt screaming.

Sarge chases Ethan through a blizzard of ash. The green figure flickers like a candle fifty yards ahead. The screams ring out across the blank empty spaces. Ethan collapses to his knees with a moan. The soldier catches up and drops to one knee next to him.

"Let me see it," he says.

Ethan moans, shaking, cradling his bloody hand.

Paul and Todd come running. They look down at him in surprise.

"Is he in shock?" Paul says.

"No," Sarge says. "Not physical shock, anyhow."

"You need help?"

Todd gapes at them. "What the heck happened to him?"

Sarge leans close to Ethan's ear. "You're okay now. Let me see it."

He's still doubting what he saw until Ethan slowly unravels his trembling hand and shows the bloody stump where the tip of his index finger used to be.

The fucker bit it off. Ate it with a crunch. Its little black eye gleaming with hate.

Ethan looks at his hand, his face pale and surprised.

"Somebody, get me the med kit," Sarge says.

"I'll go," Paul says and runs off to the Bradley.

"And plenty of water, Reverend," Sarge calls after him. He tears a strip from the teacher's shirt and winds it tightly around the wound. "We're going to take care of this," he tells Ethan. "You're going to be okay. We'll put some pressure on it for now, all right? Then we'll clean it real good, and I'll sew it up."

Todd drops to his knees next to Ethan and says, "You're alive, man. You're *alive*."

"You're fine," Sarge says. "It ain't nothing."

Ethan whispers something. Sarge bends closer to hear.

"*Kill. Him.*"

"The hell you say!"

Ethan winces in pain. "*Not murder. Not that. Mercy. Do it quick, before—*"

Back at the fuel island, Steve's rifle pops once, twice.

"Take care of this man," Sarge barks.

"Sarge?" Todd says.

Sarge jumps to his feet and runs back across the lot. "*No, goddamnit, no!*"

He finds Steve standing over Ducky's corpse, his rifle smoking and his eyes wild.

"What happened?"

Steve trembles with disgust and rage. "That thing. That fucking *thing*."

Sarge closes his eyes, but he can still see Ducky's body lying on the ground, a drained, empty husk, and the creature splattered like road kill across the asphalt.

He can still see where the parasite had begun eating Ducky's leg.

Wendy returns in time to see Sarge carrying Ducky, a limp bundle wrapped in a blanket and light as a child, into a nearby sloped field crowned with a stand of oak trees. Paul and Todd and the gunner have gathered at the top next to the hole they dug. They ask her where Anne is; Wendy shakes her head, staring in horror at the empty hole, feeling death's chill. She tells them the infected aren't far behind, coming like a flood. A heavy silence falls on them as they fear the worst has happened to Anne and turn inward to look at these fears.

Sarge and Steve gently lower the body into the pit.

"He knew he was going to die, yet he kept doing his job to the very end, saving our lives," Sarge says. "That thing was pounding us, and Ducky kept on going. He was in an amazing amount of pain, alone and without hope, but he kept on going. For us. And for that, Ducky, you have our thanks. Because of you, we're still here, and we'll remember you."

He nods to Paul, who intones: "'Our days on Earth are like grass; like wildflowers, we bloom and die. The wind blows, and we are gone—as though we had never been here. But the love of the Lord remains forever with those who fear him.' Amen."

"Amen," the survivors murmur.

Paul lowers his respirator mask to cover his face while the others lift wet bandanas over their mouths. Steve pours gasoline into the hole with the body, and Sarge lights it. They step back from the sudden fury of heat and light. Sarge insisted on burning him. That way, he said, nothing will be able to dig him up and eat him.

There's no time for mourning. Sarge knows grief is a luxury at a time like this. The survivors plod back down the slope toward the Bradley, now completely inventoried and repacked, everything in its place. Sarge watches a group of refugees break into the truck stop in search of food, water, shelter. It's time to get back on the road. The day will only bring more refugees, each more desperate than the last, and behind them, a flood of infected. They'll just have to try to find Anne on the road, if they can.

Anne waits for them at the Bradley, hands on hips, her head and shoulders wrapped in rags. Her shirt is sprinkled with fresh blood. She pulls the rags and bandana down to expose her smiling face. They've never seen her smile before and find it jarring but also oddly uplifting. A tiny voice in their heads tells them that this too shall pass. They can get through this. They're alive, and they can go on surviving.

Anne says, "Don't give up hope."

☣

The Bradley drives along the westbound lanes of the Penn Lincoln Parkway through open hill country, passing abandoned cars and files of tired refugees on foot hauling backpacks and children. The scarred, ash-filled wasteland that was once Pittsburgh recedes the farther they go west; the view here is a brilliant green, virtually untouched by Infection.

The vehicle veers onto an exit, taking them past another abandoned military checkpoint and onto a sunlight-dappled two-lane back road. They pass telephone poles staked at regular intervals and mailboxes and signs reading, SPEED LIMIT 45 and SCHOOL BUS STOP AHEAD. Rolling hills overlook the road from the right, crowded with maple and beech and dogwood. Figures march singly or in small groups across distant green fields. The air is humid and clean and crowded with the sounds of birdsong and insects.

After several miles, the Bradley passes a sign announcing, BUCHANAN EVERGREEN FARM and another marked, CHRISTMAS TREES. The vehicle turns onto a long crushed stone driveway and speeds toward the distant farmhouse. Inside, they find the desiccated corpses of a large family lying on the floor, smiling and blue and hugging each other among empty bottles of pills. They remove the bodies and burn them in the backyard, coughing soot out of their lungs and marveling at the greenery and lazy birdsong. Anne wants to put more distance between them and Pittsburgh, but Sarge tells her they'll stay the night here. Paul contemplates the fresh graves and the family photos on the wall, depicting generations that owned this land until Infection, and believes the world is slowly becoming haunted. *Or maybe we're the ghosts and don't even know we're dead yet. Survival, after all, has turned out to be a strange purgatory between living and dying.* Anne gives Ethan his glasses and a fresh T-shirt. She says nothing else, but Ethan, pleasantly numb on painkillers, knows he's accepted again. While Anne unpacks the Bradley, he searches for but doesn't find his backpack with his family photos. There's now nothing to even note they once existed other than memory. Like the others, he has no home, not even evidence of a past life outside his own unreliable mind. Todd watches the others move about in safety with a smile on his face, biting back witty quips, biding his time. Wendy cleans her Glock and exchanges a long glance with Sarge before going upstairs to take her turn washing in the antique bathtub. The soldiers fortify the house and rest on easy chairs in the living room while the others set up the stove and drink coffee in silence, feeling safe for the first time since they left the hospital.

The clock in the living room chimes the hour.

Anne tells them about the refugee camp.

The soldiers she saw on the highway were attached to the Federal Emergency Management Agency. They came from a camp called Defiance. She talked to an officer there on the Humvee radio. It's only a few hours' drive away, in Ohio, in a place called Cashtown.

Sanctuary. A place where they can finally rest. The real deal: a place where they can be finally and truly safe.

The survivors stare at her, unsure how to respond to this news. After everything that's happened, they're happy simply to be alive and clean and fed in this house. The idea they might end this journey is a lot to absorb.

After several moments of stunned silence, Paul says, "Well, Amen."

The other survivors laugh and echo the sentiment.

The night passes without nightmares.

The next morning, Anne is gone.

FLASHBACKS: ANNE LEARY

"This is outrageous," she said into the phone cradled between her cheek and shoulder as she flattened a lump of dough with her rolling pin. "Did you call the police?"

Anne had championed the bond to refurbish the park with new playground equipment. If there was one thing she'd learned, it was playground equipment wasn't cheap, as in five hundred thousand dollars' worth of not cheap, but she'd negotiated hard—people had a hard time refusing Anne Leary—and gotten the very best.

She felt a sense of ownership over it. Now here was her friend Shana calling to tell her there were two men at the playground acting suspiciously.

"The cops aren't answering the phone," Shana said.

"Our tax dollars at work." Anne trimmed the dough into a ten-inch square and expertly maneuvered the knife to cut it into strips a half-inch wide.

"The phone lines are all jammed up with that thing going on downtown. People killing each other in the streets. It's like the Screaming again. It took me eight tries just to get through to you."

Anne laid half the strips on top of her pie filling at regular intervals and pressed the ends into the edge of crust. Afterward, she'd place the other half crosswise across the top, bake it, and produce a perfect blueberry pie with a lattice crust.

"I don't understand what the fuss is about," she said. "They said on the radio it's happening everywhere, but if that's true, then it should be happening here. *I* don't see anything going on."

"I don't know, Anne. Things are apparently pretty dangerous out there. Haven't you been watching the news?"

"You know how the media is. They sensationalize everything. This is all going to blow over; you'll see. We got past the Screaming. We'll get past a bunch of people trying to take advantage by stirring up trouble. We just have to stay tough until the police sort it out. And if they don't, we will. If the crazies come here, we'll show them they aren't welcome, like last time."

"I guess you're right."

Anne looked up at the ceiling as if imploring Heaven. "*Of course* I'm right!"

After the Screaming, the city had filled with crazies. People deranged by what they'd seen, wandering about in shock and anger and loss. Others convinced the world was ending and flailing at their neighbors in panic. Criminal types looking for easy pickings. They were everywhere; some inevitably wandered through Anne's neighborhood. People were scared and stayed in their homes, but Anne toughened them up. She got them organized. They banded together and chased the crazies out.

And this too shall pass. Fear is the real enemy.

They just had to stay tough.

"Well, what are we going to do?"

Everybody in the neighborhood knew Anne Leary and looked to her to take the lead in a crisis. People didn't just call her to tell her things. They expected her to *do* something. She was treasurer for the local PTA and produced a monthly newsletter for the local homeowners association. After the Screaming, she not only organized the drive to keep out the crazies, she enlisted homeowners in her community to get their fallen neighbors to the clinics, take care of their children, tend their yards, and anything else that needed doing. It was hard work, but the people who lived here were more than happy to have something they could do to help. Anne believed a major crisis brought out the best in people, if only you asked them to step up. If only they had proper leadership.

The dog ran into the kitchen and paced in front of the glass sliding door connecting the kitchen to the backyard, whining and barking and scrabbling at the glass.

"Hang on, Shan. I can barely hear you. The dog's going berserk."

She opened the door and watched Acer take off like an arrow and disappear through a gap in the fence that her husband always threatened to repair but never did.

"I'm back," she added. "We can't have the crazies running amok in our park. Our children *play there*. If the cops are too busy to help, we're going to have to do this ourselves. Just like last time."

"Oh, Anne, don't go vigilante again."

She scooped up her pie and tossed it in the oven. "Me? I'm not doing anything. Big Tom's going, not me."

Her kids tramped by scowling. Anne followed them with her eyes, monitoring her little ducklings for signs of conspiracy.

"I've got to run, Shan. I have to go vigilante on my kids."

"Tell Big Tom to be careful if he's going out today."

Anne frowned but laughed. "Sure thing. Bye, Shan." Hanging up, she turned on the hot water tap, squirted in some dishwashing liquid, and began filling the sink. "Children, come here!"

Peter tramped back into the kitchen, followed by Alice and Little Tom. They gazed sullenly at their mother.

"Well?" she said, hands on hips. "What's wrong?"

"Dad says we can't go outside today. We're bored out of our *minds*."

Anne turned off the tap and dumped a stack of dirty breakfast dishes into the foamy water.

"Did he now?" she said. "*TOM!*"

Big Tom was in the living room, sitting on the couch watching the news, already an hour late for work. He entered the kitchen scratching the back of his head and looking worried. Her husband was a large man—not muscular, not fat, just *big*. His smile lit up his entire face. People thought he was a natural comedian, but they also respected him when he was serious. He was the kind of guy who didn't start fights but was perfectly capable of finishing them.

"The authorities are saying it's some sort of plague," he muttered. "A plague that makes you crazy and hurt people. Things are getting pretty hairy out there."

"Tom. *Tom*. We can't keep the kids locked up like this."

"They're telling everybody to stay indoors, dear."

"It's just more of the crazies. Kids hopped up on drugs."

"It's the screamers, they say. The screamers all woke up, and they're like maniacs. They're—"

Anne snorted. "Give me a break. In any case, all that stuff is going on *downtown*, not here. The only thing we've got going on *here* is two crazies hanging around the park that I want you to give a good talking to. Go kick them out of there so our kids can go play outside."

"They can play in the backyard," he offered.

"*Tom*. If you were here each day with these little darlings since the Screaming like I have been, you would know that they're wild animals and need space to roam. You can't keep children bottled up on a beautiful day like this. You want maniacs? These kids will tear the house apart. I am speaking from experience."

Anne suppressed a smile. She knew he'd obey her. He always did. The truth was he loved her more than anything, and after a good deal of token hemming and hawing, he always did as she said. Anne was the type of person who mouthed off to strangers about their driving, their parking, how they treated their kids in public. She'd gotten her husband into a fistfight once over her editorializing about a man taking two parking spaces at the supermarket with his oversized truck. Big Tom had apologized after knocking him to the ground.

"I don't think you understand what I'm saying," her husband said with a massive frown.

Her eyes narrowed. He wasn't playing. He was serious. Well, so was she. When it came to things like this, she was very much in charge. And she could be very, very stubborn.

"Go, Tom. Go be the man."

"You want me to go?"

"Don't go, Daddy," Little Tom said, his voice cracking.

"Don't you say another word," Anne warned her boy, her voice quiet and deadly. A hush fell over them all; the mood in the house became tense. She went on sunnily, "Your father isn't working today, so he can help out around the house." She looked him in the eye. "Yes, dear, I want you to go take care of that problem in the park."

Big Tom stormed out of the kitchen and returned with one of his shotguns. The kids watched this in stunned silence except for Little Tom, who choked back a sob.

"Oh, Tom, don't go Rambo or anything," she said. "It's just stupid kids, I'm sure of it. Just give them a stern warning so they leave and don't come back."

Big Tom loaded the shotgun wearing a grimace that was almost a sneer. She could tell he was scared, and it confused her. The only time she'd seen Big Tom scared was their first date, their wedding day, and the arrival of their firstborn.

"Okay, I'm going, then," he said.

Anne looked at the ceiling, almost laughing, and said, "That's what I've been *saying*."

"Lock the door after I leave the house."

She waved him off, already focused on her next task. Anne never locked her door during the day and wasn't about to start now. If she needed to lock her door, she wouldn't be living in this neighborhood.

After Big Tom left, doubt nagged at the back of her mind, a little voice whispering, *Bring him back*, which she overcame by diving back into the endless housework that constituted her 24/7 job. She washed the breakfast dishes, dried them, put them away.

She took her pie out of the oven and set it to cool. Big Tom loved her pie, and she laughed thinking about him devouring it. He'd come back feeling silly about being scared, and she'd say nothing and put a nice big piece of pie in front of him with a cold glass of milk. She tried to call her girlfriends to talk about all these things on her mind, but there was still trouble on the line. Around noon, she made sandwiches for her kids and began to seriously worry.

The kids ate their lunches sullenly at the kitchen table. Little Tom's chin wobbled as he chewed mechanically, watching his mother with big watery eyes.

"Where's Dad?" Peter said, his voice challenging.

Alice stopped chewing. Little Tom sobbed and rubbed his eyes. Anne, who'd been staring out the window wondering that very thing, realized they were all looking at her.

Fear flickered across her face, followed by a smile.

"Dad went for a walk with Acer," she said.

She stood, picked up the phone and tried to call his cell, but the phones were jammed. She tried again. And again. Always the same. Always that frantic busy signal indicating system failure. The kids studied her closely with worried expressions.

Peter understands what's happening. Perhaps even better than I do.

"Ha!" she said. The phone was ringing.

Big Tom's ringtone—Leo Sayer and the Wiggles doing the chorus of "You Make Me Feel Like Dancing"—sang out from the living room.

Anne slammed the phone down, biting back a nice, juicy F-bomb. That was just like him. He was always forgetting to bring his cell phone.

"Where's Dad, Mom?" Peter pressed.

"Go to your rooms," she said.

"*I want Daddy*," Little Tom screamed.

Alice buried her face in her hands and wailed.

"Where's Dad?" Peter said.

"I have a better idea," Anne said. "Come on, get up. You're all coming with me."

"Where are we going?" her boy demanded.

"*You're* going to Trudy's next door. *I'm* going to get your father. You all right with that?"

Peter nodded with visible relief.

"Then let's go, troops," she snapped. She bent to wipe Little Tom's tears with a paper towel. "You too, big man. Finish your juice first."

The kids got out of their chairs and put their shoes on, Peter helping his brother and Anne helping Alice. Anne noticed how grown up Peter was becoming at just seven years of age, and she swallowed hard to get rid of the sudden lump in her throat. Outside, it was a beautiful day, sunny and a perfect seventy degrees. Anne blinked in the sunshine, looking for trouble, but the neighborhood looked the same as it always did. The air was crowded with distant sirens, but there was no trouble here in the 'burbs. Just green lawns, well-kept blue-collar homes and beautiful blue sky. No people either, but they were probably all at work or inside watching the news. Even Little Tom perked up, and she had to hold his hand to keep him from becoming distracted. He'd reached an age where he became easily fascinated by anything resembling a rock.

She herded the kids across the street to Trudy's house and rang the doorbell.

A muffled voice: "Who is it?"

"Trudy, it's me."

"Anne?"

"Open up, Trudy."

The door opened, and Trudy Marston peered out at them and then past them, scanning the sidewalk and street beyond.

"Everything all right, Anne?"

"Right as rain," Anne answered, resisting the urge to turn around to see what Trudy was looking at. "Listen, friend. I need you to watch my little ones while I go look for Big Tom at the park."

Trudy opened the door further to expose her haggard face. "Jesus, is he okay?"

Anne smiled grimly. "He won't be after I get through with him."

Her neighbor's voice became shrill. "What was he *thinking* going out today?"

Anne blinked. "Never mind that. I need to bring him home. Can you watch my kids?"

"I'm sorry, I can't. Hugo is in a bad way. He's been stirring all morning, crying out in his coma. I've got to keep watch on him."

"You know Hugo is in our prayers, Trudy. If he's stirring around on his bed, that's a good sign he'll wake up soon. It's not a coma anymore if he's yelling in his sleep. Take it from me: you know I was a registered nurse before Peter came along. They'll all wake up soon. We're all hoping that."

An expression of horror crossed Trudy's face.

"You okay, Trudy?"

"Yes. I hope so, too," the woman said, her voice tired and faded. "Anyhow, I've got to keep a watch on him. I've got to be ready when he wakes up." She laughed harshly. "Even after everything, I just can't leave him. Ain't that a hoot?"

"Well, now you've got three little helpers to help you watch. Right, helpers?"

"Yes, Mom," Peter said. He scowled skeptically at Trudy.

"This isn't a good idea, Anne."

"Come on, kids, get in there," Anne said. She hustled her children through the door. She stifled a cough; the house stank like sour milk. Her poor neighbor had really let herself go since Hugo fell down during the Screaming. "Trudy, fifteen minutes is all I ask."

"Please..."

Anne looked up at the sky, almost laughing. Why was everybody being so unreasonable with her today? "Come *on*, the park is right over there. It's a five-minute walk. I'll be right back, I swear."

People had a hard time refusing Anne Leary.

She power-walked to the park, fueled by her fury at her husband for making her worry like this, and paused at the curb. If there were a couple of crazies lurking about, it might not be a good idea to run into them. She had a forceful personality and was a big talker, but she was physically small and hated violence. Talking tough could only get you so far, and she couldn't back it up without Big Tom around. She surveyed the neatly manicured lawns and trees for any sign of friend or foe. For any sign of people at all. Wind rustled in the branches. The playground stood empty. The swings moved a little in the breeze, as if haunted.

"Tom?" Anne said, hating how timid her voice sounded.

Where was everybody? Usually, there were a lot of people in the park on a beautiful day like today, even on a Monday, even after the Screaming screwed everything up.

She noticed a plume of smoke rising over downtown. The sirens crowded in a little closer. As she moved into the trees, she heard a crackling sound. *Of all things. Who would be lighting fireworks at a time like this?*

"Tom!" she yelled, feeling bolder. "Tom!"

She crisscrossed the park repeatedly, searching for any sign and finding none. She didn't wear a watch, setting her schedule by her routine alone. The sirens grew louder until she realized they weren't there anymore. Everybody seemed to be lighting fireworks downtown. Time blurred again as her rage turned into panic. She felt the day slipping away from her.

"Tom, I'm sorry," she cried. She ran blindly through the trees. "I'm sorry. Now come on out here!"

Anne stopped, sweating and panting. Her shoes were muddy, her pants scraped and torn. The sun hung low in the sky. The last sirens petered out. She had a sense of some massive unseen battle being fought and lost. The crackling sound was everywhere now.

"*I want my husband*," she said fiercely and spit.

A horrible feeling overtook her. It shot through her like an urge to vomit. She fell to her knees.

"Oh no," she said. She covered her mouth with her hands. "Oh, *no no no no no no*."

Anne rose unsteadily to her feet and ran on tired legs. She finally arrived at Trudy's door gasping for breath.

"Please," she said. She pounded on the door. "*Please*, God."

Nobody came to answer it.

She went to the picture window and tried to peer in, but the sheer curtains obscured her view. A television was on, glowing in the dark interior. She pounded on the window until pain lanced through her hand. She briefly contemplated breaking it and how she might accomplish this. Instead, she ran around to the back of the house feeling like she was about to scream. She had a sense of being out of control.

If anybody touched one hair on my kids' heads—

Anne couldn't bear to finish the thought. Couldn't bear the idea they might be hurt.

"Please God. Please God, please God—"

The glass sliding door was open. The screen door was closed, the mesh torn away.

That sour milk stench poured out of the house.

"Please," she whispered as she stepped inside.

The living room was dark. The TV was on, displaying rainbow colors and emitting the grating buzz of the emergency broadcast signal.

"Trudy? Trudy, are you there?"

Nobody answered her. Anne ran across the room to the kitchen. Three small glasses sat on the table. One still had a little milk in it.

"Trudy, where are my kids?"

There was an unmade bed in the master bedroom. The sour stench there was so concentrated it made her gag, pushing her back out of the room with an almost physical force.

"Trudy, it's me, Anne!"

All the rooms were empty. It seemed nobody was home. Where were they? She needed time to think. She needed to find them and keep them safe until Big Tom came home.

"Where are my kids, Trudy?"

Anne returned to the living room. The emergency broadcast signal continued its grating honk. She moved to turn off the TV.

Oh my God—

"No," she said. "No, no, no, no—"

Her body convulsed. She bent to vomit explosively onto the carpet.

After several moments of retching and gasping to catch her breath, Anne could look again at what had been hiding in plain sight.

The bodies were arranged on the floor by the fireplace. Trudy had died wearing an odd smile, her neck cleanly broken. Peter and Alice and Little Tom surrounded her legs.

Something had mangled them. Torn pieces out of them. There was blood and flesh everywhere. They'd huddled around Trudy for protection. They'd wanted Trudy to protect them because their mother and father were not there.

No, Anne told herself. Peter still held the poker from the fireplace. *They were protecting Trudy.*

That's my kids. This is just like them. To put somebody else's safety before their own. So brave. My big, grownup boy is so brave. My good Peter. Just like his daddy.

Anne screamed and clawed at her face until she passed out.

She found herself wandering in the middle of the street. Paul Liao called to her from the driveway of his home as his wife hustled their kids into an overpacked station wagon. Across the street, a body lay on the sidewalk at the end of a long smear of blood. Somebody screamed far away. Somebody close by fired a gun and shattered a window.

A van approached and stopped. The doors opened.

"I got her," somebody said. "Cover me."

A cop in riot gear appeared in front of her. He flinched at the sight of her face.

"*Crazies*," she said thickly. Her voice sounded alien to her ears.

"You're safe now, ma'am. Step right this way."

Another cop swept the area with his shotgun. "Jesus, look at her face," he said. "I thought she was one of them for a second."

He cursed and fired at something behind her. The gun's roar filled the world.

"*Chase them out*," she insisted.

She wanted to tell them something else important but couldn't remember what it was. The noise had scrambled her thoughts again. She was having a hard time thinking. She faded in and out of consciousness. She remembered burying her children in her backyard. She remembered the power going out. She remembered digging a grave for herself. She became angry. She wanted to yell at the big cop, but he was gone. It was dark—inside, not outside. She was in a big room now, sitting with her back against the wall. Her face felt stiff and stung from an alcohol wipe. The scratch wounds on her cheeks throbbed under thick, bulky bandages. A blanket was draped around her shoulders, and she pulled it tighter around her neck. She sensed the presence of hundreds of people in the room, coughing and whispering and snoring. As her eyes became accustomed to the darkness, she saw their bodies lying on cots and sitting huddled on the ground.

"Tom," she said, trying to find her voice. She called out: "Tom? Tom, are you there?"

"Oh Jesus, not another one," somebody groaned.

"Please shut the hell up!" another voice roared in the darkness. "We're trying to sleep here."

"Big Tom!" she cried. "Answer if you can hear me!"

"You're not the only one who lost someone, lady. Give it a rest."

People sobbed in the dark, talking to loved ones who weren't there. Somebody coughed loudly. A couple made love on a cot. A man masturbated loudly under a blanket. The tips of cigarettes glowed in the dark. Another man lay on the cool hard floor twenty feet away, huddled around a handful of photos he studied endlessly with a flashlight.

Anne stared at the flashlight until her vision washed out in a white burst. Two men were arguing. One said it was only a matter of time before the food and water ran out, and then they'd be killing each other over the crumbs. The other said they should stay put. The world was ending outside, and only a fool would try to make plans that lasted longer than a day.

It was daytime, she realized; time had blurred again. Beams of morning sunlight streamed through a row of punched windows near the ceiling. The room was a vehicle service garage. People milled around aimlessly. They bartered candy and cigarettes, settled disputes with swift and furious beatings, washed themselves with tepid water poured into plastic bowls. The air smelled like old motor oil, human waste, and fear. People huddled around radios and argued over the news before drifting away. Colorful public health notices plastered the walls, orange and red and yellow, reminding her to wash her hands, avoid the infected, and approach law enforcement and military personnel calmly, without sudden movements, and with her hands over her head.

This wasn't some type of government fortress but instead an old-fashioned refugee camp, and a temporary one at that. How long had she been here? How long had it been since her world ended? She felt lightheaded, like she hadn't eaten in days. She thought of a blueberry pie sitting on a kitchen counter, covered in flies.

"The authorities are in control," a voice said. "Help is coming. Don't give up hope."

The shell-shocked, skinny kid was some sort of government official, and he was handing out lists of evacuation centers printed on clean yellow sheets of paper.

"This one's been overrun," somebody said in disgust. "I was *there*."

"The next one is five miles from here."

"Might as well be on the moon."

"The only safe place is right here. I'm not going anywhere."

The kid ignored them. He handed out his yellow sheets and delivered his simple mantra of hope with a plastic smile.

He held one out until Anne accepted it. His dead face warped again as he said, "The authorities are in control. Help is coming. Don't give up hope. Report any suspicious behavior."

Nobody else seemed to be in charge. The cops who'd brought her here were gone. Even the kind woman who wore a blue Walmart apron and doled out the rations appeared to be some sort of volunteer. Then she saw several men working the room. They shook hands, looked concerned, and wrote things down in a notebook. This ad hoc leadership committee came close enough for her to hear one of them, a gentle-looking overweight man wearing large glasses, tell people that they had to get organized.

"Why?" a man said belligerently.

A woman sitting on a cot said: "You're just like *them*."

The overweight man adjusted his glasses and said, "Them?"

"The government."

"But we're all alive because of the government," he reasoned. "They brought us here and gave us food and water, blankets, medical supplies. We're trying to get organized in case the supplies run out and the government can't send us anything else."

"Like I said," the woman said triumphantly.

Anne shook her head in mild disgust. *At least these guys are doing something.* She recognized something of herself in them.

"But I *could* use some batteries if you got any you could spare," the woman went on.

Anne noticed an armored fighting vehicle parked at the far end of the garage and decided to take a closer look. Wrapping the blanket around her, she wandered through the dense smells and noises of the camp until she found an empty spot where she could sit with a clear view of the impressive war machine. Three soldiers stood hunched over the engine, arguing in language so technical it was almost foreign. Anne thought they looked more like mechanics than soldiers. She watched them while she sipped her bottle of water. They cleaned engine parts with rags and studied the crowd around them like engineers looking for cracks in a dam.

She planned to stay close to them. It was obvious to her that the man she'd heard arguing this morning was right: this place wasn't going to last very long. If anything happened, the safest spot in the room would be behind the soldiers and their weapons.

She hated herself for thinking this. Cursed herself for wanting to survive.

Anne watched them work on their vehicle for the next three days. During that time, the refugee population dwindled to less than a hundred souls. The cops never came back to bring in more people, and as food and water began to run out, the portable toilets filled to overflowing, and petty crime escalated, many left to take their chances outside.

On the third day, the Walmart woman brought Anne her daily ration—this time only a bottle of water and an energy bar.

"Sorry it's a bit meager this morning, dear," she said. "But don't worry. We're expecting another shipment later today, I'm told. The government promised on the radio."

"So things are getting better outside?"

An expression of fear flashed across the woman's face. A sunny smile replaced it. "Of course!"

The mood in the shelter was tense. People were furious the rations had been cut to almost nothing and looked for somebody to blame. Mothers demanded milk for babies that screamed in their hunger. Rumor spread that several women at the far end of the room had been raped in the night. Most of the refugees wanted the portable toilets cleaned and the corpses, zipped up in shiny black body bags arranged in nice neat rows against the east wall, taken out and burned. Some of the men threatened each other over accusations of using more than their fair share of supplies.

People crowded around the leadership committee demanding answers. Eventually, the overweight man with glasses fought through the mob and approached the soldiers.

"May I speak to your commander?" he said, his voice tight and thin.

"I'm Sergeant Toby Wilson, sir," one of the soldiers said in a booming baritone. He extended his large hand. "You can call me Sarge."

The man shook the commander's hand with enthusiasm, beaming at the warm reception.

"Nice to meet you, Sarge. I'm Joshua Adler."

"So what can we do for you, Mr. Adler?"

"Me and some of the other guys, we've been trying to get things organized."

"Uh huh. We've been watching you do that."

"Well, you must know that our supply situation is getting bad. The government said they would be coming back with more. Now, I've drawn up a list..."

The man fumbled with a notebook until Sarge held up his hand.

"Mr. Adler, we have nothing to do with that. We don't know anything about it. We're here to get our rig working again. It needs professional civilian maintenance. Seeing as that's not going to happen, it's on us to fix it using whatever we can find around here. That's taking time."

"I see..."

"We almost got it figured out, and we're hoping to get back in the field as soon as we can. That's our top priority."

"All right, I understand, uh, Sarge, but maybe you could tell me if you have any news of things on the outside—"

"It's bad."

"Bad?"

"Bad as in real bad. Bad as in we're losing this fight."

"So who's in charge?"

Sarge shrugged. "I guess you are."

At the other end of the garage, the doors opened. Three soldiers entered the shelter, armed to the teeth and wearing bulky MOPP suits complete with goggled respirator masks that gave them a vaguely bug-like appearance.

"Stay where you are," one of the soldiers announced, his voice muffled by his mask. "Please stay calm."

The first soldier appeared to be the leader. Gripping a pistol in his clenched fist, he walked through the people crowded among the cots looking into their faces. He was looking for somebody. The other soldiers followed with automatic rifles.

Joshua excused himself, signaled to the other men in the leadership committee, and approached the soldiers.

"Captain," one of the soldiers said.

The leader turned and raised his pistol. "Sit down, sir."

The soldiers standing behind him swept the room with their rifles.

"But we're—"

The captain slid the bolt back in his service weapon to chamber a round. "Now, sir."

Joshua sat on the ground with the other men.

The soldiers continued to walk through the crowd. The captain looked each person in the face before moving on. The captain pointed at a man and said, "I got one here."

One of the soldiers grabbed the man by the arm and pulled him roughly to his feet.

"What are you doing?" a woman demanded.

"He's infected, ma'am," the captain said. "Come on, Parker, get him up."

The people nearest the man cried out and shrank away from him, leaving him to struggle weakly against the soldiers. He was obviously sick; his face was shiny and red with fever. A soldier cracked his skull with the butt of his rifle, and he fell limp.

They dragged him toward the exit.

"Wait," Anne said. "Officer, wait! What are you going to do to him?"

The captain replied, "Sit down and shut up, ma'am."

"I think she likes you, Captain," the soldier named Parker said.

"Watch out, she's going to report you to her PTA," the other added with a laugh.

"He's just sick," she pleaded. "He's not one of them."

The captain raised his pistol and aimed it at her face.

"You're crazy, lady. Maybe you're infected too."

A tall man stood behind the soldiers and approached the officer. He wore the black suit and white collar of a clergyman.

"Now, hold on a minute, sir," the man said. "This lady is right. This is bullshit. Let's talk this out."

The captain turned, gave the clergyman a quick once-over, and said, "Are you Catholic?"

"No, son, I am not."

"Then I don't give a rat's ass what you have to say."

The pistol flashed in the man's hand and struck the clergyman in the face. Anne, still standing, exchanged a quick glance with Sarge, who stood by his Bradley with his crew, wiping his hands with a greasy rag. The man shook his head slightly.

Anne swallowed her rage and returned to her seat on the floor as the soldiers dragged the sick man out of the garage. The clergyman lay groaning on the floor.

Outside, a gun fired.

Later that day, about half the refugees packed their meager belongings and left. Those who remained were broken people. They lay on their cots and stared at the ceiling.

The following night was long and uneventful except for people sobbing quietly in the dark. The room stank with the ammonia smell of piss.

They were doomed, and they knew it.

The next morning, the doors burst open again, and a group of men and women entered carrying rifles and pistols and wearing a motley collection of military uniforms. The refugees shrank from them with shrill screams.

"Anybody here need a ride?" one of newcomers called out with a grin.

A woman flung herself into his arms. "Sam!"

"I told you I'd find you," he said, tears streaming down his face. "Didn't I tell you?"

"We've got buses outside, enough for everybody," announced another member of the gang, a woman with a bandaged head. "There's a FEMA camp near Harrisburg, and we're starting a convoy. If you want in, pack up your things now. We're out of here in ten."

The refugees crowded around asking questions. They must have been satisfied by the answers, because all of them grabbed whatever possessions they had and hurried out the door to the line of commuter buses idling outside.

As the last of the refugees headed toward the door, one called out to Anne, "Last chance, lady!"

She shook her head.

The man waved and shut the door. Anne sighed with something like relief. The atmosphere, previously tense and stifling, became peaceful. The room seemed so much larger without the others filling it.

"Why didn't you go?"

Anne noticed the clergyman had also stayed behind.

"It shouldn't be that easy," she said.

"You might be right. I'm not sure I trusted them either."

"No," Anne said. "The others had no choice but to trust them. I have a choice. It shouldn't be that easy."

The man nodded. He approached and sat on a nearby cot with a heavy sigh, touching the bruise on his face gingerly. Anne got a good look at him. He was a big man, with dark skin, white hair, and a weathered face. She guessed him to be in his mid-fifties.

"What about you?" she asked. "Why didn't you go?"

He shrugged and said, "'Long is the way and hard, that out of Hell leads up to light.' That's a fancy way of saying I agree with you."

"I liked that. Was that the Bible?"

"No. *Paradise Lost*. John Milton."

They introduced themselves. His name was Paul.

The Bradley commander approached.

"We've just about got the rig fixed," he told them. "If you don't mind, later on, we'd like to start her up and drive her around a bit. We'll open the service door a little to ventilate, but it's going to be loud and smell bad anyway."

"It's all right," Paul said. He wandered off to contemplate the rows of corpses, still in their body bags, which lay waiting for transport that would never come.

Anne said, "Sergeant, how could you be so callous when they dragged that man outside to be murdered in cold blood? You knew he didn't have the sickness."

The soldier shrugged. "I could give you a dozen reasons, ma'am. Let me ask you a question. Why were you willing to risk your life to save him?"

She thought of several answers—the man was innocent, his murder was immoral, a society is judged by how well it defends its weakest members—but all rang false and hollow in her mind. She snorted. "What was I really risking?"

Sarge nodded. "That's what I thought. In Afghanistan, when things got really bad, the only way we could get through was to accept the idea we were already dead."

She recoiled at that. "Jesus."

"Those people out there. The screamers. They're pretty much the living dead. But us? We're the dead living."

"How can you say we're already dead?" Anne thought about it for a moment. "How could you do it? Doesn't it change you?"

"Yes. It changes you. But..." The big soldier shrugged again. "You survive."

"Why?"

"Why what?"

"Why survive if it's not really you anymore? Why survive if there's nothing left to survive for?"

"Somebody's got to live, ma'am. Somebody's got to carry on. That's all we need to know. That's all we're ever going to know. Somebody's got to live, or the whole thing is pointless."

"What is?" Anne wondered.

Sarge offered a grim smile. "The human race, of course."

"That's a lot of responsibility."

"If we don't accept it, we might as well let them win now and get it over with."

He cleared his throat and told Anne how he'd taken his unit into the field to test a non-lethal weapon, and how radio dispatches suggested some type of disaster. He and his crew subsequently lost contact with the Army. They were on their own. They had a new mission in mind· for themselves. They wanted to return to the mission site and try to locate their lost boys.

"We won't survive out there long on our own," he explained. "We need infantry to protect us. In return, we offer protection. The Bradley's mobility, its armor and cannon."

"What are you saying?"

"Well, I guess I'm saying I want you to join up with us."

"I want to help you, I really do, but I'm not a soldier," she said. "Never been one either."

"I want you to pull together some civilians and run them as a squad. We have a few weapons. I'll teach you how to use them. If we find our guys, then two days, max. Maybe three."

She eyed Paul praying over the bodies of the dead. "What about him?"

"I think he's suicidal. But if you want him, you can have him. See how this works?"

"But why me?" she said. "If you knew me, you wouldn't pick me for something like this."

"I'm picking you based on what I do know. You don't fear death. You're tough; you're not looking for easy answers and for everybody else to take care of you. And you've got a good head on your shoulders. You sat down instead of getting yourself killed helping that man, so I don't have to worry about you welcoming death or even actively seeking it."

"Well," Anne said in amazement. "I can see you've thought this through."

She realized she wanted this. Had, in fact, been sitting here for days waiting for something like it to present itself. The chance to really do something. The chance to fight back and stop the plague in its tracks.

The chance to kill every one of these monsters for what they did to her kids.

"You're a survivor, Anne," Sarge said. "I need survivors."

FEMAVILLE

The refugee camp appears over the next rise. A sprawling mass of people and buildings covering the land as far as the eye can see. Distant helicopters buzz like flies through the hot, still air. Tiny figures swarm among the houses and public buildings and trailers and tents, a seething ocean of humanity partially obscured by smoke drifting from thousands of cook fires.

The Bradley grinds to a halt. The survivors emerge from its dim interior at a crouch, weapons ready. Acting like a combat infantry unit is now second nature to them.

One by one, they join Sarge on the cracked road that plunges downhill and straight to the gates of the camp. Their weapons sag in their hands as they forget themselves, overwhelmed by the view. Jaws drop as Sarge passes around a pair of binoculars. They stare at the camp in a mounting daze. It's literally tiring just to look at it.

The camp easily holds more than a hundred thousand people. At its core is Cashtown with its private houses and stores and public buildings and parks packed with rundown FEMA trailers. Beyond the core, the camp encompasses outlying farms, the fields filled with campers and vehicles, even a giant circus tent. And beyond that, acres of forest leveled to make room for this teeming horde and its miles of tents and shanties. Massive clouds of dust hang over the land like a brown veil. The camp surges against mountainous walls of heaped sandbags, tractor trailers, and shipping containers, all wrapped in miles of barbed wire and buttressed with wood guard towers. The air is filled with the white noise of thousands of people and vehicles, occasionally startled by the distant popcorn pop of gunfire. In the east, a small band of infected makes a run at the wall and is cut down by a machine gun.

Weeks ago, this camp didn't exist.

"There it is," Wendy says. Her chest heaves with emotion. "The FEMA camp."

The sight almost defies belief. It's beautiful. Beautiful and horrifying.

"Incredible," Paul says, his voice loaded with awe.

Wendy glances at Sarge. "This is good for us, right?"

Sarge runs his hand over his stubble. "Maybe. I think so."

"We're Americans," Todd says. "We're all on the same side, right?"

"We can't be sure of anything," Sarge tells him.

Steve whistles. "I wish Ducky could have seen this."

To the survivors, the camp represents the time before Infection. If they drive into that place, they'll rejoin the human race. They'll be like astronauts returning home after years in space.

But the world won't be the same. The time before Infection is gone, and anything resembling that time is a mirage and possibly a trick. Right now, they're being chased hard by the devil, but it's the devil they know.

Sarge sighs. "It's a chance. Anybody got any better ideas where to go?"

Nobody does.

"Anne would know what to do," Todd says.

"Anne ditched us, Kid," Sarge says bitterly. "We waited around for two days, and she didn't come back. We barely made it out of there alive. She's either dead or on the road. Either way, she already made her decision and has no say in ours."

"*Okay*," Todd says.

"So that's it, then," Paul says. "We're going in."

Wendy snorts. "What choice do we have?"

☣

The Bradley cruises down the road past fields filled with the stumps of cut trees and burning piles of cleared brush. Scores of pale department store mannequins wearing designer fashions strike surreal poses across the smoky wasteland, their torsos tied to stakes and old street signs planted at regular intervals, some lying in the dirt among rags and scattered plastic limbs. A hundred yards from the road, several figures in bright yellow hazmat suits load bodies into the back of a municipal garbage truck, pausing in their work to stare at the armored fighting vehicle as it zooms past.

The camp looms close now, piled across the horizon and emitting waves of white noise, sewage smells, and wood smoke. The vehicle roars past a concrete pillbox from which the barrel of a heavy machine gun protrudes, swiveling slowly to follow its progress. A man wearing a T-shirt and camouflage pants steps into the road and waves at them to stop, but the rig rolls past him. Near the gates, more men in hazmat suits toss body bags from the back of an olive green flatbed truck into a deep, smoking pit. They pause in their work to stare as the Bradley comes to a halt in a cloud of dust and sits idling in the sun.

The man in the camo pants jogs up, panting for air. He slaps his hand against the Bradley's armor. "Open up in there, goddamnit!"

He waits and adds, "If you think we're going to let you drive a tank into the camp without you telling us who you are, you're crazy. So what's it going to be?"

The single-piece hatch over the driver's seat flips open, and the gunner pops his head up. Moments later, the hatch on the turret opens, and Sarge emerges.

"We're looking for Camp Defiance," he says.

"And you found it. Who are you?"

"Sergeant Toby Wilson, Eighth Infantry. I've got one crew and four civilians inside. We were told it was safe here."

"We're still here, ain't we?" The man turns his head and roars, "Open the gates! Got a military vehicle coming in!" He sketches a rough salute. "Welcome to FEMAville, Sergeant Wilson."

The gates, pulled by soldiers with rifles slung over their shoulders, slowly grind open. The Bradley lurches forward in low gear and follows a uniformed woman, who directs them by hand signals where to park. The area smells like diesel fuel and decaying garbage. Other soldiers press in to gawk at the battered vehicle and its cannon.

Sarge stares at them in surprise as they burst into cheers at this symbol of American might. They're still clapping as the other survivors emerge into the sunlight.

Bustling with activity, the area appears to be some type of checkpoint and distribution zone. The Bradley sits parked between a beat-up yellow school bus and a Brinks armored car. A massive pile of bulging plastic trash bags awaits disposal next to rows of body bags. A large truck stacked with cut logs idles next to a cluster of large yellow water tanks, one of which is being coupled to a truck. Men in overalls unload salvage from the back of a beat-up pickup covered with a patchwork of tiny scratches made by fingernails and jewelry. Light bulbs hang from wires strung between wood poles. The Stars and Stripes sways from one of these wires like drying laundry, big and bold, making Sarge suddenly aware of a lump in his throat.

He looks down at the cheering boys and wonders if this might be home. It certainly feels like a homecoming.

An officer pushes through the throng and extends his hand to help Sarge down from the rig. He is a large man with a square build, salt and pepper hair, and silver captain's bars.

"Welcome to Defiance, Sergeant. I'm Captain Mattis."

Sarge salutes. "Sergeant Tobias Wilson, Eighth Infantry Division, Mechanized, Fifth Brigade—the Iron Horse, sir."

The captain grunts. "You're the first I've seen from that unit."

"I'm afraid I've lost them, sir."

"And your squad?"

"KIA over a week ago, sir. Pulling security for a non-lethal weapons test."

"Non-lethals," Mattis says sourly. "I almost forgot we even tried it. Seems like a year ago, but a week's a long time these days. You've been on the road with these civilians since then?"

"Pretty much. I trained them, and they did most of the fighting."

"I'll be damned," Mattis says. He sizes up the others. "Were you all in Pittsburgh?"

"We got out just ahead of the fire, sir."

"A horrible thing. Damn shame. I stayed overnight there once, you know. Years ago. Loved the rivers and all the bridges. The old neighborhoods. Beautiful city."

"Yes, sir, it was. So what's the situation here?"

Mattis smiles. "You rest up. I'll bring you up to speed after your orientation, Sergeant."

The grinning soldiers collect the weapons from the other survivors.

The captain adds, "Now please surrender your sidearm."

☣

Wendy climbs onto the school bus and collapses into one of the seats. The windows are painted black and covered in layers of chicken wire, making the interior as dark and claustrophobic as the Bradley. Her nerves feel raw and edgy. For the last two weeks, she lived with her Glock loaded and within easy reach on her hip. She now feels its loss as if it's an amputated limb.

Sarge sits next to her and fidgets with his hands.

"Are we under arrest or something?" she whispers to him.

"I don't know. They said we have to go through some sort of orientation."

She chews her lip and wonders. Orientation could mean just that—the people who run the camp want to tell them about who runs it, what the rules are, how to collect rations—or it could be a euphemism for something else, maybe even something sinister. Sarge looks worried, not a good sign.

The bus roars to life and rolls forward, trembling violently as it passes over a stretch of deep potholes.

Wendy reaches for Sarge's large hand and clasps it in hers. "Did the soldiers tell you anything?"

Sarge shakes his head. "I don't know who to ask."

"What do you mean?"

"I mean, I literally don't know who's in charge here—FEMA, the Army, some other branch of the government. Those guys you saw at the gate weren't from a single unit. I recognized patches from at least six different outfits. Mostly National Guard. The highest-ranking officer on the scene—the captain I was talking to—is a logistics officer in an ordnance company. The only real clue I saw was the flag when we came in. It was a U.S. flag."

"All right," she says. "But if they're Army and you're Army, why'd they take your gun?"

"I don't know, Wendy."

"I don't like this. Not knowing."

Without the protective weight of her gun at her side, she's ready to assume the worst.

He squeezes her hand and says, "I don't like it either."

"At least we're all still together."

Wendy flinches at a loud thud. Then another. Somebody threw something heavy at the bus. It reminds her of the monster bashing their vehicle as they struggled to flee the Pittsburgh fire. She gasps and digs her nails into Sarge's hand, which he accepts without protest. The soldiers at the front stand and finger their rifles. The window across the aisle explodes, and angry shouting and dusty sunlight penetrate the bus. Wendy half stands in her seat and catches a glimpse of camping tents and people through the jagged hole.

"Take your seat, ma'am," one of the soldiers—a clean-shaven kid with large ears protruding from under his cap—tells her. "Please, it's for your safety."

Wendy sits and shakes her head in wonder.

"Volleyball," she says. "I saw some teenagers playing volleyball outside."

"That wasn't a ball that hit us. Somebody was throwing bricks or rocks. Something's wrong here."

"It can't be all wrong if kids are playing volleyball."

"People play volleyball in prison."

The bus stops. The driver kills the engine. They sit quietly for a while, waiting for something to happen. The heat is oppressive. The smell of diesel exhaust slowly dissipates, replaced by conflicting odors of cooking and open sewage. They hear a mother shouting at her child to be careful. Somebody plays a guitar.

The door opens. A woman enters the bus carrying a clipboard, her face partially obscured by a green bandana. Her blue eyes glitter against her sunburned forehead. She pulls the bandana down to reveal a young pretty face set in a bright smile.

Wendy grunts with surprise. The camp appears to be run by teenagers.

"I'm Kayley," the girl says. "And I'll be your orientation instructor."

☣

The survivors are led into a classroom inside a brick school building. Kayley stands at the front of the room while they take their seats. The window blinds are open to allow sunlight to fill the space and provide a view. Outside, several women take a smoke break while another inventories a pile of boxes.

Ethan pauses at the teacher's desk before finding a seat. His classroom was like this one, clean and neat but low on budget and behind the times in terms of technology. The main teaching method was lecture using a green chalkboard, erasers, and plenty of chalk. For a little excitement, maybe an overhead projector with transparencies. He remembers how much he loved the squeaky sound a stick of chalk made on the board as he wrote equations for his students. He loved everything about the job, in fact. That, and his relationship with his family, defined him.

How quickly things change.

How would you solve for x?

Answer: you try to kill it.

His finger throbs with pain. He pops another painkiller.

A part of him realizes he could start over. The camp appears to offer a second chance. If they provide schooling to kids, maybe he could even teach again. Putting his skills to work here is a duty as real as Wendy's wish that she were still a cop. One might think teaching kids math during the apocalypse would be a waste of time, but the opposite is true. Kids should continue to learn and prepare for the future. Otherwise, there is no future, and the war against Infection is already lost. The other way lies barbarism.

He'll never teach again, however. He knows this. Even if the plague were to end tomorrow, he still can't imagine it. That part of him is as broken as the world.

The truth is the only reason he's here is because of the slim chance he might find his family among the camp's residents. This hope, thin as it is, has become his strongest reality. Everything else is illusion. He'll keep searching until he finds them. He'll search forever. That's what he does now. That's who he is.

Todd flops into the desk next to him and slouches with a scowl. "I just can't get away, I guess."

"Ready for some algebra?" Ethan says with a wink.

"I liked algebra. It's school I hated."

A man walks into the room and talks quietly with Kayley for a few moments before leaving. Moments later, a group of people enter in a cautious daze.

"You are all survivors of Pittsburgh," she tells them. "You are not different from each other. You're all the same. At one time, you were neighbors. Welcome each other."

The survivors size each other up and nod before taking their seats. The newcomers are filthy and exhausted. One of them sobs quietly as she hugs a sleeping toddler against her chest. Another puts his head down on his desk and falls into a fitful sleep. Dust floats in the sunlight around them. They smell like ashes.

"Welcome," Kayley says. "Welcome to Camp Defiance. You are safe here, in this room. This is a safe place, and you're okay."

The survivors settle in and look at her hungrily.

She says: "After the Screaming, the Federal Emergency Management Agency established a series of forward operations posts across the country to coordinate Federal support of local authorities. Camp Defiance was one of them, although, back then, it was simply called FEMA 41."

After the Screaming turned into the Infection, she explains, the outpost was almost overrun, but word had gotten around about its existence, and people poured in from all over southern Ohio. Almost overnight, the outpost became an armed refugee camp and exploded in size. The refugees helped keep the camp going, and now it's run by a mixture of Federal, state and local government people and protected by a mixed bag of military units.

"Today, the camp has a population of more than a hundred thousand souls and is constantly growing." She pauses to let that sink in. "I worked in a refugee camp for the Peace Corps for two years overseas. The ideal size for a camp like this is twenty thousand. It's nothing short of a miracle this place grew as fast as it did and functions as well as it has. That it came to be at all."

Ethan suppresses the urge to whistle; a hundred thousand is a tiny fraction of the population in this region before Infection, but it represents a chance. Somewhere, in this teeming horde, his wife and baby girl might still be alive.

Kayley spends the next fifteen minutes describing how they'll be processed. Newcomers to the camp must go through a brief medical exam and register to receive resident cards. Food and water are collected at distribution centers. Skilled workers may be offered jobs by the government and paid with priority access to housing and bonus allotments of food and water. The camp also has a health center and scattered health posts, pest houses, cholera camp, schools, markets, and cremation pits.

"Does anybody have any questions so far?"

"I do," Ethan says. "What kind of records do you keep? I've got family missing."

Kayley nods. "Locating lost loved ones is a big priority for us. Tell the people at Registration while you're being processed, and they'll help you out. We keep a record of every person who has ever entered this camp. They also have contacts with other camps in Carollton, Dover, Harrisburg, and other places."

Satisfied, Ethan leans back in his chair.

Sarge stands. "I've got a question. What are you hiding here?"

Kayley smiles at him. Her face shows no signs of surprise.

☣

The survivors bristle at Sarge's tone. A moment ago, they were disoriented, listening to Kayley in a lethargic daze while struggling to absorb everything she said. Now they're alert and taut as deer that smell a predator in a sudden shift of breeze. They watch Sarge and Kayley closely, their hearts racing and their breath shallow as they once again, automatically, tread the tightrope between fight and flight.

After several moments, Kayley says, "Can you be more specific?"

Sarge grunts. "Well, for one, why'd you take our weapons?"

Wendy glares at Kayley, wondering the same thing and wishing she felt the reassuring weight of the Glock in her hand right now. She feels electrified by urgency and confusion. She has complete faith in Sarge's instincts, but he sprang this confrontation without telling her; she has no idea how to back him up.

"Sergeant Wilson, almost everybody in this camp is armed," Kayley is saying. "We all know that infection spreads like wildfire. If one person catches the bug, it might bring the entire camp down. We're on constant lookout for infection and must be ready to act quickly if we see it."

Sarge crosses his arms. "I'll ask again then. Why did you take ours?"

"Your weapons were taken for the time being because, quite often, newcomers don't take to orientation. We don't have the means to enable new residents to slowly transition from the dangerous world outside to the relatively safe oasis we've created here. Some people can't accept the sudden change and become upset and irrational."

"I can see why," Sarge says. "It's like a police state around here."

"Yes and no. We're actually rather thin on policing. Surely, you don't really think this camp could function without the consent of its residents. But it's true that we're a society that is under siege. There are certain responsibilities. It's different being here than out there on the road."

"If we're not prisoners, you'd let us leave, if that's what we wanted?"

"You're not prisoners, but neither can you simply come and go from the camp as you please, for obvious reasons. Every time somebody enters the camp, there's the possibility of infection or some other disease being imported. We can't allow that, unless, of course, you're an authorized scavenger."

"You're not answering my question."

"The simple answer is you can leave any time you like. But if you do, you can't come back. Is that a satisfactory answer?"

"We can leave with all our gear?"

"If a resident decides to leave, they can go with either what equipment and supplies they brought or its equivalent value, which is the law."

"What about our Bradley?"

Kayley's smile disappears, replaced by a hard line. "I think you mean *our* Bradley, Sergeant. That machine was manufactured for the Army and belongs to the people of the United States. You're a soldier, and if you personally try to leave, your superiors may let you go, or they may decide to shoot you for desertion. I don't know. But I can tell you for a fact that the people in charge here aren't going to let you drive out of camp with a multimillion-dollar piece of military hardware that could be used to save American lives."

"This is bullshit. It's a trap."

"The trap is in your mind, Sergeant Wilson."

Sarge turns to the other survivors and says, "Come on, we're leaving. They can't stop us."

None of the survivors move, not even Wendy, who believes Kayley explained the camp's position perfectly and now feels reassured rather than threatened. Sarge gapes at them, sweat pouring down his face, seemingly disoriented and unsure of what to do next. He bumps against his desk and knocks it over with a crash that makes the other survivors flinch.

"It's not safe here," he pleads.

Wendy stands and peers into his face.

He says quietly, just to her, "This is a *bad* place."

The man is visibly shaking.

"You're among friends here," Kayley says. "You're safe."

Wendy glares at her. "Could you shut the hell up, please?"

She returns her attention to Sarge, slowly reaching out until she touches his face gingerly. She holds his stubbled cheeks in her hands. "Tell me."

His eyes avoid hers until finally connecting. He takes a deep, shuddering breath. "I don't know. I'm scared."

"I've got you, baby," she tells him. "Look at me. Look at *me*."

The other survivors look away. Nobody judges him. They've all been where he is now. Everybody has post-traumatic stress disorder, or PTSD, these days, with its bad sleep, depression, guilt, anxiety, anger, hyper-vigilance, and fear. Wendy still can't sleep at night without flashing to the infected bursting howling into the station. She's amazed that after everything Sarge endured, it's now that he cracks, and here, where he's finally safe.

But she understands. The truth is none of the survivors is comfortable in this place. The sudden change from survival to safety—not just safety, but society, with rules and customs—is nothing short of a shock to the system. None of them fully trust it. Yet it's not evil. It is, in fact, their best chance at survival.

"I'm sorry," Sarge says.

Wendy now believes she understands why Anne didn't come with them to the camp.

We're all broken. None of us may belong here.

Holding Sarge's face in her hands, she remembers the man in the SUV during the morning of Infection, when Pittsburgh woke up to fratricide. Her station had already been overrun, and Wendy walked the streets alone, on foot, shrugging off people begging her for help. Cars snarled bumper to bumper all along the four lanes of North Avenue and were even stacked up on the sidewalk and jammed into the narrow median, their horns bleating like panicked sheep. Other vehicles raced through the trees in the adjacent park, skidding across the mud and going nowhere fast.

The infected ran among the vehicles in the jam, peering into the cars as if window shopping before punching in the glass with bloody knuckles. Wendy saw the infected swarm over a nearby wrought iron fence, emitting a communal howl that made her heart rate skyrocket and her legs turn to jelly. Though her conscious mind was still in pieces, it registered that Allegheny General was on the other side of that fence; the infected were still waking up and streaming out the hospital's doors.

Wendy drew her service weapon and fired once, twice. A man yelped and flopped off the fence, quickly replaced by another in a paper hospital gown, his legs smeared with his own shit.

People abandoned their cars and ran into the park swinging purses and briefcases. The traffic jam became a parking lot. She wheeled, distracted by the sickening sound of crumpling metal and a gunned engine straining against an impossible load.

The man drove a shiny red 4x4 SUV on a lifted suspension, three tons of glass and steel with an evergreen air freshener swinging from the rear view and a specialty license plate reading

XCESS over the standard *visitPA.com*. Panicking, he tried to ram his way out of the press of honking vehicles. The acrid stench of muffler exhaust and burning rubber filled the air. He backed up his vehicle, his face and his mouth working behind the windshield, and stomped his foot on the gas. He crashed the SUV into the car ahead of him, shoving it forward less than a yard and jolting himself with whiplash.

Recovering, he backed up again, yanked on the steering wheel, and roared into a Volkswagen Jetta in the right-hand lane at an acute angle, the collision twisting the frame and shattering the driver's side windows. The driver howled in shock and pain, trying to shield her face with her arms. As the SUV backed up again, crumpling the hood of another car behind it, an infected man pulled himself into the Jetta's open window, his gown flapping and his legs kicking in the air.

Wendy's stomach turned over, and she bent to spit a gob of bile. The mindless, brutish cruelty of the SUV driver and the rabid infected was making her physically sick. The driver had a cut on his forehead now and looked dazed. He revved the engine and bucked his vehicle forward into the car in front of the Jetta, shoving it sideways against the curb and bursting its windows in the sharp impact. The passenger door opened, and a woman emerged, wailing and pulling a screaming child out of the backseat. The air filled with a sweet maple syrup smell, ethylene glycol released by a broken radiator. Wendy swallowed hard against another urge to vomit.

"Halt," she said hoarsely. She raised her arm and shouted: "Stop it!"

She marched up to the SUV as the man stepped on the gas. She didn't flinch. Recognizing her uniform, he braked with a short screech, stopping the vehicle inches from her knees. He stared down at her through the window, panting for air. His eyes, slowly focused with understanding and regret, began to fill with tears.

The cop raised her gun and fired, punching three cobwebbed holes in the windshield. Smoke filled the cab and blood splashed across the glass.

Then she's back in the classroom, cupping Sarge's face and looking into his eyes.

Wendy knows what it's like to lose control.

"I've got you, baby," she says. "I've got you."

After a brief medical exam, Todd hurries into the processing center, a hot, confusing jumble of people and tables jammed together under various signs and flags in what used to be the school gym. People sit behind the tables, talking to applicants, while others sit on the floor ringing the room and fan themselves with pieces of cardboard marked with numbers.

A wave of sour body odor envelops him. It's so hot in the room that a mist of sweat hangs in the air, rising on beams of sunlight entering the space through dirty skylights. He spots Ethan at one of the tables but can't locate the other survivors. They must have gone through processing already, leaving him behind. He was last in line for the medical exam, and, apparently, he'd spent too much time in the bathroom taking the longest dump in his life sitting on a real toilet that actually flushed, surrounded by four walls in blissful privacy. His thoughts are jolted as a man shoulders him as he walks past, offering a muttered apology.

His first impression of the place is there's still a huge number of refugees entering the FEMA camp, but he soon realizes that all sorts of government business goes on here, from job applications to replacement of resident cards to reporting crimes and more. Some of the tables are run by sharp-eyed, clean-shaven men in business suits under American and other flags indicating various agencies of the Federal and Ohio state governments. Todd figures they're the complaints department. You go there and complain, and in return they give you bad news.

He takes a number, finds a spot on the floor, and fans himself while he waits. He watches Ethan, who has moved to another table, keeping the little stump of his finger elevated as he works the room. Probably looking for his dead wife and little girl. Todd is mentally flexible enough to accept that his father is dead or infected along with all the cubicle drones at the office where he worked, and his mother is definitely among the infected, having fallen during the Screaming. He feels sorry for Ethan, but living your life like a defective CD eternally skipping during your favorite song is not living.

Eventually, Todd's number is called, and he finds himself sitting at a picnic table across from a red-haired woman who looks at him like he just hit her in the face. Slapping an index card on the table in front of her, she takes down his information—name, where he lived, social security number, gender, age, height, eye color, nearest relations, and a brief medical history.

"You were in high school?" she says, pen poised above the card.

"Yes, ma'am," Todd answers, using the respectful tone he used with teachers.

"What grade?"

"Senior," he says. He's worried the woman will check up on him and realize he lied about that and his age. Then he notices the stacks of index cards tied with rubber bands being carted by the other bureaucrats and realizes he can pretty much say anything he wants, and there'd be no way anybody could confirm or deny it.

"Do you want to go back to school? We offer schooling here. You could get your diploma."

"No, thanks," he says sunnily, his brain working hard on how to defend that decision.

The woman shrugs, does not care. "Any job skills?"

"I've had jobs before but nothing that required skills. I'm really good with computers, though. What kind of skills are you looking for the most?"

"Psychotherapist."

He laughs.

She says, "I'm not kidding."

Todd opens his mouth, but she silences him by holding up her index finger, the universal sign for *wait a minute*. The woman pulls an old mechanical typewriter toward her and starts pecking at the keys with agonizing slowness, glancing frequently at the index card. She finally yanks a business card-sized piece of paper out of machine, stamps it with a seal and hands it to him with a thick manila envelope. He notices she typed his name wrong.

"This is your resident card." She explains that he will use it to obtain his rations, access the showers and medical services, and apply for other government help. "This is your information packet. In it, you'll find a recap of your orientation—a map of the camp, the rules you're expected to follow here, and a list of services and where to find them. There's currently a small surplus in shelters, so you don't have to build your own; your allotment is marked in yellow highlighter. This is your claim ticket so you can pick up the property you brought into the camp with you. And finally, here are two flea collars. Put one around each ankle. Keeps the lice away."

"Gross! I mean, thanks."

"Do you have any questions?"

"Just one. Do you have stores, or anything like that?"

"There are six open air markets. Four are where people sell pretty much anything. Another is for produce grown in the camp, and the last is for meat."

"What's the accepted currency?" he presses. "Is it a barter system, or is the dollar—"

The woman glances over his shoulder and yells, "*Twenty-one!*"

Todd stands, trying to think of something biting, but a family approaches, wild-eyed and holding out their cardboard number to the woman like an offering, and he tells himself she is not worth it.

You're not going to get me down, lady. I survived out there for weeks while you were in here sitting on your ass typing on index cards. I fought and killed to survive.

His mind flashes to Sarge standing in front of the hospital, spitting tongues of flame and smoke with his AK47 in the dark. He remembers throwing a Molotov into a mob of the infected. The Bradley smashed through the parked cars, its gun booming. He smiles.

"Ha," he says and walks away to find Ethan standing near one of the tables and wringing his hands. He asks how the search is going.

"Slow," Ethan says with a sad smile, but he appears happy to be trying, and this is something, Todd realizes. At least there is this.

"Where's everybody else?"

"The Army took Sarge and Steve away for debriefing. Wendy got a job as a cop and is heading to where they told her she could live. She gets priority housing, being a cop. And Paul is on his way to one of the food distribution centers. He got a job there passing out food."

"Well," Todd says, feeling awkward.

"How about you? You going back to school? They offer that here, you know."

"I don't really see the advantage of learning calculus," Todd says before catching himself. "Oh, sorry, man."

Ethan nods sadly. "It's okay. I don't see the point in teaching it anymore, either."

"I've got big plans, Ethan. I've got this stash—"

"One-oh-eight!" a voice cries from one of the tables.

Ethan perks up. "That's me."

"Well," Todd says with a frown. "I guess I'll be seeing you around."

"Right," Ethan says vacantly. "Take care of yourself, Kid."

Todd collects his duffel bag, weapon, and ammunition in another room and walks outside into hazy sunlight, feeling tickled and breathless with excitement.

I'm here. I made it.

The street in front of the school is filled with people. Sweating in their helmets, some bored soldiers glance at him before going back to talking among themselves. They barely look a day older than him, just beefy kids. Several children sit on the cracked sidewalk and draw with pieces of colored chalk. Another group of kids, orphans of Infection quickly going feral, pull a red wagon filled with empty plastic jugs and bottles. Whatever grass might have grown here is now gone, trampled into dried dirt that floats in the air as dust. A military five-ton rolls down the street, ignoring a stop sign and beeping at the lazy crowds. Several men work on a large machine, their tools and parts laid out neatly on a filthy white blanket. Dogs bark inside a mom-and-pop shop across the street converted into housing. A loudspeaker attached to an old telephone pole, dangling a tangle of wires, squawks instructions on how to avoid cholera, followed by an ear-splitting screech. A moment later, an old Britney Spears song starts playing, tinny and offering more nostalgia than entertainment in this time and place.

Todd is irritated at the other survivors. They couldn't even stick around to stay goodbye. *You're on your own again, old man. You were doing just fine before joining up with them. You were ninja, surviving on your own, as you've always done. You can do it again. The improbable umbilical cord wasn't meant to last. It was a relationship born of necessity, nothing more. Now it's time to be a nation of one again.*

He consults his photocopied map, a virtual city carefully drawn in madman scrawl, his to explore. He identifies the school, situated on a road that forms one of the camp's major arteries used for motorized transport between the central hub and the distribution and health centers. He finds his new home, a speck in one of the endless shantytowns. Then he locates the nearest general market, where he intends to launch his career as a trader.

The other survivors are haggard, tired, broken. *Just look at Sarge, the man who fought a horde of screaming infected by himself and saved our lives: damaged goods.* Todd is young and taut and much, much more resilient than he looks. If anything, the apocalypse has been almost kind to him. Already lean, he's starting to put on a little muscle and with it, more confidence. He feels powerful. He looks at the kids running by in packs and the soldiers passing around a cigarette and thinks: *My generation will survive this. Will be defined by it.*

And we will define the age in turn.

☣

Paul hitches a ride hanging onto the side of a garbage truck as it grinds down one of the camp's main arteries. The truck has been assigned to collect the dead for disposal. Its sides are decorated with crowded layers of outlandish graffiti, much of it incorporating grotesquely painted skulls and bones. He let the driver bum a cigarette and in return learned why the dead are burned instead of buried in pits outside the city. The reason, he was told, goes back to the camp's origins, when many people, raised on horror films, postulated the infected were zombies—hungry things that rose from the dead. Though it was quickly disproven, the practice stuck. Even if the people here want to bury the dead now, they can't. There simply isn't enough space for both the dead and the living.

A rock hits the side of the truck with a metallic boom that makes Paul flinch. Another sails by close to his head. The cab's passenger-side window rolls down and a rifle protrudes, carefully sighting on a target among the tents.

No more rocks are thrown at the vehicle.

The truck lurches over the potholes, trembling in its metal skin. It makes three stops to pick up bodies lying stiff in the sun, their faces pale and their skin flaccid and waxy under sheets of plastic. For years, Americans sanitized death. Few people actually saw the dead in their natural state, bloated and drawing flies and emitting stench. They saw them laid out on velvet in fine caskets, dressed up in their best clothes, preserved like Egyptians.

The truck finally slows in front of a large wood church. A hand reaches out the window and points to the front doors.

Paul jumps off and pounds the side of the truck to signal the driver that he can go. The hand waves back, and the truck continues on down the road.

Free of the truck's exhaust, the camp's ever-present smells of cooking, wood smoke, and sewage return with a vengeance.

He breathes deep, figuring he might as well start getting used to it.

The doors are open, and he walks in, eager to do something. He finds himself staring down the barrel of an M16 rifle.

"Where do you think you're going, Father?"

Paul frowns. "It's Reverend, not Father, and I'm going to the place where I've been assigned by the government to live and work."

"Let's see your papers."

The soldier studies his work papers while the rest of his squad glances at him curiously and then returns to their business. Paul ignores them and takes a look around. The church is filled with children sitting on every kind of chair in front of every kind of table imaginable. The pews are gone, probably hacked up for firewood. A long line of sunburned kids holding bowls, spoons, and mugs wait their turn to receive stew being ladled out of large vats on the altar in the domed apse, like a scene out of *Oliver Twist*. Their chatter fills the grand nave and rises up to the vaulted ceiling. They chew in the light of windows beautifully patterned with hand-stained glass.

A man in clerical garb approaches with his hand extended. "Welcome, sir." He's tall and skinny, his shoulders slightly stooped, and wears a neatly trimmed beard. "I'm Pastor Strickland. This is my church."

"Nice to meet you," Paul says. He retrieves his work papers from the soldier and shakes the man's hand warmly. "I'm Paul Melvin. These kids are all...?"

"That's right. Orphans of Infection."

"So many." Paul can't help but stare at them. He hasn't seen a happy, living child in weeks. Seeing so many here, eating good food in a safe place, warms his heart.

"These kids must be nourished and protected. They're our future. But they're still wild animals, most of them. Don't turn your back on them or leave your property unattended."

"I'll keep that in mind. But they seem pretty well behaved."

"They have an abiding respect for the supernatural," Strickland says with a smile. "They think if we find the right words, God will end Infection."

Paul grunts, pleased. "That's something I have in common with them. I'll have to ask them what words they think will work."

"I'm sorry, Paul. You won't be working here. You'll be working down the street at the FoodFair handing out rations to the campers. Hard work, and thankless at that. Is that a problem?"

Paul shakes his head. He would like to work with the children, but it doesn't matter. "I just came here to work. I have to wonder, though."

"Why do we need somebody like you to do that kind of work?"

"Something like that."

"Ah, well. I'll tell you. On a weekly basis, we hand out enough food to give each camper about twenty-one hundred calories a day. They get wheat, beans, peas, vegetable oil, fortified food such as a corn soya blend, some salt and sugar. If the camp gets its hands on some cattle, we can distribute a little beef, but that's not all that often. The campers get no spices, and most people can't afford that kind of thing at the markets. Our fare will keep you alive, but it's monotonous, as you can imagine, and people get mad after a while eating the same old thing. Here's something else. We try to give rations to women only because they're more likely to pass it on to other family members instead of selling it to buy something else. That naturally produces conflicts. Plus there's the simple fact that we work for the government here, essentially, and a lot of people are resentful."

"I saw people throwing rocks at a garbage truck today."

"They're less likely to throw them at people in our profession," Strickland says. "Does that answer your question simply enough? A lot of people have turned away from God because of what happened, but they haven't gotten around to blaming us for it yet. Most of the campers see us for what we are: people trying to help."

"That's what I want to do," Paul tells him. "I want to help."

"Then you've come to the right place. This camp needs all the help it can get."

☣

Wendy enters the police station, a graffiti-covered building crowded with shouting people arguing with powerful, burly men wearing a variety of motley uniforms, from correctional facilities officers to private sector rent-a-cops. The building smells like angry men testing each other, a scent she knows well. There's an atmosphere of simplicity and brute force here. The walls are plastered with wilting public health notices, camp edicts, duty rosters, and poorly rendered carbon copies of missing persons sheets. Two bearded officers shove through the crowd, loading shotguns. Dogs sleeping on the floor raise their heads sharply as the men tramp out of the station. A man wearing a STEELERS cap, horseshoe mustache and a ratty black CASHTOWN FIRE DEPARTMENT T-shirt directs her to where Unit 12 bunks, the cost for this information a degrading moment of sexual appraisal. He doesn't care why she wants to know; he probably thinks she's somebody's woman paying a visit. He spits tobacco juice into a soda can as he watches her leave.

She walks down a corridor that smells like an ashtray. The administrative area has apparently been converted into housing for another unit; off-duty officers pad in and out of the rooms barefoot and in their underwear, scratching their bellies as they watch her struggle past with her duffel bag. The hallway is partly blocked by boxes of miscellaneous equipment. She wonders if Sarge is okay, surprised by the sudden sensation of butterflies in her gut. He seemed fine when he left with Mattis, but she's worried about him and wonders when she'll see him again.

The reality of the situation strikes her just before she reaches her quarters. The camp is overcrowded, and space is obviously at a premium. People are jammed everywhere, and skilled workers are expected to live in or near their base of operations. Unit 12 bunks in the detention area; she'll likely be living in a jail cell. Pondering the irony of it, Wendy enters the space, her foot crunching on an empty beer can, and takes in her new quarters.

She was right. Eight men occupy the detention area's processing space and six holding cells. A man snores loudly in a bunk, while another sits next to him on the floor wearing a pair of boxer shots and cleaning a rifle. A mustached man smokes a foul-smelling cigar while filling a plastic cup from a water cooler. Another has a small Coleman going; she smells coffee brewing, rich and strong, which makes her feel strangely homesick. A gray-haired man stops reading his book and peers at her over his reading glasses, a toothpick clenched in his teeth. Wendy becomes aware they're all looking at her with their lean stubbled faces. Good ol' boys. She puts on her game face and returns their gaze. Her heart soars at the opportunity to be a cop again, but she's now wondering what it's going to cost her.

"I'm looking for Ray Young," she says. "The unit sergeant."

"And you would be?" the man with the book says.

"Officer Wendy Saslove, reporting to the unit."

The man glances at the others before chuckling. "How about that," he says, chewing on his toothpick.

"Christ, Jonesy, I could have sworn she was one of yours," a voice behind her says.

Wendy recognizes the mildly sardonic tone. She turns and sees the man with the STEELERS cap filling the doorway, smiling and holding his soda can.

"I'm, uh, working on that, Ray," the young man called Jonesy says. He licks his hand and straightens his hair.

Ray spits into the can and says, "Well, Officer Saslove, I guess that's your room right there." He gestures to one of the holding cells.

"Thank you, Sergeant."

Wendy picks up her bag and takes it to the cell. The toilet is dry as bone, and the sink has been removed. Instead, she has a washing bucket with soap and sponge. A shit bucket with a bag of lime and roll of TP. The bunk looks serviceable enough and will actually rate as four-star comfort after sleeping on the ground for the past few weeks. The walls are plastered with photo spreads of big-chested blondes; those will obviously have to go. The main problem will be privacy in this male zoo. She rolls out her sleeping bag on the bed and opens her duffel, noticing for the first time the name DEVEREAUX written on it in black marker.

After she unpacks, Wendy realizes the sergeant followed her and is standing in the doorway to the cell. The others watch closely, wearing half-smiles.

"Officer Saslove, if I may," he says. "It's not that I mind having a pretty face like yours hanging around, but I look at you and I wonder: what are you doing in my unit playing cop?"

She ignores him as she pins her badge to her belt. Ray squints at it and adds, "So what were you then, a meter maid?"

One of the other cops walks up to the cell and leans against the bars, peering in with a smile.

"Hey, I'm talking to you." Ray crumples the soda can in his hand. The room tenses and Wendy with it. She will eat the sergeant's shit; she's the rookie here, so she expects some unit hazing. But if any of them touches her, if that's how things work in this shithole, she's going to break bones. She pulls on her Batman belt, taking comfort in the weight of the Glock on her hip. She pulls her collapsible ASP baton out of the bag next and slides it into place, flashing back to its last use at the hospital.

"Where'd you get that gear, Saslove?"

"From the Pittsburgh Police Department."

He glowers at her. "Is that so? How'd you get it, exactly?"

"It's standard issue, Sergeant. I worked patrol for nearly a year."

"You'd better be telling me the truth, so help me. Are you shitting me?"

Wendy stares back at him, saying nothing.

He takes a step forward and she places her hand on the handle of her baton, already planning where she's going to hit him and how hard.

"Jesus Christ," Ray says gently, with something like awe.

The other cops gather around. "Pittsburgh," they whisper among themselves, almost chanting the word. "She's a cop." One of them reaches and touches her shoulder lightly, while another holds out a warm can of beer with a friendly wink.

"Welcome, Officer Saslove," Ray says, his eyes big and watery. "And God bless you."

☣

The open air market is set up at the site of the old Cashtown Flea Market on the outskirts of town and serves as the closest thing to a mall the camp's residents can get. Now situated in the middle of a vast shantytown, the market's boundaries are roughly marked on the west by Christmas lights and light bulbs hanging from wires strung between poles, and on the east by one of FEMAville's many foul canals. These canals were once part of a medieval-style defense system of staked trenches dug around the old town by the original refugees to stop the infected, but were slowly absorbed by growth, the stakes removed and burned for firewood. Wood planks form bridges over the rank canals, now filled with sewage and garbage and even a few bodies, some always burning, day and night. Solar landscape lights thrust into the dirt mark its edges to ensure night travelers don't fall in. The canals are deadly; if drowning in the toxic sludge itself doesn't kill you, any number of diseases will.

Todd wanders awkwardly among the crowds of people browsing the wares stacked on the tabletops, as if testing his legs on the deck of a ship. He's not used to crowds. He's especially not used to crowds where almost everybody is carrying a gun, axe, hammer, bat, or other weapon. The people here are angry and desperate and stink of fear. He feels exposed, vulnerable, a little disoriented with something like vertigo—that weird sense that everybody knows each other and is aware of you, and that you don't belong. It's high school all over again.

Come on, old man. Nobody here gives a crap about you. They have their own problems. Boy, do they ever.

The vendors near him shout out products and prices while others haggle with customers or chase away children and beggars. The products include batteries, condoms, cigarettes, sewing thread, spices, seasoned firewood. Commodities, rarities, and plenty of junk. The prices are based on whatever the seller wants—dollars, gold, services in kind, barter—and the market appears to be thriving. Like the earth, trade abides. Barter appears to be most popular form of exchange; one merchant sells playing cards, board games, and dice but accepts only cigarettes as payment.

Nearby, a line of people wait their turn to get into one of a battery of portable toilets. They erupt into spontaneous applause as a truck drags an emergency generator down the road. Electricity means progress. Two men in orange jumpsuits pull the bottom section out of one of the portable toilets, where the waste reservoir is located, mount it on a wheeled cart, and push it up a ramp onto the back of a wagon drawn by a horse.

Todd takes in every detail with a keen eye. More than anything, the people here want and need electricity. That, and plumbing. In the shanties where he lives, he saw people everywhere using car batteries, sometimes wrapped together in banks, to power DC devices as well as AC devices using adapters. One enterprising mechanic has two cars wired together with jumpers and juices up failing batteries as a service. As for water, the only option is to wait hours in line at a government water tank.

As he explores the booths, Todd takes notes of merchants and what they buy and sell. Water purifiers, baby supplies, vitamins, tampons, propane, garden seeds. Ammo, sugar, porn mags, bug spray. Little bits of comfort and convenience and civilization.

Pieces of an America that has fallen down. Products from other countries that no longer exist. Consumable relics of a past age.

Todd has a lot of DC-powered appliances from the truck stop store that could make life much easier for at least a few people here. They're heavy, though, and liable to break. He wants to dump them in exchange for a different product. The most successful merchants, he notices, specialize in a particular item that everybody needs. The item should be small and lightweight to be easily portable. Something like cigarettes would be ideal, but then he'd need to be constantly on guard against addicts. Sugar and coffee would be good, but the sellers are dealing them in plastic baggies, creating a risk of spoilage due to water or infestation. Garden seeds should be a popular item right now, but he doesn't know a thing about gardening.

Something like candles, on the other hand, would be perfect.

"So what are you supposed to be?"

The girl is talking to him. Time slows as their eyes connect. His heart takes a flying leap. She is a petite, fiery thing, her skin white as a sheet, with long, curly red hair that rages about her head like a lion's mane. She looks about seventeen or eighteen. She has a sly mouth and a button nose and laughs easily, her blue eyes sparkling, betraying an appealing brand of feminine insanity.

"I'm Todd."

"I'm Erin. I asked you what you're doing."

"I'm going to be a merchant. I have some stuff I'd like to sell."

"Really? You should definitely hire me then."

Todd laughs. "And why should I do that?"

"You're new. I can show you how things work around here so you don't get conned."

He stops laughing. "How do you know I'm new here?"

Erin flashes him a glance that tells him she thinks it's obvious. "Do you know about the gangs? They'll try to collect a tax from you."

"How much should I give them?"

"Nothing, you dodo bird," she says. "It's just a con. If the sellers paid every gang what they asked, there'd be no market. They can't really do anything to you. The sellers look out for each other, and everybody here is armed to the teeth. The sellers are the biggest gang of all. Now, aren't you glad I told you that?"

"Yeah," he admits.

"You need somebody. Every day, you have to collect water and firewood and cook your food. Once a week, you pick up your rations, and they let you take a shower. That doesn't leave much time to be a seller. All these sellers have somebody helping them out."

He has to agree she makes a good argument.

"You could do all that for me?" he asks her.

She shrugs. "I'm doing it anyway for me. Might as well get paid."

"And what do you want in return?"

Erin smiles as she leans in close. His heart pounds.

"I want in on the action," she whispers close to his ear.

☣

The school gym is hot, crowded, and noisy. The tired volunteers and professional bureaucrats manning the tables feverishly write and type information that nobody will read and hand out poorly mimeographed information that few will actually use. The main thing people seem to come here for is decisions, but they appear to be in short supply. After days of working the system to try to find his family, Ethan is beginning to see the processing center as a flea market for dying government. One big going-out-of-business sale. Waiting for his number to be called again by the records people, he wanders among the tables, finally pausing in front of a clean-cut young man under a U.S. flag and a sign that says, ASK ME ABOUT RESETTLEMENT.

"Would you like to hear about Resettlement?" the man asks him.

Ethan shrinks back and shakes his head.

"It's all part of the President's policy for a fresh start," the man says. He is clean shaven and wears a business suit with a neatly ironed white shirt and blue tie. "When the pandemic is over, we're going to have to put Humpty Dumpty back together again. This means people who still have assets out there, somewhere, will recover them. Those who lost everything will be given the means to start a new life. This is Resettlement in a nutshell."

"You're going to do what, then? Tell me where to live?"

"Only if you sign up," the man says with a smile. "If you enroll in the Resettlement Program, we'll match you with a good community and give you a job as close to your old profession as possible, respecting of course your preferences, special needs such as any health problems, and surviving social networks. But of course the final decision is yours."

Ethan laughs. "And the incentive is you're going to give everybody a house and a car?"

"Everything you need to start a new life."

"How can the country afford this?"

"The nation is filled with dispossessed property, sir, previously owned by individuals and corporations. Property owned by individuals who die intestate will be passed on to the nearest surviving heirs in accordance with state and local laws. But in cases where there are no identifiable heirs, the property will escheat to the Federal Government for redistribution."

"My God," Ethan says.

The man behind the table is talking about a massive seizure of property on an unprecedented scale, to be distributed to the survivors.

"Not God," the man says. "The Wade Act."

This Wade Act will conflict with numerous state and local laws. With the amount of power and assets on the table, it might even be enough to trigger a civil war.

Ethan doesn't care about any of this, however.

"I'm here trying to find my missing family."

"Resettlement is about looking to the future, but there will be a full accounting. Every person, every dollar, every asset. If your family is alive, you'll find them, and you'll be able to live together again under Resettlement."

"Good."

The man holds out a clipboard. "Just fill out these forms."

"Let me ask you a question first."

"Of course."

"You mentioned a full accounting. How full will that accounting be?"

"The fullest."

"I'm speaking of the dead. We all have blood on our hands."

"Don't ask; don't tell, sir." The man smiles, still holding out the clipboard.

Ethan stares at it longingly. "Perhaps later."

The man frowns and drops the clipboard back on the table.

Ethan adds, "Sorry."

"You know, we'll survive this. It's okay to hope."

Ethan says, "Not yet, it isn't."

☣

Angry, shell-shocked, and dressed in filthy clothes, mobs of people wander among the densely packed tents and shanties built on grass long trampled into dust.

Ray says this place is going to blow.

"It's fucked up, but it works—barely. And for now. You know the old saying about America always being three days of lost meals away from a revolution? Here, it's a matter of hours."

Wendy nods. "What are the biggest community problems?"

Ray barks a laugh. "Everything. Wendy, we got people packed in here like sardines. The place is an open sewer that serves gruel for breakfast, lunch, and dinner. We have to truck in clean water for half the camp. Outside supply is obviously touch and go. Then there's the constant threat of fire, disease, and of course Infection. Everybody's carrying a gun. We got gangs, prostitution, drugs, con games, rapes, murders, suicides, you name it. All right?"

Just two weeks ago, this place didn't exist. There was a sleepy small town here in the middle of eastern Ohio. Outlying farms. Open fields and woods. All of it now absorbed into a camp with the same population as Independence, Missouri and the poverty of Calcutta, growing with the speed and resilience of a weed.

"I get the picture."

"Don't worry about them. Worry about you. The main thing you got to realize is there are a lot of unhappy people in this place who had everything, and now they have nothing. They're mad as hell and looking for somebody to blame. Every once in a while, some asshole gets an itch to take a shot at a cop. So you keep a sharp eye out there."

"I will, Sergeant."

"My name is Ray. Use it. Damn it, Wendy, you should be calling the shots, not me."

"I'm just fine with the way things are, Ray. So when does my training start?"

The man snorts. "This is your training. You got a question?"

"Okay. How are arrests processed for trial? Where's the courthouse?"

"Stop right there," Ray says. He takes off his grimy STEELERS cap and wipes sweat from his forehead. "I guess I need to make a few more things crystal clear. Wendy, I know you were a cop back in the real world, but this is the far side of the moon. We just don't have what you want here. It's frontier justice. We're holding this ground by force."

They approach long lines of people waiting their turn to fill their jugs at a bright yellow water tanker guarded by a squad of kid soldiers with M16 rifles. A cloud of dust hangs over the scene. Ray changes the subject, pointing out landmarks on what will become her night beat—shower facilities, health tent, food distribution center, and a feeding center where new mothers can breastfeed and collect extra rations. The latrine area, a large battery of portable toilets, is especially dangerous at night. Women who come here after dark are often raped. Men too, sometimes. As a result, many people drop their waste into the nearest canal.

"So what am I supposed to do if I see a crime? Just rough them up?"

"If you want." Ray stuffs a pinch of chew in his cheek. "Or you could take them to the Judge, who will probably give them hard labor such as shit disposal. They get an electronic bracelet that tags them. It's pretty much the same punishment for any offense, so only bring in the hard cases you really want punished. The worst offenders get put outside the wall."

"What about proof? Is it just my word?"

"Yup. That's how it is here. You got to understand, though, that our main role is not to solve and punish crimes. The locals mostly do that for us. The people here all watch out for each other. They usually know if somebody commits a crime and sort it out themselves without our involvement. We're not really in the justice business. Our job is to keep the peace."

"We're not cops," Wendy says. "We're armed thugs."

"Yup. You want out?"

She doesn't even have to think about it. "No."

"Our unit's shift starts around sundown. Then we get to patrol a Third World shantytown in the dark for twelve hours. Memorize your beat, don't get lost, don't fall in the canals, don't get killed. Especially don't get killed. We need people like you, Wendy."

"I'm nothing special, believe me. Especially for this work."

Ray stops and spits a gob of tobacco juice into the dust. "You don't understand. We need people like you to *survive*. Listen: one day, this thing is gonna end, and things will get back to normal. To do that, we'll need people who can remember what normal was and make things right again. There aren't many cops walking the earth right now. Every time one dies, all those memories of how things used to be dies with them."

"I'll live, Ray. I survived out there for weeks. I'll make it in here. This is nothing."

"Just know the original cops in this town were good men, and they died trying to hold this place when it was first being built. Not all of them died by the hands of the infected."

Wendy smiles at him, touched by his concern. "I promise I'll be careful."

"You do that, Wendy," Ray says. "You do that."

Speakers mounted on poles in the area squawk, *We are winning; ask what you can do to help*, before screeching loudly and resuming a tinny rendition of Madonna's "Like a Virgin."

Paul leaves the FoodFair supermarket, dog tired and enjoying the night air after hours of handing out food packages, shifting boxes, and mopping floors. The food distribution center has no air conditioning, and keeping the camp supplied is hot, sweaty work. His tattered clerical uniform, recently cleaned and patched, is already getting ripe again. He could use a shave and a haircut. But he did good today. He digs into his pocket for his wilted pack of Winstons and lights one up with a sigh. The cool air feels good. He's happy for the opportunity to finally rest. After his smoke, he'll brush his teeth and hit the sack with the other workers, lying on his old bedroll with bags of rice as a mattress.

The camp is still noisy but is slowly settling down for the night. The parking lot of the FoodFair is covered in tents and campers and people huddled around their cooking fires. He takes another drag and exhales, enjoying the relative peace. He remembers that the last time he had a cigarette like this, Pittsburgh was on fire. The infected streamed through the cars. He threw a Molotov. He cut somebody in half with his Remington. The Bradley roars in his head.

He stills his mind with a short prayer of thanks that he remains alive to do this good and useful work. Maybe God doesn't want to listen, but being omnipresent, the Almighty can't help but hear it.

"Is that you, Paul?"

Paul sees a figure sitting on a bench and approaches. It's Pastor Strickland. The man holds an old photo in one hand; the other is cupped around the flame of a candle.

"Do you think it's impossible to still love somebody who is infected, brother?" Strickland asks him.

"No. I think it's not only possible, but unavoidable. But they hate us in return. That's the hardest thing to bear."

Strickland rubs tears from his eyes with the palm of his hand. "Loving them is just as hard." He adds, "You did good work today, Paul."

"Thank you."

"This means something to you, doesn't it? The work, I mean."

"It's the only way I know how to be me," Paul answers, surprising himself with the sudden insight. He wants to think about it more, but his tired mind can't hold onto the threads.

"There will be a march within the next few days. A march of Christians trying to make things right around here. There's more that can be done working together than by one man alone. You might want to give a listen to what they have to say. I'll be there too."

Paul slaps the back of his neck to kill a mosquito. "I'll do that."

They pass the next few moments in silence. Paul finishes his smoke and grinds it out on the asphalt with his boot. Strickland blows out his candle. A dog howls in the distance.

"Can I tell you something, brother?" the pastor says quietly in the dark. "Can I speak to you as a man of the cloth? Will you hear a short confession?"

"Of course."

"I always wondered if you could be a Christian and cry at a funeral. I mean, if somebody is going to Heaven, shouldn't we be celebrating? Shouldn't that be a happy day? It's the same here. The world is dying. Why are we so sad? Why do we cling to this miserable life? Maybe this is it, Paul. Maybe the Lord is calling us all home. If so, why do we resist the call? Why are we fighting God's will? And why does it feel so horrible? Why does it taste like ashes? Why does it fill us with sadness?"

Paul has no answer, but he understands the essential question. He has asked himself the same question in the past.

Sara would have an interesting answer. His mind flashes to the battle between the infected and the mob and what happened after the infected overran the last knot of fighters: sketchy images of himself walking down the road, returning home to his wife. But he can't remember what happened after that. He's beginning to worry that he may have killed her.

☣

Ethan runs between the shanties, his finger itching and throbbing. He hears his pursuers shouting to each other. He believes he has lost them.

The woman was telling him the Marines landed in New Jersey when her friends noticed what he was wearing.

He still wore scrubs from the hospital—the pants, anyway.

They thought he was a doctor.

Ethan spent the last few days at the processing center trying to locate his family, sleeping on the floor and living on handouts. The arrangement wasn't so bad. The school still has electricity and plumbing, the government's way of demonstrating its strength. In some ways, he has been living in luxury compared to many people in the camp.

They sat on folding chairs, fanning themselves with their cardboard numbers. The woman told him she heard the Marines landed in New Jersey. He already heard the rumor several times while waiting in the processing center. The Marines established bases along the coasts, and the Army is striking inland, reinforcing the refugee camps and using them as forward operations bases in the campaign to retake the country.

It sounded a bit wishful, to say the least.

"If it's true, then where are they? Why aren't they here?" Ethan asked and didn't bother listening to the answer. Rumors about the Army held no interest for him. All that mattered was the search.

While the woman continued talking, he noticed how attractive she was. He realized that he could always move on. He could find somebody else and start a new family.

He didn't want to do that. What was it Paul said to him when they talked about the people who left behind photos of their loved ones? *I wouldn't even know how*, he said when asked if he could ever let go of those he left behind. Right.

Thinking about Paul triggered memories of hours sitting in the hot dim belly of the Bradley fighting vehicle, rolling through a dying city on screaming treads.

The memories made him feel oddly homesick.

Ethan was wondering how the other survivors were coping when the woman's friends approached. They noticed he was wearing scrubs and asked if he was a doctor. They had a sick friend, and they were there to try to get him placed on the list for surgery—a service provided only to the most needy cases in this time of scarcity, as so many medical professionals were either killed or infected. The hospital sent them here, only to be told by the government to return to the hospital.

They reminded him that it was against the law for doctors to avoid work. Their eyes were gleaming, desperate.

When he told them he wasn't a doctor, they asked if he'd been a hospital patient. How could he have survived when the screamers rose from their beds? Maybe he had the disease but didn't know it. Was he a carrier? Was he infecting all of them even now?

Ethan doesn't remember how things became violent. His memories blur at that point. He may have lashed out at them first; his mind simply blanked out. He became aware of shacks flying plastic, grim faces staring at him from doorways and over the flames of cooking fires. Lawn ornaments, hanging laundry, buckets, plastic jugs. He knocked something over. Curses filled the air.

He remembers when he used to be a pacifist. At school, kids would occasionally fight, and he'd have to get between them and break it up. He hated doing it. Sometimes he'd have night terrors over getting punched by a kid. In these visions, he would lose control, lash out, and lose everything.

A truck rumbles alongside, filled with men laughing down at him. A brown giant in T-shirt and jeans stands and shouts, "Hey you! You want a job for the day?"

Better to ride than run. He nods, gasping for breath, remembering that horrible day in the department store, as he ran blindly among the mannequins.

Calloused hands reach down and pull him up into the truck.

"*¿Qué onda?*" they ask him.

He sits on the trembling bed of the truck as it lurches over the potholes. One of the men hands him a bottle of water. He takes a drink and winces at the metallic taste. He hands it back.

"You got a trade?" the giant says to him.

"I was a teacher. Now I just kill people."

The men laugh, ringing him with their bearded faces. They spit over the side. He can smell onions on their breath. Some of them speak English, while others chatter in Caló, an argot of Mexican Spanish common in the Southwest. Somebody passes around a flask, and he smells distilled alcohol, probably made from the wheat and rice distributed in the weekly ration.

The truck stops in a cloud of dust in front of a large barn. The men jump out. The building is being used as a slaughterhouse. Cattle pace around a holding pen, agitated by the smell of blood. Draped in plastic garbage bags, butchers work on animals hung upside down by their hind legs. Ethan watches them drain the bodies then remove the head, feet, hide, and internal organs. The ground is soaked with blood.

The giant tells Ethan the beef is cut, wrapped, and sent out immediately to the food distribution centers. The men here are paid in meat. A lot of it ends up in the market, bought and consumed fast before bacteria take hold. Most refugees put it into an eternal stew they keep continuously bubbling over fire along with rice and anything else they can find, such as wild onions and beans. The bones are fed to the camp dogs—pets brought by the refugees who now can no longer afford to feed them—whose presence is tolerated by the authorities because their hatred of the infected makes them good sentinels. The fat is used to manufacture soap, candles, and biodiesel.

Other slaughterhouses in the camp process chickens, sheep, pigs. This one, the giant says, handles only cattle—steers and heifers mostly. The men here know cattle, how to stun them with a hammer, how to cut their throats and drain their blood with a knife. How to strip the carcass.

"So what do we do?" Ethan says.

"We move the cattle that comes into the camp into the pens."

"From where?"

"The truck pulls up over there."

"And we move the cattle about fifty feet into the pens? That's it?"

The giant grins down at him. "That's it. We were told some trucks are coming in today. Here comes one now."

The massive tractor trailer comes to a halt near the holding pens. Inside, the cattle bellow sadly.

"*Águila*, boys," the giant says. He winks at Ethan. "Sharp eyes. Like an eagle."

The men take their weapons and form a semicircle around the rear of the truck. Two men clamber up and tie a nylon net in front of the trailer's doors. The driver, sweating in a camouflage cap and hunting vest bulging with shotgun shells, gets out and leans against the cab.

"What do you want me to do?" Ethan says.

"*Caile*. I want you to stand right here, *bolillo*."

"Do I need a weapon too?"

"We protect you."

The giant moves to the doors, removes the bolts and flings them wide. He quickly steps out back and to the side. A wave of heat pours out of the trailer. Ethan winces at the rich smell of dung. Lowing, the cattle jostle and raise their heads. Their eyes gleam at him from the dark.

Ethan wonders why nobody is doing anything. Two of the men continue to hold the net taut. He realizes the others have moved away from him, stepping back from the trailer.

"*A ponemos chancla*," one of the men whispers behind him.

The creature lunges hissing out of the dark, claws outstretched. Ethan cries out in fear and revulsion as it smashes into the net and plunges to the ground at his feet, shrieking and straining and reaching for him. A massive stinger protrudes from between its legs and stabs at the dust. The men surround the thing with spears. They shout obscenities in multiple languages as they thrust their weapons into the monster, which thrashes and keens.

Finally, the thing lies still, dead. The men continue to stab it until it becomes a featureless pile of road kill.

"*Mono*," one of Chicanos says to Ethan. He draws his finger across his throat. "Jumpers."

Ethan shakes his head, trying to clear it of the blind terror he felt when the thing sprang out of the dark. And rage at being used as bait.

"Now you are one of us," the giant says with a grin. "*Machín*."

Ethan holds up his finger. "I was already one of you."

The giant's face goes pale. He nods, transfixed by the jagged stump.

Ethan stares at the thing lying dead on the ground. The men spit on it.

"So what happens next?"

"Now we check the cattle for infection, *vato*."

They lead the cattle into a special quarantine pen. Two of them are infected. They're easy to spot: thin, silent, listless, staggering a little when forced to walk. A heifer has one of the monkey things growing out of its side, while a steer has two, both on its right flank.

"Jumpers," the giant says. "Little fuckers."

The infected cattle are separated, killed, and dragged to a large smoking pit behind the barn. The heat rises from the scarred ground in blistering waves. Charred legs stick out of the blackened piles of meat, slowing crumbling into ash blowing away in the wind.

There, the dead cattle are burned with all of the others.

☣

Todd lights a candle in his small, sweltering one-room shack and stares at its intense glow. *This candle is possibly the only beautiful thing in this entire horrible place.*

Candles would be an ideal specialty as a merchant. Everybody needs candles. They're simple, small, and necessary. The only thing to watch out for is breakage. That, and a match shortage. He might have to sell matches too.

But he's not going to buy and sell candles.

He has an idea he believes will make him rich. He remembers Philip telling him a good businessman buys low and sells high. But how do you do this with a barter system?

The answer may be that you acquire lots of something that is almost worthless now and sell it later on when it becomes virtually priceless.

Winter clothing, for example.

A few people sell winter gear in the market, mostly for scrap value and as substitute pillows and stuffers for bedrolls. Coats, hats, scarves, gloves, sweaters.

Almost nobody here believes Infection will last until winter. They have been here for less than two weeks, and many of them have no idea what things are like outside now. They believe the rumors the Army is coming to save them. They believe the government propaganda that things are getting better.

Things are not getting better. They are getting much, much worse. The people here will be in for a rough winter. If Todd can build up a big supply of winter clothes, he can trade them for pretty much anything he wants. He'll be a rich man.

"Knock, knock," a voice says from the doorway.

"Hey, Erin," he says with a grin. "Come on in. Welcome to my humble abode."

The girl walks into his shack and looks around.

"Humble is right. *Yeesh.*" She holds up a plastic baggie. "I scored some weed. It's not very good, but it gets the job done. You want to get high?"

Todd looks at the bag. "Okay, I guess."

Erin sits on the ratty carpet covering the dirt floor and rolls a joint. "I am in dire need of entertainment. My need is *dire*. You know, before everything went to shit, I was going places. I was one ugly duckling as a kid. And then I got older, and I wasn't ugly anymore. Just like that: suddenly, I was popular. I had like eight hundred friends on Facebook. Then the bug comes along, and I'm cut off from the world. Sometimes, I feel like I don't even exist anymore."

Todd watches her come up for air, but she says nothing more. She lights her joint and tokes on it. She hands it to him, and he kisses it, taking little puffs and wondering about the strange strong smell of it.

"I used to do a lot of war-gaming with these college guys," Todd offers tentatively. "I'm wondering if there are any war-gaming clubs around here. You know, *Warhammer 40,000...*"

Erin stares at him. His voice trails off. Time appears to slow. He coughs loudly on the smoke.

She smiles and beckons the joint to return. "I don't know anything about that stuff. Can we light another candle?"

"Sure," he says with relief.

"Cheer this place right up. How about beer? You got any alcohol?"

"No, but I have some candy, if you're interested."

"Oh *God*, yes."

Chewing on Gummi Bears with an expression approaching bliss, she asks him what things are like on the outside. He tells her about escaping his house during the first day of Infection, surviving on his own, finding other survivors. Riding in the belly of the Bradley, spilling out to fight and scavenge. The stories are so fantastic that instead of embellishing them, he tries to downplay their drama, afraid she'll accuse him of making it all up.

Erin stares at him wide eyed. "I wish *I* had done all that." Her eyes gleam in the candlelight.

"I'm not sure you would. We came very close to dying—well, almost every day."

"Man, it's so *cool*. You're like some kind of superhero."

"Um," he says.

"Is that how you got that wound on your arm?"

Todd remembers the worm monster lunging out of the dark, its shark-like jaws snapping.

"Yeah," he says gloomily. He covers the bandage with his hand. "So how about you? What's your story?"

"I've been here almost since the beginning."

"What happened?"

"I came to the camp with my dad, and I got bored," she mutters. Then she brightens. "Let's play truth or dare."

"Okay."

"I'll go first. Go ahead, Todd. Ask me."

"Um, truth or dare?"

"Truth," she announces.

"All right." Todd's not sure if he's high or not from the joint, but he wants to think he is. "Okay, what's the most embarrassing thing that ever happened to you?"

"Oh my God, I've got a *great* answer to that one." She starts laughing, and Todd smiles along. "One time, in study hall, me and my friends were updating the status on our Facebook pages, right? I had to run to the ladies' due to some women's trouble. That night, my Blackberry started ringing nonstop with these guys wanting to do some really gross things to me. Turns out I'd left myself logged on to Facebook, and my jerk friends wrote as my status that I love to give blowjobs, with my phone number."

She laughs loudly while Todd smiles politely, wondering why she finds something so cruel to be so funny.

"Oh, man," she adds. "That happens to everybody sooner or later, right? Okay, it's your turn. Truth or dare?"

"Truth," he says, hoping she won't ask him the same question.

"When was the first time you did it with a girl?"

Todd stammers briefly before inventing an elaborate story about his junior prom and how he scored with his date in the backseat of his friend's car.

His voice trails off. She can tell he's lying.

"It's okay," she says.

His mind scrambles in search of something light and witty to say to recover the mood, but none is needed; Erin deftly rescues him.

"Want to see one of my cheers, Todd? A really good one?"

"Okay," he tells her, feeling overwhelmed.

Erin jumps onto her feet, shakes off a wave of laughter, and then stands erect with her arms stiff and muscles tight.

"Sharp and snappy. One, two, three, here it is: Go Cougars!" She claps to the beat, keeping her hands under her chin. "Go Cougars! We are the Cougars, hey, we're number one; our cougar roar has just begun." She punches the air. "Rawr!" She claps again. "Rawr, rawr! We are the Cougars, yeah, we'll say it loud; we're stepping up because we're proud. Rawr! Rawr, rawr! We're the best, all right, we're here to win—"

Erin finishes a kick and flops onto the ground laughing. Todd claps his hands.

"Wow," he says, his heart pounding with sexual excitement.

Outside the shack, somebody yells at them to keep it down, which makes her laugh even harder.

"Let's pretend that was my dare. Now it's your turn."

"Dare."

"Kiss me."

Todd was hoping for this. Truth or dare, after all, is a kissing game. He moves toward her on hands and knees, feeling lightheaded and breathless, unsure where to begin. He has never kissed a girl before. She meets him halfway. It's like falling into a warm pool, smooth and jolting. He holds her shoulders and kisses her. He probes her tongue with his, wondering if he's doing this right. His erection strains against his jeans, sending waves of pain and pleasure through his body. Finally, she pushes him away.

He falls out of the kiss, amazed.

"And," she adds, "take off your shirt. I forgot to mention it's a two-part dare."

Still dizzy, he obeys, and she appraises him.

"No tattoos. Wow. My boyfriend has tats everywhere."

Todd frowns, alarmed and jealous. He half expects a bunch of jocks to enter the shack pointing at him and laughing and congratulating her on setting him up for a fall.

"You have a boyfriend?" he says, trying to control his tone.

"He's one of *them*. Outside."

Well, then he's not really your boyfriend anymore, he wants to say, but holds his tongue.

She smiles coyly at him and says, "Maybe I need a new boyfriend."

He smiles back.

"Dare," she says.

"You too," he says bravely.

Erin crosses her arms, hesitating with a teasing glance, and pulls her shirt over her head in one swift motion. Todd expects her to be wearing a bra, but there isn't one. Her pert breasts are perfect. Her smooth body burns in the candlelight. He stares at her in awe.

"Dare," he whispers.

"Come here. Kiss me again."

Wendy turns on her flashlight as she approaches the latrines. Jonesy does the same. She prefers to patrol by moonlight, letting their eyes adjust to the dark and becoming hunters instead of mere night watchmen. But the latrine area is dangerous at night even for cops, and the nearby canal is poorly marked by solar-powered landscape lights. A flare arcs over the horizon, and she hears the snarl of distant small arms fire. The pickets are busy tonight. Then the shooting stops as suddenly as it began. Wendy radios their position to Tyler, the gray-haired book reader back at the station.

Roger that. You guys be careful, now. Keep a sharp eye.

She smiles at the men's protectiveness as she keys the walkie-talkie and says, "You too."

I most certainly will, young Wendy.

Another flare arcs over the distant shanties.

"Sounds like a real battle out there tonight," Jonesy says, chewing loudly.

"Give me some of your gum."

"What do I get?"

"Jonesy, my boyfriend could break you in half. And if he couldn't, *I* could."

"Okay, okay," he laughs. "Can't blame a guy for trying."

She pops the piece into her mouth and starts gnawing on it with a vengeance.

Her third night on foot patrol with Unit 12, and she's already bored.

Last night, a little excitement: an explosion on the far side of camp, a flash in the sky followed by a boom and slight shock that she could feel in her feet. Later, she found out a homegrown crystal meth lab had blown sky high. She almost wishes something like that would happen here.

Flares burn as they fall in the night. A machine gun rattles on the wall.

They walk along the edge of the canal in search of planks that will allow them to cross. Their flashlight beams flicker along the rough ground. Somebody plays a harmonica in the nearby shanties. A couple moans loudly, having loud sex in one of the shacks.

Jonesy chuckles.

"Guess you're not the only ladies' man around here," Wendy says.

He laughs. "Here's the bridge. Watch your step."

They tramp over the planks and find themselves among the batteries of portable toilets.

"Police," Wendy says loud and clear.

"Police coming through."

"So, Jonesy, how did you end up becoming a cop?"

"Well, Ray started the unit, and Tyler and Ray are on the same bowling team, and Tyler's my dad. When Infection started, I was finishing high school. I was going to college too. I was going to learn how to be a veterinarian."

Wendy smiles. Tyler was not being protective of her, but of his teenage son. "Being a vet is a good job."

"Yeah, but then—"

A man appears in their path. He shields his eyes from the glare of their flashlights.

"Can you all get that light out of my eyes, please?"

They lower their flashlights a little. Wendy places her other hand on the handle of her baton.

"Stay where you are, sir," she says.

"You're cops, right? I thought I heard you say you were police."

"Do you need assistance?"

"My wife is missing. She came out here to use the bathroom an hour ago."

"All right, sir. Can you describe—"

Her instincts scream, *Fight*.

She draws her baton and wheels as Jonesy falls moaning to the ground. A man stands over him holding a length of pipe. A slab of wood glances off her head with a meaty thud. Her vision goes black and floods with stars.

She reels as the shapes close in.

The training takes over, and she moves.

She flails with the baton and smashes one of the men in the face, then backhands the other man in the ear. The first stumbles back and she pursues, beating him furiously to the ground while the second thrashes in the nearby canal, coughing and spitting.

Another blow to the head.

She falls into a deep blackness.

Sarge. Sarge, help me.

When Wendy regains consciousness, she's aware of a heavy weight on her body and a stabbing pain in her genitals. She opens her eyes and sees the infected thing leering down at her, its face gray and wet with blood, its eyes red with virus.

Wendy screams.

She no longer sees an infected on top of her, just a man telling her to shut up or he'll kill her. She smells his rancid breath, hot on her face. He strikes her savagely once, twice.

She blinks and sees an infected. She screams again.

His hand clamps over her mouth. She works her teeth around it and bites down hard. He hits her again, but with little force; she clamps down harder, growling like a dog. The man howls with pain and rage. She feels blood spray down the back of her throat and releases the mangled hand, coughing wetly.

She screams again. And again. But the man is gone.

☣

The crowd of thousands pours down the road past the food distribution center, singing hymns and waving poorly made signs announcing, GOD IS STILL WITH US and LUKE 21:11. Paul grinds out his cigarette and joins their ranks. His mind flashes to the suburban mob marching down the road back in Pittsburgh, thronged together with their weapons and shouting their slogans to make themselves feel stronger. Air Force jets roared overhead in a sky filled with black smoke, dropping bombs on distant targets. He remembers how he spoke to them: he blessed them just before the infected attacked. He told them their war was just.

They march past the camp's feeding center and the pest house. They pass a swing set displaying flags for various government agencies and services housed inside a small red brick building that used to be the town post office. The refugees pause in their daily routines to watch the marchers stream by singing, "Onward, Christian Soldiers." Some join the march while others laugh or shout at them to go stir up the dust somewhere else. Nervous soldiers watch the marchers and finger their weapons.

God isn't very popular these days, Paul knows. These people here are the hardcore Christians. The true believers. Their faith astonishes him. It makes him feel a bit ashamed. Yet he can't help but see them as a woman who defends the alcoholic husband who beats her regularly, making excuses for his psychotic behavior.

"Did you hear?" a man says behind him. "The Marines are in New Jersey."

"Who needs 'em?" another man snorts.

"I heard the Feds are going to try to take our guns away from us after the Army shows up," a woman says. "We'll be defenseless."

"That's just a rumor. Just like the Marines landing anywhere is a rumor."

"I heard it was Washington, not New Jersey," somebody cuts in.

"But what if it's true? Don't they understand the Second Amendment saved this country? If it weren't for the Second Amendment, we'd all be infected by now. God bless the NRA."

Paul hears babies crying. His mind flashes back to the giant fanged worm slithering out of the gloom, mewing for food. He marvels that even now, children are being born in the camp. No matter what, it seems, life goes on. Perhaps the human race abides too.

Near the front of the crowd, a man shouts into a megaphone. The march slows, congealing around several figures standing on the roof of a van in front of the old high school, the nominal seat of government in the camp. Paul continues to push forward. He recognizes Pastor Strickland and several other clergy standing behind an overweight man wearing a white collared shirt with the sleeves rolled up and massive sweat stains at the armpits. Black pants and tie. Paul has never seen him before but recognizes his voice. The man is a popular talk show host on the AM dial in the Pittsburgh area. McLean. Thomas McLean.

"We thought we were invincible," McLean is saying. "Like the Romans. We were consumed by money and pleasure and sex. Infection is happening because God is punishing us."

The mob roars its approval, drowning him out.

"They want you to believe we can live without God. Without our faith. They want us to ignore God. But God ain't ignoring us, folks. No, sir. God is talking to us loud and clear. And do you know what he's saying?"

Paul strains to hear, wondering who "they" are.

"He's saying we have insulted him, yeah, we have *insulted* him, and he's not going to take it!"

The crowd roars. Pastor Strickland and the other clergymen behind McLean nod and applaud with grim smiles.

"We have insulted him by celebrating the spirit of the Antichrist, and we are reaping the whirlwind. Insulted him by allowing feminism to destroy the American family, murder children, and promote lesbianism. By allowing homosexuals to destroy marriage and corrupt our children. By desecrating this great nation with our greed, pop culture, liberal universities, public education, separation of church and state, and persecution of Christians."

"No," Paul sighs. "Not this. Not now."

The crowd is angry. He can feel the energy surge through them like a wind. They wave their signs and cry out to McLean to tell them what to do.

"We must repent, for the end is nigh. I think we can all agree that it's pretty darn nigh. But how does one repent? Do you even know what that word means? It means to make yourself *righteous*. It means to become *pure*. We must purify ourselves as a nation and forge a new covenant with God."

Hundreds of hands reach into the air and wave gently like wheat in a breeze.

"To the atheists, I say, banish them from the camp!"

"Cast them out," the people chant.

"Banish the homosexuals!"

"Cast them out."

"Banish the elitists who look down at you!"

"This isn't right," Paul says to the faces around him as McLean continues to run down his list. "God doesn't want this. God doesn't want us to hate each other. We're all Americans."

"He wants us to hate sin," a woman snaps at him.

"It ain't a rally until the devil shows up," a man observes. "Here he is in the flesh."

"This is deranged. Infection has deranged us. Can't you see that?"

"All I see is a nigger with a death wish," the man replies with a grin.

"Keep that racist crap to yourself," another man warns.

"God is punishing us for our wickedness," the woman says. "Why is it deranged to think that?"

McLean points at the processing center, his voice raised to a scream. "Those people in there, they tell us how to live, but nobody voted for them! Now they want to silence me for speaking out! They see me as a threat! They can kill me, but they don't understand that the fire has been lit, that the fire is you, and the fire is spreading, and we will burn the corruption from the body of this great nation, and an even greater nation, a true Christian nation, will rise from the ashes!"

The crowd surges forward. The soldiers guarding the processing center push them back from the front doors with their rifles.

"Tell them to pass the Sodomy Ordinance. Tell them loud. Tell them now. Tell them—"

A metallic shriek drowns him out. The crowd pushes, compresses, loosens as people scatter at its edges. A Bradley armored fighting vehicle approaches at forty miles an hour.

A wreath of wildflowers trembles on its metal chest like a necklace. An American flag waves from one of its antennae. McLean points at the vehicle, shouting into the megaphone, but nobody can hear him.

The vehicle flies past the crowd and continues on its path.

Paul grins as he watches it pass. It's his Bradley, he's sure of it, and it can only be Sarge and Steve driving. He ducks out of the mob into one of the narrow alleys between the rows of shacks, intent on following the vehicle. It would be nice to see a friend right now. One of his people.

☣

The Bradley rolls past the sentries and into the military compound. Sweating in their helmets and uniforms, the soldiers admire it as it passes. The Bradley slows as it turns onto Main

Street, whose small retail stores and upper story apartments now provide barracks, mess, and headquarters facilities. The street is filled with soldiers wearing different uniforms, merchants and mercenaries, prostitutes and drug dealers, and olive green five-ton trucks carrying food and ammunition.

Even here, the command structure is confused, with many different Army and National Guard units mixed together, large numbers of raw recruits, and with several different headquarters displaying their loyalty to the United States, State of Ohio, and/or Commonwealth of Pennsylvania. A banner hanging from the barracks windows announces simply, PRAISE THE LORD AND PASS THE AMMUNITION.

The Bradley slows again and executes an abrupt turn into the service garage. The grease monkeys surround it, hoping something is wrong, itching to work on its engine again. They love the machine. There are so few of them left operating on American soil.

The hydraulic ramp drops. Sarge emerges holding Wendy in his arms. On the other side of the garage, a squad of recruits practices firing M16 rifles at paper targets set up in front of a wall of sandbags. The shooting tapers to respectful silence as they catch sight of the Bradley's commander carrying the beautiful sleeping woman into his quarters.

☣

Todd enters FEMAville's military compound and asks where he can find the man who commands the Bradley.

He and Erin laid in the shack staring up at the ceiling, sweaty and panting. For the first time in his life, he felt truly accepted. She'd seen him naked, and he'd lost his virginity. Now he'd love her until the day he died. His body continued to shudder with the aftershocks of the incredible explosion of pleasure. The shack filled with her unique musky scent. She lit the remainder of her joint and chattered about her smart phone and Twitter account and how she wanted to exist again. Todd nodded and studied the curves of her body, feeling strangely envious of her effortless beauty. He was already sad he might never have her again. He was suddenly starving. Moments later, she asked him if he wanted to do it again. After the third time, he passed out.

When he woke, Erin was gone, and so was his stash of electronics. His capital.

Suddenly, he had nothing.

She left him an enigmatic note that read simply, *Sorry. You are very cute.*

He thought about his options all morning. He could try to find her and get his stock back, or he could forget about it. Confronting her would be problematic, to put it mildly. Todd is terrible at confrontation, plus he believes he might be in love with her. The agony of wanting to see her again is already beginning to overtake the anger he feels at her robbing him blind.

Screw this. I know a cop. I'll get Wendy to help me. The cops will get my stuff back, and I'll forgive Erin, and then we'll be together again.

He knows he'll never have her, that he was used. But he can't stop himself from hoping.

By the time he reaches the military compound—where he believes he'll find Sarge, who in turn will be able to tell him where Wendy is—he has replayed the events of the previous night dozens of time in his mind. He has imagined many conversations they are yet to have. The angry one where he asks her why she used and hurt him, forces her to take a good hard look at herself, and makes her cry over her misdeeds. The calm one where he gazes upon her coldly and tells her he forgives her and pities her, and then wishes her a nice life. The happy, highly improbable one where she brings his stuff back and they fall into each other's arms.

The garage is filled with soldiers sitting on the hard cement floor writing letters, reading books, and making coffee on Coleman stoves. Chickens cluck in a series of cages against the far wall next to neatly stacked cordwood. Todd smells gun smoke, coffee, and chicken shit. The quiet soldiers frequently glance at the office in the corner where Sarge has made his home. He treads carefully among them, ignoring their hostile stares, still muttering to himself as he knocks on Sarge's door. No answer. He pounds angrily.

The door opens, and a glaring Sarge steps into the entry wearing his camo pants and a T-shirt. His expression softens with recognition.

"Hey, Kid. Good to see you."

Todd flushes at hearing his old nickname.

The soldier thrusts out his hand, and Todd shakes it.

"You too, Sarge."

"What brings you out this way?"

"I have some bad news. Can I talk with you for a minute?"

"Come on in then. I got some bad news too, Kid."

Todd stops in surprise at the sight of Paul and Ethan standing over a cot where Wendy moans in a fitful sleep.

Wendy wakes up with a massive headache and an overwhelming sense of dread. The small room is filled with men staring at her. Sarge presses a cool, damp cloth against her forehead and looks at her with love and fear. Paul, Ethan, and Todd are here, and so is Ray and all the cops of Unit 12 except Jonesy and his dad. Their faces light up at seeing her awake.

Ethan looks like somebody punched his lights out, smiling with a black eye. Somebody asks her how she's feeling, and she struggles to concentrate on the voice. She wants to wake up. She's not sure she's awake now. If this is a dream, it's a good one; she feels happy having Sarge close and safe being with the other survivors. Odd that she should spend the two worst weeks of her life with this group and feel so bonded to them. They are her people. She remembers how, at the hospital, she began to think of them as a tribe.

She wonders if she's dying.

Sarge asks her if she needs anything. *Do you want some water?*

After she drinks, she asks them how she got here. Her voice sounds funny, and she thinks there might be something wrong with her ear. The men glance at each other and avoid her eyes. The truth is she remembers nothing. Whatever happened to her was so bad, they can't bear to say it out loud. Ray sits on an ammo crate next to her bed and tells her she and Jonesy were attacked. Jonesy has a concussion and is in bad shape. She got banged up pretty good, but physically, she's fine. Wendy takes this in and wonders why she can't rise from the cot. She feels feverish. She can't shake the feeling that she's dying.

You should see the other guys, Ray says. *You really did a number on them. We caught two of them. We know who the third guy is, and we'll have him in the bag soon. You don't worry about them, Wendy. We'll take care of it. They deserve to die for what they did, and we're going to take care of it.*

Ray places her badge on the pillow next to her head.

We found this at the scene.

Her head pounds. She feels confused. Her dreams were filled with nightmares, and now she's wondering if some of them were real.

Ray asks if she has a problem with them taking care of things the Defiance way.

Wendy surprises herself by saying clearly, "Do it."

She leans over the side of the bed and vomits onto the floor at Sarge's feet. Then she plummets into nauseating darkness lit briefly only by a few tiny sparks.

☣

Smiling like wolves, the Unit 12 boys leave the room in single file to deliver justice to the men who attacked their people. They nod to Ray as they pass by with their black shirts and bulletproof vests and guns.

Wendy tosses and turns on the bed for the next few hours while Sarge sponges her face with a wet cloth. As evening approaches, soldiers bring steaming bowls of beef stew. The survivors sit on the floor in a circle to eat by candlelight.

"Just like old times," Paul says. "Except for this good food."

"Must be nice to have a job that pays in raw beef," Ray says.

Ethan grins. "You don't know what I had to do to earn it."

"Something dangerous, from the looks of your face," Sarge says, squinting at him as if trying to figure out a puzzle.

"It's nothing," Ethan tells him happily. "Some people at the government center thought I was a doctor and attacked me. I ran, found a crew unloading cattle, and worked the day."

"Ah," Ray says in understanding. He knows about the cattle crews and how they use people as bait for the monsters that infect the animals.

"When I got back to the government center, the same people were waiting for me and gave me this," Ethan answers, pointing at his face and laughing.

Todd chuckles with him. "Why are you so happy about it?"

"I'm happy because I may have found my family."

The other survivors glance at each other and offer weak smiles.

"That's good news, man," Ray says.

Sarge pats his shoulder. "Yeah, it's good, Ethan."

Ethan glares at them. "I'm serious."

Ray bristles. "And I'm taking you seriously."

"I spent several days at the government center. The records people found one Carol Bell in the camp, but it wasn't my wife. I kept pushing until I finally convinced somebody to check some of the other camps. Turns out there is a C. Bell and two M. Bells at the FEMA camp near Harrisburg. Three days after Infection, a C. Bell and an M. Bell arrived on the same day."

He looks at the others for a reaction.

"It sounds hopeful, Ethan," Paul says. "I mean it."

"It sounds *awesome*," Todd tells him.

Ethan turns to Sarge. "I was wondering if you could take me there. There, or as far as you can."

Sarge believes it's appropriate the other survivors are here with him again, as he never really left them. His mind plunges against his will into the past during every still moment, forcing him to relive the horrors of Infection, the Screaming, Afghanistan. The worst is when he finds himself standing in the dark alone in front of the hospital, shooting the infected swarming across the parking lot while every atom in his body screams at him to run. He surfaces from these terrifying flashbacks drenched in cold sweat, his heart clenched in his chest. He's not stupid. He knows he's suffering from post-traumatic stress. He also knows that getting back out in the field will cure it, at least temporarily.

"I might be able to take you as far as Steubenville."

"What's in Steubenville?"

"Bridges."

Ethan nods. "The infected of Pittsburgh."

"What's that mean?" Todd asks.

"That big fire that chased us out? It also chased out all the infected," Ethan explains. "Many of them are walking west, straight to the bridges. Straight to us. Right, Sarge?"

Sarge nods. "I'm leading a mission out there to blow the bridges. Specifically, the Veterans Memorial Bridge. Six lanes across the Ohio River."

"You can't help but hear them," Paul adds. "They've been attacking the camp ever since we got here. The gunfire has become almost constant, day and night. After a while, it gets to be background noise. If they get inside, we're done."

"We're the last refugees that made it to the camp from Pittsburgh."

"Can the infected swim?" Ray asks him.

"Our intelligence says they can't," Sarge answers. "If we blow the bridges, they'll be stopped cold at the river."

"What they'll do is go north and south."

"That's not our problem."

Ray shrugs. "Yup. It's not."

"The migration will be deflected, and that's all that counts as far as we're concerned."

"I want in," Todd says. "Let me come, Sarge. Please."

"I might as well join in too," Paul says, eyeing him with hope. "I could be useful."

Sarge shakes his head in disbelief. The truth is he would be happy to bring them on the mission. The boys he commands are good, but they don't know what the survivors know. He's just surprised they'd want to leave the safety of the camp to go back into the jaws of the beast. And after just a few days, no less. Wasn't that the point of their journey together, after all—to find this sanctuary and try to live a normal life?

He says, "It's going to be incredibly dangerous."

He remembers driving through Steubenville, the town eerily quiet. No sign of life, not even a dog barking. The infected are there, all right. And with many of the infected of Pittsburgh migrating west, the place is going to be swarming.

"I'm coming too," Wendy says from her cot.

"Wendy!" Todd says happily.

The men launch themselves to their feet as she stands painfully, visibly trembling. She touches the back of her head and winces. She shrugs off their hands and walks to where they were sitting. She takes a place next to Sarge and accepts a drink of water in a plastic cup.

"Well, then I'm going too," Ray says.

"The hell you are," Sarge growls. "You're not one of us."

"But she's one of *us*. If she goes, I'm going. It's that simple. I made a promise."

"Yeah?" Sarge glares at him. "To who?"

"To a lot of fucking dead people," Ray snaps back.

"If he wants to come, he can come," Wendy rasps.

Sarge scowls. "Are you all sure about this?"

"Yes," the survivors murmur, looking down at their bowls.

"What about you, Wendy?"

"You were right. It's not safe here for us."

"Can you do it?"

"You're not going without me."

"All right."

The room falls silent as they consider their reasons for wanting to go.

"I hate it here," Todd says finally.

Ethan says, "I love it. But I have to get to Harrisburg."

"We'll get you as far as we can, Ethan," Sarge tells him.

"It will be good to get out of here for a few days," Paul says. "Maybe I'll go all the way to Harrisburg with you. This place is unclean. God doesn't live here."

"Where exactly does he live, Preacher?" Ray asks quietly.

"Where? Out there, friend. With *them*. They're his agents."

"Get your sleep tonight," Sarge says. "We're training tomorrow. The morning after that, we're going to drive out there and blow a hole in that bridge."

FLASHBACKS: REVEREND PAUL MELVIN

He remembers seeing the half-eaten remains of the children defiling the altar of his church, blood running down its sides like the afterbirth of some grisly sacrifice to a pagan god. He remembers his shoes squishing on the wet carpet, stepping over the bodies of his congregation surrounded by clouds of buzzing flies. He remembers the mob marching out of the haze singing and waving their guns and banners. He remembers how they hung the infected on a traffic light at the intersection of Merrimac and Steel, how they demanded he bless them, how he told them their fight was just. He remembers the screams, the popping guns, the newly infected twitching on the blacktop, the final shouting as the last of the mob made a stand in the smoke. He remembers telling them not to be afraid as they died.

He remembers walking through the smoke while the screams rose up from the city all around him. He remembers going home intent on letting Sara infect him so that they could be rejoined. He remembers finding his house on fire.

Like Job, Paul lost everything he loved.

As with Job, God allowed it.

THE BRIDGE

When the survivors left Pennsylvania in their flight from Pittsburgh, they crossed a sliver of West Virginia, a piece of ground stabbing north like a spike, before finally entering Ohio. The Veterans Memorial Bridge connects Steubenville, Ohio and Weirton, West Virginia—six lanes of modern superhighway carrying U.S. Route 22 across the Ohio River. Nearly twenty football fields in length, the cable-stayed bridge consists of steel girders and beams supporting a composite concrete road deck, the entire structure suspended by cables fanning out from the two support towers. A common design for long bridges.

Before Infection, thirty thousand people crossed this bridge every day. Now it's a funnel for more than a hundred thousand infected moving west away from the still-burning ruins of Pittsburgh.

☣

The Bradley roars east on Route 22, leading a convoy of vehicles including several flatbed trucks stacked with explosives, armored cars, and four school buses fitted with V-shaped snowplows on their grilles.

The rig slams into an abandoned minivan and sends it spinning onto the shoulder of the highway without breaking its stride. The crash makes Wendy flinch.

"Let's practice a rapid scan," Sarge says.

Wendy blows air out her cheeks. She moves her left hand to wipe sweat from her forehead and bangs her elbow again.

"Mother," she hisses. Sitting in the commander's seat directly adjacent to Sarge in the gunner's station, her body is surrounded by hard metal edges. Not much room to do anything except work the joystick that controls the turret and weapons systems.

She peers into the integrated sight unit, which provides a relay of what Sarge sees, overlaid with a reticle to help aim the Bradley's guns. The highway slices through rolling green hills to the horizon. Smoke still pours out of Pittsburgh and darkens the eastern sky. The horizon shimmers and pulses with heat waves.

"You're sightseeing," Sarge says.

"It's hard to take my eyes off the road."

"You have to get used to the fact that somebody else is driving. While Steve will obey our commands to stop and go and so on, we're a self-contained world up here, just you and me. You help scan and identify targets, and I'll track and kill them."

"Yes, sir."

"I'm not a sir. I work for a living, ma'am. Now let's do a rapid scan with overlapped sectors."

"With who, what?"

"That means I'll be scanning roughly the same ground ahead as you. First, scan center out, near to far, then left and right to center. I'll be scanning far to near."

Gum cracking, Wendy studies the highway ahead and identifies two abandoned vehicles in the grassy median. They pass a billboard on the right that tells her to *Tune in to Channel Seven News at Eleven with Janet Rodriguez*. Janet grins confidently down at her in a power suit with her arms crossed. Beyond, power lines and trees.

The opposite lanes of the highway are occupied by a long column of infected that stare grimly at the rig as it rolls by on its grating treads.

"Identified," she says.

"Confirmed. Range?"

"Fifty meters?"

"I'm asking for the range to the nearest target."

"I thought that's what I was giving you."

"See that billboard up there on the other side of the highway? That's about a hundred."

"Oh, then seventy, seventy-five?"

"Bingo. You're learning fast. You should be proud, babe."

She turns and flashes a smile. "That's Corporal Babe to you."

"What can I say, girl. You do look good in cammies."

"Settle down, Sergeant," she laughs. "This Army uniform is like two sizes too big for me."

"You wear it like a dress."

"A tent, maybe."

She laughs lightly, feeling good for the first time since she kissed him at the hospital. Sarge is a good man. He gives her precious moments in which she can forget about Infection and everything else. She believes she could easily fall in love with him, if they live long enough.

THE INFECTION ♦ 237

The Bradley hums with the stresses generated by dozens of moving parts. She can feel the beating heart of the engine, converting controlled explosions into the raw horsepower needed to turn the treads and propel the vehicle's twenty-five tons. The vibrations flow through her body, reminding her she's riding a metal bull with the strength of five hundred horses and a mind of its own. Yet she feels powerful sitting here in its brain. More in control than she has ever felt, in fact. She's in an armored box with wheels, somebody else is driving, and she's got the big guns. She laughs again as she considers there are few better places one could be in the middle of a zombie apocalypse.

The exhilaration she feels, however, is tempered by a growing weight on her chest. Running the rig is a lot of responsibility. The soldiers, the other survivors, and all the people back at the camp will be counting on her to make good decisions when they hit the bridge in ninety minutes, and she simply doesn't have enough training or experience to do it right. She's scared.

"You ready for more?" Sarge says.

I'm ready for a hot bath with real soap, scented candles, some Alanis on the CD player, and a tall glass of red wine.

"What else you got?"

She wonders again why she wanted to come on this mission, but another glance at the man beside her in the gunner's station reminds her. They're a tribe.

☣

Todd smiles at the almost surreal sense of *déjà vu* he feels at being back inside the hot noisy belly of the Bradley. He has butterflies in his gut, the humid air is dense with the smells of nervous sweat and diesel combustion, and he has to pee. Just like old times. It feels oddly right. The big difference is Anne is gone, Wendy is up in the front with Sarge, and there are two new faces in their unit—Ray Young, the rent-a-cop with the hard eyes and horseshoe mustache, and Lieutenant Patterson, the combat engineer with the buzz cut and earnest clean-shaven face.

"Once more into the breach, huh, Rev?" Todd says with a laugh. He wants to show off his easy familiarity with the group to the newcomers, but the two men either didn't hear him over the Bradley's engine or are simply lost in their own thoughts. As usual, nobody cares.

Paul smiles weakly but says nothing. Todd looks at him and realizes how grounded he feels here with the other survivors. The Bradley feels like home. Yet he still doesn't know these people. He suddenly wants to talk to the reverend about something important, something philosophical, man to man at the edge of the abyss—the nature of faith during war or whatever—but he can't think of where to start such a conversation. A little more grounded, but he's still floating, away from others as well as himself.

The survivors' role in the mission is to help clear the bridge and then keep Patterson safe because the lieutenant is going to blow the bridge using more than two tons of TNT and C4.

The engineer told them that cable-stayed bridges are a little harder to blow a hole in. The cables fanning out from the towers pull to the sides instead of up like a suspension bridge, requiring a stronger deck to compensate for the horizontal load. That means more force will be needed to blow a hole in it that the infected won't be able to cross.

What's more, they won't have time to attach the charges under the bridge for a bottom attack. Instead, they'll have to lay the explosives directly on the road deck, tamp it with a hill of sandbags, and blow off the concrete to expose the steel reinforcements. A second round of charges will cut the steel rods and beams. It'll be a lot of work and take a long time.

Here's what will happen: After the bridge is secured, the trucks will pull up. Workers will unload the explosives in piles across the eighty-foot-wide, six-lane bridge. These piles will be laid out in two lines covered in sandbags used as tamping to direct the force of the blast down into the concrete. The engineers will apply shaped C4 charges to the exposed steel elements.

Then boom. The unsupported piece between the two blast lines will fall into the Ohio River, and the resulting forty-foot gap will stop the infected from crossing.

They have to do all this while potentially holding off hordes at both ends of the bridge.

"Hey," Todd says to the combat engineer.

The glazed eyes flicker and focus. "Hey, what?"

"Why forty feet?"

Patterson grins. The transformation this brings is almost alchemical. A moment ago, he looked like a hardened killer on death row waiting for his lawyer. Now he looks like a frat boy about to explain how he spiked the professors' punch at the party.

"Mike Powell," he says, his accent deep Louisiana.

"Oh yeah," Ray says.

"Who's Mike Powell?"

"He set the world record in the long jump back in the nineties," Ray explains.

Patterson nods. "Almost thirty feet. We're going to do forty—just in case one of those little hopping sumbitches can beat old Mike Powell's record."

Todd grins with the other men, filled with awareness that history is being made today. It's the end of the world, but a new one is beginning. He can't help but feel excited. It's epic, ninja, like living in a video game. He's already forgotten the crushing sense of death he felt back at the hospital when Wendy held her Glock against his head and Ethan counted down to zero.

You made it this far, old man. You're lucky. You're good. Hell, you're practically immortal. You're earning your place in the new world. There will be historians in this new world, recording the heroic deeds of people during the dark time of Infection for future generations to understand and respect.

The bridge they're blowing is the Veterans Memorial Bridge. *What buildings and bridges and monuments will they build to honor our sacrifices? What day will they set aside for our memory? They'll look at us as the Greatest Generation, the people who fought the Infection and rebuilt the world. Every war has a turning point. Ours is here, now.*

He thinks about John Wheeler and April Preston and the ghosts of his high school. Most of them are by now certainly infected or dead.

But not me. I survived for a reason.

Maybe, this time, he'll reap the rewards when he returns. Maybe he'll get a little more respect. Erin was impressed by his tales of survival and the wound on his arm but ripped him off anyway. Inside the camp, he felt powerless and small, his life reduced to stories nobody could truly believe even in these times.

Out here, he feels powerful, somehow more real, part of something again. He'd never say such a thing out loud to the other survivors, but he's here because he wants to find himself.

Paul signed up for this mission on impulse, but he's old enough to know that nothing happens purely that way. There's always a reason. It's not loyalty to the others. He feels safer with them, but not really safe, and certainly not very safe out here, in the lion's den. He loves them in his own way with whatever love he has left to give anybody, but they can make their own decisions and take care of themselves. It's not disgust with Pastor Strickland and his ministry of bitterness and resentment, either. He doesn't approve it, but he also has no interest in fighting it. Strickland still loves the infected that he lost but hates people he doesn't understand. A kingdom divided will be ruined, and a house divided cannot stand, as Jesus taught. There have always been false prophets like Strickland and McLean, and there always will be.

It's not even a simple desire to find a better place to live. If he continues on with Ethan to Camp Immunity near Harrisburg, it'll be as filthy, hungry, and violent as Defiance. When they were leaving, the people cheered and blew whistles. The rumors the Army was coming achieved a critical mass. But nobody cared about the convoy of vehicles leaving the camp, filled with people ready to sacrifice everything to save them all.

If God can appear cruel and vindictive, well, we're made in his image. God should have told Job that he had no right to question him because as bad as God is, people are even worse. When the chips are down, the best and worst are on full display.

The funny thing about the story of Job is that Job never questioned Satan. In Hebrew, Satan has two meanings. One is the Adversary. The other is *ha-Satan*, the Accuser. In either case, he is an Angel of the Lord. Maybe Job didn't question Satan because he didn't have to do so. If God is everything, he is also Satan. The Adversary. The Accuser. Creator of Heaven and Earth.

The fact is Paul hated leaving only a little less than he hated staying. Perhaps that's why he's here. *Anne had the right idea. Just keep moving.* He feels like he finally understands her decision to abandon them.

If you keep moving, they can never get you. You might even outrun yourself.

Stay still, and curse the day you were born.

We try to live with as little pain and as much pleasure as possible. But pain makes us realize we're alive. We truly live one moment to the next when we live with pain. When pain stops, we become afraid. And we remember things we don't wish to remember that are themselves painful.

Long is the way and hard, right, Anne?

The Catholics believe there is Heaven and Hell and between them a place called Purgatory, in which souls are purified and made ready for Heaven through a period of punishment. Similarly, there is a state of existence between living and dying: survival.

These days, God has no use for charity and good works. God demands everything now. These days, the Lord only calls those who have been baptized in blood.

And that is why Paul joined this mission. Not to be tested, but to put an end to these tests.

"I came naked from my mother's womb, and I will be naked when I leave," Job said upon hearing that his family died and all his earthly possessions destroyed. "The Lord gave me what I had, and the Lord has taken it away. Praise the name of the Lord!"

Sara, I will be with you soon, wherever you are.

☣

Ethan remembers holding Carol's hand while she pushed Mary out into the world, counting between pushes, trying to pour all of his strength into her by will alone. He'd always wanted children but felt ambivalent about the amount of responsibility they required. He wanted kids to be like library books, something enjoyed for a while and then returned. Something he could manage over time, not maintain every hour of every single day. The idea of wiping puke and changing diapers for the near future overwhelmed him. Mostly, he worried about his relationship with his wife. They had a good life, and he didn't want to see it spoiled.

"It's a girl," the doctor told him.

"It's a girl," he said to his wife, his heart bursting with pride.

Still holding his hand, Carol cried with relief and joy.

Later, the nurse asked him if he wanted to hold his daughter for the first time.

"Yes," he said without hesitation.

The woman handed him the tiny swaddled creature, and his heart opened. Just like that. A visceral, almost painful love surged through him and poured into the child in his arms.

Change diapers? Hell, he'd eat this kid's shit, he realized.

Anything. Anything for you.

This person will die without me. But more than that: *Everything I do to this child from now on will reverberate through the rest of her life.* He never felt so needed. So responsible.

"Your name is Mary," he told her in a singsong voice, not caring how it sounded.

From that point forward, nothing mattered except family.

They're going to the bridge to blow a hole in it, and then he's going to travel two hundred miles to Camp Immunity near Harrisburg. He'll have to get there on his own this time, and the journey promised to be difficult, if not impossible. Carol and Mary might as well be in Australia. But he hasn't felt so close to them since Infection started. There's a chance *they exist.*

The operation itself appears equally hard. Two school buses loaded with troops will lead the way. The buses are forty feet long, almost exactly the span of each set of lanes on the bridge. They'll drive to the end of the bridge and block it to create a wall of firepower against the infected. The Bradley will follow at a walking pace with the survivors and another squad of soldiers. They'll clear the bridge and set up the charges while another pair of buses parks behind them, sealing both ends of the bridge.

The combat engineer and his people will plant the charges, strip the concrete, and set the next round of charges. Then they'll begin the countdown. The soldiers in the buses will make a run for it. Machine guns will cover their retreat.

The final charges will blow.

Mission accomplished. Bravo, bravo.

Impossible.

A million things can go wrong, not the least of which is the infected might brush them off the bridge with ease. Monsters walk the earth now. The bridge might be packed with giant worms, swarming with malevolent little jumpers, or occupied by the terrifying demon that kicked the crap out of the Bradley and almost burst their eardrums just with its roar.

He won't even be able to launch his journey to Immunity on the West Virginia side of the river. He's going to have to find a boat. Even that seems impossible to him.

But he'll do it.

He'll do anything, kill anybody, sacrifice everything, to find his family again.

Sarge is glad to be back in the Army doing his duty, though he's not sure who he's actually working for at the moment. Captain Mattis is regular Army but got the operational orders for the mission from the provisional government of the Commonwealth of Pennsylvania. The Federal government nationalized the Guard, while Ohio claimed control of Federal troops currently fighting on its soil. The refugee camp is run by FEMA, at least nominally, with people from different levels of government claiming jurisdiction over different things.

Even here, in the field, things are not perfectly clear: Sarge is in charge of security, but Patterson, the combat engineer and a first lieutenant, is nominally in charge of the entire operation. Mattis gave him a half-strength, watered-down National Guard infantry company for the mission, two-thirds under Sarge's direct command for the assault on the Veterans Memorial Bridge, the remaining third to be deployed for a separate operation to destroy the smaller Market Street Bridge a few miles to the south. The soldiers are weekend warriors for the most part, supplemented by volunteers from the camp, but most are well trained, disciplined, and equipped, and some even did time in overseas wars.

In the end, it doesn't matter to him where he got his orders. The mission is sound as far as missions go, and he's simply happy to be back in the field commanding troops. Out here, ringed by death on all sides, appears to be the only place where he can feel truly calm and in control. He's terrified by what that means. He's glad Wendy came along because he's not sure he's going back when this is all over.

"Identified," Wendy says, adding, "What the hell is that thing, Sarge?"

The giant hairless head totters on spindly tripod legs. It stops and drops a load of dung that falls onto the highway like a wet bomb. Grimacing with a wide mouth and oversized, bulging eyes, the thirty-foot-tall monster leers down at the infected streaming around its legs.

"*Shaw chonk*," it says, its deep voice booming through the air.

A long and thick tongue lashes out, wraps around the torso of an infected woman, and pulls her up into its cavernous mouth. Chewing loudly, the thing chortles deep in its throat, the heavy bass sound vibrating at its edges like an idling motorcycle.

"*Shaw chonk, groomy lactate.*"

"Christ," Wendy says.

In any other time, the vision of this monster tottering down Route 22—its skinny legs supporting a bloated sphere of mottled flesh with its grotesque visage—would have irreparably damaged Sarge's mind. Today it only fills him with revulsion and hatred. The thing is a trespasser on his planet and must be destroyed. Anne used the perfect word to describe these things: *abominations*.

Sarge gives the general order to halt the convoy.

"What are we going to do?" Wendy says, her voice quiet and breathless.

He switches to high magnification for a closer look at the thing. The monster's wart-covered face fills the optical display. Revolted, he switches back to low magnification.

"*Groomy!*" it bellows across the landscape.

"We're going to kill it."

He estimates the range to target at two hundred meters using the rule of thumb method of picturing a distance of a hundred meters and ranging to the target in hundred-meter increments. He adjusts the RANGE-SELECT knob to two.

He presses a switch on the weapons box, illuminating the AP LO annunciator light. He selected the 25mm gun with armor-piercing rounds firing at a low rate of fire, about a hundred rounds per minute.

"Line up the shot, Corporal Babe."

Wendy presses the palm switch on her joystick with her fingers, which activates the turret drive and releases the turret brakes. Then she puts pressure on the stick. The turret rotates in response. The reticle centers on the monster's legs.

"Now give me elevation to center mass on that thing's hideous goddamn head."

She feathers the stick until the reticle is centered between the monster's eyes.

"Got it."

"You're drifting."

"Sorry."

"Don't say sorry; stabilize."

She pushes the drift button to stabilize the turret.

"Good job."

"Sarge, if something happens—"

"Nothing's going to happen," he says, his eyes glued to the optical display. He presses the arming switch for the cannon. "But if you really want to know, I love you."

"So we'll be together no matter what."

"No matter what, if you want me." He adds: "*On the way.*"

He depresses the trigger switch, and the Bradley's main gun fires.

He says, "Tell me what you see."

The rounds arc up the highway, the path illuminated by tracers. The thing is moving again.

"Um, lost?" she says, meaning she thinks the rounds are passing over the target.

"Correction," he murmurs. "I'm taking over the turret."

He corrects the elevation and shoots again, leading the lethal fire into the beast using the tracers. The rounds, designed to penetrate Soviet tanks and concrete bunkers, enter the monster's skull and burst in flashes of light. Geysers of blood and brain rocket into the air.

The thing screams shrilly and topples, trailing black smoke. The pulped remains splash across the lanes and into the median. One of the legs twitches, and then it's still.

Despite the noise of the Bradley's engine and systems, they hear the soldiers in the buses cheer. Sarge's heart pounds at the sight. These things die like anything else.

"Target destroyed." He smiles at Wendy, who beams back.

"Holy crap, that was exciting," she says. "I think I'm addicted. And I think I love you, too."

"We're going to get through this. We're going to win."

His smile fades. The truth is, a part of him hopes that they never win. The truth is he wants the war to go on and on and on, because he may never be able to return to peace.

The Bradley idles after the shooting stops. Sarge gets on the intercom and tells them they just destroyed one big ugly monster. Ray Young glances across the smiling faces and wants to scream at them for being complete morons. They're driving to a place where the big ugly monsters will be thick as fleas. They're going there by *choice*; they're idiots.

The idea of driving onto that bridge and being greeted by the entire infected population of Pittsburgh fills him with pure bowel-evacuating terror. America has become a killing floor, and there are things out there that want to eat you. They'll eat you while you're still alive, and then you'll be dead, and you'll never see the sun again or kiss a girl or laugh at a joke or drink a beer.

Ever again. As in *forever*.

And nobody will give a shit about your famous last words and heroic deeds. These days, if you're lucky, your friends will burn you in a pit. If not, then you're food.

Only a lunatic would put himself in that situation.

These motherfuckers are crazy.

No. YOU'RE the looney. You're here because you made a promise, which you actually didn't literally make, to a lot of dead people, who are, well, DEAD, to make things normal again, which means asshole cops back being asshole cops, and if it's one thing you hated from the time before Infection almost as much as credit card debt, it's ASSHOLE COPS.

These maniacs don't know any better, apparently; you do. Which makes you an even bigger fool.

He swallows hard as he fights the urge to retch.

Todd leans toward him and says charitably, "It's going to be okay, man."

"Shut up, kid," he says.

Just because you're suicidal doesn't make you any braver than me. In my time, I started fights over anything from noble causes to petty grievances, and more often than not, I ended them. I fight to win, and I fight dirty. Bravery has nothing to do with this. This is about living and dying. There is nothing in between.

Cashtown had so many ne'er-do-wells like him that the upright citizens were hard to tell apart from everybody else unlucky enough to have been born there. Once, the town prospered in steel and timber, but like so many places in America, it fell into ruin due to overseas competition and decades of betrayal of the American worker by big business and the country's politicians. People passing through left with impressions of rusting, abandoned steel mills, smokestacks, and rail yards. Deteriorating housing drenched in American flags. For years, it was just another town in a depressed region where people lived paycheck to paycheck with as much pride as they could muster.

Ray worked as a rent-a-cop for a self-storage facility and frequently got into trouble with real cops. He drank, he smoked, he brawled, he broke things, he screwed anything with two legs. He lived in his mom's basement and broke her heart with bad behavior and general lack of a future. Probably the only decent thing he ever did was volunteer for the local fire department.

When the Screaming happened, he was sleeping one off. He found his mother dead hours later. She caught the Screaming while taking a bath and drowned all alone. There were so many dead, the mortuary couldn't bury her. The county zipped her up in a body bag, tagged her, and drove her away in a truck for burial in a mass grave—to be dug up later and buried properly when things returned to normal.

Of course, things never did.

During the morning of Infection, he was driving home from his shift when he saw a pack of lunatics in pajamas tackle and tear apart a child fleeing on a bicycle. People fought everywhere. The couple who ran the bakery looked out the window of their store, trying to call somebody on the phone. As Ray drove by, he saw another pack of pajama-wearing lunatics crash through the window and tear them apart.

All Ray could think at the time was, *I don't want that to be me.*

The truck radio shouted at him until he turned it off.

He drove home and loaded his rig with everything he could get his hands on. Food, beer, liquor, cigarettes and dip, jugs of water, packets of Kool-Aid, burritos, and TV dinners. He restarted his truck, turned on the radio, and flipped across the shouting voices until he found the local AM news station, which emitted the emergency broadcast signal.

He turned off the radio. *It's better this way. I really don't want to know.* People were killing and eating each other. He had all the information he needed.

He drove back to the storage facility, locked the chain-link fence behind him, and sealed himself inside one of the storage sheds with somebody else's dusty old shit.

Ray stayed in there for five days until he ran out of booze, the last set of batteries failed in his flashlight, and he could no longer stand the dark and the stench of his own waste.

He opened the garage door and emerged into a brave new world.

The camp was already sprawling, bursting out of Cashtown until it reached the self-storage facility and the ruins of the old steel mills. Some of the storage units were being plundered to make room for refugees. He stood there for fifteen minutes, blinking in the sunlight with his mouth open, trying to understand it, his head pounding with the worst hangover of his life. After what he'd seen that first day of Infection, he'd thought he'd find the town abandoned by the living. Instead, he found a thriving refugee camp with the population of Boulder, Colorado.

Not a very noble way to survive that first deadly week of Infection, but the point is he *emerged*. The point is he *survived*.

There's no honor in survival, but life goes on, and life is everything. Nothing else matters. And anybody who thinks differently is a fool—a fool who probably won't live very long.

He found out most of his friends were dead. The town had five governments. Four families lived in his mother's house, which had already been looted top to bottom. Some of them he recognized as his former neighbors. Many of the locals had tried to cash in, selling land to the government and basic necessities to the refugees at outrageous prices, trading everything they had for a pile of paper money that rapidly declined in value until it became worthless.

Some of the more important and civic-minded locals, however, became entrenched with the government. They knew Ray as a badass, and they needed men like him on their side to maintain law and order.

So Ray became a lawman and, in the process, a true believer in making the world right again. He was good at it. His only regret was his mom wasn't alive to see him do it.

When he found out Wendy was a Pittsburgh police officer, it was like meeting an angel. The news of the city's burning had struck the camp like a thunderbolt. People walked around in a daze, unable to comprehend it. By the time Wendy showed up at the police station, the fire was already legend. That made her something of a miracle, rare and precious.

Which is why he came—to protect her. The part of Ray Young that he's been finding out is good believes if he can protect her, he can help make the world right again.

As for the part of him that's bad, the part he knows all too well, that part also wants to see the world return to normal. Ray is tough and morally ambivalent; he can be a bully and violent on a whim, but he has no wish to live in a world in eternal fear of being wiped out by a horde of diseased, homicidal maniacs. He longs for the day when he can get drunk on payday, throw a bottle through a window, and take a swing at good, honest cops who come to arrest him.

He was a loser back in the day, that's true, while he's an important man now. But he was a loser who was certain to live a long life of petty amusements in a town he loved. He wants the world to get back to normal: a world where beer is manufactured and sold cheaply in mass quantities, tobacco farmers are free to harvest their crops unmolested, and women are loose and fun and have easy access to birth control.

He came for reasons both selfless and selfish, but none of that matters now.

Now that he's here, all he wants to do is live.

☣

The numbers of infected multiply as they approach Steubenville along Route 22. The Bradley breaks their bodies with sickening thuds. The buses send them flying with the V-shaped highway truck snowplows welded onto their grilles. They bypass the town along the north, their view of it obscured by a treed slope that gradually turns into a concrete wall. The fronts of the vehicles are splashed with blood; the windshield wipers work full time. The Bradley crashes into a guide panel mounted on a sagging overhead gantry—ROUTE 7 SOUTH STEUBENVILLE—and smashes it into flying green shards that scatter across the highway. The infected race toward the buses, squealing and pounding sides painted with special messages: HELLO, NOW DIE and NONE SHALL PASS and INSTANT CURE! INQUIRE WITHIN.

Sarge says into the intercom, "We're approaching the bridge. Stay frosty."

Wendy glances at him with wide eyes. Her face is pale and pouring sweat.

"Eyes forward." He adds in a gentle tone, "You're okay, babe."

"This is different than before. This isn't just survival. This is a mission." She shakes her head before returning her attention to the ISU. "We're fighting a war now."

"Don't matter what you want to call it. Either way, people's lives are riding on what you do, so you make sure you do it right. You do the best you can."

"It's too much this time. I'm scared."

"Only crazy people don't get scared. Being scared is perfectly normal. You just have to control it so it don't control you."

"How?"

"You take things one step at a time. Each minute as it comes. And breathe."

She licks her dry lips. She takes a deep breath. "Okay."

"Small steps. Right now, all we got to do is drive."

The bridge appears in the distance on the left and grows larger by the second. Sarge glances at the instrumentation, pleased that none of the critical annunciator lights are lit up or flashing at him.

He activates the intercom. "Get into your battle rattle. We'll be in the shit in less than ten and back home in a few hours."

No macho cheering or theatrical complaining comes back to him from the passenger compartment, just cold silence and a reminder this is a different kind of war.

The bridge looms on the left, dominating the view against a gray sky that darkens toward the horizon like a distant storm. Waves of heat ripple at the horizon's edge, a cremated Pittsburgh giving up its ghost. The appearance of the bridge itself, a wonder of modern engineering appearing suddenly after miles of empty country, is almost as startling as the memory of the fire. An overhead road sign declares, EAST 22 NORTH 2 WEIRTON PITTSBURGH. The convoy slows as it comes together in single file and exits for the interchange.

Honking loudly, a platoon of Brinks armored cars and flatbed trucks at the tail of the convoy breaks off and continues south along Route 7 into Steubenville. These troops are headed to the Market Street Bridge, an old light rail suspension bridge built in 1905 that was later upgraded into a two-lane crossover for vehicles. Seven thousand cars and trucks crossed that bridge every day before the end of the world. Now it's used only by monsters.

The Bradley rolls onto the Veterans Memorial Bridge. Sarge sighs with relief.

The operation has officially begun.

☣

The two leading buses race ahead to the other end while the rest of the convoy slows and stops. The other two buses deploy laterally across the Ohio side and form a steel wall blocking access to the bridge. Within moments, the soldiers in the buses start shooting out the windows, cutting down the infected following the convoy. The Bradley idles on the asphalt. Inside, the survivors listen to the occasional pop of rifle fire as soldiers on the bridge take down stray infected.

A voice bursts on the radio: *Oh ... oh, Jesus Christ.*

Sarge keys his handset. "Negative contact, Immune 2. Say again."

There ... thousands ... them.

"I repeat: Negative contact, Alex. How copy?"

Over the Bradley's idling, Sarge hears the splash of small arms fire from the other end of the bridge nearly six hundred meters away. Next to him, Wendy scans the bridge for threats. The Immune 2 unit, comprising the two buses that moved ahead, are supposed to plug the West Virginia end of the bridge by creating another steel wall. Once both ends of the bridge are sealed by buses manned by combat troops, Sarge and his force will walk the bridge from one end to the other and clear it.

Then Patterson and his engineering team can do their work.

Sergeant Horton popped back onto the radio frequency, loud and clear. *We're trying to set up the buses, but they're everywhere, Sergeant. Not just the infected but the monsters, too. Hoppers. The giant heads with legs. Elephants with tentacles growing out of them.*

"Copy that," Sarge says.

"Should we go and help him?" Wendy says.

"Our job is to clear the bridge. Alex's job is to secure the other end."

I think we got it! Yeah, he's got it. Holy shit, we're in place. We're in place, Immune 1.

"I copy, Immune 2. Sierra hotel." Army lingo meaning, "Shit hot," a compliment.

We'll hold them here as long as we can.

"We'll see you in a few minutes."

Roger that.

Wendy activates the Bradley's intercom system before Sarge can reach for it. "It's time to go, guys. I just wanted you to know that I love all of you. Good luck, and come back safe."

Sarge nods. "You heard the lady."

He presses the button to drop the exit ramp.

The survivors dismount into May sunshine. Nearby, a squad of National Guard and two machine gun crews stare at them with expressions of barely concealed disdain. Covered by the Bradley, they're all going up the bridge together. Their job is to clear it of anything breathing so that Patterson and his people can do their work. The big five-ton trucks, loaded with tied-down boxes of TNT and C4 covered in plastic tarps, stand idling, surrounded by burly men waiting their turn in the game. Patterson walks over to them and barks instructions. A moment later, the men strip off the tarps to expose enough explosive to rip the bridge in half.

Todd checks his M4 carbine and waits for the order to move out, chomping at the bit for some action. He saw the way the Guard looked down their noses at him and wants to show them what he can do.

The firing at the other end of the bridge increases in volume. Todd wonders what those men up there are seeing, what they're going through.

Paul nudges him. "This is going to be a shit storm, boy. You stay close to me."

"I'm not worried, Rev," Todd says with a smile. "If God is with us, who can be against us?"

"That's what I'm afraid of. I think God might be on *their* side."

"Got an extra smoke for me, Preacher?" Ray says.

"Here you go."

"Thanks. Feel that breeze. Man, that feels good."

Gunfire crackles in the distance. The survivors crane their necks and squint at the Market Street Bridge, clearly visible to the south. Vehicles and soldiers move along the road deck. The crackle becomes a steady pounding roar. Sparks flash along its length, tracer rounds streaming to contact. Pale figures fall off the bridge into the muddy waters below. A rocket explodes at the far end, a flash followed by a deep boom and a mushroom cloud.

There's a hell of a fight going on over there. The other team is in action.

Todd fingers the handset the Army gave him for the mission and keys it with a squeeze. "Uh, Sarge?"

Todd, unless this is an emergency, stay off the comms.

"Sorry about that, Sarge."

Todd hesitates but can't help himself. He's already committed. And he can't resist using the radio.

"I was just, uh, wondering when we're going to get moving," he adds. "Um, how copy? Over."

You move when I tell you to move.

Todd smiles. He heard Wendy laughing in the background.

A minute, Sarge gives the command to advance.

It's show time, folks. Godspeed.

The Bradley crawls along the bridge, keeping pace with the Guard unit led by Sergeant Hackett. On the far right, near the edge, Paul looks down at the brown torrents far below. *The water seems a good place to be, especially if the infected can't swim. A man could get a boat and disappear.* He thinks about how the Ohio is formed by the Allegheny and the Monongahela meeting at Pittsburgh, and travels all the way here; downstream, it feeds the Mississippi. He asks Todd to swap weapons for a moment and uses the close combat optic to get a magnified view of the far shore. The land swarms with infected as far as the eye can see. Corpses and small islands of plastic garbage float in the water, collecting in piles on the riverbanks. The infected gather at the water's edge to drink among scores of bloated corpses washed up onto the mud.

Paul lowers the rifle, feeling sick, and hands it back to Todd.

"You look like you saw a ghost, Rev," Todd says. "What's going on over there?"

"The usual," Paul tells him. He saw them eating the dead.

Behind them, Ray says, "Hail Mary, full of grace," repeatedly until doubling over. He vomits loudly onto the road.

Sergeant Hackett frowns at the survivors and shakes his head.

Todd flushes with embarrassment and hisses at Ray, "Come on, man. Be cool."

Ray wipes his mouth and says, "Fuck this."

"Contact!" one of the soldiers calls out.

The Guard go to guns. The Bradley slows even further, almost coming to a halt. The survivors slow their pace as well, waiting until the threat is eliminated.

"Clear," the soldiers shout. The motley little army resumes its advance.

Ray is right to be scared, Paul thinks. *The hordes of hell are waiting for us at the other end of this bridge.*

As if reading his thoughts, Ray says, "You don't look too scared, preacher. What's your secret?"

"There isn't any secret, Ray."

"You think if you die, you go straight to Paradise to be with the virgins, right?"

Paul smiles and answers, "No, boy. I'm not scared because I'm already dead."

Ray stares at him in disbelief for several moments before shaking his head. "You people are crazy."

"*I'm* not crazy," Todd says.

Paul notices Ethan frowning as if trying to solve a difficult puzzle. The reverend pauses and raises his shotgun. He knows that look well. Todd sees them and shoulders his carbine.

"What you got?" says Todd.

Ethan looks up and roars, "Heads up!"

His voice is drowned out by a flurry of screams, gunshots, and curses. Paul looks up in time to see a flash of pale gray flesh. He pulls the trigger, and the shotgun bucks hot in his hands. The little creature flops to the deck, rolling and hissing and bleeding. Paul aims and fires again. The hopping thing explodes, leaving a trail of smoking gore splashed across the asphalt.

He senses motion in the corner of his eye, turns fast, and cracks another of the little monsters in the skull with the butt of his gun. The thing squeals and stumbles away until Ray Young pumps two rounds into it with his pistol.

Killing the infected is hard because they're people. These monsters are something else. When Paul kills them, he feels no remorse at all. Just a deep satisfaction doing the Lord's work.

He scans the area with his shotgun but sees no other threats. The gunfire around him sputters.

"Cease fire, cease fire!" Hackett calls out.

"Man down!" one of the soldiers cries.

"We need a minute to take care of our people," Hackett shouts at the survivors. "What you got?"

"We're all okay here," Paul yells back.

The Guard pause after this announcement and glare at the survivors with open resentment.

"Guess they thought we'd all be dead or something," Paul says.

"Sorry to disappoint them," Todd grumbles.

"The hoppers were up in the cables," Ethan says with a shrug. "These cables that hold the bridge together. They were up there waiting to drop down on us. A pretty basic ambush."

Paul nods. "Good one, boy."

Ray laughs and spits on the ground. "Batshit crazy. But you seem to know your stuff. I'll give you that."

Sergeant Hackett pulls a can of spray paint out of his leg pocket, shakes it and sprays a bright orange X on the back of one of the two men in his squad who were stung by the hoppers. The man weeps and nods, accepting his death sentence. He'll keep fighting, but he'll have to be killed when it's all over.

The other soldier was stung several times and lies curled on the ground with his face clenched in mortal pain. Ethan looks at him and wonders what must be going through his mind right now. Wonders if the man can feel infection proliferating in his blood. Can feel his body slowly being converted into an alien life form.

Hackett crouches, talks to the man, pats his shoulder. Then he stands, draws his 9mm, and shoots him in the head. The other soldiers tense, and Ethan thinks, *This is it, they're going to shoot Hackett now and go home*, but the sergeant growls at them to get back in line and prepare to advance, and they obey.

The Bradley revs its engine and resumes its slow crawl toward the center of the bridge. Ethan glances at the other bridge to the south, now almost concealed in a haze of smoke lit by muzzle flashes. As the survivors pass under the overhead WELCOME TO WEST VIRGINIA sign, the remaining infected race toward them in a flying horde.

We kill them, and the bridge is ours. This is it.

He raises his rifle. Paul pushes the barrel down.

"What?"

"Wait," Paul says, his eyes on Hackett.

The sergeant has called for a halt and to hold fire until his command.

"What's going on?"

"He's afraid of hitting the buses and killing our own people," Paul tells him. "We're going to let the infected get close and take them out with aimed shots."

The infected bolt down the bridge, arms splayed at their sides. It takes every bit of strength Ethan has not to empty his rifle at them. Or run like hell.

"Hold the line," Hackett cries.

This is ridiculous. There are too many. If they get close, we're going to have to make every shot count.

He sees no old faces in the swarm. The virus is a harsh mistress, driving its hosts to constant exertion in its never-ending effort to spread infection. The bodies of the old failed long ago. There are no children. The Screaming spared the children, but Infection didn't; the infected refuse to spread the pathogen to them, preferring instead to kill and, if they need food, eat them.

What's left are healthy adults who were once Americans and had lives. He sees a man running at him wearing a tattered business suit, his tie still knotted around his throat. A Sikh with a long beard, dressed in a turban and greasy mechanic's overalls. A cop still wearing his bulky Batman belt, dead radio and all. A beautiful naked woman with a gray face and the remains of a hospital gown dangling from one wrist.

A wave of stench washes over the survivors, the characteristic sour milk stink of the infected.

"Give the order," Ethan murmurs.

"He's got this," Paul says.

"Why is nobody firing?"

"Don't panic," Ray mutters. "If you start panicking, I'm going to shit myself."

"Give the goddamn order already!"

"*FIRE!*" Hackett screams across the highway.

The line erupts with a volley. The first wave of infected collapses in red spray. Ethan gasps, caught off guard, and fires his first shot, shooting the mechanic through the throat. He adjusts his aim and puts two into the woman. He backs up several steps, firing at the businessman and missing until he shoots out the man's knees and puts him down.

The line trembles. Then they're all running, streaming back toward the Ohio side of the river, firing as they run, trying to keep distance between themselves and the infected.

Hackett holds out his arms. "Halt!"

The soldiers show good discipline. They stop and open up on the remaining infected. Ethan keeps running. For a moment, Ray runs alongside, and it feels like they're racing. Then Ethan is jerked back. He struggles against the hand grabbing at his shirt.

"Fire your rifle," Paul shouts in his ear.

"Leave me alone!" Ethan screams in a panic. He wrenches out of Paul's grasp and spins in time to see the swarm bearing down on him, hands outstretched, their howl turning his legs to cold jelly.

Paul's shotgun crashes in his ears. A man wearing pajama bottoms collapses in a heap.

Ethan feels drained. He can't run anymore. A part of him wants to sit and let the infected take him. His mind flashes back to Philip, who sat in the cinders of a half-burned convenience store in Wilkinsburg after seeing a newspaper with an old date.

He pictures his daughter's face. He reminds himself he has something to live for. To fight and even die for.

He screams and fires. The cop's face explodes, and the man continues running, almost decapitated, until collapsing to the ground at Ethan's feet.

The team returns to the center of the bridge. The survivors walk among the twitching, dying bodies in a slight daze, as if through a dream, their shoes soaked through with the blood of the dead. Killing is exhausting work. They feel numb. The wounded infected crawl after them, coughing blood and growling until finished off with mercy shots given without a second thought.

The machine gun crews set up their guns at the edges of the bridge and aim them toward West Virginia. There's a sea of infected on the other side of the two buses up there, and if that line fails, the MG teams and the Bradley will become the main line of defense for the engineers. The five-ton trucks are already backing up toward the center line. Men clamber along their beds, cutting into the boxes and dumping piles of sandbags onto the road.

Ray sighs loudly. He feels strangely blessed. He has been ambushed and bum-rushed, and he's standing next to a bunch of morons fooling around with more than four thousand pounds of high-grade explosives, but he's still alive. When Patterson tells him to grab some sandbags and distribute them along the two lines in the road he drew with chalk, he's almost grateful. Mindless labor, he understands. He's perfectly fine with that. A little work won't kill him.

"Yo, Ray. Ray. *Ray Young.*"

He turns and sees the Bradley commander gesture at him from the open hatch of the vehicle.

"You need something, Sarge?"

"I've lost contact with Sergeant Horton. He's in the right bus. I need a runner to get up there and report back on what's happening."

"Christ, Sarge, you can hear the firing from here. They're still there."

Sarge glowers, and Ray glares back, setting his jaw, feeling mean. He's afraid of dying, yes, but not fighting. He never backs down when it comes to a fight.

Anytime, Sarge. Anytime you want, you let me know.

"Ray, there's blood on the windows," Sarge says. "I need to know if he's got casualties. I need to know what he's got in front of him. I need to know if he needs ammunition."

Ray understands bullying very well. Sarge isn't being a bully. It's a reasonable request.

"All right, all right," he grumbles.

"You sure it's okay? Sure you don't mind?"

"I said all right, I'll go."

"Then move your ass, shit for brains!"

Ray grins, checks the magazine on his M16, and starts jogging. After fifty feet, he's already flagged and wheezing.

He feels a hand on his shoulder and almost screams.

"What's up, dude?" Todd asks him.

"What are you doing here, kid?"

"Thought you might want some company."

"Why don't you just do it, and I'll go back?"

Alarm crosses Todd's face. "Sarge wouldn't like that. Come on, it'll be cool."

It'll be cool. Crazy, stupid kid.

They slow as they approach the bus. Several of the windows are sprayed with blood on the inside. Two are open, and gun smoke drifts lazily out of them. Dark shapes move inside. The constant pop of gunfire is so hot and loud here that it almost feels like a physical barrier.

Ray and Todd glance at each other.

"What do you think?" Todd shouts at him.

"I think we should get this over with."

Ray pushes open the bus doors and climbs aboard, looking down the aisle and coughing on the smoke. Soldiers fill the aisle and seats on the right side, firing and reloading and screaming obscenities. Dead men occupy several of the seats on the left, their eyes staring at nothing. Empty shell casings clatter to the floor, already covered in brass and links. There's an atmosphere of madness here. The soldiers wear wild expressions, like they've completely lost it.

But they're holding.

He finds Sergeant Alexander Horton sitting in one of the seats, his eyes bulging with fear and his chest torn out and dripping onto the floor. Dead as a doorknob.

Mission accomplished, now let's get the hell out of here.

Todd taps him on the shoulder and points.

Ray looks past the nearest soldiers and sees the horde.

It surges toward him in a vast shrieking swarm, an endless freak show of monsters and zombies converging on the bridge. He spots packs of hoppers with their absurd walk, occasionally leaping to sting one of the infected. Giant leering faces loping on bony stilted legs. Bellowing titans waving their tentacles. And flowing among them, mindlessly marching and occasionally serving as food for the monsters, thousands of infected waiters and students and housewives and cashiers and investment bankers.

He wakes up outside the bus, running, gasping for air.

Paul rushes to meet them halfway. They fall to their knees together.

"Talk to me," he says.

"He freaked out," Todd says. "Reverend, there's like *a million* of them over there."

"Ray?"

"Tell your boss that Horton's dead. In fact, one out of four soldiers on that bus is dead. And every infected bastard from Pittsburgh is beating at their door."

☣

Sarge sits on the Bradley's turret and aims his binoculars at the school buses at the end of the bridge. They have been on the bridge for over an hour, anxiously watching the engineers do their job. Patterson bangs on the armor to get his attention and tells him he's almost done setting up the charges. The TNT is arranged in two lines in front of the Bradley. All that remains before the show, the engineer explains, is finishing the tamping and pulling back the wires for each series of explosives to where they'll be detonated.

The distance between the Bradley and the end of the bridge is about three hundred meters. Sarge has the Bradley's battle carry—pre-selected range and ammunition—set up to establish a kill zone around the buses. He looks at his watch.

It's going to be close.

He sees Todd working with the other survivors and Guard to pass sandbags along a human chain. He waves at him.

Yeah, Sarge?

Sarge smiles. For a moment, he forgot he has radio communication with the survivors.

He keys his handset and says, "Todd, I want you to go up to the buses and tell those boys we need twenty more minutes from them."

Cool! Todd, out!

Todd snatches his carbine and takes off at a sprint.

He hears a colossal crash of thunder and looks south. The center of the Market Street Bridge, shrouded by a drifting cloud of black smoke, collapses into the Ohio River.

The soldiers let up a ragged cheer. Sarge grunts with satisfaction. Half the mission is over. But it won't be successful unless they finish the job and destroy this bridge.

He returns his binoculars to the buses. He sees fresh streaks of blood on the windows. The dead sit patiently in their seats, as if waiting for their next stop.

Just hang on a little longer. He marvels at the bravery and endurance of the men inside those vehicles. He can't even imagine what they must be going through in there.

The engineers shout in alarm. Sarge shifts his gaze and sees one of the towering things leering down at the bus. Ropes of drool leak between its massive teeth.

The monster's tongue lashes out and pulls the broken body of a National Guardsman into its chomping mouth. The monster chews greedily with a blissful expression, its eyes closed and leaking tears. The creature is so happy, it's crying.

Another chortling thing appears on the right. Its tongue lashes out, and a man screams.

The bus is *moving*.

"Todd, get back here now," Sarge says.

But I'm almost there.

"Get back here now! The line is breaking."

The gunfire sputters and stops. Soldiers emerge from the buses and race toward the safety of the machine guns at the center of the bridge. One of the monsters lashes out over the roof of the bus, grips a fleeing soldier by the ankle and yanks him up and into its mouth. The man screams and fires his weapon until the teeth crush his body into paste.

The bus is moving, swinging to the side like a pivoting door. Something big is pushing it. Tentacles wave in the air behind the vehicle. One of the giants. A limb as thick as a tree trunk, knotted with thick pale muscle, emerges. Then the behemoth pushes past and lumbers onto the bridge, bellowing like a foghorn.

"Prepare for action," Sarge says into his radio. "Hold the line!"

So close. We're so close to winning this.

He drops into the telescoped seat, lowers, it and seals the hatch.

Immunity 1, this is Immunity actual, he hears over his headset.

"Go ahead, LT."

I still need fifteen minutes.

"You got your fifteen, out." He shouts, "Get those MGs up!"

The thirty-cal machine guns placed at the edges of the bridge open fire. The tracers stream down the causeway and converge on the bellowing titan. The monster staggers back a few steps, its massive head trembling. The infected swarm around its feet.

"Hackett, I want that MG fire directed at the foot mobiles," Sarge says.

Roger that, Sergeant.

"What about us?" Wendy says.

"On the way," Sarge says and squeezes the trigger.

The rig trembles as the cannon fires, *BUMP BUMP BUMP BUMP BUMP*. Empty shell casings spill down the Bradley's chest. The HE rounds crash into the giant and the area around it and explode in a series of flashes.

"Target," Wendy says, letting Sarge know his aim is good. "Target."

"It's like shooting at a barn," he mutters.

Immunity 1, this is Immunity actual, we're about ten from detonation. How copy?

"Solid, LT," Sarge says. "Ten minutes to detonation."

The giant collapses, shivering, gushing blood.

"Target destroyed," Wendy announces.

Nice work, Steve says from the driver's station.

"Mark the time, Wendy. Officer or not, if the LT isn't ready in ten, I'm going to put my boot up his ass."

Smoke billows at the end of the bridge. The horde runs out of the smoke and throws itself into the machine gun fire, driven by endless rage.

"Shifting fire to area target," he murmurs as he switches to the coax MG. "On the way."

Keeping the reticle in the same place, Sarge fires horizontally across the target area, then again diagonally, then again horizontally, forming a repeating Z pattern.

"Jesus," Wendy says, almost retching.

Hundreds of rounds fall among the ranks of the infected and cut them down. The bodies collapse in groups, often in pieces. Smoking fingers and hands and heads and feet and legs fly through the air in a bloody mist. Some of the bodies literally disintegrate under the withering machine gun fire, flesh and bone exploding wetly across the asphalt.

Ten minutes. A long time. Too long. But we can do it. The soldiers and the survivors can handle the infected, while the Bradley can handle the larger monsters.

He winces as the Bradley fills with a hellish roar he remembers all too well.

☣

The monster's screaming cascades across the bridge. The shooting sputters as the soldiers and survivors flinch in primordial terror. The screaming fades as the engineers remove sandbags and rows of TNT blocks in front of the Bradley. The rig revs its engine and trembles like a bull stomping its feet.

"What in the hell is that?" Ray says.

"We don't know," Paul tells him.

"But you've met."

"Yeah. We've met."

Thick clouds of smoke hover at the end of the bridge, concealing the buses. The infected have stopped coming for the moment. Then the monster screams again, rending the air in its pain and drawing the smoke clouds into strange swirling patterns.

Todd catches a glimpse of a massive horned thing. Then it emerges, a thickly muscled mass of armor and spikes and giant horns instead of eyes set almost directly over its chomping jaws. Todd can feel each step it takes send a tiny vibration up his spine. The thing is so ugly and terrifying his eyes glance off it.

The Bradley's cannon fires. The monster staggers under the blows but doesn't appear harmed. It screams, blanking out Todd's mind for a moment, literally eliminating his memory of the last few seconds. Then it advances. The smoke follows it in swirling patterns, clinging to its limbs.

The engineers finish removing the array of charges from the Bradley's path, and Patterson shouts into his mike. The rig jolts forward. Todd reads BOOM STICK on the side of its turret as it roars full speed toward the demon, its cannon pounding.

"What are they doing?" Todd demands. He runs after the Bradley and waves his arms. "What the hell are you doing?"

Paul grabs his arm and pulls him back. "Let them go."

"No! They'll be on the wrong side of the bridge when it goes up!"

The Bradley disappears into the clouds of smoke swirling at the end of the bridge. The thick haze lights up with flashes of cannon fire, the reports echoing back as booming thunder. Then it's gone. The engineers return the charges to the road.

"No!" Todd screams. "No!"

Waves of infected run howling out of the smoke.

"They had no choice," Paul shouts into his ear. "Patterson isn't ready, and we don't know what that thing can do to us. We've got to finish this, boy!"

One of the behemoths lumbers toward them, groaning under the MG fire. Then it roars and gallops forward blindly until crashing through the rail and falling into the river below.

Ray appears at their side and empties his rifle into the swarm. "Fire your damn guns!"

The towering things step ponderously among the infected, their giant faces grinning.

"Shaw chonk?"

"Shaw chonk, mute chonk."

"Fire in the hole!"

Trailing a line of smoke, an AT4 rocket streams from the Guard unit and scores a hit on one of the monsters. The top of its head erupts in a geyser of blood and brains.

"Holy shit," Todd says in amazement.

He drains his magazine, reloads, fires again.

Hoppers drop from the cables onto one of the MG teams.

"They're above us again," Ethan yells into the noise. He fires at the targets over his head.

"On it," Todd says. He adjusts his aim to shoot at the things clambering up the cables. Two of the creatures fall to the ground with a wet, meaty sound.

The soldiers scream and shoot their rifles as the hoppers leap into their midst, fangs bared and stingers erect. Ethan sees more climbing the cables.

Ray tugs on Paul's arm. "We fall back, or we're screwed."

"You go, Ray. I'm not moving until this bridge is down."

"You may already be dead, preacher, but I'm not."

"You will be if we don't blow this thing, understand? We all will!"

Todd glances behind them and sees the engineers run after the retreating five-ton trucks, joined by some of the soldiers. Patterson backs away slowly at a safe distance, uncoiling wire as he goes. He waves at them. The charges are in place, tamped, primed and ready to explode.

Hackett blows his whistle to call the retreat. It's time to blow the bridge.

Another AT4 missile zooms down the span and detonates on the far side. A score of infected disintegrate in the blast, raining blood and flesh on the rest. A severed arm comes to a skidding halt at the survivors' feet.

"Now can we go?" Ray asks.

The survivors turn and sprint after Patterson, who is already splicing the firing wire. The engineers wave at them.

"Fire in the hole!" they shout.

"Down, get down!"

Ray tackles Todd to the ground as the blasting machine sends an electric pulse through the firing wire.

The blasting caps explode. The explosions detonate nearly a ton of dynamite in the far right lanes.

The bridge erupts with a cataclysmic peal of thunder. The bodies of the survivors leave the ground as the shockwave hiccups across the bridge. The massive jolt tears the cables, sending them flying through the air like the metal tentacles of a colossal beast. One of the bridge's towers shifts and slumps with a groan. The sky goes dark as a massive wave of dust billows overhead. Then another section of TNT erupts and sends a second shock wave through the bridge. The ground bucks under them again, and for a moment, if feels like they're all falling into the water.

After the third explosion, the bridge falls silent. Coughing on dust, Todd raises his head and looks behind him. The world is dark and filled with swirling particles, and he can't see five feet in any direction. His ears ring. Then he can hear the tramp of thousands of feet. Monstrous shapes move through the clouds of dust. The Bradley's cannon booms in the murk.

"We did it," he rasps.

"Almost," Ethan says. "That was the stripping charge. Now we have to go back and finish it."

☣

The demon punches the Bradley with a crash that reverberates through the hull and the bodies of the crew. The thing circles the vehicle one step ahead of the turret. Wendy presses the fast turret switch, increasing the speed of its response, and wrenches the joystick. The monster's body comes into view. As the reticle passes over the thing's spiky flank, Sarge fires the cannon point blank with armor-piercing rounds. The monster roars in pain and stomps away with a series of deep booms. They catch a glimpse of its tail terminating in a spiked ball, then it's gone. Moments later, they hear the infected pounding everywhere on the hull, trying to get in. The LO AMMO indicator light pops on and flashes. Sarge overrides the system but has no target.

"Where is it?" Wendy cries. "We almost had it!"

Boom boom boom boom boom boom...

The demon rushes them from the right on stomping feet. Wendy yanks on the stick, pulling the turret as fast as it will go. The monster roars and slams the hull, and she blacks out for a moment, seeing stars. When she comes to, she can't remember why she's here.

"I have no shot!" Sarge tells her. "Move the turret!"

She frowns at him. Why is he yelling at her? Then it comes back. She pulls on the stick. Sarge fires again and curses. The sear indicator light is blinking.

"What's wrong?" she says.

"Misfire!"

Sarge presses the misfire button, returning the 25mm gun bolt to the cocked position, but the sear light continues to blink.

"It's still jammed," he says. He stares at the instruments in helpless rage.

"What now?"

"Now..."

Boom boom boom boom boom boom boom

"Look out!"

BOOM!

The next punch makes her vomit against the instrument panel.

"Sorry," she moans. She wipes her mouth and wags her head to fight the continuing nausea.

"What?" Sarge says. "What's going on?"

"What do we do now?"

"Where's Randy?" he says, laughing.

"Sarge, knock it off!"

She shoves him hard, twice. The Bradley commander stares at her blankly, then shakes his head to clear it. He presses a button, and another light pops on. Wendy recognizes it. Sarge is dropping smoke grenades.

"Reverse! Steve! Back the hell up!"

Wilco, Sergeant.

The rig jolts backward on screeching treads as the demon stumbles screaming through the thick white smoke.

"We still got the TOW," Sarge says.

The monster emerges from the smoke, its head bobbing as if smelling the air, and then roars and charges.

"Fire it now!" Wendy screams.

"We can't!"

They hear a series of thuds from behind as the Bradley slams into the infected during its retreat.

The Launcher UP and TOW indicator lights are on. The TOW launcher is deployed and ready to fire missiles from its firing tubes. The MISSILE TUBE 1 indicator light is on, indicating its missile is ready to be fired.

"It takes sixty-five meters to arm. We need distance."

"Go, Steve, go," Wendy says, virtually praying to the driver to go faster.

The demon gallops at them. Then it stops and jerks its head back to lick the bleeding wounds on its flank.

Sarge presses the arming switch for the TOW.

"Put the reticle center mass on that abomination and keep it there."

The monster rolls back onto its feet and resumes its chase.

"Come on, come on," Sarge adds.

"We need more distance."

"Yeah," he says. "Yeah, we do."

Wendy looks over her shoulder, but there's no back window, no rear-view mirror. Somewhere behind them, Patterson blew two cratered trenches in the bridge, each more than two meters deep. She isn't sure the Bradley will be able to drive over them.

The thought fills her with claustrophobic panic.

"Um, Sarge?"

"On the way!" He presses the firing switch on the gunner's right control handle.

The TOW missile flies down the bridge and strikes the demon in the chest in a fraction of a second. It detonates in a burst of light.

"Target!" Wendy shouts, laughing and crying.

Cowabunga! Steve says.

The MISSILE TUBE 1 light flashes. Immediately, the TOW system indicator lights burst across the board: TRCKR, CGE, PWR SUP. The TOW system has failed.

The monster lies on the bridge keening and thrashing in a widening lake of thick black blood. One of its arms dangles by a few ropes of cartilage.

"I think we killed it," Sarge says. He takes a deep breath and blows air out his cheeks. "We killed it."

"Thank God," Wendy says. "What now?"

Swarms of infected pour around the dying monster and race toward the Bradley.

Sarge selects the coax machine gun, arms it, and puts his finger over the firing switch.

"Now we hold them off here as long as we can with the machine gun," Sarge tells her, adding, "On the way."

☣

The soldiers gather around Patterson and Hackett, filthy, their faces drawn and tired, their eyes wild, their hair and uniforms coated with white dust. Several wince and massage body parts where they've been stung and are even now gestating another generation of monsters.

"It's just us now," Hackett says. He reaches into his pocket, pulls out the can of orange spray paint, and throws it over the side.

The survivors gather at the edge of the crowd. Paul coughs on the dust, feeling a hundred years old, tired in his bones. He removes a wilted-looking cigarette from his battered pack of Winstons and lights up with a sigh.

Hackett spits on the ground and glares at the lieutenant. "LT, I need an honest-to-God, no-shit assessment on what it's going to take to finish this."

"I need thirty minutes up there to lay the second round of charges," Patterson says.

Hackett nods slowly, apparently weighing fight or flight.

"They're coming, Sergeant," one of the soldiers says.

"Sergeant, if it's all the same to you, I'd like to stay," another tells him.

"Me too," says one of the engineers.

All the men who've been stung want to stay and do their duty. They have literally nothing else to live for. They know that within several hours, they'll be dead.

They want to die for something.

"We still got the Bradley up there," one of them says. "I can hear it shooting."

"And the MG," another offers.

"I have a few rounds left for the AT4."

Most of the men here have been infected. They're dying. For them, the search for the meaning of life is over. Now they want to find meaning in death.

"We also don't have a lot of bullets left," Ray points out. "What are we supposed to kill them with?"

Hackett ignores him. "Your orders, sir?" he asks Patterson.

"I want you to get my team to the center of the bridge and hold it for thirty minutes."

"Yes, sir."

"Hooah," the soldiers shout with hoarse throats.

They scramble for one of the five-ton trucks and climb onto the back among the boxes of shaped C4 charges, sitting with their legs dangling over the sides, rifles loaded with safeties off.

The truck revs its engine and starts down the highway with a burst of exhaust, speeding toward the onrushing horde. Paul stands on the back, leaning over the roof of the cab, blinking as the dusty wind blasts his face.

"You may want to start praying again, Ray," he says. "Say another 'Hail Mary.'"

"I gave that up," Ray tells him. "I think you were right."

"What about?"

"God's on their side, preacher."

"Something's working," Paul says with a smile. "You're still alive, aren't you?"

Ray snorts.

The air fills with the pop of aimed rifle fire as the truck wades into the horde. The soldiers begin clearing the bridge.

At the center, Hackett blows his whistle and the soldiers jump down from the truck and charge. "Go, go, go!"

The soldiers fan out, covering the MG and giving it time to deploy. Moments later, the air fills with its staccato bark. A rocket streams into the open mouth of one of the towering things and explodes; smoke pours from its eyes and mouth as it topples to the ground. The dust settles, and they see the Bradley among hills of dead and dying infected, its coax machine gun still blazing. Waves of infected topple in heaps in front of it.

The engineers drop ladders into the trenches and place the charges. Patterson primes them with blasting caps connected by firing wire unreeled from a cardboard spool. The soldiers hurdle the trenches and deploy in a firing line, occasionally shooting but letting the machine guns do the hard work for now.

The minutes tick by.

The Bradley stops firing.

☣

The vehicle has either suffered a malfunction or, more likely, has simply out of ammo. The endless horde surges around it and rushes toward the soldiers. Tentacled titans and towering froglike things and hopping monkeys and squat crablike creatures with enormous clacking scissor hands mingle with the infected—thousands of them, needy, wanting, hungry.

Hackett roars an order. The soldiers stand and fire a volley that sends the front ranks of the infected crashing to the ground in a lake of blood.

"Reloading!" the MG crew calls out.

"Pour it on, boys!" Hackett roars, his M16 popping. "Keep it hot!"

Tracers stream downrange in a pounding roar of gunfire. Todd aims center mass at a woman running at him and fires a burst, knocking her over. He spares a quick glance down the line and sees fewer than twenty tired men screaming like maniacs and firing rifles. Beyond, at the edge of the bridge, the MG team feverishly reloads their gun.

He aims at a man running at him in hospital scrubs and fires again. His vision shakes; the man falls. Nearby, Ray shoots on full auto, the rifle spitting empty shell casings and puffs of smoke, while screaming every obscenity he knows. The rifle jams. He throws it away, still roaring his endless string of profanity, and yanks two handguns out of their holsters, emptying them at the horde that is now less than twenty yards away and coming fast.

The hoppers leap into the air with hisses. They land on several of the soldiers and send them toppling back into the trench. A tongue lashes down, wraps around the machine gunner and yanks him roughly into the air to land in a salivating mouth.

The infected drop like flies while the rest close the remaining distance and surge against the firing line with a general howl.

Their horrible sour milk stench fills Todd's nostrils moments before he's shoved to the ground.

Shoes and bloody bare feet slam into his body. He glances up and sees the hateful, shrieking faces of the infected glaring down at him. He gasps at the lancing pain.

It's not fair. He wishes he never came on this mission. He wishes he stayed. *It's not fair. I'm too young to die like this. It's so stupid.*

He curls into a ball and covers his head with his arms. The infected scream down at him.

Their chests explode, and they flop to the ground in a smoking ruin.

"Don't you touch that boy," Paul roars. He chambers another round and fires. More bodies collapse all around Todd, spraying him with blood.

"*GROOMY,*" one of the monsters bellows over their heads.

"Don't you touch that boy, I said!"

Ethan rushes in, his rifle popping. "Get him up."

"We'll cover you!" Ray says, firing with both fists.

Todd opens his eyes, his vision blurred by hot tears, and sees Paul's face.

"Hey, Rev."

"You're all right now, son. I'll get you out of here."

They hear a rumbling sound they can feel deep in their chests. Paul gasps, his eyes wide with recognition.

"You all right, Rev?"

Paul smiles weakly.

"God bless you, Kid—"

He lurches high into the air and into the gaping maw of one of the towering things, which bites down with a sickening crunch.

"No!" Ray screams.

"The legs!" Ethan calls to him. "Shoot it in the legs!"

Todd tries to stand, his eyes flooded with tears. "Rev?"

Ray nods and rushes at the monster, shooting down the infected running at him until he stands almost directly underneath the monster.

"Die, you piece of shit," he says. He takes careful aim and shoots out one of the thing's knobby knees.

The thing squeals, its leg collapsing under its enormous weight, and falls into the horde with a meaty splash.

Another sound pierces the air.

Hackett is blowing his whistle.

Ethan and Ray and Todd leap across the trenches, trailing clouds of dust. The infected spill into the open pits behind them, squealing and clawing at the walls. Todd stumbles on the other side, screaming for the reverend, Ray half dragging him.

Ethan turns and walks backwards while pouring lead into the snarling faces of their pursuers. "Go on, I'll cover!"

On his left, Hackett and two soldiers run toward him from the opposite lanes, chased by a group of infected. He slaps a fresh mag into the rifle and cuts down the infected.

I think I'm finally getting the hang of this. He turns again to provide cover fire. Constantly aware of the other survivors, he wonders where Paul is, and feels a sudden stab in his heart as the fact of his friend's death strikes him again.

He lowers his rifle for a moment, panting with exhaustion.

"I'm sorry, friend." *I hope you're in a better place.*

Hackett collides with him, and he feels the air rush out of his lungs. The world spins, and he hits the ground hard. His rifle is gone.

"Jeez, Sergeant," Ethan gasps. "You okay?"

A boot strikes his ribs and knocks the air out of him again. Another sinks into his back and sends lancing pain up to his neck. The soldiers stand over him and kick him.

They're infected.

Hackett slowly rises to all fours with a groan.

"Run, run, run," Ethan hisses at him.

Hackett turns with a snarl and bites into Ethan's ankle.

Ethan screams. The pain is incredible. He remembers the pistol on his hip and squeezes two shots through Hackett's skull. His eyes stinging with tears of regret, he looks down at his torn ankle smeared with blood and saliva.

The soldiers have stopped kicking him.

The pathogen has entered his nervous stream and is already flowing into his brain. Within moments, he loses control of his limbs. His body twitches. The pain in his ankle recedes as his body responds to infection by flooding his brain with endorphins.

The soldiers grin wolfishly and run after the others.

Probabilities. He was a math teacher. He understands probabilities. It works like this: you take enough risks on a long enough timeline, and you'll probably lose. It's that simple.

He looks at the gun still gripped in his hand. Despite the weakness and spasms, he retains some control of his body. He should end it now, before he becomes one of them.

He raises the pistol to his head.

Infected race past snarling. Their feet slap on the wet asphalt and splash through puddles of blood. Ethan raises himself onto his elbow, aims, and fires methodically. A running figure spins like a top before toppling to the pavement. Then another.

His hand flops back to the ground, the gun forgotten.

The world is bathed in shades of red, terrifying and beautiful.

The first wave of despair passes through him. Now he understands why the infected cry out at night. They're filled with sadness. Incredible, impenetrable, inconsolable sadness.

The sadness of memories of an entire life, just out of reach.

The sadness of slaves.

Then the rage begins. The pure hatred.

The hunger. The need.

The urgent, directive hum of the BROOD.

To create. To make perfect. To *evolve*.

Ethan hisses, spraying spittle, and struggles to stand. He knows there are things on this bridge that have not yet received the viral gospel.

There they are, murdering his people, each death an extinguished vector. He sees figures running toward him. Small arms fire crackles across the bridge.

A woman stands over him now. She looks down at him wearing a sad expression. She holds two smoking pistols in her fists.

His face contorts into a hideous grimace.

"Anne," he growls. "Good to see you."

The small moment of pleasure passes almost instantly. He glares up at her with hate and tries to push himself off the ground. She falls to one knee, meeting him halfway.

"Ethan, listen to me," she says close to his ear.

He shakes his head and snarls. "Go..."

He's already forgotten who she is. All he knows is she's a terrifying monster in the eyes of the BROOD. A monster that destroys vectors for the BROOD. A monster that is a threat to the BROOD. A monster that must be tamed by becoming a host for the BROOD.

Assimilate, the BROOD hums. *Assimilate and grow in safety in a fertile host.*

The monster says: "Your family is still alive."

The red veil lifts. The faces of Carol and Mary flash through his mind. He sees Mary in a bathing suit running through a series of sprays in a water park, Carol laughing as she unpacks lunch on a picnic table.

"Mary," he growls deep in his throat.

Mary turns and rushes toward him.

Daddy!

The sun in his eyes, so bright.

What a perfect day that was.

Ethan's head bursts as Anne pulls the trigger.

Todd staggers through hell, shouting for Paul and Ethan while the engineers retreat with pistols, crowbars, and baseball bats. They form a protective circle around Patterson, who struggles to connect the firing wires to the blasting machine, the right side of his face swollen to twice its normal size.

Help is arriving. Fresh troops have formed a ragged line and shoot into the ranks of the infected, which break apart under the withering fire. The soldiers are from the two buses they left behind at the Ohio end of the bridge. Civilians are here too, whom he doesn't recognize. He wanders among the infected, which drop bleeding to the ground around him.

He shouts the names of his friends.

A voice calls out: *Get down, get down!*

Fire in the hole!

The trenches in front of him erupt in a blinding flash, followed by a deafening crash. A massive tremor buckles the bridge and knocks him off his feet.

He lands hard on the asphalt. He struggles back onto his hands and knees, feeling lightheaded.

Come on, kid, a voice says, tiny and distant.

Ray Young grabs at him, his mouth working, his STEELERS cap smoking. The man hauls him roughly to his feet.

The garbled, muffled sounds of the world rush into his ears with sudden clarity.

Ray is screaming: "The bridge didn't blow! It didn't work! We've got to move! You hear me? It didn't blow!"

Todd turns and sees a giant lumbering toward him, bellowing its foghorn call, its tentacles swaying like whips. The horde follows close behind, an endless throng of infected.

"We've got to get out of here!"

They failed. It's over. And his friends died for nothing.

"Come on, kid!"

"No," he says.

"Come on!"

"No! No!" He pushes the man away and shakes his fists at the infected. "You killed my friends! I hate you!"

"We're going to die here if we don't move!"

Todd stands shakily, shrugging off Ray's hand again, and draws his pistol. "Come on! I'm right here!"

Todd aims his pistol at the behemoth crashing toward him and fires. Ray stands next to him and fires with both hands, screaming his head off.

The giant lunges into a gallop with a roar.

Within moments, the monster looms over them.

And falls through the earth with a groan.

The broken section of the bridge detaches and tumbles seventy feet until swallowed by the waters below. The monster falls with it, lowing plaintively as it crashes into the river.

Todd raises his fist and whoops. The infected run at him and topple over the edge into the river below, shrieking like bats.

"Ha!" he screams at them. "Ha! That's what you get!"

Then he falls to his knees among the rubble and bodies and cries. "You killed my friends."

I didn't know you very well, but you're the only ones who really knew me. You listened to me when nobody else did. You saw me. You depended on me. You accepted me.

Like nobody ever did.

"All for a goddamn bridge," Ray says in disgust. He drops his pistols onto the road and walks away shaking, leaving Todd alone.

Anne kneels next to the boy and puts her arm around him. After some time, he curls up on the ground, his head on her lap, and falls asleep.

From somewhere in the distance, over the stomping feet and snarling breath of the infected hordes, Anne hears the metallic shriek of armored treads.

☣

Ray sits on the edge of the bridge among the dead and dying, his feet kicking in empty space. He briefly ponders the water, the clouds, the sun hanging low in the sky. The wind whistles through the gap. Across forty feet of open space, hundreds of infected still crowd the other side of the span, moaning and reaching out to him as if pleading. He resurrects a mangled cigarette from the crushed pack in his shirt pocket and lights it. He takes a deep hit and blows a long stream of smoke. A cigarette never tasted so good. *What I wouldn't give for an ice cold beer*, he thinks, almost salivating.

Ice. Cold. Beer.

Life is good. It's even beautiful.

And way too short.

The pain in his side is incredible. He can feel the pathogen growing there, converting his cells into a monster waiting to be born. One life ends, and another begins.

I'll fight it. And maybe I'll win.

He heard the hoppers grow right out of your body as if it were topsoil, sucking it dry, and then eat what's left after they're born. By that point, you're so drained, all you can do is watch.

It's a lousy way to go. He'd rather die of bone cancer.

The first time he does something really good in his life, he has to die for it.

A noble sacrifice. Right. Big fucking deal.

We ain't the three hundred Spartans. There ain't no legends being born here. The country is filled with heroic chumps sacrificing themselves for a future that will be dominated by all the ignorant and selfish assholes who hid and did nothing. In a week, most of the good citizens of Camp Defiance will forget all about it. And even if they don't, even if they build a goddamn pyramid here in my honor, I'll still be dead. I gave my life when all that matters is staying alive.

It's too bad. He really wanted to see what he could do. He was just starting to feel like he had some potential as a human being.

THE ROAD

Sarge and Wendy sit on the Bradley's warm metal skin on a thickly treed hilltop overlooking the desolation that was once Steel Valley. Sarge inspects the scorched land with binoculars while Steve stands guard nearby with a rifle. They see no sign of life, infected or otherwise. The entire region appears to be dead, barren. They'll be driving past Pittsburgh today along a southern route, and they need to take a look at the road to see what's ahead. To the northeast, the city still blasts heat into the sky like a massive furnace while bleeding its toxins into the Ohio River. The land is carpeted in gray ash and cars half melted into the road.

They're refugees forced from everything they consider home, nomads living on whatever they can find. But mostly, they're survivors. They're good at surviving because they're on the road, and they're still alive.

They have a new mission now. They're going to Camp Immunity, near Harrisburg, to find Ethan's family and tell them he's dead and that he never gave up searching for them. That he never gave up hope. His little girl has a right to know who her father was, how he died so thousands might live.

They don't intend to stay in Immunity. The only sanctuary they trust now is the Bradley.

Wendy runs her fingers along the deep scratches in the turret made by the claws of the demon. The grooves remind her of the empty spaces inside her that appeared when she learned Paul and Ethan were dead. It's still unfathomable to her that they could die, even in this dangerous world. They'd become larger than life in her mind, closer than family, in such a short time. Now she feels their absence like an amputated limb or a missing gun. Her mind still wants assurance they're there, covering their sectors, with her world being a little safer for it.

Sarge touches her shoulder. Wendy wipes her eyes with the palm of her hand and tries to smile.

He touches his heart. "They live here."

"It should have been me."

"No," he says. "It shouldn't."

Wendy looks down at the charred wasteland that was once a thriving city and wonders why she's alive when so many died. She doesn't see anything special about her. She can't accept that she deserves it.

Sarge adds, "They didn't die for nothing. They died so many more could live, and that's the noblest way to die."

She squeezes his hand and sighs. She feels sick and empty, starving but unable to eat anything, her mind searching for its own sanctuary.

Maybe she'll find it on the road.

The Bradley wasn't trapped on the West Virginia side of the river. The vehicle has an inflatable pontoon that encircles the rig and can turn it into a boat propelled by its treads at four miles an hour. But they didn't go back to Defiance.

Anne radioed to tell them the mission succeeded. She was leading another group of survivors to the camp, taking them through Steubenville for supplies, when they heard the sounds of battle. She found the soldiers at the buses on the Ohio side of the river arguing over whether to abandon their position and support their comrades. Anne rallied the soldiers and led both them and her team of survivors in an assault that bought Patterson enough time to finish blowing the charges.

Just what Wendy would expect her to do. She's a natural leader.

Anne said she was going to take Todd back to Defiance with the other survivors and then head back out to find more.

After breaking radio contact, Sarge told Wendy and Steve he could never go back. That he could never feel safe there. That the only place he can stand being is here, on the road.

They agreed to come with him.

"I believe in you, Toby," she says.

"It's just us now," he tells her.

"We'll find others and start again."

"A tribe, right?"

He puts his arm around her, and she snuggles close.

"A tribe," she agrees.

"We'll be together."

"No matter what."

They're rejecting the security of the camp for the brutality of the road, which just claimed two of their friends. They know it's insane, but they feel safe out here. They understand it. It's strange, but they feel they must go on facing it in order to continue earning the right to be alive when so many died.

Survival, it seems, is also a state of mind. And it carries a steep price.

"Sarge!" Steve calls out.

"What's up?"

The gunner grins. "Listen."

The pounding of rotors in the distance, growing louder.

Sarge and Wendy turn and see five black objects glide across the sky in formation.

"God," Sarge says. He raises the binoculars for a closer look. "I can't believe it."

"What is it?" Wendy asks him.

He lowers the binoculars, smiling in a daze. "Chinooks. Big helicopters, troop carriers. Moving west."

"How? Who are they? Where are they going?"

"It's the Army, babe. The Army. Here, take a look."

Sarge hands her the binoculars. She watches the helicopters move across the sky. There's an elegance to the ungainly beasts she finds inspiring.

"See that?" he says, sounding wistful.

Behind the first formation, another approaches, five black dots in the sky heading west.

Wendy nods. She swallows hard. Tears roll down her cheeks, and she smiles, filled with new hope.

"Look at them go," he adds.

America's far-flung armies are coming home.

The fight isn't over. It's only getting started.

The counterattack has begun.

WANT MORE?

Thank you for reading!

If you enjoyed *The Infection*, kindly review the book on Amazon and be sure to check out the next book in the series, *The Killing Floor*.

Learn more about Craig's writing at www.CraigDiLouie.com. Be sure to sign up for his mailing list to learn about new releases.

And turn the page to read the first chapter of *The Killing Floor*!

OUTBREAK

On the second floor of the West Wing of the White House, the meeting adjourned for lunch early because the machine gun was too loud.

Dr. Travis Price, assistant director with the Office of Science and Technology Policy, stared out the window into the smoky haze that had settled onto the city.

Outside, the Marines shot the infected off the fence.

The conference room doors opened and servers entered in crisp blue suits, pushing carts across the carpet. They flinched at the machine gun's coughing bark.

"Oh my God," said Sanders, who stood at another window.

"What?" somebody said, his voice edged with panic.

"It's one of the gardeners."

Travis looked down at the green lawn but saw nothing except an infected woman climbing the fence. She flopped to the ground. The machine gun stopped firing.

"What happened to him?"

"Nothing. He's down there pruning the rosebushes."

A few people laughed.

"Now that's loyalty," somebody else said.

"Hope he's getting time and a half."

Amazing world we now live in, Travis thought, *where the mundane shocks us*.

The Continuity of Government Task Force had been thrown together on the epidemic's first day. The President wanted more authority to deal with the spread of the Wildfire Agent, the official name for the Infection. Congress had to approve everything.

The room was packed with bureaucrats, policy wonks, and congressional staffers; Travis had been attached to the task force as science adviser.

They argued *posse comitatus*, the Insurrection Act of 1807, the lessons of Operation Noble Eagle. Mostly, they fought over the boundaries of executive authority and ways to legitimize mass slaughter. Busts of George Washington and Benjamin Franklin, placed in niches on the far wall, observed the proceedings with mild disdain.

Travis wondered if all this debate over legal interpretations was some kind of institutional denial, the equivalent of Nero fiddling while Rome burned.

His stomach growled. He'd eaten little over the past few days. His body needed food.

He approached the lunch table, picked up a sandwich, and stared at it. Tuna fish, he observed, with the crusts expertly cut off. He marveled at the amount of care in its preparation. He took a bite, chewed, forced himself to swallow. Packs of infected ran through the nation's cities on a series of TV screens recessed into the wall just above his head. One of the stations scrolled evacuation instructions to people in the DC metro region.

So far, he'd been asked to contribute little to the meeting—which was good, since he had no insights to offer. Everybody knew what he knew: seven days ago, one in five people around the world fell down screaming. Four days ago, they awoke from a catatonic state and began attacking others and infecting them with some type of disease, plunging the world into hell.

It was all right there on the TV screens.

The big question was why, and nobody had an answer to that.

CNN showed a mob charging a squad of police in Chicago. The infected were like animals. The cops pushed them back with their riot shields and flailed with their batons. Then they were overrun.

"No, no, no," somebody sobbed.

"Hey," Travis hissed to two men standing near him. Fielding and Roberts, clean-cut men with hard faces and astronaut builds. They worked for the Office of the National Security Advisor. "Should we be allowing this on the air?"

He felt sure the government should be trying to control the flow of information in a crisis like this. Censorship was wrong, of course, but could also be practical to prevent panic.

Fielding and Roberts exchanged a glance.

"Why try to cover up or deny something that's happening everywhere?" Roberts said.

"Stick with science, Doc," Fielding said.

Travis turned away, his face burning with embarrassment. He wondered why he'd bothered. Outside the realm of science in which he excelled, he was awkward around other people, always saying the wrong thing.

On the TV screen, three of the five fallen cops got back on their feet. While it took three days for the screamers to awaken and attack their caregivers, once bitten, conversion took mere minutes.

Heads jerking, the cops ran to join a pack of infected.

"The biggest question is why they run so fast."

"What's that, Dr. Price?" Roberts asked him.

Travis blinked, unaware he'd voiced the thought aloud. "Uh, the biggest question on the tip lines. Why the infected can run."

The men stared at him blankly. Travis moved aside to allow other people access to the sandwiches. The crowded room buzzed with gossip and debate.

He went on, "A lot of people think the infected are zombies. Like zombies in movies. Dead people who've come back to life. Zombies are slow, right? People don't understand."

"Probably a good thing too, Doc," Fielding said. "If people think their loved ones are already dead, fewer of them might hesitate. They'll kill them on sight if they have a weapon."

"But we're not telling people to kill the infected."

"Of course we're not telling them that."

"I guess if they were zombies, they'd be dead and have no rights, and then it would be okay to tell people to kill them. Too bad about that."

"Interesting," Fielding said flatly. His hard eyes betrayed his contempt.

"Dr. Price, do you mind if I talk to you alone for a moment?" Roberts asked.

"Certainly," Travis said with relief he hoped didn't come across as too obvious.

The man gestured to the window. They moved away from the others. Travis winced at the man's breath, sour from endless tension.

"My wife fell down," he said.

"SEELS?" Travis asked. Sudden Encephalitic Lethargica Syndrome, or SEELS, was the formal, if somewhat broad, term scientists were using to describe the mystery disease that made more than a billion people collapse screaming, bringing the world to a crashing halt.

"Yeah." The man ran his hand over his buzz cut. "I got her into a hospital. Now she's one of those maniacs out there."

"I'm sorry," Travis said mechanically.

"Listen, she's pregnant. Eight months."

"Oh."

"My kid—is he one of them or one of us?"

Travis opened his mouth and shook his head. Theories flooded his brain, fighting to be spoken, but he held them back. Roberts wanted some type of assurance, some sign of hope, but Travis didn't know the right words. He was as bad at platitudes as he was at small talk.

"The President," Fielding called to them. He pointed to the TV screens.

President Walker had spent most of the crisis underground in the Situation Room. Since the epidemic started, they'd seen him only on television. Somebody boosted the volume, filling the room with the President's address to the nation from his desk in the Oval Office.

"—functions of our government continue without interruption."

Roberts turned away to watch. Travis suppressed a sigh of relief.

The President said, "Federal agencies in Washington are evacuating and will reopen at secure locations within the next few days. To ensure the safety of personnel critical to the continued functioning of our government, I am also ordering the immediate evacuation of the White House."

The room erupted with gasps and murmuring and people shushing each other.

"Quiet!" somebody shouted.

"Excuse me," Travis said. He stepped through the crowd. "Please."

They moved aside readily, staring at the screens.

"—evil acts of terror perpetrated by people who were once our family, friends, neighbors."

He closed the door behind him.

A human train hustled past, shoving him aside. He caught a glimpse of the Attorney General flanked by stoic Secret Service agents and trailed by pale staffers clutching briefcases.

Travis fell in with them. He glanced over his shoulder at the conference room doors. Fielding, Roberts, and the others were still listening to the President's speech. He didn't need to hear it. He'd already gotten the message loud and clear: *Get out. We're leaving now.* Six thousand people worked for the White House. He had no idea how many were in the building right now, but it was a lot. He was taking no chances at being left behind.

A large man, wearing a business suit and ear piece, appeared at the end of the corridor and waved them forward. "The stairs are clear. Let's move it."

The group quickened its pace as people poured into the corridor from multiple doors. Everybody was getting the same message: *Evacuate.*

The lead agent pushed through the mob. "Make way for the Attorney General, people."

Travis tried to follow in their wake but was blocked. He was now at the rear of a large crowd filling the corridor and trickling down the stairwell. Behind him, the thirty people from his working group caught up. A large portrait of Andrew Jackson frowned down at him from the wall.

The line ground to a halt. The staffers cracked open laptops and tried to make calls on their cell phones. People sat on the steps and shared what they knew. Rumors rippled down the line.

Helicopters are taking us out. Marine One is in the air.

The President was already gone.

The line moved and then stopped again. Travis chafed. He felt trapped. He had a bad feeling about the evacuation. He looked at the worried faces around him and wondered if they felt it too. He loosened his tie and tried to control his growing panic.

Get me OUT OF HERE.

They finally reached the bottom and exited the building. Exhausted from working day and night to help steer the White House's lumbering decision-making process, officials and bureaucrats and secretaries blinked at the gray sky, looking for the sun. Ahead, more people streamed through the trees under the sentinel gaze of Marine guards with automatic weapons. A sniper on the roof fired his rifle with a sudden *bang*, making the crowd flinch in unison like startled deer. Travis hurried after them, coughing on hot, smoky air that smelled like burning chemicals.

For days, he'd watched the apocalypse on TV, and now here he was hurrying right into it. It was strange, but he thought he'd been in the safest building on the planet.

Emerging from the trees, Travis was greeted by the cathartic view of a massive Chinook helicopter standing on the broad South Lawn, the metallic chop of its rotors competing with the crackle of gunfire. The door folded closed. Travis scanned the black haze drifting across the sky. Past the familiar sight of the Washington Monument, he saw the black dots of one helicopter receding, another approaching.

The helicopter on the ground lunged into the humid air, blasting the mob below with a strong, hot wind. A briefcase spilled open and shed hundreds of papers that fluttered in the air. *This isn't an evacuation. This is a meltdown.*

The Secret Service waved the crowd back as the next helicopter landed hard and fast. Travis pressed ahead, ducking at the booming shots of the sniper rifles. He was so close now. If not this ride, he'd make the next. Instead of assuring him, this idea inspired more panic. The people around him continued to shout into the roar of the blades, scream at the *crack* of Uzis, point at the infected being shot down as they climbed the makeshift fence surrounding the landing zone.

"Come on!" he shouted into the noise.

People were moving again. Those ahead of him boarded. Then the Secret Service closed ranks. The helicopter was full, the agents shouted. Wait for the next one.

So close, Travis thought. He looked at the sky past the Washington Monument and saw one helicopter disappearing, but none coming.

Somebody screwed up. There's not enough transportation to get everybody out.

They're going to leave us behind to die.

He pushed forward until he stood face to face with one of the Secret Service agents. The crowd heaved and Travis found himself looking into the barrel of a large handgun, one short squeeze from oblivion. He dug his heels and pushed back at the bodies pressing against him, staring wild-eyed at the big gun in the agent's hand.

"Please don't shoot me," Travis said.

"Back," the agent told him.

"Listen to me. You have to get me on this helicopter."

The large man's expression remained inscrutable behind mirrored sunglasses.

"I'm a science adviser," Travis added. "The President needs me, do you understand? If you want this thing to end, the President is going to need me at his side. I'm a *scientist.*"

The agent said nothing.

"You really think bullets are going to stop this?" Travis said in disgust, giving up.

The agent frowned, and Travis winced, thinking he was going to be shot. Instead, the man turned and boarded the helicopter, grabbed the arm of a young woman seated near the door, and pulled her to her feet. She burst into tears and obeyed meekly. Then she stood in the doorway looking dazedly at the crowd, mascara running down her face, her hair frayed around braids coiled into a bun. The roiling mob glared back at her in a state of fierce panic. The agent said something; she screamed and clawed at his face until he shoved her off. People surged around to help her. She continued to wail. The sound of it made Travis want to throw up.

Then he realized what was happening.

"Hey, wait," he said.

The agent slid his hand under Travis's armpit and propelled him toward the open door of the helicopter.

"You can't do this," Travis pleaded. "You have to let that woman on too!"

The agent said close to his ear, "Don't try my patience."

If you want to live, live, he was saying. *If you want to die, die. Don't play games with me. I have to stay here. I'm a dead man doing his duty.*

His face burning with rage and shame, Travis climbed into the helicopter and took the woman's seat. He sensed somebody staring at him. He glanced up and locked eyes with John Fielding. He looked away.

The helicopter lurched into the air.

He felt Fielding's cold gray eyes bore into him as he fought back another urge to vomit. The machine banked in its long ascent and offered a window view of the crowd surrounded by swirling debris. A sob ripped through him.

I just want to live. Why is that bad?

The helicopter was still turning. Below, Travis saw a shiny black Lincoln Town Car, little flags flying on its hood, approach the South Lawn at high speed. Some high-ranking official or foreign diplomat seeking sanctuary. A horde of running people chased it. The vehicle accelerated as it neared the fence then veered sharply as Secret Service agents opened fire on it. The car crashed through and coasted to a smoking halt among the trees.

The infected streamed across the lawn into the guns of the Secret Service when the helicopter straightened out and cut off his view.

ABOUT THE AUTHOR

Craig DiLouie is an author of popular thriller, apocalyptic/horror, and sci-fi/fantasy fiction.

In hundreds of reviews, Craig's novels have been praised for their strong characters, action, and gritty realism. Each book promises an exciting experience with people you'll care about in a world that feels real.

These works have been nominated for major literary awards such as the Bram Stoker Award and Audie Award, translated into multiple languages, and optioned for film. He is a member of the Horror Writers Association, Science Fiction and Fantasy Writers of America, and International Thriller Writers.

Other books by Craig:

The Killing Floor
Tooth and Nail
The Aviator Series
Crash Dive Series
Armor Series
The Children of Red Peak
Our War
One of Us
Suffer the Children
The Retreat Series
The Alchemists

Printed in Great Britain
by Amazon

33237617R00171